Rough Wrangler, Tender Kisses

Dell Books by Jill Gregory

Rough Wrangler, Tender Kisses
Always You
Cherished
Cold Night, Warm Stranger
Daisies in the Wind
Forever After
Just This Once
Never Love a Cowboy
When the Heart Beckons

Rough Wrangler, Tender Kisses

Jill Gregory

A DELL BOOK

A Dell Book
Published by
Dell Publishing
A division of Random House, Inc.
1540 Broadway
New York, New York 10036

Front cover photo by James Randclev/Visions of America, LLC/PictureQuest
Insert illustration by John Ennis

For information, address Dell Publishing, New York, New York.

Dell® is a registered trademark of Random House, Inc., and the colophon is a trademark of Random House, Inc.

ISBN: 0-7394-1372-4

Printed in the United States of America
Published simultaneously in Canada

To my beloved father,
the best dad in the world—with love forever

Rough Wrangler, Tender Kisses

Prologue

Cloud Ranch
Wyoming, 1867

For as far as the eye could see, snow blanketed the valley. The sturdy log ranch house nestled among the trees looked as tiny as a bug against the backdrop of snow-glistened mountains and pine trees. In all that wide lonely space and deep dark quiet, nothing moved or broke the stillness except the woodsmoke curling from the chimney.

Inside the ranch house he had built with his own two hands, Reese Summers leaned against the desk in his lamplit office and studied the three Barclay boys. Seven-year-old Nick, nine-year-old Clint, and Wade, who was eleven, were lined up before him, standing shoulder to shoulder like wooden soldiers. They looked so touchingly young, so vulnerable, and yet, somehow, so united. Just as Linc Barclay would have wanted, Reese thought as he gazed into the young faces full of painful uncertainty.

"Boys, let me tell you something." His voice was gruff, but a thread of gentleness ran beneath it. "Your father was the best friend I ever had."

Young Wade nodded. The others didn't move a muscle.

"Your father was also the bravest man I knew. He died trying to save your mama's life, and I want you boys always to remember that—to remember both of them as two of the finest people who walked this earth."

The boys all nodded, but none of them said a word. As the wind rose, whistling at the windows of the square, sturdy Wyoming ranch house, and the fire blazed with cheery ferocity in the hearth, the three dark-haired boys, orphaned only a few weeks now, clenched their jaws and watched their father's old friend in silence.

Nick, the youngest, hadn't said a word since they'd arrived at the ranch just before supper. But he heard and noticed everything with those dark, long-lashed eyes of his. Clint, the middle child, was the spitting image of his father, his hair the same shade of deep mahogany, his features sharp and handsome. Wade, the eldest, was clearly in charge. He'd inherited his mama's raven-black hair, but even at this young age, had the rangy toughness and the promise of height and muscularity that had been Linc's.

"We 'preciate your taking us in, Mr. Summers," Wade said at last, stepping forward and meeting the man's keen brown eyes.

Reese put a hand on his shoulder. "Call me Reese, son."

The boy nodded. "Reese," he repeated uncertainly.

Then his jaw tightened. With pride, Reese noted.

"We'll earn our way," the boy said with dignity. His hands were clenched at his sides. "I promise—we won't never be a burden to you."

"That's right," Clint piped up. "I know how to pitch hay. And throw a rope."

Little Nick, the one who had witnessed the stagecoach attack and seen his parents slaughtered, the one who had not yet spoken since that day, merely nodded, though there was wonder and a touch of hope in those huge, sad eyes as they remained riveted on Reese Summers.

Reese knelt down before all three boys. "Listen to me. You'll never be a burden to me. I want you here. You understand? You're not hired help. You're . . . family. That's what I've got in mind." He cleared his throat. "You'll be my family, and I'll be yours."

"But what about *your* family, Mr.—er, Reese?" Wade asked.

Reese's gaze shifted to the bronze-framed photograph on the mantel across from his desk, lingering a moment before returning to settle upon his young charges. "Well, you see, boys," he said quietly, "I lost my family, too."

"You did?" It was Clint who spoke. He turned suddenly to glance at the photograph that showed an elegantly gowned woman seated on a flowered wing chair, with a small, golden-haired girl on her lap.

"Are they dead too, like Ma and Pa?" Wade ventured.

Reese shook his head. "No." His voice was heavy, almost as heavy as his heart. "They're not dead. But they're gone just the same."

Suddenly young Nick inched forward and pushed his small hand into Reese's big, callused one.

Reese met the child's eyes, then a lump rose in his throat. He looked from Nick, to Clint, to Wade—three brothers trying so hard not to cry, to be strong, but each of them hurting badly.

"It's going to be all right, boys," he said slowly, his warm gaze encompassing all three of them. "Cloud Ranch is your home now as much as mine. We're going to be a family—you hear? A real family, just you wait and see."

He didn't know if they believed him. He vowed to make his words come true. It would take time, but he would make it work. Not like the last time.

Once the boys were settled in their beds in the big room down the hall from his, he tossed back a shot of whiskey and thought about this chance he'd been given. The chance to help out his old friend, and to end his own agonizing loneliness.

Slowly, like the plume of smoke rising from the chimney, his heart lifted. It was good to be needed. Wanted. There would be children and noise and laughter in the ranch house again.

Maybe with someone other than himself rattling around in here, it would actually start to feel like a home once more.

He picked up the photograph and stared at it, longing in his eyes. He was going to have sons now, three fine sons. But that didn't stop the hurt as he gazed at the tiny daughter whose absence made a hole in his heart.

Caitlin . . . if only . . .

He closed his eyes and let the pain rock him.

And with it came a renewed determination. Someday, somehow, he'd win his daughter back, bring her here to Cloud Ranch. Home, where she belonged.

Chapter 1

"Oh, Miss Summers, do remember what I said. Don't ever, ever, *ever* fall in love with a cowboy."

As the stagecoach lumbered to a shuddering halt in the center of the tiny Wyoming town called Hope, the stout woman wearing the feather-trimmed hat and the puce traveling gown leaned forward, and nodded wisely at the blond girl seated across from her. "If you do," she sighed, "he'll only break your heart."

"Don't worry, Mrs. Casper." The blond girl's tone was reassuring. She straightened the satin bow atop her smart pink hat, smoothed her pale lavender skirt, and managed a smile for the woman who had talked incessantly since boarding the stage, mostly about her niece in Kansas who'd been left brokenhearted by a smooth-talking wrangler. Despite her tendency to babble, Mrs. Casper was kind, and Caitlin appreciated kindness. She hadn't seen much of it lately.

"I promise you, there's no need to worry about me." The girl spoke quietly as the stagecoach driver clambered down from his perch and the coach swayed. "There is absolutely no chance of my falling in love with anyone."

Ever again, she thought firmly.

Once had been more than enough.

Caitlin fought the pain that squeezed around her heart as Alec Ballantree's sensitive, beautifully handsome face surged into her mind. She didn't want to think about that, or the fact that her reticule contained only a meager twelve dollars and forty-seven cents, all the money she had left in the world—or about any of the countless other ways her life had fallen apart in the past few months. She wanted to think only of what must be done, only about Becky, the little sister who needed her. Only about the future.

But her stomach clenched at the thought of all the responsibilities facing her. Her eleven-year-old sister's wan little face and worried brown eyes lingered in her mind and she knew she must not fail.

She turned her attention to the sights beyond the stage-coach window, trying to concentrate on the town, to forget her weariness, the length of her journey, and the uncertainty of the future. She was here now, in Hope, and it was only a matter of hours before she reached her father's ranch.

Cloud Ranch. Reese Summers's pride and joy.

The town looked small, but bustling. Laughing children ran along the boardwalk, while men in chaps and spurs and Stetsons strode up and down the street. Women wearing bonnets and bright gingham dresses bustled in and out of various shops. And there were wagons and buggies and horses everywhere she looked. From the saloon came the tinny plinking of piano keys and the sound of deep raucous laughter.

Mrs. Casper's high-pitched voice overrode everything else.

"Mmm, take that one there for example. Isn't *he* a handsome devil? Just the kind to steer clear of, dear. Mark my words."

Caitlin spotted him even as Mrs. Casper spoke. For a moment her breath caught in her throat. The dark-haired man leaning against the railing outside of Hicks Mercantile was eyeing the stagecoach, his thumbs hooked in the pockets of his dark pants, two six-shooters slung in the gunbelt fastened across his lean hips. *Handsome devil* didn't begin to describe him. *Dangerous, gorgeous, intimidating*—those words *did* describe him, Caitlin thought faintly.

Well over six feet tall, he was deeply bronzed and muscular, with sharp, even features, wide shoulders, and an air of nonchalance.

Was he a gunfighter perhaps? she wondered a bit uneasily. There was something undeniably dangerous about him. His looks and demeanor didn't shout danger—but instead whispered it.

He was certainly handsome, but in a completely different way from Alec, she thought as she recalled her former fiancé's curling light brown hair and debonair smile, his quick laughter and smooth elegant hands, hands befitting the gold signet ring that had been in his family for four generations. This man, this cowboy, appeared to be about as different from Alec Ballantree as a slab of steak from a lobster patty.

This man, with his pitch-black hair just long enough to brush his shirt collar, and the cool diamond-blue eyes that glinted from beneath the brim of his hat, was rugged as rock and looked as if he'd never seen the inside of an opera house or a tearoom, never had a servant shine his shoes or draw his bath.

Never danced a waltz with a woman beneath a crystal chandelier and told her he loved her . . . told her he would always love her . . .

He looked tough and capable—and just a tiny bit angry.

About what, she had no idea—and wouldn't even try to guess. There was no time to waste speculating about handsome strangers, especially cowboys, whom Mrs. Casper had spent the last few days of the journey warning her about.

She had to find Wade Barclay, her late father's fore-man, and get to the ranch.

"Hope, Wyoming!" the stagecoach driver bellowed, and threw open the stagecoach doors. As he let down the steps with a grunt, she bade farewell to Mrs. Casper, clutched her pink satin reticule between her gloved fingers, and carefully stepped down into the dusty street.

Hope. That's what she wanted, what she needed. *Hope.* Hope that the sale of the ranch would go smoothly and swiftly, hope that she could return to Becky as soon as possible.

Hope that no more trouble would catch up to them.

Caitlin peered up and down the street. The handsome cowboy had straightened and was studying her, but she resolutely ignored him. When she spotted the older, pot-bellied man in the huge white Stetson ambling toward her, she felt a wave of relief.

He looked exactly as she had pictured her father's foreman. Genial, easygoing, avuncular. And punctual. She was grateful he had met the stagecoach on time.

"You're Miz Summers, ain't you?" He squinted at her, but it wasn't his close-set eyes or the mole on his chin she noticed but the beet redness of his bulbous nose. "I'm—"

"Yes, of course, I know who you are. Good afternoon, Mr. Barclay. I appreciate your arriving here on time."

"Huh?"

The man stumbled as he reached her, and Caitlin instinctively shot out a hand to steady him. She tensed though as she smelled the liquor on his breath.

"Mr. Barclay . . . are you all right?"

"Wha? Never better, little lady. But call me Wesley."

"Wesley? I thought your name was Wade—"

"Hell, no, honey, I reckon I know my own name."

He chucked her under the chin, playfully, then as she drew back and stared at him in amazement, he threw back his head and let out a ripsnorting belly laugh. "Just bein' friendly-like, honey. So you're old Reese's long-lost little girl. And a right purty filly you are, too."

Gracious, he's a drunk, Caitlin thought in dismay. Bitterness filled her. She should have known Reese Summers would have had a drunk for a foreman. "I'd like to get to the ranch as quickly as possible." She tried to keep the anxiety from her voice. "If I'm able to complete my business tonight, I can purchase a ticket on tomorrow's stage and return to Philadelphia—"

"Tomorrow . . . Aw, honey, so soon? You just got here."

"Mr. Barclay . . . take your hand off me, please."

"I'm just bein' friendly. You're about the purtiest little gal I ever did see—"

"Mr. Barclay!" Caitlin slapped his hand away as it slid up her arm. Before she could order him again to keep his hands to himself, a gust of wind seized her hat and blew it clear off her head. She whirled to chase it and ran smack into a wall of rock.

It took a moment for her to realize that it wasn't a wall of rock after all—it was a man. A tall, lean, dark-haired man with an iron chest, a fierce scowl, and a body that was pure steel. *The cowboy.*

"Take it easy, princess."

Stunned, she couldn't do more than stare up into those clear blue eyes. For a moment, as his cool gaze commanded hers, she felt a wave of heat rush through her. Perhaps because she'd banged into him so abruptly, she felt light-headed.

Up close, she realized, he was even more mesmerizing than he'd been at a distance. And certainly . . . bigger. He towered over her, with his black hair and rugged features and that dark stubble shadowing his jaw. Beneath a blue chambray shirt almost the exact same color as his eyes, his chest was broad and muscular—and every bit as unyielding as the rest of him.

Caitlin took a step back, feeling overwhelmed. That little bit of distance helped—suddenly she recalled her hat—and tore her gaze from his. Peering past him, she was just in time to see it sailing into the horse trough across the street.

"No!"

She dashed after it, but it was too late. As she watched, the fetching, oh-so-fashionable hat with its dainty satin bow, ivory lace, and tiny pink and white silk flowers landed in the murky water.

Caitlin's mouth quivered as she watched the sodden ribbons and the once-beautiful little flowers sinking into the horse trough. She felt bereft. That hat was one of the last remnants of her once-privileged life in Philadelphia. Now it was gone too, ruined—just like everything else that she had once had and had taken for granted.

Gritting her teeth, she turned back toward the foreman.

"Mr. Barclay." Caitlin saw the cowboy watching her, a frown upon his face, but she ignored him as she addressed the potbellied man. "Kindly retrieve my bag from the driver at once and let's start for the ranch. I assume you've brought a buggy—"

"Buggy? Hell, girl, I don't got no buggy. And why do you keep calling me Mr. Barclay?" the drunken man whined. He teetered and would have fallen, but the cowboy's arm shot out this time to steady him.

"She's not thinkin' straight, Wade," the man complained. "And neither am I . . . right now. You explain, will ya? I think Reese's little girl is thick-headed," he added in a loud whisper that brought rosy color surging into Caitlin's cheeks. "What do you think, Wade?"

"Wade?" Caitlin stared from one man to the other and at last her stunned gaze fixed on the tall cowboy.

"He . . . called you Wade."

The cowboy nodded.

"Do you mean . . . *you're* Wade Barclay?"

"Reckon so."

"But . . ." Something dropped like a stone in the pit of her stomach. Her gaze flew to the other man. "Then who is *he*?"

"Wesley Beadle. Faro dealer at the saloon."

"Faro dealer . . ." Caitlin's voice trailed off.

"Mighty confused, ain't she, Wade? And she ain't even drunk." The potbellied man grinned, then burped, and with a vague wave in Caitlin's direction, he wandered off toward the saloon.

Another gust of wind swept down from the mountains and snagged several strands of golden hair loose from the chignon at Caitlin's nape. They whipped into her eyes and she brushed them back in frustration as she rounded on the real Wade Barclay.

"I don't understand. Why didn't you speak up sooner? You saw me walking toward him—you let him make a fool out of me!"

"Miss Summers, I reckon you did that all by yourself." Those impossibly cool blue eyes raked her dispassionately for one long moment, a moment in which, despite her pretty lavender gown and proper chemise and stockings, she felt as exposed as if he'd stripped her naked. She couldn't breathe as that hard stare traveled up and down the length of her body, skimmed every curve, burned through the silk of fair skin and delicate features and even through the icy exterior that was her only armor against the world. She knew by the faint contemptuous curve of his lip that this cool, tough-eyed cowboy found her profoundly lacking—stupid, graceless, an object of scorn.

How dare he.

She had just decided to try to wither him with a stare—the way Miss Culp did to all the students at the Davenport Academy for Young Ladies—when he jerked a thumb toward the brass trunk the stagecoach driver had unloaded. "That yours?"

"Yes, it is, but—"

Before she could finish the sentence, he was stalking away from her, toward the trunk.

Caitlin shook her head slowly. *Buck up*, she told herself, tightening her spine as she felt a raindrop from that wide cloudy sky plop down on her nose. *Don't let a rude, arrogant, uncivilized ranch foreman rattle you. Just get out to the ranch and take care of your business.*

She jumped though when a woman's booming voice rang out from the boardwalk.

"Wade—Wade Barclay! Is that Reese's daughter?"

He turned, squinted beneath his hat at the two women hurrying along the boardwalk. "Reckon so. Didn't see any other females get off the stage today." He swung back toward Caitlin, his handsome face half-hidden by his hat, carrying the trunk as easily as if it were a plate of pie.

"Miss Summers," the stout woman with the basket over one arm called out. "I'm Edna Weaver—my husband owns the bank here in Hope. How do you do?" Waiting only for a wagon to roll past, she stepped briskly off the boardwalk and hurried forward, the basket swinging. A reed of a woman followed, studying Caitlin with wide, searching eyes. "This here is Winnifred Dale—she works in the post office." Edna Weaver made a sympathetic clucking sound. "We're pleased to make your acquaintance, honey—only sorry it's under these circumstances."

"Oh . . . yes. Thank you." Had the entire town been anticipating her arrival? First the faro dealer and now these two women. Caitlin was surprised that anyone in Hope even knew of her existence—considering that her late father had never even written to her in the past eighteen years.

Warily, she studied the two. Edna Weaver's steel-gray hair was twisted into a practical bun, her gown was muted plum and trimmed with jet buttons, simple, yet stylish as it hugged her plump figure. Her deep-set brown eyes met Caitlin's green ones with steady appraisal and there appeared to be genuine friendliness in her smile. But Caitlin had learned that people weren't always what they seemed and she wasn't about to let her guard down. Not with Edna Weaver—not with anyone, however friendly they appeared. The other woman, shorter, and slightly younger than Edna, perhaps in her forties, had a nervous, mouselike quality. She kept touching the high neck of her green and white gingham gown and peering at Caitlin through narrow spectacles that rested on the bridge of her delicate nose. Wispy brown hair that looked soft as taffy curled around her small, pointed face.

"Your father was a fine man, dear." Regret tinged Edna's words as Wade Barclay set down her trunk. "Reese didn't get to town much—but I can guarantee you he'll be sorely missed around these parts. Isn't that so, Winnie?"

The brown-haired woman was gazing at Caitlin as if transfixed. "Yes, yes, it's so." A shy smile emerged. "Your father was a dear friend . . . a very dear friend," she murmured sadly. "He . . . he would have been so proud to see what a beautiful young lady you turned out to be."

Caitlin stiffened. However kind Winnifred Dale might be—or meant to be—she was misguided. Reese Summers wouldn't have cared how his daughter turned out. He didn't care about her at all.

The woman rushed on. "If you need anything while you're here in Hope, Miss Summers, anything at all, you must call on me—or on Edna here. We'd be happy to lend a hand in any way we can."

"Hope is a neighborly place," Edna added. "So is all of Silver Valley. You'll like it here, I'm sure."

"That's kind of you, but I won't be staying. I've only come to settle my father's estate."

Both women's eyebrows rose simultaneously in surprise. Wade Barclay went still as stone.

Caitlin's chin shot up a notch. "I didn't come to pay my respects—or to settle in Wyoming. I came to sell Cloud Ranch."

"Sell . . ." Edna made a choking sound.

Winnifred's hands flew to her heart. "Oh, no! My dear, you can't do anything like that! Gracious! That ranch is such a big, successful, wonderful place—the largest in the territory! It meant everything to your father," she gasped. And looked at Wade Barclay.

He said nothing. Only stared at the blond girl in taut, deadly silence.

"I am well aware of that." Caitlin's voice was tight. She knew exactly how much Cloud Ranch had meant to her father. More than her mother had meant to him, more than *she* had meant to him . . .

"However, it doesn't mean anything to me." She managed an airy toss of her head, a pretty gesture she had perfected in dozens of Philadelphia ballrooms. "I intend to sell it lock, stock, and barrel and return back east just as soon as possible."

"The hell you will," Wade Barclay said in a low tone.

Edna Weaver jumped in. "What he means, honey, is that you *can't* sell the ranch—I mean, you *mustn't*—" Edna flashed the foreman a helpless glance.

"Wade, dear," Winnifred murmured in distress, her eyes darting back and forth between Caitlin and the cowboy, "do you mean she doesn't *know*?"

"Who's had a chance to tell her *anything*?" he growled.

"What do you mean? Tell me anything about what?" Caitlin fought the alarm sweeping through her. She stepped forward. "There is no reason why I *shouldn't* sell Cloud Ranch," she said breathlessly. "I have a letter from a lawyer telling me that it was bequeathed to me in my father's will. It's right here in my reticule—"

But as she began to dig frantically through her handbag, Wade clamped a hand over her arm.

"This isn't the time or place to go into this. Let's go," he said curtly.

"G-go?"

"To the ranch. I'll explain everything there."

He looked toward Edna Weaver and Winnifred Dale, still watching in consternation. "Ladies," he said, nodding.

"Oh, yes, do go, Wade . . . show her the ranch." Winnifred bobbed her head. Edna grimaced and started to move away.

"I'm sure . . . Wade can explain it all, Miss Summers. And we'll see you again," she said quickly. "Didn't mean to interfere, Wade," she added worriedly, her head drooping as the foreman shot her an exasperated glance.

Caitlin watched them move off, their skirts rustling as they hastened along the boardwalk. She was rigid with shock. She couldn't imagine what impediment there could be to her selling the ranch, but the very idea of something keeping her from executing her last desperate plan filled her with fear. For a moment she stood rooted to the spot, trying to summon what remained of her composure.

A bay horse tethered to a hitching post beside the mercantile neighed suddenly, then fell silent. Hope's main street appeared suddenly deserted, perhaps, Caitlin realized, because of the darkening horizon and the rain that threatened. The high, gray sky had begun to fill with tumbling clouds and the wind starting to gust down from the mountains smelled of damp earth and pine.

A dusky tension gripped the air as Caitlin's lavender skirt whipped about her legs.

"Miss Summers? You all right?"

Wade Barclay was still holding her arm. He was gazing at her warily. "You're not going to faint or anything, are you?"

"I never faint, Mr. Barclay." She took a deep breath and met his glance with big green eyes ablaze with purpose. "Nor do I cry. Neither one accomplishes anything constructive. That much I've learned in my experience of the world."

"That so? Well, fine then. Let's go."

"I'm not going anywhere with you until you answer my questions."

"Want to bet?"

His grip on her arm tightened. With his other hand he lifted her trunk easily and without another word began to propel Caitlin along the street.

"How dare you! Let me go." She tried to wrench free and gasped when she couldn't. "Listen, Mr. Barclay—I want answers and I want them right now!"

"Maybe it's time you learned, princess—you can't always get what you want."

Caitlin's mouth dropped. "Let me go!" she demanded furiously and dug in her heels. "I refuse to accompany you another step until you tell me what those women were talking about." It was either downright drag her or stop, and Wade Barclay, his eyes narrowing, stopped.

"Do you always behave like a spoiled brat?"

"Do you always behave like an obnoxious *bully*?"

"Reckon you just bring out the best in me." Wade scowled. He hadn't meant to let his temper get the best of him, hadn't meant to let Reese's daughter know how much he disliked her. Reese wouldn't have wanted that. But somehow, from the moment she stepped down from the stage, all golden angel hair and creamy skin and bewitching eyes, he'd felt his chest go tight inside.

The tiny little girl he'd looked at so often in the framed photograph on the mantel was all grown-up. No longer merely the pretty dab of a child who had gazed sweetly back from her mama's lap, she was every inch a woman now. A woman whose beauty shone from every exquisite feature, who smelled faintly, deliciously, of violets.

A woman who had broken Reese Summers's heart.

She and her mother both, Reese reminded himself, his gut tightening.

Remembering how Reese had yearned for this girl, this daughter of his, how he had worried over her, dreamed of her, even whispered of her with his last breath, made Wade's gut clench.

He wanted to hit someone—but he couldn't hit her. He'd never hit a woman in his life and he wasn't about to start with Reese's daughter. Even if she did deserve a good spanking.

Reese had made him promise to take care of her. Damn it, what he really wanted to do was haul her pretty butt back onto that stage and slam the door in her face. But instead he curbed his temper, tensed his jaw, and spoke to her with all the cool detachment he could muster.

"Look, Miss Summers, it's going to rain. Could even

storm. Do you want to be stuck out in the middle of nowhere when that happens or do you want to be snug and dry at the ranch? It's up to you. But if we don't head out right now, we're not going to make it back before the storm hits."

"On the contrary, Mr. Barclay, it's up to you. I'm not going anywhere until you answer my questions. As soon as you do that, we can leave. What aren't you telling me about Cloud Ranch?"

"Whatever you need to know you can find out soon as we get there." He reached for her arm again, his expression purposeful, but Caitlin jumped back out of reach.

"I won't go anywhere with you—not until you answer me."

That did it. His mouth tightened. Blue eyes glittered. "Suit yourself."

He dropped her trunk in the street. Dust sprayed as it struck the earth. And then he strode off. Scarcely able to believe her eyes, Caitlin could only gaze in consternation at his back.

He was leaving her, actually leaving her, walking toward the opposite end of town. Every long stride left her farther and farther behind.

A wagon rattled by. A door slammed somewhere. The clouds tumbled lower.

Caitlin felt dazed. And a little ill. Wade Barclay wasn't looking back, wasn't slowing his steps at all. He was actually abandoning her. He would no doubt get in the buggy and drive right back to Cloud Ranch—without her.

Then what would she do?

She gritted her teeth, straightened her shoulders, and

with a slight groan, hefted her trunk. She started after him, with as much dignity as she could muster.

The wind whipped at her dusty gown and blew the wayward strands of her pale curls. Anger flamed through her—anger at the man who was supposed to have greeted her and taken her to her father's ranch, treating her with respect and consideration. Instead he had insulted, bullied, and abandoned her.

Fuming, she marched down the main street, the trunk dragging at her arms, random raindrops spattering her path. By the time she reached Pete's Feed Store and saw Wade Barclay standing at the heads of two gray horses hitched to a wagon, she was out of breath. Droplets of perspiration glistened at her brow, and her face was flushed like the pink wildflowers that had dotted the plains just outside the town.

"A wagon?" she huffed as she came up beside him, and dropped the blasted trunk in the dust. "Why didn't you bring a . . . buggy?"

"Had supplies to buy. Needed a wagon." He spoke the fewest words possible as he moved from the team's heads and shoved a few sacks around in the back of the wagon. "Does this mean you want to go to the ranch after all?"

"Brilliant, Mr. Barclay." Caitlin's arm burned from carrying the trunk. "I see your powers of reasoning are only exceeded by your manners and charm."

"Don't have much use for manners or charm in my line of work," he drawled. "And this is what I'm doing right now. Work. Hauling you back to the ranch isn't a social nicety, princess, it's just part of my job."

"Something my father would have expected you to do, you mean."

He eyed her, coming around the side of the wagon toward her, his movements easy.

"That's right."

"And do you think he would have expected you to make me carry my own trunk, to chase you down the street, to have to endure your insufferable rudeness?"

Wade stared at her, opened his mouth, then shut it.

Damn it all to hell, she had him there. Reese would have expected a lot more from him and he knew it. But this selfish, spoiled, damnable little beauty didn't deserve his respect, or sympathy, or kindness. She deserved a kick in the butt.

"Let me help you into the wagon, Miss Summers," he said, forcing himself to be civil. "If you're not too proud to ride in it."

"I don't have much choice, do I?" She allowed him to help her onto the seat. There was such strength in the hands that lifted her that she trembled a little.

She stared straight ahead as he tossed her trunk into the back of the wagon, atop a sack of potatoes.

"One more thing, Mr. Barclay," she said icily as he sprang up beside her and picked up the reins. The team of gray horses started smoothly forward.

"What's that, Miss Summers?" Even that lazy drawl of his gnawed on her nerves.

"I'm giving you notice." She spoke each word with clear precision. "The moment we reach Cloud Ranch, you're fired."

Chapter 2

"Fired?"

"Correct."

"Fired." Beneath an increasingly overcast Wyoming sky, Wade Barclay gave a crack of laughter. He flicked the reins and the horses picked up their pace to a fast trot, kicking up showers of dust as their hooves flew over the trail. They left the little town of Hope behind and headed west across a vast treeless plain.

Caitlin twisted upon the seat to glare at him when he continued chuckling.

"How nice that you find this amusing. I do hope you're still laughing when you begin searching for another job, hat in hand, hungry, desperate—"

"You're a real charmer, aren't you, princess?"

"Stop calling me that. It's Miss Summers to you. I'm your employer," she retorted, grabbing the wagon seat suddenly as they jolted over a rut in the trail. "Or at least I am for the next little while—how long until we reach the ranch?"

" 'Bout two hours." The way he said it made her realize that he felt this was going to be the longest two hours of his life. Caitlin felt exactly the same way. She could scarcely wait to reach the ranch and be rid of this man forever.

"When we arrive you will immediately gather whatever personal belongings you possess and you will vacate my property. I'm sure that someone else will be there to attend to the horses and the . . . the supplies and . . . everything."

"Quite the boss lady, aren't you?"

"Not for long. Only until I can sell the ranch to the highest bidder."

"Don't count on that."

"I beg your pardon?"

His next words chilled her. "No one is selling this ranch."

"You have nothing to say about it."

"That's where you're wrong."

Caitlin couldn't bear it any longer. If there was a reason why she couldn't sell the ranch, and Wade Barclay knew what it was, he was going to tell her here and now. She would burst if she waited until they reached the ranch. All she could picture in her mind was Becky's face the last time she'd seen her—sweet and pale, and so very worried.

And her voice—quavering so softly that damp gray afternoon when Caitlin had gone to the Davenport Academy to hug her and say good-bye.

"But you will come back and take me away from this place, won't you, Caity? I hate it here—everyone is whispering about me. About P-Papa. Even the teachers have been horrid."

"I'll come get you as soon as I possibly can. Don't pay any attention to the whispers. Just hold your head up high and pretend you don't hear." That's what Caitlin had done, too. She knew from experience that it wasn't easy.

"I'll try." Becky had clung to her hand, giving it little pitiful squeezes. *"Everything is going to be all right, isn't it, Caity?"*

She'd kissed Becky's cheek and promised her that everything would indeed be all right. And she would make it all right—no matter what.

"Stop the horses right now." Caitlin glared at Wade Barclay's grim profile. "You keep giving me hints and warnings and being horridly mysterious without giving me any information. I refuse to put up with it a moment longer. We're not going farther until you give me some answers. Do you hear me?" Her voice rose as he continued on as if she hadn't spoken. "Answers!" she shouted. "This is too important—I can't wait hours. Stop the wagon right this minute or I'll—I'll jump out!"

The glance he threw her was skeptical, but her flushed cheeks and quickened breaths must have convinced him of her genuine agitation because to her surprise, he actually obeyed her command. The horses drew up. The grassy trail stretched before them, and beyond rose a series of rolling sage-colored hills. Three deer darted past some brush to her left and bolted away, and the sky darkened to an even more ominous shade of green as she turned on the wagon seat to face him.

"It's about time you started listening to me—"

"I'm not doing this for you." He cut her off. "I'm doing it for Reese."

"What are you talking about?"

His eyes flicked over her. "He wouldn't want you getting yourself all upset."

At the thought of how wrong he was, a sharp pain twisted through her, but she wouldn't let Wade Barclay see it—not a glimpse. She smoothed her skirt. Shrugged.

"I highly doubt that."

"You're wrong."

"My father was too selfish and self-centered to give a damn about me when he was alive, so I can't see that he would care much now that he's . . . Oh!"

He seized her so suddenly that Caitlin gasped as his strong fingers clamped around her arm.

"Not another word against him." Wade spoke in a low, angry tone. "You'd better not bad-mouth Reese to me or to anyone else."

"How dare you threaten me." Her rich green eyes were wide with alarm, but her voice was steady, if a little breathless. "Take your hands off me this instant!"

Wade stared into those flashing, fiery eyes and felt a heated tension shoot through him. Damn, did she have to be so beautiful on the outside when she was such a nasty little witch on the inside? If he didn't know what he did about her—if he hadn't seen and heard himself just how cold and callous she was—and how irritatingly bossy—he might have been ambushed by that beautiful face.

As he glared at her, fighting the fury inside him, he suddenly noticed that her lower lip was trembling. Dark pink and full, it quivered and he couldn't seem to stop staring at it.

She had a luscious mouth, and a body that would tempt any man but a blind preacher—yet she was nothing but a she-devil, he reminded himself.

Reese's she-devil.

And he'd promised Reese that he'd take care of her.

"Take your hands off me!" the she-devil screeched again, and this time, he did as she asked.

In fact, he pushed her away.

"I think we'd both better settle down," he said.

Caitlin took a deep breath. "It's very important to me that I understand something right now. Is there some reason why I cannot sell Cloud Ranch?"

"You won't be selling Cloud Ranch." His answer was as firm and purposeful as the set expression upon his face.

"That's ridiculous." But fear clutched at her. "I have every right. The letter from my father's attorney says plainly that I inherited the ranch including the land, the house, the cattle, and all buildings and property—"

"Do you want me to finish answering your question or do you want to listen to yourself babble on about something you don't know squat about?"

She flinched at his harsh tone. The anger rose in her again—anger and the beginnings of real unease. She *had* to be able to sell the ranch. She needed the money it would bring so that she and Becky could get away, so that they could manage until she could find a job and get them settled in a decent place to live . . .

"You're making no sense," she told the foreman, her voice low and shaking with the apprehension tearing through her. "But go on. I'm listening."

"Abner McCain, Reese's lawyer, was supposed to meet us at the ranch today. He had some business in Laramie and thought he'd be back, but I got a telegram right before the stage pulled in. He can't make it until tomorrow, so it looks like you're going to have to hear this from me."

"Hear what?"

A rumble of thunder shook the air. The clouds seemed to grow even darker, heavier, lower in that great sky. Wade frowned at them, then shot a glance over at Reese's daughter, weighing his options. She'd explode like a lit firecracker when he told her. Probably yell. And cry—despite that nonsense she'd spouted about never crying. And then she'd yell some more.

She deserves this shock, he thought grimly. *She has it coming.*

Yet great as the temptation was, he couldn't bring himself to tell her now, here, in the middle of nowhere, with a storm bearing down on them. That didn't seem right.

She'd want to be alone after she heard, have a chance to calm down and sort things out in private. And if they headed home fast, maybe they could beat the storm.

"The terms of your father's will are complicated. Too complicated to explain right now. You'll want to look the will over yourself. Not that it will change anything," he said evenly.

"But you—"

"Look, there's some real bad weather moving in fast." Wade took up the reins again. "You'll get drenched if we don't make tracks. Reckon you wouldn't like that much. Besides," he added as the horses pranced restlessly, "you'll probably need a good strong shot of whiskey once I tell you exactly what that will says. Trust me."

"I don't drink whiskey and I don't trust you and I want to hear the terms right now."

"Too bad." Wade sent the horses into a trot, then quickly took them to a gallop as a gust of wind lashed down from the mountains and shook the thick grass and the limbs of all the trees.

Long wisps of gold hair whipped free of Caitlin's chignon and swirled across her cheeks. She felt a splash of rain. Just what she needed. To get soaked on top of everything else. On top of finding out there were complications in the will.

"Very well, Mr. Barclay, when we reach the ranch, first you'll tell me the terms and then I'll fire you," she informed him. Suddenly she gasped as the team surged forward and the wagon jolted hard and fast over the rough trail.

He was trying to beat the storm, she realized, not trying to frighten her, but she couldn't help the alarm that rushed through her as the wagon tore across the vast open plains, and the cool, damp wind pelted her face. She jolted in the seat and wished she had her hat—even more tendrils of hair blew loose of their pins as the horses raced for home.

She stiffened her back and said nothing, refusing to cry out, to let Wade Barclay see how uncomfortable, alarmed, and miserable she was—not only at the breakneck pace they were traveling but at the complications looming before her.

Wasn't her life complicated enough? She should have known her father would have made it even more so. Even in death, he was a source of hurt and doubt.

She was only three when her mother, Lydia, fled the tiny cabin deep in Wyoming Territory, taking Caitlin with her to find a better life. Reese Summers cared for nothing but his precious ranch, her mother told her later. He was set on building Cloud Ranch into the biggest, most profitable cattle ranch in the territory, no matter that his wife and child were stranded in the midst of vast, lonely mountainous country, no matter that Lydia was dreadfully unhappy, that the winters were savagely cold, brutal, and spent in isolation deep within Silver Valley. Reese refused to give up his dream, to budge from that wild outpost of land wedged in the shadow of the Laramie Mountains. So her mother left him, fleeing east, where she met and married Gillis Tamarlane, the dashing scion of a railroad magnate. Gillis not only arranged for Lydia's divorce, but also promised to raise Caitlin as his own.

And Caitlin never saw Reese Summers again—not since the day that Lydia packed her up shortly after Reese set out on a cattle drive. Her mother simply took the wagon into town, used the money Reese had left her for supplies, and boarded the stagecoach headed to St. Louis. And never looked back.

Caitlin looked back though—or tried to, but throughout the years, her memory of those early days in Wyoming blurred and faded. She could remember very little about her real father. Her impression was of a large man with a very deep voice and—cigars. She remembered the strong aroma of his cigars. But not much more.

There wasn't even a photograph of him . . .

Not that she didn't ask for one. She wrote to Reese for the first time when she was eight, asking if he would send her a photograph, asking if he would write to her, asking if she might come to Cloud Ranch sometime and ride a pony.

There was no reply.

She tried again a few years later—and again that brought no response.

Not once did he even acknowledge her letters.

She didn't even know that Cloud Ranch indeed became the most prosperous ranch in the territory until Reese's letter arrived, the letter where he told her he was dying—and requesting that she come to see him.

The letter arrived the very same day the news reached her that Lydia and Gillis had perished at sea.

The day her entire life changed forever.

Her mother and Gillis Tamarlane were charming, good-natured, fascinating, and elusive parents. What with the hectic social whirl they delighted in, they didn't have much time to spare, certainly not enough to spend at home with either Caitlin or her young half sister, Becky. Growing up, she and Becky never wanted for anything that money could buy—they had the finest of homes, and a plenitude of clothes, toys, schools, nursemaids, cooks—and there were parties and outings galore. But their parents' time and attention were noticeably absent. Lydia and Gillis never seemed to have more than a few moments to spend with their daughters, for there was always a ball or an opera or a house party to attend, always a friend to visit or a trip to take.

As a matter of fact, they were enjoying an extended house party at the Earl of Wyslet's estate in Suffolk before their fatal voyage back across the Atlantic.

A voyage that changed Caitlin's life in every possible way.

For despite the fact that they were forever gallivanting from one party or event to another, that they were often too busy to pay attention to the everyday lives of their daughters, and that they packed them off to fine boarding schools the moment they were of age, the loss of those two beautiful and dashing parents struck both Caitlin and Becky deeply.

No wonder that in the aftermath of grief and confusion there was no time or strength or will left to ponder the wishes of Reese Summers, a man who had ignored Caitlin completely over the past eighteen years. Particularly since the next blow to fall sent her reeling: the shock of discovering the mountain of debts Gillis Tamarlane had left behind—debts that, once settled, rendered Caitlin and Becky virtually penniless—and turned them into objects of pity and scorn, whispers and silence from those whom they'd once counted as friends.

A spatter of rain shook Caitlin from her reverie and she realized that the horses were now crossing a hillier, steeper terrain—plunging up a zigzagging trail, flying past a narrow red ravine on a path that left her breathless. Drizzling rain fell sporadically but gathered strength as another crack of thunder boomed, even louder and nearer than the first.

"Bet right about now you're wishing you had that hat of yours," Wade Barclay remarked over the rush of the wind.

Caitlin didn't deign to answer.

They entered a long valley where the tall grass blew in the wind, where distant pine-covered mountains cut the sky and a waterfall tumbled down from high black rocks in a splash of silver. A valley where cattle huddled in bunches upon the wide grassland, and upon ledges, rocky slopes, along ravines—even more were visible in the distance, in the flower-bright foothills, as far as the eye could see.

Caitlin caught sight of antelope darting across a hilltop. Vivid wildflowers bloomed—Indian paintbrush, buttercup, forget-me-nots, their colors brilliant against the ominous purpling of the sky. The horses sprang forward, the rain rushed down, and jackrabbits scurried through the brush in search of their burrows.

"Is it much farther?" she gasped at last, shivering, rain streaming like tears down her cheeks, her gown plastered to her body.

"Not much. The house is set back behind that big ridge up there."

"So we're nearing my father's land."

"We've been on your father's land for miles," he retorted. "All of this is Cloud Ranch."

Shock ran through her.

"All . . . of this?" She waved her hand, vaguely encompassing the long valley, the rangeland dotted with cattle, the hills and ridges they'd been traversing, even the distant waterfall far to the west.

"Every blade of grass, every rock and hill, every steer and calf—those canyons way across the valley, the buttes back of the stream, all the prairie as far as the eye can see—and beyond. Cloud Ranch."

Stunned, she hugged her arms around herself, swaying as the wagon rolled along at its relentless pace. *All of this?* Something in the wild, desperately beautiful land struck a cord in her—it *was* beautiful, in an awe-inspiring way. It was big country, huge, and they hadn't passed another human being or dwelling of any kind since leaving Hope.

On a clear day with the sun shining it would be magnificent. Today it was almost terrifying. Should lightning strike . . .

It did, at that very moment.

Caitlin bit out a scream as the fiery slash of gold exploded across the sky.

"Easy. We're all right." She saw the cool glance Wade Barclay threw her and bit down on her lip to contain herself. Not that she cared what he thought of her—he would be off her property in a very short time anyway and she'd never have to see him again—but she didn't want to give him the satisfaction of thinking her a frightened ninny, of laughing at her . . .

She had a quick sudden flash of others who had laughed at her—particularly Mavis Drew and Annabella Pratt, laughing behind their hands after they learned that Philadelphia's most sought-after belle was poor, penniless, and adrift—that she'd lost everything, including her fiancé Alec Ballantree. They'd laughed when she'd found there was no place for her in the world she once had dominated like a radiant sun among lesser stars.

Oh, how they'd laughed.

Her throat tightened. Her lovely mouth set with resolve. She didn't care what she had to do, what obstacles she had to overcome—no one would ever laugh at her or Becky again.

Another lightning bolt blazed across the sky, illuminating the mountains, their craggy, pine-covered peaks, the slopes of yellow and blue flowers dappled with pink, but this time Caitlin swallowed the scream, swallowed her fear.

"Almost there!" He had to shout over the roar of the wind as suddenly gusts of rain began to slant down in streaming torrents and Caitlin hugged her arms around herself and yearned to see shelter . . . any kind of shelter.

Then they were at the peak of the great ridge and galloping wildly across level land, a rich green meadow high with grass, studded with cattle.

As the rain slashed down the wagon bounced across

the trail, which swerved through a belt of trees that shook like matchsticks, then across a sloping plain, over a rise, and then, at last, she saw it.

A house. A wonderful house. Not the tiny square wood cabin she'd expected—the one her mother had described long ago, but a long, sprawling, magnificent two-story log house with wide windows and a slanted roof, surrounded by outbuildings and corrals, barns and sheds. Plumes of silver-gray smoke curled from the chimney, and golden light glowed cheerfully at the windows. There was a long, white-painted shaded porch out front, she saw as the wagon careened closer, turning up a winding drive and then past the corrals and a low building where a russet-haired cowboy in the doorway waved his hat at Wade Barclay in greeting.

The cowboy immediately sprinted forward as the wagon halted before the house. A great black dog with two white feet bounded off the porch and wagged its tail as Wade jumped down from the seat.

"Hey, there, Dawg." Wade strode around to heave Caitlin's trunk from the back. Another boom of thunder shook the sky.

"Fine weather we're havin, Wade." The cowboy grinned, hurrying straight to the horses' heads.

"Couldn't be better, Rooster." Wade helped Caitlin alight. He did it so effortlessly she might have weighed no more than a pin. The instant her feet touched the ground she pulled away from him and swept toward the porch.

"You must be Miss Summers." The cowboy tipped his hat, rain pouring from the brim as his gaze skimmed over the wet lavender gown that clung to every single one of Caitlin's lush curves. He had the grace to blush. "Uh, pleasure to meet you, ma'am. Only sorry about the circumstances."

"So am I." Caitlin stepped onto the covered porch, not even glancing at the cowboy, or at the black dog sniffling around her heels and at the hem of her soaked gown. She had meant to dash inside as quickly as possible, but now that she was here, at the very doorway of her father's precious Cloud Ranch, her feet wouldn't budge. She could only stare, frozen, at the huge double doors of sturdy oak, at the gleaming brass knocker shaped like a horseshoe.

This was the house where she'd been born. Her mother had always described it as such a tiny place. She realized suddenly that Reese Summers must have kept the original log cabin where he and Lydia had lived and added the other sections of the house after the ranch became successful. After his ambitions had come true—at the expense of his wife and daughter.

She swallowed.

"Go on in." She jumped at Wade Barclay's deep voice beside her. "Reese is gone, you don't have to face him," he said coldly.

She couldn't reply. The sight of the house, the impact that this place, Cloud Ranch, had had on her life, loomed before her as she tried to will her feet toward the entrance.

For years, Cloud Ranch and her father's neglect had ached in her heart—an ache that had never gone away. Coming to this ranch, which had meant more to him than his wife and his daughter, brought all the pain of those unanswered letters back again, and made her wonder, as thoughts of it always did, how her life might have been different if Lydia had never left, or if Reese had cared enough about her to keep in touch . . .

Go in, she told herself as the rain pelted down beyond the shelter of the porch and the wind blew her skirt around her knees. *Just push the door open and walk in.*

"Something wrong?" Wade asked sharply.

She tore her gaze from the heavy doors and gazed into his handsome, frowning face.

"N-no . . . nothing at all." She noticed that Rooster was leading the horses toward the barn, that the dog had trotted after him, his black coat slick from the downpour. And that she and Wade Barclay were all alone on the porch, with the wind and rain whipping in at them. Suddenly she became aware that the foreman was studying the curves of her body through the sodden gown that stuck to her. Her breasts, her hips, all clearly outlined by the wet clinging silk. His blue eyes were narrowed, and there was a keen glint in them that made her flush.

She wanted to slap him. And she wanted to run away from him . . . and this wild, desolate place.

"You came all this way to claim your inheritance," he said, and she heard the fierce quiet anger back in his voice. He shifted his gaze from her body, focusing with piercing intensity on her face.

"Don't you want to see where your father lived—and where he died? Or are you too squeamish to go inside?"

"Don't be ridiculous."

His lip curled. Suddenly he pushed the door open. Before Caitlin even realized it, he grabbed hold of her arm and dragged her inside, then kicked the door closed behind them.

"Consider yourself safely delivered. Welcome to Cloud Ranch."

Chapter 3

Caitlin couldn't speak for a moment as she gazed around the wide, oak-floored hallway.

For a moment she forgot all about Wade Barclay, his roughness and rude treatment. A sense of comfort, spaciousness, and warmth enveloped her. So this was Cloud Ranch, this big house with its high-beamed ceilings and gleaming wood floors.

With a lump in her throat, she realized that this expansive area must have once been the entire main room of the cabin. The room where she and her mother had lived with Reese Summers.

Now it was a huge entry hall, its oak floor polished to a high gleam, and an elaborate brass chandelier descending from the ceiling. A walnut table and square mirror stood against one wall, and a wide stairway led to the next story.

She took a deep breath. The house smelled of lemon polish. And . . . beef stew, she realized. And fresh bread. A tantalizing combination.

The sensation of spaciousness, hominess, and cozy

warmth enveloped her—she had a glimpse of large, comfortably furnished rooms branching off the entry hall: a parlor with gold-framed watercolors upon the walls and an elegant stone mantel, and a study or office of some sort, with shelf after shelf filled with books, as well as a great oak desk and a Turkish carpet that covered almost the entire floor.

Cloud Ranch was not primitive or spartan in any way, she realized. It was every bit as comfortable and fine in its own way as her former Philadelphia home had been.

Somehow this only made the knot in her chest grow tighter.

"Francesca? We're back!" Wade called out, setting her trunk down beside the walnut table.

"Who's Francesca?"

"Our cook and housekeeper—here she is now." Wade's stern features relaxed for the first time as the short, olive-skinned woman bustled into the hall. She looked to be in her mid-sixties, pretty, with dark graying hair twisted into a firm coil atop her head and strong, chiseled features.

"Senor Wade! *Por Dios,* you are soaked to the bone," she scolded, a Spanish flavor accenting her brisk words. Her floury hands flew in dismay to her cheeks. But as her gaze fell upon the bedraggled blond-haired girl all the soft concern faded from her face. "Ah, so this is the senor's daughter," she muttered.

Francesca's dark, thick-lashed eyes swept Caitlin from head to toe. There was patent disapproval in her stare. She sniffed. "On behalf of Senor Reese, I welcome you, senorita." She spoke with a noticeable lack of enthusiasm. "If you wish, I will show you to your room."

"Thank you." Caitlin spoke quietly. "I'm afraid that I'm dripping water all over your floor."

"Hmmph." The housekeeper shrugged, her expression stony. "You are not responsible for the storm. Besides," she added, "I have been told that the floor now belongs to *you*."

And you couldn't be more displeased about that, Caitlin thought. She turned to Wade. "I've decided that you may stay on until after we've had our discussion—and until the storm has passed. Then I want you to leave my property at once."

"You don't say."

"I do say."

She spoke haughtily, but some of her composure slipped when she suddenly noticed that his chambray shirt was every bit as soaked as her own gown. It clung to the muscles of his chest and arms—*and what powerful muscles they are,* she thought in a gulp. They could only have been built and toned by an immense amount of hard work. She felt her breath catch in her throat. *Don't stare,* she ordered herself, and with iron resolve, dragged her gaze away from his powerful body and focused instead on his face. That dark, quiet handsome-as-hell face.

"Kindly carry my trunk to my room. That will be the last of your duties here."

"'Fraid it won't be that easy to get rid of me, Miss Summers."

"We'll just see about that."

"Yep, I reckon we will." Hefting the trunk, he strode past her to the staircase. "I'll meet you in Reese's study in an hour. Don't keep me waiting. We'll go over the will before dinner."

Caitlin's mouth dropped. One would have thought *he* was the owner of Cloud Ranch—not merely its foreman, she thought indignantly as he strode up the stairs two at a time and disappeared around a corner.

Well, she would soon put an end to that bit of presumption.

"Come, senorita." The housekeeper gestured toward the stairs. "You must be weary from your journey. Senor Reese would want you to rest."

Weary didn't begin to describe how she felt. She feared she might actually burst from all the swirling emotions racing through her. Caitlin followed the woman up the stairs, to a room at the end of the upstairs hall. There was no sign of Wade anywhere, but the door was ajar and her trunk was in the center of the floor, beside a brass four-poster bed.

"I will bring you some hot water for your bath," Francesca said brusquely at the doorway. "Then I must return to my cooking."

She started to turn away.

"Francesca—wait," Caitlin said suddenly.

The housekeeper paused and studied her with those dark eyes.

"You don't seem to want me here." She shrugged. "I don't understand why, but it doesn't matter. Because I won't be staying long. Only long enough to sell the ranch."

There was a pause during which Caitlin heard only the rush of rain and wind at the window. Then, slowly, Francesca shook her head. "It is not that I don't want you here, senorita. That is not for me to say." She drew herself up very straight. "It is that it took you so long to get here. Too long. That is all."

She swept out the door and down the hall before Caitlin could respond.

Drawing in a deep breath, Caitlin closed the door and leaned against it. The room was large, with a wide-paned window graced by crisp yellow and white curtains, and there was a plump yellow quilt upon the bed. Everything looked pretty and fresh. But the thing she noticed immediately and which drew her quickly forward was the fire blazing in the small stone hearth across from the window. Wade Barclay must have lighted it when he'd brought her trunk.

Shivering, she hurried toward the dancing golden flames and began to strip off her wet clothes.

Perhaps the man isn't so bad, after all, she thought, grateful for the kind gesture and trying to be fair. But then she shook her head. Of course he was bad. Bad news all the way around. He was too handsome for words, impossibly rude, arrogant, and ridiculously domineering. The last thing she needed was a man trying to control her— she'd had enough of that. No man would ever wield power over her again, she vowed as she leaned toward the flames, her bones aching for the warmth.

She had a sudden sickening vision of Dominic Trent, of the cruel triumph in his face that night when he'd thought he'd cornered her, when he'd tried to force her . . .

She let out her breath and pushed the ugly memories from her mind.

Dominic Trent had learned the hard way that she wouldn't be controlled so easily. And Wade Barclay would too.

Rubbing the chill from her arms, she turned her thoughts to what lay ahead. She'd deal with these stupid complications and then she'd send Wade Barclay packing from Cloud Ranch faster than he could say "Giddyap."

And then she'd head back east to Becky. Perhaps she could still leave tomorrow, if all went well.

And nothing Wade Barclay could say or do was going to stop her.

"What do you mean the ranch doesn't belong solely to me?" Caitlin sat upon the green leather sofa that took up one wall of Reese Summers's study. She gaped at Wade as if he'd just tossed her a lit stick of dynamite. "There must be some mistake!"

"No mistake. See for yourself."

He opened the desk drawer, removed a packet of papers, and brought them over to her.

But as he held them out to her, Caitlin stared wordlessly at them, as wary of touching them as she would be of touching a snake.

She had thought she was prepared for anything when she came down here to meet Wade. She had bathed, brushed her hair, and coiled it atop her head in a smooth, perfect chignon. She'd donned a tight-sleeved gown of dark blue silk and her pearl and garnet necklace with its matching dainty earbobs. She'd come downstairs feeling strong and confident and ready to face whatever difficulties Wade Barclay threw her way, but some of her composure had vanished when she'd entered Reese's study. For a moment the faint scent of cigar smoke had assaulted her nostrils and brought back hazy memories. Pleasant memories of being held and cuddled, of feeling safe, happy, of a deep voice speaking to her, *singing* to her . . .

She'd shaken them off. She didn't want those memories. They didn't matter.

The scent of cigar smoke had wafted away. But then Wade Barclay had made his stunning announcement and the rest of her composure flew right out the window.

She stared at the packet of papers he held out to her, feeling her hands grow clammy.

"Do you want them or don't you?"

She snatched them from his grasp. "Perhaps you would be so good as to tell me who else this ranch could possibly belong to?" she snapped.

"My pleasure, ma'am." Wade met her flashing eyes with equanimity. "Me."

She went cold all over. *"You?"*

"That's right." He sauntered to the desk and leaned against it, his thumbs hooked negligently in his pockets. "Me. And my brothers. Clint and Nick Barclay."

"Brothers? You mean, there's more than one like you in this world?"

"Do you want to hear about the will or not?"

"Go ahead," she bit out, a dreadful panic shooting through the center of her stomach.

Wade picked up a pencil from the desk and began to roll it between his fingers as he spoke. His tone was quiet and steady.

"The fact is, Reese left you forty percent of Cloud Ranch. And he left the same to me. Ten each to Clint and Nick." His eyes flicked over her, unreadable in the study's amber light. "That means the Barclay boys own sixty percent of this ranch, compared to your forty percent, princess."

"I can count!" she snapped. She felt dizzy. "My father would never have done that." She stumbled to her feet. "Why in the world would he leave his ranch to his foreman?"

Wade studied her for a long moment as rain drummed at the windows and the wind snarled like a wolf. "Because I was more than his foreman. I was—I am—his son."

Her green eyes flew to his lean, hard face, searching it in disbelief.

"I was told . . . he never married again . . ."

"No, he never married again. He adopted me. And Clint and Nick. When we were just young boys. He raised all three of us as his own sons."

Caitlin stared at him, speechless. Each word struck her like a stone.

"Reese Summers was the best father any of us could have had," he continued quietly. "We were orphaned when I was eleven years old. Clint was nine and Nick . . . Nick was only seven. He took us in, gave us a home, taught us ranching . . . and a whole lot more." He stopped, but not before she heard the pain in his voice. Pain over the loss of Reese Summers. Then he cleared his throat and continued in a firm, steady tone.

"As it turned out, I was the only one who shared the passion he felt for this land, for this ranch. Don't get me wrong, Clint and Nick love Cloud Ranch—they grew up here, and consider it their home, but they wanted to follow different paths. Reese gave them his blessing. Yet he wanted them to know they'd always have a home here." He set the pencil down and fixed his hard gaze on her.

"Your father was quite a man, Miss Summers. The

finest man I've ever known. I was proud to consider him my father."

There was silence but for the quick drum of rain. Caitlin struggled to speak.

"He . . . took you in—three of you—left this ranch to you . . ."

She felt ill. Suddenly her legs wouldn't support her anymore and she sank back down upon the sofa, trying to breathe past the painful lump in her throat.

Reese Summers didn't answer a single one of her letters, refused to visit her or see her, even to send her a damned photograph of himself—but he took in the three Barclay boys. He raised them as his sons, bequeathed them his ranch—and never once bothered his head over his daughter.

Knifelike pain sliced through her and mixed with a boiling anger as she clenched the will between shaking fingers.

"I hate him," she whispered. "I hate him so." Her lips began to tremble. "I'm only happy I didn't trouble myself to come to him when he finally got around to sending for me!"

He reached her in two quick strides. The next instant she was seized, hauled up from the sofa, and the will flew from her grasp as she was imprisoned in a grip far too powerful to break. Shock pierced her. She saw the fury in Wade's eyes, felt the tension in every muscle of his tall, powerful frame, and knew that he was filled with an anger every bit as potent as her own.

"Enough," he warned.

"L-let me go."

"Not till I'm ready. We need to get a few things straight."

"You're hurting me," Caitlin gasped out, and she saw his eyes dart down to where his fingers dug into her shoulders. Instantly their excruciating grip relaxed, but he only slid his hands to her wrists, and held them in a steel grip instead.

"I told you once. I won't hear a word against him."

"I'll say whatever I please."

"Not in this house. Not to me."

Caitlin tried to wrench free of his grip, but couldn't. Wade smiled grimly. "Now do you want to hear the rest of the will's terms or not?"

"What I want is for you to let me go!"

"My pleasure, Miss Summers." He said it with contempt, but when she lifted her gaze, she saw something more than scorn in his eyes. There was a burning intensity that might have been part anger, part something else— something that was keen and dangerous and indefinable, but which sent a wave of heat through her, and for some inexplicable reason, her heart began to race.

"Let me go *now*," she whispered, all too aware of his strength, his anger, and the all-too-palpable heat pulsating between them. The glitter of his eyes seemed to cut her soul.

Wade wanted to let her go. Hell, he *meant* to let her go. But he held on. For a moment he was lost in those stormy green eyes. Distracted by the perfect swell of her breasts beneath that pretty, tight-fitting gown. Caught in her scent of sweet, wild violets.

But Caitlin Summers was hardly wild, he reminded himself, and she was certainly not sweet. A city girl used to every privilege, who only knew how to stamp her feet, give orders, and adorn herself. The girl who had broken Reese's heart.

He released her, his hands dropping to his sides. "Just remember what I said."

How could she forget? Every word he had said about her father, about the Barclay brothers, was branded into her mind.

She walked quickly toward the fireplace, trying to gather her thoughts, to calm her thudding heart, and it was then that she saw the two photographs side by side atop the mantel.

One was framed in bronze—a photograph of Caitlin as a little girl, seated upon her mother's lap in a flowered chair. The other was of three young men in their teens, standing with a handsome, broad-shouldered man—all four of them straight-faced before the camera, holding cigars aloft between their fingers.

Reese Summers and the Barclay boys.

She whirled away from the photograph, wanting to stare at it, to study it, to study the man who had been her father and cared nothing for her, but she'd be damned if she did it with Wade Barclay in the room.

"So we both own Cloud Ranch—no, *four* of us own Cloud Ranch," she said, her eyes flashing angrily. "Fine. I'll make it easy for you— and your brothers. I'll sell you my share."

He leaned against the desk again, regarding her coolly. "No."

The downpour outside suddenly abated to a soft thrum. The wind faltered. Inside the firelit study where Reese Summers's books and papers and whiskey decanters were lined up on shelves, where the faintest whisper of tobacco scent still mingled with the smell of worn leather, and where Wade Barclay leaned against her father's desk as if he'd been doing it all his life—which he no doubt had—Caitlin's eyes desperately beseeched his.

"Why not? I don't know anything about running a ranch, and I could care less. I—I have a life to lead back east." It wasn't totally a lie, though it wasn't the glamorous life he no doubt thought awaited her.

"Surely," she plunged on, trying not to let him see how desperately important this was, "you don't want me interfering with your decisions, telling you how to do this or that . . ." She searched for words. "Or generally interfering with your business."

"Reckon now it's your business too."

"But you don't want me as a partner!"

"You got that straight, lady. Only it's not what I want that matters, it's what Reese wanted. And for some reason I don't understand worth a damn, he wanted you on this ranch."

She flew toward him, wishing she could smack that smug, set-in-stone expression from his face. "He did this to me on purpose—he is trying to destroy my life. Don't you see that? He was an angry, bitter man—angry because my mother left him, because she hated this place back then as much as I do now! He wants to punish me because she refused to stay on this wretched ranch in this barbaric land, so now he's trying to force me to—"

She broke off at the cold rage in his face as he came away from the desk and towered over her. She stepped back instinctively, bracing herself to feel those powerful hands on her once more. But he must have seen the flash of fear in her face and realized that if he touched her again in anger, he might not be able to control himself. He didn't touch her, but his voice was full of soft, dangerous warning. "That's enough."

Caitlin's breath eased out. "Let me sell you my share." Her voice throbbed. "Then you'll be rid of me for good! You can run this place into the ground for all I'll care."

Brilliant green eyes implored him. Eyes that were almost impossible to resist. And all that blond angel hair pinned up so tight—Wade found himself dry-mouthed suddenly, wondering what it would look like if she ever let it all tumble down.

Hell. She was so beautiful, and so shallow. He wanted to throttle her.

"Let's get one thing straight. I'll never let you do anything that would run Cloud Ranch into the ground. I call the shots around here; I run the ranch."

"Not if you force me to keep my share, if you refuse to buy it." Sudden hope lit her face. The solution was so clear, she couldn't believe she hadn't thought of it before. "I'll just sell to someone else," she breathed. She nearly laughed with relief. "When that lawyer gets here I'll have him make all the arrangements. He can find the highest bidder—and then you and your brothers can own Cloud Ranch and deal with some stranger as a new partner, instead of having it all to yourselves."

He strode to the mantel and leaned a shoulder against it.

"You don't understand the terms of the will, Miss Summers, so let me explain them to you. You can't sell the ranch to an outsider without approval from me and both of my brothers. And that's something you'll never get. Your only hope is to sell to one of us. And none of us will buy your share—not for a year."

"A year? But why . . ." Dazedly she tried to understand.

"Reese wanted you to live here for a year. Don't ask me why, but that's what he said, right here in black and white. After the year's up, if you want to sell, me or Nick or Clint—or all three of us—can buy you out."

"I can't stay here for a year . . . I won't . . ."

"I forgot to mention," he said coolly, "there's a nice little stipend for you for each month you stay. It's damn generous. Not that you seem to be wanting for anything," he added, taking in her necklace, earbobs, and the elegant dark blue silk of her gown. "Looks to me like you've probably got all the fancy duds and doodads you could possibly need, but I reckon a woman like you always wants more."

The way he said it was an insult. *A woman like you.*

He had no idea who she really was, what she'd been through. And he must never find out.

People only pitied you or took advantage of you if they knew your vulnerabilities—that was one of the lessons Caitlin had learned in Philadelphia. And she'd learned it the hard way.

She considered what Wade had said about a monthly stipend. If she stayed on at the ranch, she'd receive money each month. A generous sum. Caitlin felt as if a noose were slowly tightening around her throat, choking her. She needed money, and she needed it immediately. She owed the last semester of Becky's tuition and room and board at the Davenport Academy; she owed back wages to servants at her Philadelphia home who'd been turned out without the money due them after Gillis Tamarlane's other debts had been paid first by the bank. She needed to purchase train tickets for her and for Becky so they could leave Philadelphia, and then there was their living expenses until she could find some sort of salaried position—perhaps a governess or a shop clerk—in a new city . . .

But now Wade was telling her that in order to receive any money at all, she'd have to remain at Cloud Ranch!

"How much is this—this monthly stipend?" She tried to sound calm. Let him think it was for bonnets and bows.

"Enough. More than enough, even for you, I reckon."

"I want to see the will—I want to read it for myself."

"Fine with me." He came away from the mantel, hunkered down, and retrieved the will from where it had fallen under the desk when he'd grabbed her and sent the documents flying. Just as he handed it to her, Francesca appeared in the doorway.

"*La comida,* Senor Wade, it is ready."

"Be right there, Francesca. *Gracias.*" He raked a hand through his hair and threw Caitlin a taut glance. "Our grub is ready. Coming?"

She spread open the papers, peering intently down at the long rows of even black print. "No. I'm not hungry."

"McCain will be here tomorrow. He can explain it all to you."

"I prefer to read it myself."

For a moment Wade thought he heard a thread of panic in her voice. What the hell did she have to be so worried about? Upset, yes. Angry, yes. That he could understand. She had wanted the ranch and the fortune it would bring—he'd already pegged her as the type who worshiped money and all it could buy. And finding out she'd have to wait to sell would have put a crimp in her high-falutin' plans.

But she sounded almost . . . scared.

He looked at her more closely. She appeared calm.

Then he saw it. Her lower lip was quivering. He stared at it. Yep. Definitely quivering.

"Maybe you'd like that shot of whiskey I mentioned earlier."

"I told you before." Her eyes were still fixed on the paper. "I don't drink whiskey."

"Right. So you did."

He gave her one last glance as she moved around the desk and slipped into Reese's deep maroon leather chair, her gaze lowering once more to the papers she spread before her.

She was so intent upon them he was certain she never even noticed him leave.

The long handsomely carved oak table in the dining room had been set for two. But as Francesca served up platters of thick steak in hearty brown gravy, mashed potatoes, corn bread, and buttered green beans, he felt glad that Miss Caitlin Summers wasn't joining him for dinner after all. It would be much more peaceful without her.

Not that he especially enjoyed eating by himself in the dining room. Since Reese had died, he'd either had Nick or Clint here to share his meals, or after they left, he'd often eaten in the bunkhouse with the men or at the homes of friends and neighbors. Silver Valley's new schoolmarm, Luanne Porter, had invited him most often. Sitting in this room, at this table, reminded him too much of Reese, of countless family dinners together when they'd talked, argued, joked, and made plans for the ranch. The big house seemed empty enough without the man who had built it—but this room seemed even emptier.

Francesca's cooking was delicious as always. He finished off the dinner with hot coffee and apple pie. When all was said and done, Caitlin never even put in an appearance. Wade knew she must be half-starved after her journey. But she was obviously more stubborn than sensible. He frowned, remembering her determination to read the will for herself. If she thought she could find a way to sell the ranch without fulfilling Reese's terms, she'd be disappointed. Wade had gone over everything with Reese, line by line, and promised him things would be done exactly according to his wishes. No way was he going to buy her share—or let her sell it to Nick or Clint—until the year was up.

After scraping the last bits of pie from his plate, he pushed back his chair and wandered into the study. He found her still at Reese's desk, bent over the will, staring intently at the page before her.

"If you're hungry, you'll find what's left of supper in the kitchen."

"I'm not." She rose as he entered, and he saw the fatigue in her eyes, the weary droop of her slender frame, and he saw something else too. Defeat.

"I'm going to my room."

Her fingers were clenched around the papers as she swept past him. How many times did she plan to read the damn thing, looking for a way out?

"This place isn't so bad," he remarked, and saw her shoulders tense.

"Sunrises are mighty pretty—sunsets too. Winter's

hard, but hell, it's only spring. You don't have to worry about the cold weather for a long time yet."

She stared at him wordlessly. His words had been meant to ease the pain he saw in her eyes, but it had only intensified. Wade's gut clenched. There was nothing of Reese in her after all. She only cared for a cultured, privileged life, for the world she'd always known. If Reese had thought to touch something in her, to bring out the part in her that was his, the part that loved the land, the open range, the sky and wind and sheer raw beauty of this valley, he had failed. He would fail. When the year was up, she'd sell. If not sooner.

Unless she was really greedy, she might not even stick it out through tomorrow, he thought suddenly. She'd forfeit her forty percent share, the stipend, everything—and run back to her rich friends and fancy home back east.

"I wish to see Mr. McCain the moment he arrives tomorrow," she said in a low tone. Her eyes were full of an unutterable sadness that made him feel uncomfortable for some reason.

"Suit yourself. Good night."

She left him alone, only the faint scent of violets lingering in her wake.

In her room, Caitlin blinked back her tears. The rain had ended and she opened the window, breathing in great draughts of mountain air, trying to calm herself. She wanted to read the will again, but she was too exhausted. It would have to wait until morning.

Tomorrow, she thought, rubbing her aching eyes. *Tomorrow I'll figure something out. Find a way.* She couldn't stay in Wyoming for a year. She couldn't. She needed the money—all of it—now.

Of course the first month's stipend would help, but it wasn't nearly enough. And what would she do about Becky? She couldn't drag her sister to this huge, awful, lonely place, miles and miles from even that speck of a town.

Hopelessness descended upon her when she at last sank into bed. She expected not to be able to fall asleep. She couldn't remember the last time she had slept deeply and well—every night she tossed and turned, haunted by her worries and the uncertain future. But instead, that night, lulled by the song of a thousand crickets and the rush of damp, sweet-smelling mountain air blowing in her window, and the great, heady silence of the Wyoming wilderness, she fell asleep in a twinkling and didn't stir until the morn.

Chapter 4

Caitlin didn't know where she was.

She lay upon soft pillows and stared at the ceiling, breathing in sweet pine-fragrant air and enjoying the caress of cool sheets against her skin. Faint sounds reached her ears. Horses neighing. The melody of birds. Men shouting to one another. A door slamming, and the happy bark of a dog.

Cloud Ranch.

She sat up, smoothing back her hair.

Pale gold sunlight spilled across the floor, gilding the white-painted bureau and the silver-framed mirror above it, shining across the fringed rose and blue rug that covered much of the wood floor, and sending slender beams of light across the bed.

Yellow and white curtains fluttered in the breeze as she sprang up and scurried barefoot to the window.

The view stunned her. Yesterday she had seen the ranch through the gray of a downpour, today she saw it in full light, the view beyond her window shimmering and resplendent.

It took her breath away. Gray-blue mountains in the distance, cut by waterfalls, their towering peaks magnificently gowned in shawls of pine and crested with snow that shone and glittered in the morning light. Amethyst foothills, studded with flowers, a valley long and deep and green, the land rolling and graceful and seemingly endless.

Caitlin's senses tingled. She took in a great gulp of the pine-scented air, watched the huge black dog bounding from the corral toward the plains, and felt something squeeze around her heart.

This place was beautiful, she could not deny that. More than beautiful, it was magnificent. For the first time in her life, she felt something akin to a bond with the father she'd not seen since she was a child. Oh, yes, it was easy to see why Reese Summers had loved this wide, majestic, sun-sparkling country.

But not why he had favored it over her mother and her.

Giving herself a tiny shake, Caitlin drew back from the window. Perhaps this land was seductive, with its wildflowers and antelope, its mountains and sparkling waterfalls and endless green-gold prairies that beckoned in the wind and sunshine, but she would not be seduced.

She was here on business, and she would leave by the end of this day, she vowed, having arranged one way or another for the sale of her share of Cloud Ranch.

Just as she started to turn away from the window, however, she caught sight of Wade Barclay coming out of the barn. He strode to the corral, where a tall roan stallion frisked, and called orders to a small group of ranch hands riding past.

He looked more handsome than ever in a work shirt of dark blue, dark pants and boots, that somber-looking holster and pair of guns he wore low on his hips, and a black Stetson.

She felt her heartbeat quickening.

He looked so *comfortable,* so completely at home in these rough, noisy, bustling surroundings.

And why shouldn't he feel comfortable, she asked herself angrily as she whirled away from the window to begin her toilette. He'd grown up here—the son of Reese Summers. To him, this place was home.

She reminded herself that she and Becky no longer had a home—any home—as she readied herself to leave her room and face the day ahead. That steeled her resolve. After breakfast she'd continue to scour the will.

The house was cool and quiet, with no sign of anyone around. Downstairs, she found the dining room empty, the long table polished and bare. Francesca was in the kitchen, her hands full of bread dough.

"Senor Wade and the men finished breakfast hours ago," she sniffed in greeting. She dumped the dough into a metal pan and wiped her hands on her apron. "I will fix more for you now."

"Don't trouble yourself," Caitlin replied coolly. Her stomach was growling its hunger but she hoped the woman couldn't hear. "I'll wait until lunch."

Francesca snorted. "No, senorita. What would Senor Reese think if I didn't feed his daughter proper meals? You will have the flapjacks and eggs and toast just like the rest of them, but tomorrow you must come earlier and eat with Senor Wade." She grimaced then, and added reluctantly, between clenched teeth, "If it pleases the senorita."

"I probably won't be here tomorrow." Caitlin sat down upon the bench that faced the long trestle table and helped herself to one of the oranges in a ceramic bowl in the center of the table. "I'm leaving after I meet with Mr. McCain today. Do you know when he's expected?"

The woman merely shrugged and shook her head. Caitlin didn't try to engage her in any further conversation. Obviously Francesca resented her presence here, and didn't want her to stay on at Cloud Ranch any more than she cared to remain here. Well, that was fine with her. Now all she had to do was find a way to sell her share of the ranch—then she could leave.

By the time she'd finished a plateful of scrambled eggs, slices of bacon, thick bread served with rich fresh butter and strawberry preserves, and coffee sweetened with sugar, she felt fortified and ready to do battle. And even better, she had a plan.

She hurried to the window as a horse and buggy came into view, trotting up the long drive.

"Mr. McCain," she called to the tall beanpole of a man in a well-cut black suit as she let herself out the front door and crossed the porch toward him.

"Yes, Miss Summers." The buggy halted and he touched the brim of his hat. He wore gold spectacles that sat upon a razor-thin nose. "I apologize for not being able to meet with you yesterday. I trust this isn't an inconvenient time."

She assured him it was a perfect time and eagerly ushered him into the parlor she'd glimpsed the day before. Part of her hoped Wade Barclay would be off somewhere and she wouldn't have to suffer his presence at this meeting, but these faint hopes died when he appeared in the doorway just as she invited Mr. McCain to be seated upon the horsehair sofa.

"Morning, Abner." The foreman spoke easily. "Miss Summers."

The attorney came forward to shake Wade's hand, but Caitlin only proffered a cool nod. Then she excused herself to retrieve the copy of the will from her room, brushing past Wade as if he didn't exist.

When she returned, Wade noticed a determined gleam in her eyes. She swept past him and flashed the attorney a dazzling smile.

"We have a great deal to discuss," she announced. She slipped gracefully down upon the flowered wing chair opposite the sofa where the lawyer had taken a seat, prettily arranged the moss-green skirt she wore with a soft, lace-trimmed white silk blouse, and bestowed upon the bespectacled lawyer a sweetly helpless smile. "I'm afraid I have a problem with my father's will, Mr. McCain—it is not at all suitable." She leaned forward slightly, her breasts straining against the white shirt. "But I'm sure *you* will find a way to help me."

"You already *know* about the contents?" He looked surprised.

"I told her." Wade spoke from the mantel, ignoring the icy glance Caitlin shot at him. "Gave her my copy to read last night. Reckon by now she knows what it says as well as you do, Abner. Probably got it memorized. She just doesn't like it much."

"I see. Well—"

"Surely a man of your experience can help me," Caitlin

said quickly, that lovely smile snapping back into place. "I know you have a kind heart and you'll take pity on my circumstances. Of course I wish to claim my inheritance—the inheritance my father wanted me to have—but I simply cannot stay in Wyoming for a year."

Wade Barclay leaned against the mantel, arms folded across his chest, watching her. He'd seen women work their charms on a man before, but none as smoothly and sweetly as this one. McCain would no doubt be eating from her dainty little fingertips before they'd gotten through the first paragraph, but that wouldn't help her one damn bit.

The will was ironclad. Except . . .

He tensed suddenly, and hoped to God the lawyer kept his wits about him.

Abner McCain removed his own copy of the will from a leather folder, pushed his spectacles higher up his nose, and blushed a delicate pink as he regarded the beautiful daughter of his deceased client. "I'll try to assist you in any way I can, Miss Summers."

"I knew you would," she breathed, and her eyes positively glowed at him.

His blush deepened. "Shall we begin? It is customary to read the contents of the will aloud."

"That won't be necessary." Wade heard the tinge of impatience in her voice, but the next moment she had iced it over with more sweetness. Enough to choke an ox.

"I know what the will says, Mr. McCain. Mr. Barclay explained it to me and I read it carefully myself. But now I need to know what *you* can do to change it."

He looked shocked. "Change it? That's impossible. I can't change a man's will. I've been entrusted to carry out your father's wishes . . ."

"But what about my wishes?" Caitlin allowed her voice to quiver. "Please, Mr. McCain, my future is in your hands. I can't stay here for a year—it's impossible. Anyone can see I don't belong here. And Mr. Barclay certainly doesn't want me here."

"Of course he does. He wants to honor Mr. Summers's wishes as much as I do." He shot Wade a startled glance and was rewarded with a snort.

"She's staying, as far as I'm concerned," Wade said curtly. "But that doesn't mean I want her here."

"Well, if you don't want her here, you know, that could solve . . ."

"Abner!" Wade cut him off abruptly. He pushed away from the mantel and fixed a steely blue gaze on the lawyer, who gave a sudden gulp. "I do want her here," he said slowly, deliberately.

Caitlin stared at him. *Liar,* she thought contemptuously. Then she turned back to the lawyer who looked more than a little flustered. He was shifting his gaze from her to Wade, swallowing hard past his Adam's apple, and shuffling the papers in his hands.

"Well, then," he said quickly. "I'm terribly sorry, Miss Summers, believe me I am, but that's all there is to say about the matter." He gave her an apologetic smile. "To keep your inheritance, you must stay on the ranch for a year, and after that amount of time has elapsed, you may sell your share to any or all of the Barclay brothers—or to any other party to whom the Barclays all give approval. Really," he tried to sound encouraging, "that isn't so bad. Is it?"

Caitlin felt her throat tightening. She felt more and more trapped. She glanced down once more at the papers in her hand as the lawyer's voice droned on.

"And I need your initials, Miss Summers, upon each page, to show that you have been informed of all the contents and understand what is contained herein." The lawyer dug into the pocket of his black suitcoat and with a wide smile produced an elegant silver pen. Which he promptly dropped, and snatched up again, flushing beet-red. "Here, why not sit comfortably at the writing desk and we'll make everything official."

Caitlin would rather have eaten a toad than signed the papers. She wasn't ready to admit defeat, but she had little choice but to seat herself at the writing desk, take up the pen, and glance down at the spot where her initials were required.

"Here," the attorney said kindly, removing the first page and pointing to the margin of the second. "There are only four pages—your father's will was not as complicated as some others I have seen," he said with pride, but Caitlin was no longer listening.

She had frozen, the pen in midair.

"*Four* pages? My copy of the will only contained three pages."

There was a moment of horrible silence and then she heard a choking sound from McCain. Then came a muttered oath from Wade Barclay.

"Now you've done it," the foreman growled and Caitlin felt a surge of excitement.

Quickly she peered at each page the lawyer had set before her. The first three were identical to the copy she had read—the fourth was one she had never seen before.

Her heart leapt when she saw that it was titled *Addendum*.

Chapter 5

She read the text swiftly as her heart pounded with renewed hope. When she finished she pushed back the chair and rose, whirling to confront Wade Barclay.

"How dare you keep this from me!" Rushing forward she waved it beneath his nose.

"It was none of your business." Wade frowned. "It was meant for me."

"None of my business? It says that you—*you*—Mr. Wade Barclay—may at your discretion cancel the clause that requires me to stay here for a year. If you deem it necessary and appropriate, you can override that clause and allow me to sell *you* my shares *at any time!*"

"So?" His jaw clenched. "It doesn't matter a damn, princess. Because your father only put that in as a contingency—for an emergency situation he couldn't foresee, an escape clause. He didn't plan for me to use it. He wanted you here on this ranch, he intended for you to make it your home for a year, and that's the way it's going to be."

"No! You can release me from that and I demand that you do so!"

"Miss Summers," Abner McCain interjected, placing a tentative hand upon her arm. He flinched as she shook him off, her eyes flashing at him.

"Don't you 'Miss Summers' me! I asked you if there was any way at all around the will and you told me there wasn't—you lied to me!"

He paled. "It wasn't a lie, precisely. That clause was private, meant only for Mr. Barclay—"

"Well, now that I know about it, you can just go ahead and start drawing up some purchase papers." Caitlin's mind was racing. She *would* be able to leave today after all. "I need to know what is a fair market price for my forty percent of the ranch—that is, if I can trust you to tell me that!"

Looking stung, the lawyer took a step backward, then began to speak again, trying to reassure her as to his honesty and integrity, but Wade interrupted him.

"McCain, you can go now."

"Go? B-but I haven't finished. This is all quite unsettled . . ."

"The hell it is. It's settled. She stays. For a year. Just the way Reese wanted it—though I damn well don't know why he did."

"He wanted to torment me!" she cried, pain and anger throbbing through her. "That's the only possible reason he could have inserted such a monstrous stipulation—"

"No, no, Miss Summers." McCain looked shocked. "Your father was most concerned about you—he truly wished you to make a home here at Cloud Ranch and learn to love it as he did. I know, because he told me so as I drew up the will."

Caitlin knew perfectly well that her father had not been the least bit concerned about her. His actions during his lifetime proved that. "It's a bit late for me to start feeling at home here." Caitlin's voice shook. All those years when she yearned to visit her father, to come to Cloud Ranch, and he ignored her—then, at the end of his days, he invited her, and designed his will so that she would be forced to come live here—when he was *gone.*

But he hadn't forced her. Not really, not completely. Thank God, there was the escape clause.

Fighting to keep her voice steady, she whirled back to Wade Barclay.

"You know this will never work. You know my living here is going to be an impossible situation for both of us. Why don't you invoke the emergency clause right now and save us both a great deal of trouble?"

"Not on your life, sweetheart."

"But . . ."

Diamond-blue eyes nailed hers. "I respected Reese when he was alive, and I'll damn well continue to respect his wishes now that he's . . . gone." He seemed incapable of saying the word *dead.* His jaw tightened. "Personally, I don't give a damn what you do—you can stay or leave— as you wish. But if you want either the monthly stipend, or the money your share of the ranch will bring a year from now, you'll stay put. Those are your only options."

Oh, no, they're not. Caitlin went very still as an idea, a lovely, wonderful idea, flashed into her brain. *No, Mr. Wade Barclay,* she thought triumphantly, *those aren't my only options. Not by a long shot.* She suddenly had a whole different option, a new plan that was guaranteed to work—but she wasn't about to tell Wade Barclay about it.

He'd find out soon enough.

She turned away from him to address the attorney. This time her tone was brisk, polite, nothing more. "Thank you for your time and for explaining everything to me so thoroughly, Mr. McCain. That will be all—for now."

He looked crestfallen but there was nothing more to say. Caitlin saw him out, then noticed that Wade had retreated into the study. She followed him there and watched from beneath her lashes as he opened a leather ledger book.

"What is that?"

"The ranch accounts," he answered coolly, without glancing up at her.

"Hmmm." She came forward with the smooth feline grace of a cat. "I'd like to look them over when you're finished," she said evenly.

He did look at her then, his brows shooting up. The damned girl looked so beautiful and innocent. But he wasn't fooled. She was up to something. "And what do you know about ledger books, Miss Summers?"

"It so happens that I attended one of Philadelphia's finest schools for young women," she informed him airily. "I acquired a splendid education there and I was particularly adept at arithmetic." Caitlin came right up to the desk, placed her palm smack in the center of the ledger book, and leaned toward him. "I think that as part owner of this ranch I should learn every aspect of the cattle business. I've decided to begin with the finances. Then, of course, I'll want to question all the men who work here."

"Question all the men?" His startled expression nearly made her grin. "Why?"

"Perhaps we've hired more than we need. Perhaps we

can cut back and save money on our payroll. Or perhaps some are not pulling their weight." She shrugged daintily. "Who knows what I'll discover? There's always room for improvement, that's my motto."

"Like hell it is."

"Mr. Barclay, you doubt my word?"

He shut the ledger book with a snap and sprang from the chair, moving with surprising swiftness and grace for such a large man. "It won't work," he said, looming over her.

"What won't work?" In spite of herself, she had to resist the urge to back away from him. He was entirely too big, too imposing.

"Whatever you're up to."

This time the smile she bestowed upon him was pure sugar. "You have no idea what I'm up to," she murmured. But he saw the glimmer of resolve in those entrancing green eyes just before she twirled away toward the door, and it filled him with an impending sense of disaster.

As he watched her go, he found himself unable to resist staring at the seductive yet elegant swing of her hips.

Damn, she was up to something. Something he wasn't going to like. But what?

Pacing around the desk, he picked up the account books again, then tossed them back down. Restlessly he prowled to the window and stared out at the valley he knew as well as his own name.

The land, endless and magnificent, somehow soothed him, filling him with a renewed sense of peace. This ranch, this place he loved, with its sagebrush and sunsets and distant pine-crested mountains, had meant everything to Reese and it meant everything to Wade. His brother

Nick was born with wanderlust in his blood and had never been able to settle down, and his brother Clint found his own path as a lawman in a town that needed him. Cloud Ranch would always be a home to them, but not in the same way it was to Wade. For Wade no place on earth was as beautiful, wild, and meaningful as this huge, open Wyoming Territory and every living thing that flourished on Cloud Ranch.

Now his beloved valley had been invaded by a spoiled woman, too shallow even to appreciate what she'd been handed. Someone who only wanted to sell her parcel and leave.

Why'd you want her here so badly, Reese? he mused silently as he watched an antelope leap across the stream and disappear through the cottonwoods. *Her mother didn't want to be here and broke your heart, and this daughter is just as bad. I ought to just cut her loose and let her run.*

The wind rose at that moment, rushing through the study, ruffling the pages of the ledger book. Wade grinned. *Don't worry, old man. I won't. She can cry, beg, yell, threaten, whine, or try to bribe me with all the money in the world, and I won't budge. I made you a promise to look after her, and I'll keep it.*

But it was going to be a helluva chore—and a helluva long year.

Chapter 6

When Wade walked out to the bunkhouse for his weekly poker game with Rooster and old Baldy and some of the other wranglers that night, he found them all making bets on how soon the new part owner of Cloud Ranch would bolt.

"Me, I give her one week," Miguel, the handsome Mexican cowpuncher announced, tossing a greenback onto the pile.

"Naw, I give her a day." Rooster added two silver coins. "She'll be gone by suppertime tomorrow. I saw the look on her face when she first got here, soaking wet and all, and that lady was never meant for livin' on the land. She's the tea party and toast type, if ever I saw one. She'll be gone by tomorrow," he said sagely.

"Wal, she's Reese's daughter." Baldy's rheumy old eyes fixed on each man in the group. "She's got to have some of his stubbornness in her, no matter where she was raised. I bet she'll stick it out for aboot ten days or so.

Then"—he blew smoke from his cigarillo—"she'll light out of here so fast your haids will spin."

"I hope she stays." Jake Young sighed lustily. He was the newest wrangler, fresh-faced, clean-shaven, best man with a rope Wade had seen in years. "She's about the purtiest gal I ever did see. I'd rather look at her than any of them fancy ladies down at the Dixie Dance Hall in Laramie."

"Someone's in love," Miguel jeered, and Wade joined the others who began to grin at the flushing cowhand.

"Well, maybe yes and maybe no. But if Miss Summers stays around for the May Day dance over at the Crooked T, I just might ask her to let me be her escort," Jake boasted.

"You might have to get in line, old friend." Dirk Watkins, who'd done some tracking and some gunslinging before settling into ranch work, shot him a cool glance. "Could be someone else might ask her first."

Wade frowned. "The lady might be pretty, but she's got the heart of a vulture," he growled. "Myself, I prefer the softer type."

"Like Miss Luanne Porter?" Rooster nodded knowingly. "How many times you had supper over at her place this past week?"

"None of your damn business."

"She looks plenty soft to me," Dirk murmured.

"What's that?" Jake asked.

"Miss Summers." The former gunslinger's dark eyes were unreadable in the dim lantern light of the bunkhouse. "She looks plenty soft to me."

Wade's jaw clenched. If he heard one more word about

Caitlin Summers tonight, he'd punch somebody. "Are we going to play poker or not?"

Caitlin stood by her window, gazing at the cool, glittering stars, thinking how best to drive Wade Barclay to distraction.

It was nearly midnight when she left her room, tugging a shawl around her shoulders as she let herself out the kitchen door and wandered toward the stream that ran and dipped about fifty yards behind the bunkhouse. Immersed in her plans, she sat down on a tree stump in a clearing flanked by cottonwoods and pondered the shimmering ribbon of water, where moonlight glistened and unseen frogs chirruped in the night.

"We'll see how much fortitude you possess, Wade Barclay," she muttered to herself.

Something cold and wet pushed against her hand, and she gave a gasp. Glowing eyes stared up at her, and a tail wagged in the starlight.

"Dawg," she breathed and with a sigh of relief, she reached down to let the animal sniff her hand.

The tail wagged harder and Caitlin began to stroke behind the dog's ears.

"Looks like you're my only friend right now in the world." She smiled down into the animal's eager face as his tongue licked at her fingertips. "But that's all right. It's not always easy to find a friend. A real friend. Is it, boy? People aren't always what they seem."

"Talking to yourself?"

Her head flew up and her eyes widened as she saw Wade standing there. Moonlight illuminated his dark hair and slanted across his broad shoulders. But no moonbeam could have matched the cold bright glint of his eyes.

"What are you doing here? You nearly scared me to death!"

She was annoyed to see that Dawg had deserted her to amble over to Wade and nudge at his hand.

"You don't seem like the kind of woman who scares that easily. I mean," he corrected himself, advancing toward her slowly in the darkness, "that you might look all soft and helpless, but from what I've seen, you're a lot tougher than you appear."

Caitlin didn't feel all that tough suddenly. He looked so strong, so formidable there in the darkness, a dark, dangerous figure capable of anything.

"I'll take that as a compliment," she retorted only a little breathlesssly, "though I doubt you meant it as one."

Something flickered in his eyes. He shrugged unexpectedly. "Don't be so sure. I may not like you much, princess, but I've got to hand it to you. You stand your ground."

He halted right before her. Close, so close. Again she wanted to step back, to give herself some space because his presence seemed to fill the small clearing and it was having a strange effect on her. She couldn't take her eyes off of his rugged face.

"You said you didn't cry, didn't faint, and so far, from what I've seen, you told the truth." He was studying her, taking in the shawl flung across her shoulders, her lips parted in surprise, even the soft rise and fall of her chest as her breathing quickened. "You've had a hard shock, but you didn't crumble. I'll hand you that."

"I fight for what I want, if that's what you mean. No matter what it takes," she added quickly, thinking of Dominic Trent lying on the floor in a pool of blood, after she'd been forced to hit him with the candlestick. Caitlin saw that Dawg was trotting away, back toward the bunkhouse. Only she and Wade and the moonlight faint as fairy mist occupied the clearing now.

"Which I suppose puts us on opposite sides," she finished defiantly.

She started past him, but he grabbed her arm, stopping her. "It doesn't have to be that way. You can't win this fight because I gave Reese my word—and one thing you need to know about me, I don't go back on my word."

She had a sudden all-too-vivid memory of Alec Ballantree's low, unhappy voice. *I don't believe in going back on my word, but I can no longer marry you, Caitlin. It just isn't possible . . .*

A man of his word. She no longer believed in such things. She spoke icily. "You'll change your mind—when it's in your best interest to do so."

"No. I won't." His tone was calm, purposeful. "So you're just wasting your time trying to fight this. You may as well accept the terms of the will and try to—"

"I have a sister, Mr. Barclay, an eleven-year-old sister." There was a warm tingle where he was touching her arm. She pulled away from him and plunged on, "I am responsible for her upbringing now. Perhaps you don't know, but our parents," and she deliberately emphasized the last word so that he would realize she did not consider Reese her parent in any way, "died recently and now she is depending solely on me."

A startled look crossed his face. "I heard something

about that—an accident at sea—but I didn't know anything about a sister," he said sharply.

"You don't know anything about my life, or about me, Mr. Barclay. You just think you do."

"I know that when your father—Reese—when he sent for you, you turned your back on him."

"His letter came the same day the news arrived about my mother and Gillis!" she burst out. "I couldn't have come to him then, even if I'd wanted to!"

He looked stunned. For a moment there was silence, but for the croaking of the frogs on the streambank and the sharp, sudden intake of her breath. "I'm going back to the house now. At first light, I'll conduct an interview of the men in the bunkhouse—to see if they all meet with my approval," she flung at him. "And then I want to go over the ledgers with you—all of them. I've found three errors of addition and subtraction having to do with the February accounts—your numbers are off by a total of twenty-seven cents."

Wade's eyes narrowed. "That's not possible. I've double-checked every page of the accounts. There're no mistakes."

"Would you care to place a wager on that?"

Suddenly his eyes gleamed in the moonlight. "Sure. What are you in for?"

"In for?"

"How much—money?"

Caitlin hesitated. She only had twelve dollars and forty-seven cents left in her reticule. As certain as she was that she was right, she couldn't afford to risk even a penny of it.

"Money is so boring," she said haughtily. "Let's wager something more interesting than that."

"Oh, yeah? So what do you find more interesting than money?" The question was slow and speculative, and there was a mocking challenge in his eyes, but Caitlin had him exactly where she wanted him.

"If I'm correct you'll buy my share of the ranch immediately," she stated.

He stepped closer, a slow grin curling the corners of his lips. "Nuh-uh. Sorry, princess, but that clause of the will is off-limits."

"Then . . ." She took a deep breath. "If I'm correct, you'll advance me two months' worth of my stipend immediately." With that she could pay what was overdue for Becky's tuition, room and board, send her sister some spending money, and still have something left over for the servants who'd been let go unpaid.

Wade wondered why an heiress who'd no doubt just inherited a damned fortune back east was so interested in money.

"All right—done," he agreed. He couldn't help noticing the pretty way she smiled with excitement at the prospect of the wager. She looked delectable here in the moonlight, all soft and sweet and tempting as a dainty little iced cake. "What do I get if you're wrong?"

"I'll promise not to fire any of your wranglers." She gave him a cool nod. "That's fair."

He was about to point out that he wouldn't allow her to fire a single one of them anyway—he needed every last man on this ranch. They were a handpicked group who worked well together as a team, and each had his own special skills that made him invaluable. But she looked so pleased at having come up with this suggestion that he forgot about arguing with her and suddenly found himself standing right in front of her, his hands at her waist.

"Maybe we should leave the wranglers out of this. Maybe this should be just between you and me."

"You . . . and me?" Suddenly she felt light-headed. His touch seemed to melt her brain—and everything else in her body. "I don't understand . . . what could we possibly . . . have to wager between . . . us?"

"Reckon we can think of something." Wade barely knew what he was saying. He was lost in those dazzling green eyes, lost in the soft feel of her beneath his hands. For once, her blond hair was not pinned up in a damned knot, it flowed over her shoulders. He wanted to stroke it, see if it felt as soft as it looked. And her mouth . . .

"We could wager a kiss." He didn't know where the words came from, all low and hoarse like that—they just popped out. Probably because he was staring at her mouth.

But it sent a quiver of panic through her that he felt beneath his palms.

"We . . . most certainly could *not*!" Alarmed, she started to pull away, but Wade's arm slipped around her waist and held her tight, while his other hand cupped her chin.

"Whoa, don't go all skittish on me, princess, I was just fooling."

Was he? Even he wasn't sure and he saw the wild doubt and suspicion in her eyes as they searched his. That one word—*kiss*—had been like taking his spurs to a filly he was trying to gentle. It had spooked her but good.

"How about if I'm right—and the ledger's free of mistakes—you wear that pretty hair of yours down for a whole week. Nice and loose, just like it is right now."

Those bewitching eyes gazed at him in bewilderment. "Why could you possibly care . . . about how I . . ."

"Deal or no, princess," he interrupted softly, and without realizing it pulled her even closer against him.

A sudden urge to kiss her assaulted him, and Wade had to use all of his self-control to resist. He didn't want to kiss her, he told himself—hell, he didn't even *like* her. But that beautiful lush mouth was putting loco ideas in his head. He actually felt himself lowering his own mouth toward hers . . .

Caitlin broke away with a low cry. "Don't!"

Her breathing was ragged. And she was staring at him with fear in those big green eyes—as if she thought he would throw her down on the ground and rape her.

Chagrin and anger—anger at himself—rushed through him. "Hold on," he said. "I'm not going to hurt you."

"You tried to kiss me!"

"Why the hell would I do something like that?"

"You tell me!"

The hell of it was, he couldn't. He didn't know *why* he had tried to kiss her, he only knew it was a big mistake. So he did the only thing he could think of: he changed the subject.

"Look, I've got to get some shut-eye. Are we going to get this wager set and check the books tonight or not?"

"F-fine." Uncertainty swept over her. Had she been wrong—had he really *not* tried to kiss her? Caitlin wasn't at all sure. "But you—you keep your distance from me. I'm warning you!"

"My pleasure," he muttered. "So what do I get if I win?"

Caitlin cast desperately in her mind for something. Why was she letting this man make her so nervous?

"I'll bake you a pie," she said at last, pulling her shawl more tightly around her shoulders.

"*You* can bake?"

He sounded so astonished her temper heated up all over again. "I reckon you'll find out. *If* you win," she tossed over her shoulder as she headed back toward the ranch house.

"What kind of pie?" he asked, falling into step beside her.

"Poison berry."

He chuckled. The sound of it almost made her smile in response, but she managed to smother it by remembering how much she disliked him.

"So you agree on our terms?"

"Sure, princess." He caught her arm and steadied her as she tripped over an unseen twig in the grass. "Reckon I can almost taste that pie right now."

When they reached the study, Wade confidently turned up the lamp, strode to the desk, and lifted the ledger books.

"Go ahead then. Show me these so-called mistakes."

She took the books from him and flipped through the pages, her face set with determination in the golden light.

"Here." Triumphantly, she slid one slender finger to the bottom of a row of figures. "And here."

Wade bent closer to peer over her shoulder. Her hair felt like silk as it brushed his chin. And . . . damn. Ever so delicately, she smelled like violets.

"And here."

He forced himself to concentrate on the numbers

before him, but it was difficult when she smelled so sweet and felt so soft and she was standing so close. He snatched the book from her and went around to the far side of the desk.

With this bit of distance between them his powers of concentration heightened, and he saw exactly what she was talking about. He stared at the columns—and did the figuring again. And again.

"What the hell."

Damned if she wasn't right.

"I told you!" Caitlin nearly clapped her hands in glee, but dropped them as he scowled.

"So . . . I'll accept that stipend—two months' worth—first thing in the morning," she informed him haughtily. "*After* I've interviewed the men."

The scowl deepened. "Forget about interviewing the men." He tossed the ledger book back down on the desk. "If you take it into your head to fire anyone, I'll just rehire 'em."

It was her turn to narrow her eyes. "We'll see about that, Mr. Barclay. I own equal shares and have equal say. If I want to fire someone, I will."

"You thought you were going to fire me too," he pointed out. "Or have you forgotten?"

Caitlin gritted her teeth, remembering how he'd laughed when she'd said that in the wagon. She'd never imagined the rude and arrogant foreman would own equal shares of her father's ranch. That he'd been raised as her father's *son*. "Too bad I *can't* fire you," she muttered under her breath as she spun away from him and headed for the door.

"Be sure to let me know if you find any more mistakes in the ledgers," he called out after her. "If you want I can dig out the books from last quarter too and let you take a look."

"Maybe I just will. As you can see, I'm merely taking an active interest in this ranch—my ranch," she shot back.

"I'm sure Reese would be glad to know you're so committed to the place that he gave more than twenty years' worth of sweat, blood, and tears. Too bad you wouldn't deign to set foot on it till he was dead."

The moment the words were out, a heavy silence thundered through the room. A silence that weighed on Wade's shoulders like an anvil. He watched her face tighten, saw her swallow, and noticed the way her hands suddenly gripped her skirt so tightly her knuckles whitened.

"Don't be obnoxious, Mr. Barclay," she said at last. Didn't he know how completely Reese had rejected her, that he'd never answered a single one of her letters, much less invited her to visit the ranch? Well, she wasn't about to let him in on *that* particular humiliation. Especially since Reese had raised all three Barclay boys in this house as his sons. "I've had my fill of obnoxious men."

She whirled and left the study without waiting for him to reply.

When she was gone, Wade could have sworn that the lamplight seemed dimmer. The room flat, empty somehow.

I've had my fill of obnoxious men.

He walked around the desk to one of the crystal whiskey decanters and poured himself a shot glass. Tossing it back, he remembered the bitterness around her lovely mouth when she'd said that.

He also remembered something else she'd said tonight, when she'd told him about her younger sister. *"You don't* know anything about my life, Mr. Barclay. You just think you do."

Don't start getting sentimental over a dazzling little beauty who ignored Reese for the past eighteen years, tried to manipulate his attorney into changing the will, and is probably now fixing to turn her machinations on you, he told himself.

She was up to something with this annoying checking of the books and interviewing the men. He didn't quite understand the point of it all, but it sure was wearing on his nerves.

Think about something else. Think about Luanne.

Luanne Porter, the schoolteacher who'd arrived from St. Louis a few months back to teach the children of Silver Valley who were too far away to attend the schoolhouse just outside of Hope, had gingery-red hair, a dash of becoming freckles, and a smile as big as all of the valley. She lived close by, with her aunt and uncle at their Hanging Circle spread, and not only had she been inviting him to supper since Reese died, but she'd brought over pies and cakes and cookies on a regular basis. She'd done all she could to cheer him up.

Her kisses had helped too. Sweet, vanilla-tasting kisses.

When Clint and Nick were here, they'd teased him and said he'd be married within the year.

But Wade didn't see it that way at all. He was in no particular hurry to get tied down, though he'd always wanted a wife and family someday. But he'd always thought of it as something far off and in the future. So sweet as Luanne Porter was, he'd been careful not to be too attentive. There were too many pretty girls in the saloon who liked fussing over him, sitting in his lap, inviting him upstairs to one of the private bedrooms wallpapered in red and gold. Too many fine daughters of ranchers in the valley and merchants in Hope—hell, he hadn't gotten to know half of them as well as he'd like to.

But when the time came, he knew he *would* marry someone like Luanne. Someone sweet and easygoing, someone who'd make his life as comfortable, convenient, and pleasant as a day out fishing.

He sure as hell was never going to fall in love. He'd rather crawl on his belly through a snake pit than that. Wade had watched Reese suffer and grieve for Lydia, watched the man's heart bleed and his soul ache for years, and he'd made up his mind way back when he was fourteen that he'd never give any woman that kind of power over *him*.

He was never going to love anyone that much, need anyone that much. Miss anyone that much.

Because Lydia Summers had been more than a beauty who'd flitted in and out of Reese's life—she'd owned his heart. Even though she'd left him, run off while he was away on that trail drive and taken their daughter with her—Reese had never stopped loving her. He'd never married again, never even courted another woman, unless you counted squiring Winnifred Dale now and then to a barbecue or the May Day dance, or spending an occasional night with a saloon girl upstairs in the Silver Star Saloon.

No, Reese had never gotten over Lydia, and had ached for her until the day he died.

But Wade wasn't going to make that same mistake.

Think about Luanne.

He tried to picture her face then, but it was a bit fuzzy. Must be the whiskey.

He went to bed, remembering the taste of Luanne's kisses well enough—but not before wondering if Caitlin Summers's kisses would taste like violets.

Another man was thinking of Caitlin Summers at that very moment. Dreaming of her kisses. And of her moans.

In his three-story brick mansion in Philadelphia, Dominic Trent paced up and down the huge front drawing room, wincing with every step.

Finally he sank upon the green velvet settee and leaned his powerful shoulders back against the cushions. The drawing room was in darkness, only a faint light from the chandelier in the hall filtering into the magnificent and ornately furnished room. Trent poured himself another brandy from the half-empty decanter on the table and downed the burning red liquid in a long gulp.

He closed his eyes, leaned back against the cushions once more, and pictured the exquisite face of the gold-haired woman he could not forget.

The pain swirled through his head just like the brandy had swirled in the goblet. The bandage had long since come off, the goose egg she'd left on his skull had long since dwindled to the smallest of lumps, but the pain—the pain had not gone completely away.

And it wouldn't, Dominic reminded himself, not until the woman who had caused it was completely under his power.

He'd wanted Caitlin Summers since the moment he saw her at the opera the season of her coming-out. He'd tried to court her in the usual way and had been rebuffed, but not before learning she was more steel than spun sugar, no matter how delectable she looked.

That, of course, only made her more desirable. Which no doubt was part of her plan. Deep down, she had wanted to torment him, wanted to bewitch him. She knew that her very coldness toward him only made her more exciting, her very elusiveness was the most potent of lures. Trent was an avid hunter—in his younger days he had traveled west and hunted elk and black bear and buffalo with some of the finest hunting guides that side of the Missouri. Though he'd dutifully returned to civilization to assume the mantle of his family's shipping empire upon his father's death, he had never lost his fascination with the primitive—or his love of the hunt. And Caitlin Summers, from that first moment he had seen her, had seemed like the most wonderful creature ever to be hunted.

She was the ideal prey—beautiful, independent, elegant—a woman as graceful as any antelope he had ever seen upon the plains, a prize to be tracked, stalked—and captured.

He hadn't planned on his lovely prey actually hurting him though. That night when he'd thought he had her trapped, when she was here in this very drawing room, exactly where he wanted her, completely vulnerable and without a soul in the world to help her, he'd never dreamed she would strike out at him as she had.

She'd violated the rules. Struck him over the head, nearly killed him, and left him with this wretched ringing pain that came and went, but always returned.

The doctors said it might never go away.

She would pay for that. Dearly.

Perhaps she'd imagined she'd escaped, but she would soon learn that there was no escape. From him.

That was only one of the things he would teach her when he finally tracked her down.

And track you down I will, sweet Caitlin, Dominic thought, rising from the settee, striding through the darkness into his velvet-papered hall.

"Thomas!" he called in a silken voice that for all its softness held the menace of a flicked whip.

"The housemaid who cleaned my bedroom today is to be dismissed," he told the butler who hurried into the hall in response to the summons. "She broke a goblet and spilled champagne upon the carpet."

"Yes, sir. A clumsy mistake, to be sure. But she is new—"

"Dismiss her."

"Yes, Mr. Trent." The butler bowed his head. "Will there be anything else?"

"Have Forbes bring the carriage around at precisely eight o'clock tomorrow morning."

"Yes, Mr. Trent."

"Tell him that I shall expect him to know the directions to my destination."

"Of course, sir. And where is it you wish to go?"

Dominic Trent strode toward the stairs, his brow creased with pain. Yet he took pleasure in speaking each word. "Someplace of utmost importance to my future. The Davenport Academy for Young Ladies."

Chapter 7

In the end, she couldn't do it. She couldn't fire a single one of the ranch hands. Not Rooster with his silly blushes and bow-kneed walk; not Jake Young, whose big brown eyes and clean-cut handsome features reminded Caitlin of a drawing of Billy the Kid she'd once seen on the front of a dime-store novel; not Miguel with his white-toothed smile and faultlessly polite manners; not Dirk Watkins, whose thin black mustache, elegant black clothes, and intricately tied black silk neckerchief were almost as memorable as his low, gravelly voice.

And certainly not old Baldy, whose leathery skin, rheumy eyes, and gnarled, callused hands showed evidence of years of hard work out in the sun, years of having worked, he told her, for Reese Summers "right from the very beginning when this place was nothing but a pile of mud."

She couldn't do it.

But on her way into town later that day, with Rooster

driving the wagon this time, and a plain muslin-tied bonnet protecting her from the brilliant Wyoming sun, she devised a far better plan.

And she couldn't wait to see the expression on Wade Barclay's face when she instituted it.

In the meantime she opened an account at the bank, deposited her two months' stipend, and arranged to wire money to Philadelphia. That done, she visited Hicks Mercantile and made the acquaintance of Nell Hicks and her father, who owned the establishment.

She also had a pleasant little chat with Miss Dale, whom she found sorting mail at the post office counter.

Winnifred peered at the envelope Caitlin handed her, and her gentle gaze settled on Caitlin's face. "Miss Rebecca Tamarlane at the Davenport Academy for Young Ladies? A friend of yours, Miss Summers, I presume? How nice."

"Not a friend. My sister. My half sister." Caitlin watched as Miss Dale set the envelope in a bulging mail sack. She hoped Becky wouldn't be too upset when she learned Caitlin wouldn't be returning quite as soon as she'd first hoped, but she'd assured her that the delay would not be long.

"Oh, perhaps she will come and visit you at Cloud Ranch," Miss Dale suggested with a smile.

"No. She won't be doing that. I'd never ask Becky to travel all the way out here to such an uncivilized . . . I mean, to a place so far from home," she amended quickly. "Besides, I won't be staying long enough to entertain any visitors."

"Really?" Miss Dale looked distressed. "But . . . the will? Surely by now, you are well aware—"

"Yes, and it seems everyone else in Hope is aware as well." Caitlin tried to contain her irritation. "Why is it, Miss Dale, that everyone seems to know my business?" she asked with a sigh.

Winnifred's dainty cheeks had turned pink, but she struggled to explain. "This is a small town, dear. Word travels fast and there are few secrets. Especially among friends." She pushed her spectacles up her nose and met Caitlin's gaze squarely. "Your father told me you would be coming here, for example."

"He did?"

"Oh, yes. I visited him in his last days. He told me he had left you a share of the ranch—that he had done all in his power to encourage you to make Cloud Ranch your home. He asked me," she added, her chin trembling a little, "to do all I could to make you welcome."

"I see." She studied the woman. "You must have been quite close to him."

"Yes, we were very dear friends." Winnifred's eyes misted. "Of course, it wasn't anything romantic or anything of that sort," she hurried to add, her cheeks growing even pinker. "All of Silver Valley—and Hope, for that matter—knew there was never any other woman for Reese besides your mother." She turned and began sorting through a basket of letters. "I do believe he loved her with all his heart up until the very day that he died."

A small shock ran through Caitlin. Perhaps all of Silver Valley knew that, but she hadn't. Reese had still loved her mother, even after she'd abandoned him and married another man?

"But that's neither here nor there," Miss Dale continued quietly. "It's all in the past, isn't it? Today, I'm just pleased to see you getting settled in. That would have made your father very happy."

"I can't imagine why it would matter to him." Bitterly, Caitlin wondered why her father had tried to convince everyone in Hope that he did have some feeling for her. She was baffled that he'd bothered with the charade.

"I'm only staying here right now because I must. But I don't intend to remain in Wyoming for long."

"I do hope that perhaps you'll change your mind." Miss Dale paused in her sorting to offer a shy smile. "I know of course that Hope can't compare to Philadelphia, but we are becoming a fair-sized town—for Wyoming—and we have a good many businesses here now, including stores which boast fine goods," she said. "Hicks is particularly well stocked, thanks to Nell. She's been running the place for years. And ever since the trouble cleared up last year, new businesses and citizens have been settling in Hope quite briskly. We have a shooting gallery now, and a land office, and . . ."

"Trouble? What kind of trouble?"

Winnifred Dale pushed her spectacles higher and gave a small shudder. "Why, the Campbell gang. They terrorized this town some time back—killed poor Sheriff Owen and almost ran off with Nell Hicks—!"

She broke off as Edna Weaver strode in, carrying a basket full of letters to be mailed. She greeted Caitlin warmly, and when Winnifred explained that she was telling the girl how much the town had grown since the recent trouble, the banker's wife nodded vigorously.

"Oh, yes, Hope is a far safer and more pleasant town now, thanks to Quinn Lassiter and the other men, including my husband, Seth. They all joined together and got rid of the Campbells for good. If they hadn't, who knows what would have happened. Hope might have become a ghost town. As it was, lots of folks left during all the trouble. Even Winnifred left for a number of months—she went to stay with her sister in Iowa until the trouble died down."

"It was most frightening." Winnifred nodded. "And since my sister's husband had fallen ill and she needed help running their farm, it was a good time for me to go away—but what a relief when the gang was wiped out. And when I returned I found that our little town was booming again. Why, we even have a library now!" she exclaimed with pride.

But Caitlin was scarcely listening—she was thinking about the Campbell gang, and all the terrible things she'd just heard about. Never, never could she consider bringing Becky to a place where such things could happen.

Edna's next words convinced her even further. "Yes, and though there's still a little problem with rustlers raiding some of the larger ranches right now, it's really nothing at all compared to the troubles with the Campbells."

"Rustlers?" Caitlin stared from one to the other. She'd heard stories about cattle rustlers during her journey west. "My father insisted that I live in a place being terrorized by rustlers?"

"Oh, heavens, no, it's not that bad." Edna waved a hand in the air. "They work mostly at night and only shoot at someone who comes upon them, dear. You're in no danger, I'm sure—but didn't Wade warn you about venturing out after dark?"

"Wade Barclay would be thrilled if I got myself shot by rustlers!" she rejoined.

"Oh, good heavens, no—he wouldn't!" Edna declared staunchly and Winnifred looked aghast.

"You misjudge him, dear. Wade is one of the finest men in this entire territory. In any territory, I'd say. And he was a devoted son to Reese." Gently, Winnifred shook her head. "He'd never ever wish you harm."

He will after I execute my plan, Caitlin thought with grim satisfaction, but she couldn't very well tell Edna and Winnifred what she had in mind for Cloud Ranch's impossible foreman.

So she bid the ladies good day and turned to leave, but as she headed to the door, it opened and a pretty red-headed young woman in a pale yellow calico dress stepped in.

"Well, good morning, Luanne. How nice to see you." Edna bustled over and took Caitlin's arm before she could edge past the woman out the door. "Have you met Miss Summers yet?"

"I'm afraid I haven't had the pleasure."

Edna performed rapid introductions, explaining to Caitlin that Luanne Porter was the new schoolteacher in the valley and she hailed from Boston. "She was raised in the East just like you yourself. You two ladies ought to have a great deal in common."

"How do you do?" Caitlin murmured. The school-teacher was pretty, with her heart-shaped face, soft cloud of hair threaded with yellow ribbons, and a trim figure shown off to advantage by the calico gown.

"I'm so happy to meet you," Luanne exclaimed

warmly. "I've heard from Wade all about the plans for your arrival."

"I beg your pardon?"

"Oh, Wade and I are close friends." The schoolteacher blushed. "He told me you were expected and that everyone at Cloud Ranch was in quite a tizzy over your impending arrival."

"I see."

Luanne smiled, her brown eyes sparkling. "Perhaps you'd care to come to supper at my aunt and uncle's home on Sunday? Wade's already accepted the invitation—and perhaps"—her smile widened to include the other women—"we could make it a small party. I do miss the parties we used to have back east when people lived much closer together and weren't separated by such great distances, don't you?"

"I haven't been here long enough to miss anything yet," Caitlin murmured, wondering how in the world someone so sweet could tolerate a man as insufferable as Wade Barclay.

Luanne Porter was already turning hopefully to Edna and Winnifred. "Won't you join us for supper? Mr. Weaver too, of course," she told Edna.

Before Caitlin even realized it, the evening was all arranged. She left the post office a bit dazed, but shook off the feeling as she hurried up the street, reminding herself of the final, most important errand of her day. By the time Sunday rolled around, she might very well be unable to attend the supper party—she might be well on her way to Philadelphia, flush with money from her share of Cloud Ranch.

What she was about to do might solve all of her problems. If she did it right.

Moving with swift, determined steps she headed toward the saloon.

"What the hell?"

Caitlin had just finished buttoning the emerald-green jacket of her riding habit the next morning when the ruckus began. Her heart beginning to pound with excitement, she rushed to her window and gazed down toward the corral.

A small knot of men were gathered there. Wade—who'd been in the process of saddling his horse—old Baldy, Jake Young—and five newcomers.

These were as disreputable-looking a bunch as any she'd seen along the route of her stagecoach journey. Her heart swelled with pride just looking at them. Several were in various stages of a hangover. All were unshaven, unkempt, their clothes filthy—none of them had likely known a bath in weeks—perhaps months. She'd found them all in the saloon in Hope—well, almost all of them. She'd had to walk clear across town and half a mile down to Opal's Brothel to find the one-eyed drunk called Otter Jones. He had the meanest eye she'd ever seen—and she'd heard in the saloon that he'd shoot his own grandmother in exchange for a pint of red-eye whiskey.

Eager excitement filled her as she surveyed the motley group. And especially as she saw the thundercloud of anger descend upon Wade's face.

She hurried downstairs and out to the corral, tingling with anticipation.

"Maybe you'd care to explain?" Wade growled as she approached.

"What is there to explain? I see you've met our new wranglers."

She guessed that the look he gave her must have curdled the blood of more than one grown man. It did make her knees tremble, but she leaned against the corral post, assumed a casual pose, and smiled at him. "I figured extra hands would make the ranch run more smoothly and result in even greater profits. So, just tell these men what you need done and I'm sure—"

"Clear out." Wade didn't even wait for her to finish speaking before he confronted the unsavory bunch of men before him. "We've got all the wranglers we need on Cloud Ranch."

Otter Jones, a patch on one eye, glared belligerently through the other one. "Well, that's not what that there lady said. She told me you'd pay thirty dollars for me to mend some fences and uh . . . somepin' else . . ." He scratched his head, squinting, trying to remember.

"She said you needed cowpunchers to ride out for a few days and round up strays." A short, barrel-chested man with a shaggy black beard that covered the entire lower half of his face staggered forward. "And she said we'd git thirty dollars fer it!"

Wade's tone remained even, but it held a note of unmistakable finality. "She made a mistake. We've got all the hands we need."

"I disagree. I hired these men," Caitlin said staunchly. "And I expect you to give them some work to do and pay them accordingly."

"Yeah, you heard the lady." Otter wheeled toward the foreman, a menacing light sparking in his small black eye. "She hired that there wagon and the horse so we could get out here. She said we'd each"—he hiccuped suddenly, spat, and continued—"she said we'd each git our own horse. And thirty dollars. I don't know about anyone else, but I got a helluva lot of whiskey I could buy with thirty dollars, and some dandy rolls in the hay with Opal's gals, and I ain't leavin' till I get my pay."

By now the rest of Cloud Ranch's wranglers had come out to the corral to see what all the fuss was about, and as Otter finished speaking, they each stood up straighter, wariness in their faces.

"Ma'am, maybe you should go back to the house," Jake Young addressed Caitlin in a low tone.

Dirk's hand brushed down toward his gun though he didn't pull it out of the holster.

Caitlin felt the tension crackling through the air. She hadn't expected this. She'd thought Wade would confront *her*—not these men. And she hadn't realized the men would be so upset about not getting the jobs she'd promised. It hadn't appeared to her that any of them cared to do any work—she'd heard from the bartender at the saloon that they were all notorious drunks who picked up odd jobs now and then and often didn't even show up.

Perhaps her mistake had been in offering them so much money. But she'd wanted to guarantee they showed up—otherwise how could she have harassed Wade?

The trouble was, she now reflected uneasily, thirty dollars was a hefty sum. Maybe too hefty for these men to give up on without a fight.

"You'll all receive your thirty dollars," she said hurriedly, turning to the men with what she hoped was an appeasing smile. "I apologize for the misunderstanding, but . . ."

"The hell they will." Wade's eyes were cold. "Two dollars apiece for your trouble." That icy glance touched each man in turn. "And a ride back to town in the wagon."

"Hell and damnation! Damn your two dollars, Barclay!" Otter exploded. "She said thirty and I ain't leavin' till I get it!"

"Me, either!"

"Me, too!"

Several others stepped forward angrily, and Otter suddenly rounded on Caitlin and grabbed her arm.

"You're a damned liar, lady!" he shouted into her face.

Wade's fist caught him hard in the jaw and sent him sprawling into the dust. "That's about enough out of you, Jones," he said quietly. "Apologize to the lady and get the hell off my land."

"Apologize? Like hell!" Uttering a string of oaths Jones tried to surge to his feet, but Wade knocked him down again. When the barrel-chested man suddenly swung a fist at Jake Young, he too was sent flying with a hard right punch from the youthful cowboy.

Suddenly Dirk had drawn his gun. And so had Miguel and Rooster.

"Anyone else have an objection to a wage of two dollars?" Dirk drawled softly.

Caitlin swallowed hard. Despite the warm sunshine sparkling across the corral and blazing off the surrounding grassland, she was chilled to the bone. She hadn't expected any of this. She'd thought Wade would be annoyed and angry at having to waste time sending the men away, but never that the situation would become this dangerous and volatile.

"We're goin' . . . I reckon. Keep your shirts on." The barrel-chested man was eyeing the drawn guns.

"Do we still git the two dollars?" another man asked, pushing straggly brown hair out of his eyes.

"Yes." Wade spoke evenly. "If you leave without any more trouble." He swiftly surveyed the group, as calmly as if he were counting chickens in a coop. He pulled a money pouch from his pocket and peeled off several bills. In total silence, each man accepted what was offered and slouched away toward the wagon, grumbling. One or two threw baleful glances Caitlin's way. At last Otter Jones stumbled to his feet.

He reached out a grimy hand for the money, but Wade closed his fist around the last of the bills. "Apologize to the lady."

Jones shook his head. "Damned if I will."

Wade stuffed the remaining money back into the pouch.

Otter Jones shot him a look full of hatred, then fixed that vicious glance on her. "Sorry, ma'am," he muttered, but there was no mistaking the venom underlying his words.

Wade yanked the money out once more and thrust it at him. "You steer clear of Miss Summers," he said softly. "If you know what's good for you."

"Mebbe I will and maybe I won't," he muttered as he headed toward the wagon.

Humbled and uneasy, Caitlin turned toward the foreman. "I'm sor—"

But before she could get the apology out, Wade Barclay seized her arm and began dragging her toward the barn.

"Boss—take it easy," Baldy called. He'd seen that look

on Wade's face before. He knew it meant trouble, trouble for that little bundle of blond femininity. Big trouble.

Jake knew it too. "Hey, boss, maybe you should cool down a mite before—"

"Get to work!" The snarl encompassed all of the wranglers. They knew better than to argue with Wade when he was in this mood. He was a fair man, far more steady-tempered than most, but when he got riled, watch out.

"I wouldn't want to be in that little lady's shoes," Dirk remarked, and then swung up onto his bay horse.

The others all agreed. The last thing they saw before riding out was the barn door slamming on their boss and on Reese's beautiful little handful of a daughter.

Chapter 8

The barn was dim, with only two high narrow windows letting in any light at all. In the hay-scented darkness, Caitlin wrenched away from Wade and stood her ground.

"How dare you drag me in here like a sack of potatoes!"

"I wouldn't drag a sack of potatoes—I'd toss it over my shoulder. Maybe that's what I should have done to you."

"Why don't you try it?" she invited, a challenging light in her eyes. She plopped her hands on her hips in a defiant posture, too angry to care how far she pushed him. "You'll regret it if you lay one hand on me. The last man who tried to . . ." She broke off and bit her lip. She wasn't about to tell Wade about Dominic Trent. He didn't need any ammunition about her past to use against her.

"Well, you don't want to know what happened to *him*," she summed up grimly.

"Probably he got what he deserved." Wade regarded her steadily. "What did he try to do?"

"That's none of your business. I was only attempting to give you fair warning, but it's not important." Caitlin took a deep breath, remembering Becky, remembering what *was* important. "Suppose you tell me why you didn't take advantage of the extra hands I hired." It wouldn't do to be defensive—she had to revert back to her original plan. "It's my opinion that the ranch could benefit from—"

"From employing irresponsible drunks who only care about where their next bottle of red-eye is coming from?" he interrupted her. "From offering those same drunks more money than our wranglers make in a month—stirring up unrest and dissatisfaction?" he continued, each word striking like flint.

"As part owner I have every right to—oh!!!"

She gave a gasp as he caught her wrist and yanked her toward him. She landed hard up against his chest.

"Do you know what you need?"

Eyes wide, she was positive she didn't want to know. "I need you to release my arm this instant."

"You need a good paddling, princess."

"P-paddling?"

"Spanking," he told her grimly, and the gleam in his eyes made her breath catch in her throat.

"You wouldn't dare." She tried to jerk free of his grip, but it only tightened.

"Don't push me," he said very softly. "I know what you're up to and it won't work. I'm not buying your share, not for a year—no matter how much of a damned nuisance you make of yourself."

So he'd figured it out. Satisfaction surged through her. It didn't matter if he knew what she was up to—he would still be driven to distraction by her plan. What had happened this morning was only the beginning—there was much, much more she could do to disrupt both his life and the running of the ranch, until he gave in and agreed to let her leave.

"You may not agree with my decisions about the ranch but I have as much right as you to make them." Still caught in his grasp, Caitlin lifted her head so that she met his gaze squarely. Standing this close to him was having a powerful effect on her heartbeat—for some reason it was racing. And her breath seemed trapped in her chest as she gazed into his blue eyes, but that must be due to the intense anger he stirred in her by his very existence. "And I will continue to make decisions about the day-to-day business of Cloud Ranch, despite your objections—so don't think you can use brute force to intimidate me."

"Intimidate you?" He threw back his head and laughed. "I can't imagine anything intimidating you. You're made of rock, of steel." Suddenly his gaze flickered over her with a keen scrutiny somehow different from the way he'd glared at her before. "Or so you'd have me think."

This time she really did try to wrench away from him. When she couldn't break free, she kicked at him and heard his indrawn breath as her boot connected with his shin. But his grip was still ironclad, and he jerked her even closer against him, so close she could feel the granite strength of his chest. Suddenly one arm imprisoned her waist, and unexpectedly he grinned.

That grin made her tremble. It transformed his face— before he'd been handsome in a stern, intimidating way— now he looked so devastatingly appealing—almost boyish—that she could well imagine a row of women swooning over that grin.

Which is exactly what made her angry enough to shove against him with all her strength, trying to knock him off-balance but she may as well have tried to knock over a stone wall. And her attempt somehow backfired. He whipped both arms around her with lightning speed and dragged her down with him into a wide pile of hay.

He rolled atop her and pinned her beneath him, ignoring her gasped protests.

"You . . . let me up . . . right this . . . minute!"

"Not until I've had my say. If this is the only way I can get your attention, princess, then that's how it's going to be."

Caitlin fought. She twisted, writhed, and squirmed, trying to kick him, hurt him, escape any way she could, but Wade wasn't even breathing hard and he held her helpless beneath him without any effort at all.

At last, breathless and frustrated, she finally stopped struggling.

"That's better," he said, but she thought his voice sounded hoarse.

"Listen up," he continued, his fingers still clamped around her wrists, his gaze riveted to hers. "I want you to stop trying to cause trouble and to just look around you. Try to appreciate where you are, the gift you've been given. You and I have to try to get along. I'm willing, if you are. Reese would want it that way—"

"I'm sick of hearing about Reese!"

He frowned. "If Reese were here right now, he'd be plenty worried about you. You made an enemy today."

Caitlin was finding it difficult to think straight. A small ache had begun deep inside her and was spiraling through her. She wished Wade would let her up, put some distance between them.

"You mean . . . Otter Jones," she murmured, summoning her wits.

"That's right."

"I'm not afraid of him."

"You should be." The sternness returned to his face and he shifted his weight as she gave a small squirm of frustration beneath him. "Just the same, you shouldn't wander off alone for a while," he warned. "Give me a chance to find him in town and let him know he'd better leave you alone—"

"I don't need you to protect me." With renewed determination, she began to struggle again. Coming to her senses, she called it. For a few moments, lying upon the hay with his breath warm on her cheek, with his big, muscled body atop hers, she had gone completely mad. Now she was sane again, back in the real world, trapped beneath the most infuriating man in the world, and furious at her own helplessness.

"You obviously need someone to look after you," Wade said sharply, but there was a strange tightening in his chest as he studied the angry fire of her eyes and the stubborn set of her lushly beautiful mouth. "Looks like I've been elected to the job," he muttered, but suddenly his head flew up as the barn door swung open and Baldy stuck his head in. The old wrangler peered through the dusk.

"Who's here? That you, Wade?"

In a flash Wade had released Caitlin and sprung to his feet. He strode forward as the ranch hand stepped into the barn.

"What is it, Baldy?"

"Miss Summers ain't still in here with you, is she? I got to ask you about them calves in the south pasture."

"Let's go outside then." Wade brushed past him, leading the way out of the barn. "We can talk on the way down there. I need to check myself and see how many strays are . . ."

Their voices faded as Wade led the old wrangler away from the barn. Caitlin rose slowly to her feet.

Her confrontation with Wade had gone further than she'd ever anticipated. In fact, the entire situation had gotten entirely out of hand. *But,* she thought shakily as she brushed hay from her riding habit and then tugged some more from her hair, *I can't afford to stop now. If anything, I have to press on even further. If Wade thinks he can intimidate me into giving up the fight, I'll never get away from Cloud Ranch and back to Becky.*

More than ever, she had to show him that she wouldn't let up until he'd given her what she wanted.

She went back out into the sunshine, blinking a little in the light. The sky was a brilliant turquoise, huge and endless. Upon the horizon, blue-gray tips of mountains touched pristine white clouds.

The wranglers and Wade had all ridden out. Chickens squawked in a pen, and Dawg was barking at a squirrel scampering across the limbs of a tree, but no one else was around except Francesca, who was walking sedately toward the house, head bowed, from the direction of a group of aspens some fifty yards away.

Caitlin headed toward the house as well and as Francesca approached, she saw the woman's face was wet with tears.

"Francesca, what's wrong?"

The housekeeper glanced at her briefly, then lifted a lace-edged handkerchief and wiped at her damp eyes.

"Nothing, senorita," she said in a low tone that bordered on surly. "I was putting flowers on your father's grave. That is all. I go there every week to do this."

"Oh." The revelation stunned her. "You must . . . have been very fond of him."

Francesca nodded, pursing her lips. "He was a good man, senorita. Kind, so kind, with feelings that come deep from the heart. There are not many men like that. Mr. Wade—he is like that, too."

She turned away and trudged up the ranch-house steps. Caitlin suddenly remembered that she hadn't yet had breakfast, but she didn't feel hungry. For some reason, she kept walking in the direction from which Francesca had come.

In the end, it wasn't difficult to find the grave.

It was just beyond the stand of aspens, in a pretty clearing where birds sang and the grass grew high and thick. Flowers curled around rocks and at the base of the nearest trees. There was a white headstone with Reese's name carved upon it and the date of his death, and vivid pink and yellow wildflowers had been placed carefully just beneath the base.

Caitlin approached slowly. For some inexplicable reason, a lump rose in her throat as she stared at the lettering, at the solemn white headstone, at the brightness of the flowers. She closed her eyes and saw an image of the photograph she'd seen—of the broad-shouldered, weathered-looking older man smoking a cigar with the three Barclay boys.

Her father.

Her hands were trembling as she bent down and plucked a single wildflower from the grass near her feet.

She hesitated, then began to kneel down and place the bloom alongside the others, but she couldn't. She froze with her arm outstretched.

"Why didn't you write to me, not even once?" she whispered. Anger and pain throbbed through her. "You didn't bother with me until you were dying. And why then? Why did you want me here, in this place you never cared to share with me for eighteen years?"

The tears nearly broke from her then, bitter, stinging, angry tears, but she choked them back. She flung the flower aside into the waving grass, then ran all the way back to the house.

There were no answers, there would never be any answers.

And she vowed to herself as she bolted upstairs to the sanctuary of her room that she would never visit Reese's grave again.

Chapter 9

"Where do you think you're going?"

Wade had been just about to ride out toward Black Bear Point to start rounding up cattle for the spring branding when he saw Caitlin leading Star, the palomino mare, from the barn the next morning.

He couldn't deny she made an exquisite picture in her full, dark blue riding skirt and frilled white shirt. With the sunshine pouring down the way it was he couldn't help noticing the way that shirt outlined her full breasts, or the way the sun gilded that soft, daisy-gold hair of hers. Or the way it enhanced the vivid green sparks in her eyes as she led Star to the corral fence.

He was trying not to remember the intoxicatingly soft way she had felt beneath him in the hay. Better to forget about that.

"I'm going out for a ride to survey my property," she replied airily. "Not that it's any of your concern."

"Don't wander too far. You don't know your way around yet."

"Nor will I need to—I won't be here long enough for that," she retorted sweetly and stroked a hand along the mare's flowing mane.

Wade spurred his horse away, but then reined in and turned back to watch her mount at the fence post. A knot punched through his gut at the graceful way she mounted and then sat the mare. Any doubts he might have harbored about her ability to handle a spirited western horse dissipated as he saw the sure, easy way she handled the mare.

"Something you should know," he said as she trotted toward him. "We've been having a problem with rustlers."

"I do know. Winnifred told me about it when I was in town—right after she told me about the Campbell gang, and how Hope was so unsafe for a while that she had to leave for several months until things calmed down."

"Well, things have calmed way down. You're safe as a baby at Cloud Ranch."

"So why are you warning me about these rustlers?"

As she tilted her head up toward him in that breezy, mocking way, he couldn't help staring at her mouth. It had to be the sexiest, most alluringly shaped mouth he'd ever seen. A mouth that belonged on a saloon girl—not on this irritating little snob with her proper manners and tight, buttoned-up-to-the-throat shirt and her elegant riding skirt that fell all the way to her ankles.

"Uh, what's that you said?" he asked distractedly, then scowled as he saw her smile. She repeated her question.

"If I'm so safe here, why are you mentioning these rustlers now?"

"Because you're a tenderfoot and you don't know a damn thing about life out here. If you see any strangers, anyone messing with the cattle, skedaddle out of there fast. Don't ride up and ask them what they're doing or some other damn fool thing."

A tiny stab of apprehension penetrated the cool facade she'd been wearing for his benefit. "Do you think the rustlers would actually . . . shoot me . . . or something?"

"Doubt it, but you can't be certain. Mostly they're out at night, but they've been getting bolder. So stay close to the ranch. I don't want to have to send a search party out for you."

"Heavens, I'd hate to inconvenience you," she flung back at him.

And then she was sorry she'd said it because for the second time that devastating little boy's grin flashed across his face and she felt as if someone had slammed her in the stomach.

"See that you don't." He quelled the suddenly mischievous impulse to tug that pretty little black Stetson she'd bought in Hope right off her head and toss it in the horse trough. "Rode into town yesterday," he added hastily, leaning back in the saddle and surveying her from beneath the brim of his hat. "Ran into Luanne Porter. She said she invited you to that little supper of hers."

"That's quite true." Caitlin patted the mare as the animal pranced, restless to be off. "Surely you don't object to that also?"

"I think it's fine that you're settling in, making friends." This time the grin was wicked. "Next thing you know, you'll be joining the Hope Sewing Circle. And organizing the town quilting bee."

With that, he spurred his roan and rode off before she could spit out a reply. "Quilting bee, my foot!" Caitlin fumed, staring indignantly after him as a cloud of dust rose behind his horse's hooves.

Wade Barclay would be ruing those words by the end of this day.

She called out to Miguel, who was chopping firewood near the barn. "Where is Jake Young working this morning?"

He straightened and eyed her in surprise. "Rounding up strays over near Cougar Canyon."

"Where's Cougar Canyon?"

Miguel set the ax down and approached her. "Due north. 'Bout ten miles."

"Um . . . north?" Caitlin squinted at the sky, then at the horizon in each direction.

Miguel pointed. "That way, senorita. But the boss wouldn't want you to—"

"You've been a wonderful help, Miguel." Caitlin bestowed on him a smile as brilliant as the spring sunshine and a moment later she and the mare were galloping north, kicking up dust of their own.

It was a magnificent day for a ride. Caitlin let the mare have her head and the gorgeous Wyoming grasslands whipped by. A sense of freedom and peace and exhilaration filled her as the warm breeze fanned her cheeks and the wild, open beauty of the landscape embraced her.

She eventually slowed the mare to a canter and began looking around more closely. The plains had given way to a hilly landscape dotted with cattle, and there was a canyon ahead, but no sign of Jake Young.

She rode toward the canyon, glancing in every direction.

"Jake!" she called, breaking the stillness of the hot afternoon. "Jake Young!"

There was an answering shout and a moment later the wrangler appeared on horseback upon a low ridge. Waving his hat over his head, he rode toward her.

"I was just exploring a little," Caitlin said with a dazzling smile, "and I remembered that someone mentioned you were working out this way. How is . . . everything going?" she asked, not quite understanding what he was supposed to be doing, but figuring she ought to pretend she did.

"I've rounded up about a dozen strays, Miss Summers—got 'em in the canyon. I'll be bringing 'em back shortly. There's a few more farther back in the trees. I was just going to get 'em when I heard you call."

She tilted her head at him and regarded him through glowing eyes that had beguiled far more sophisticated men. "Wade Barclay was so angry with me yesterday for hiring those other men. You're not angry with me, are you, Jake?"

"Angry? With you? No, ma'am." The young cowboy grinned from ear to ear. "Don't reckon I could ever be angry with a lady as pretty as you."

"Why, aren't you sweet." He *was* sweet, Caitlin thought. She felt a bit guilty about using him in her plan. *But it's necessary,* she told herself. "I brought a canteen of lemonade and some of Francesca's sugar cookies." She patted the small saddle pack she had tied to the mare's saddle earlier. "Why don't we have a little picnic—maybe you'd be kind enough to give me some advice."

Jake choked. "Me? Advice?"

"You see, Jake," she said earnestly, "I don't really know much about ranching—and I'm afraid to ask Wade Barclay. He isn't exactly an easy man to talk to."

His brows shot up in surprise. "Really? I'm surprised to hear that, Miss Summers. Wade's usually real good at answering questions and explaining things. And he's the best wrangler I ever did see."

"I suppose we got off on the wrong foot," she mused, and lifted her shoulders in a pretty shrug. "But you— you're so nice—and you're obviously highly skilled at your job. So perhaps you could spare me just a little of your time? And knowledge?"

"Sure thing." The wrangler flushed with gratification. "It'd be my pleasure, ma'am." Quickly he dismounted and hastened to help Caitlin from the saddle.

They found a smooth clearing shaded by aspens and it was there, seated upon fresh spring grass, that Wade Barclay found them some time later. Jake was listening spellbound as Caitlin, on her knees with a buttercup tucked behind one ear, was gesturing gracefully and reciting a poem.

"How do I love thee? Let me count the ways.
I love thee to the depth and breadth and height
My soul can reach, when feeling out of sight
For the ends of—"

"What the hell is going on here?" Sitting astride his horse, Wade stared at the picturesque scene with a muscle throbbing in his jaw.

"Oh! Mr. Barclay! Goodness gracious, you scared me!" Caitlin exclaimed, clasping a hand to her heart, but it was clear from the sparkle in her eyes and the overly innocent smile upon her face that she hadn't been frightened at all. "Heavens, I was so caught up in this entrancing poem I didn't even hear you ride up. Do you know it? The poem,

I mean. Sonnet Number Forty-three from Elizabeth Barrett Browning's *Sonnets from the Portuguese*—"

"Young," Wade interrupted in a taut voice. "Where the hell are the cattle?"

He sprang down from the saddle even as Jake Young scrambled, red-faced, to his feet.

"Boss . . . I . . . we . . . was just . . ."

"Loafing on the job?" Wade's hard glance took in the half a cookie still clutched in the cowpoke's hand, and the canteen lying upon the grass.

"We don't pay you to eat cookies."

"I know. I'm sorry, boss." Jake dropped the cookie as if it were a poison arrow. "We were just going to sit a spell and Miss Summers wanted to ask me a few questions . . ."

"I just bet she did."

"And we started talking about . . . poetry and . . . it was my fault, boss," the cowpoke rushed on. "All my fault."

"No, Jake." Caitlin shook her head and the buttercup fell from her curls into the soft grass. "You're too sweet, far too sweet, but you know that isn't true." Gracefully she rose to her feet and brushed an imaginary blade of grass from her skirt.

"It was my fault, I'm afraid." She couldn't quite succeed in sounding regretful as she gazed into Wade Barclay's blazing eyes. "It was all my idea. Jake was just being polite. But I'm afraid that once we started discussing poetry, I became quite carried away. The time seems to have escaped me. It seemed like we were talking for only a few moments—"

"Poetry." Disgustedly, Wade eyed the wrangler, who looked stricken. "What about rounding up those strays and driving them back to the corral for branding?"

"I plumb forgot. I . . . I never did that before. Boss, I'm sorry—I don't know what came over me."

"I do."

Jake flushed clear up to the roots of his dark sandy hair, but Caitlin Summers only opened up her eyes all wide and innocent.

"When you didn't show up to help with the branding, Miguel told me Miss Summers had been looking for you." Wade shifted his gaze to the lovely face of the angel-haired blonde he wanted to strangle.

"Reckon you'd best see to those steers now," he said, still gazing hard at his "partner."

"Yes, boss." Jake threw Caitlin a quick glance. "Thank you, Miss Summers. I sure enjoyed our talk. And that nice poem," he said in a rush and then bolted toward his horse.

When the wrangler had ridden off hell-bent after the strays, Wade spun around and stalked back to his horse.

Caitlin shot him a look of surprise and followed him.

"Where are you going?" she demanded.

"Home."

"Isn't there . . . anything more you wish to say to me?"

"Like what?"

She couldn't help feeling a bit indignant that all of her efforts to disrupt Jake Young's work had been for naught. Aside from that one little outburst, directed at poor Jake, Wade didn't even seem to be that upset.

"You know, it *was* all my fault that Jake didn't get his work done on time. I needed to ask him some questions about roundups. It was fascinating. I'm not quite sure how we came around to Elizabeth Browning, come to think of it, but it was most enjoyable. I miss the intellectual stimulation available to me back east."

"Fine."

"And I'll just bet some of the other men would appreciate a chance for a cultural discussion as well." She gave him a great big smile. "And in return, they could no doubt teach me quite a bit about different aspects of ranching." She clapped her hands together as if hit by sudden inspiration. "Now why didn't I think of it before? I could accompany a different wrangler each day of the week and watch him work—possibly even help him, you know, until I learn every aspect of the cattle business."

If she'd been hoping to stir him into a state of fury with visions of cowhands picnicking with her and reciting poetry instead of attending to their work, she was disappointed.

Wade swung into the saddle and took the reins. "Go ahead," he retorted evenly. "Do whatever the hell you want, Miss Summers."

"You mean . . . you don't mind?"

"I don't give a damn."

"Wh-why not?"

His smile was cold and hard as a barbed-wire fence in February. "Because I'll fire any man who stops work to talk to you—and they're all going to be told that in no uncertain terms tonight." His voice was infuriatingly calm.

But his words shook her. She didn't want anyone getting fired on her account. "Wait a minute, that doesn't seem fair," she objected, but he interrupted her.

"Fair? None of this is fair, princess. It's not fair that I'm saddled with a spoiled, frivolous female who's determined to be a burr under my seat; it's not fair that Jake got a dressing down because you used him to try to get at me;

it's not fair that I have to sit here and listen to you pretend that you care about anyone but *yourself*."

The contempt in his eyes cut her almost as deeply as his words. Stunned, Caitlin could only stare at him.

"And," Wade continued coolly, meeting her stricken look without a shred of pity, because he was certain that it, too, was all part of her act, "it's not fair that Reese died without ever setting eyes on you again, because that's what he wanted more than anything in the world." He jerked at the reins and turned the roan sharply.

"I only wish to hell *I* didn't have to set eyes on you— ever again," he muttered. Each word struck her so forcibly they might have been rocks bruising her flesh. She felt all the color draining from her face.

Wade spurred his horse and rode for the ranch without looking back.

Caitlin couldn't move. She stood rooted to the spot as fury and frustration and a great hollow bitterness rushed over her.

Her temples throbbed. Her throat ached. Somehow she mounted the mare and rode off, riding blindly, frantically, needing only to be gone from this sunlit place, to be alone with the torment of her thoughts.

Why should Wade Barclay's ill opinion of her matter? *It shouldn't,* she told herself as scalding tears threatened behind her eyelids. She wouldn't cry. She wouldn't! She had nearly wept yesterday at Reese's grave—she wasn't going to let Wade Barclay turn her into a sniveling little weakling.

"I never cry," she whispered desperately, and urged the mare on faster.

Chapter 10

She wasn't exactly sure when she realized she was lost.

The world had become an angry chaotic blur where there was only the whipping wind that tore at her hair, the thunder of flying hooves, the choking whirl of dust—and the anger and pain in her heart—anger and pain that stung her soul like a thousand pricking needles. All those things had risen up and engulfed her in a great dark storm, whirling round and round like the scattering dust and veiling the hard, wild landscape through which she rode.

Eventually the veil fell and the blurring haze cleared and she glimpsed the world again, returning to her senses only to discover that she didn't recognize a single element of her surroundings.

She was in a deep canyon, on a stony trail, with a high rock wall to her right and a sheer drop to her left. Star was cantering briskly along, but Caitlin gasped and reined her in as she took stock of her surroundings.

Beyond the canyon the foothills rose. But which was the way out—and how did she get back to the ranch?

A hawk circled high above but there was no other sound. No hint of any living creature.

Panic gripped her but she fought it back. Once she was clear of the canyon, she'd be able to figure out where she was. Surely there would be some familiar landmark, some ridge or butte or something she'd recognize.

"Come on, girl," she muttered, putting a shaking hand to Star's mane as the mare began to walk forward. Caitlin peered around in the hot silence, searching this way and that for a trail that would lead her out.

An hour later she finally managed to reach the rim of the canyon. Her throat was parched, her chest tight as she set out across a track overgrown with grass and studded with rocks. She was deep in the foothills, surrounded by pines and firs and spruce, by craggy slopes and empty ridges where now and then a deer or antelope appeared.

Far below there was a deep open plain of grass and sagebrush like the one she had ridden across before, but it rolled endlessly in every direction to end in high black-shadowed mountains—and she was no longer certain from which way she had come.

How would she ever get back to Cloud Ranch?

With a sinking heart she realized that she had left the canteen in the grass at Cougar Canyon. She had no water. No food. At least it was still only early afternoon, she guessed. She glanced toward the sun, a molten bronze ball in the sky. It would set in the west, she told herself, so south would be . . . *that* way?

She had to get back before Wade Barclay noticed her absence. The last thing she wanted was to have him gloating over her having become lost after he'd warned her not to go too far.

I'll reach the ranch before supper, Caitlin vowed, her hands clenching the reins, *or die trying.*

A half hour later she began to fear this might really happen. She'd been riding north—she hoped—but there was still no sign of Cloud Ranch cattle, or of the stream, or of any human being anywhere.

Despair filled her. And that's when she heard the gunshot.

She froze in the saddle. The mare's ears pricked up. She pranced sideways, and Caitlin stroked her neck again. "Whoa, girl. Easy," she whispered.

After the gunshot there was no sound. Caitlin waited with her heart in her throat. Suddenly she heard a shout, and then another angry voice that echoed off the rock walls. But the sounds seemed to originate from beyond the next ridge.

She didn't know whether to ride away or ride closer. Perhaps it was some of the Cloud Ranch wranglers and they could tell her how to get home.

Perhaps it is the rustlers, she told herself. *Or some other horrid outlaws. Or Indians . . .*

Perhaps Wade Barclay would be satisfied if he found her bloody, scalped body being eaten alive by coyotes and buzzards and snakes, she thought. Perhaps then he'd be sorry for all those hateful things he'd said to her.

But what would happen to Becky . . .

You're not going to die, she told herself, biting back the panic. *And you're not going to be a coward either. You're going to . . . investigate.*

She rode on slowly. Nearing the ridge she noticed a dip in the trail and realized that there was a narrow valley. Perhaps the gunshot and shouts had come from there.

Cautiously she urged the mare forward through the cottonwoods and down the valley slope.

That's when she saw them—four men standing, arguing, beneath an old scarred pine tree.

And one man down on the ground beside them, lying unmoving in a pool of blood.

He's dead. Shock jolted through her and she felt the blood draining from her face. Just in time she bit back a rising scream.

She couldn't make out the men's faces—they were too far away. But they were dressed in plaid shirts, bandannas, and denim pants, and they all wore guns. The tallest man, who had reddish hair, held his gun drawn and pointed at a shorter man in a gray hat.

"You knew what he was doin', didn't you? You helped him double-cross me."

"No . . . I swear. I didn't know nothing about it . . ."

"Someone was helping him—how many head of cattle did you two cut out for your own herd?"

The wind rose and the rest of the words were carried away. But suddenly, as Caitlin watched in horror, the tall man fired.

The shot cracked like thunder as the bullet struck the shorter man in the chest. Blood spurted and he went down in a heap.

Star reared at the sound of the gunshot and let out a frightened neigh. Even as the short man fell to the ground, the other three men whipped around toward the sound of the mare and saw Caitlin watching them even as she tried to bring her mount under control.

For one heart-stopping moment she met the red-haired man's vicious gaze. His features were blurred, but there was no mistaking the ferocious intensity of that stare. He smiled and she caught a glint of gold. Terror bubbled inside her throat, but there was no time to scream, no time to think. With fear pulsing through her, she yanked on the reins and spun the mare around, then dug in her heels.

"Go!" she shouted. "Go!"

Sagebrush, pine, and rock flew by in a blur as the horse galloped up the slope of the valley, back the way they'd come. The pounding of Star's hooves matched the pounding of Caitlin's heart as she leaned forward over the mare's mane and held on tight with hands and knees.

When she heard the sounds of pursuit behind her, she glanced back over her shoulder and gave a gasp.

Three men thundered after her, their horses galloping hard. With every stride they closed the distance. A gunshot roared past and she realized in shock that they were shooting at her. Desperately she spurred the mare on, driven by the frantic single-minded will to survive.

Suddenly there came a curve in the trail and the mare took it too fast. She stumbled and went down. Caitlin flew from the saddle, miraculously free from the mare's hooves. She hit the ground with a jolt that slammed through every bone in her body. The mare was already scrambling up, shaking, and Caitlin, still breathless from the impact of the fall, tried desperately to rise and get to her.

She staggered to her feet just as her pursuers thundered toward the curve.

Despair choked her. She'd never make it. She couldn't reach the horse in time, mount, get away. All she could do was stand frozen and terrified, her hands cold with sweat as the plaid-shirted men bore down on her. The leader smiled again and she saw that glint of gold once more—and then he lifted his gun.

Suddenly, more shots exploded, filling the air in a staccato, but they didn't come from the men chasing her—the shots came from the lip of the canyon she'd circled earlier. As she jerked her head in that direction, she saw two riders with shotguns leveled, firing at the men bearing down on her.

Then everything changed, so rapidly that Caitlin could scarcely take it in. Her pursuers turned tail and fled—galloping back toward the way they had come.

And her mare took off—bolting ahead past a stand of pines and brush, disappearing over a rise.

Shaking all over, Caitlin stared wildly up at the rim of the canyon. Somehow, even from this distance, she recognized Wade Barclay on his tall, muscular roan. And behind him rode Miguel.

She felt weak, dizzy, and breathless, but as Caitlin brushed her tangled hair back from her face she tried hard to remain standing. She would not collapse. She would not cry or whimper. She would not *faint*.

She closed her eyes, and the image of the murdered men filled her with nausea. She couldn't help but sink to the ground. In a moment, she told herself, she would try to stand.

She didn't know how long it was until Wade and Miguel reached her. When she saw them bearing down on her, she used every ounce of willpower she possessed to climb to her feet. She was standing, her arms at her sides, like a limp doll, when they reined in.

Wade took one look at her and his insides knotted. The spirited, defiant beauty who had baited him earlier in the day was nowhere to be seen in the pale, dazed face of the girl who stood wavering before him as if the tiniest breeze would knock her down.

He sprang from the saddle with more speed than grace and reached her side even before Miguel's mount had halted.

"Somebody ought to have named you Trouble," he muttered, grasping her by the arm. When he realized how she was trembling he slipped an arm around her waist, fearing she'd slip to the ground if he didn't help support her. "It's all right. I've got you."

"Let . . . go of me. I'm . . . f-fine. I don't need your help."

"Right. I can see that." But with unexpected gentleness he led her toward the stump of a tree that had been blasted by lightning, and sat her down. Ignoring Miguel, who had followed him, he pulled a flask from his pocket, opened it, and handed it to her.

"Drink this."

"I don't want—"

"Drink it, princess. You look like you're about to keel over."

"No . . . I'm . . . fine . . . just a little . . . upset."

He knelt down and pushed the flask into her hands. Caitlin stared at it. Just stared.

"Caitlin . . ."

Suddenly those stricken jade eyes gazed straight into his. "They might have been the rustlers. I don't know. I got lost. The canyon . . ." She shook her head. "Then I heard a shot. From the valley. They killed one man—he was dead when I got there. Blood . . ."

"Easy, now. It's all right. You can tell me later." Wade covered her hand with his. "Later, when we're back at the ranch—"

"And then the man with the gun, the tall man, started arguing with another man and then he shot him too." She rushed on as if Wade hadn't spoken, her eyes wide, anguished, while Wade and Miguel listened in grim silence. "And then the mare neighed and they saw me . . . they . . . came after me . . . they . . ."

"Did they hurt you?" Wade asked so quietly that his words penetrated her shock.

For the first time she seemed to really see him. The shock in her eyes cleared a little and he saw the depths of fear and horror beneath. "N-no. I got . . . away."

"You did," he agreed quietly. "You did just fine."

She swallowed then and glanced down at the flask in her hands.

"My throat is . . . so dry. Is this water?"

"It's whiskey."

"I don't—"

"I know—you don't drink whiskey. But just this once, since your throat is dry?" He didn't add that it would help ease the shock she'd suffered, as well as the chill of her fear.

She looked at the flask, then at him. "All right," she whispered. She lifted the flask to her lips and took a sip.

"More," Wade said roughly when she made a face and pushed the flask at him.

"It's awful."

"Trust me, it'll help."

To his surprise she sighed, but raised the flask again and this time took a long deep gulp.

Wade felt a strange crazy urge to wrap his arms around her, hold her tight. He wanted to smooth the tangled mass of blond curls from her face, stroke her cheek, and tell her over and over that she was safe.

Instead he scowled at her. When he thought of what had almost happened here today, cold fear gripped him. She'd almost been shot, probably by rustlers.

Why in hell had he left her alone back at Cougar Canyon?

Why had he ridden off and left her to find her own way back? She was unarmed, a tenderfoot, and . . .

This was the worst of it . . . She'd been angry. He'd made her angry on purpose. And that anger had led to all this.

Wade was so furious at himself that he felt every muscle in his body tense up. Reese had entrusted her to him, and he'd nearly gotten her killed.

He dragged his gaze from her and spoke curtly to Miguel. "Follow their tracks back to that valley. We'll meet up later at the ranch."

Miguel met his glance briefly and then nodded without speaking a word. Best not to mention in front of the woman that he was going to take a look at the dead men, see if he recognized them.

Wade stood, and scanned every direction for the mare. There was no sign of her. If she didn't find her way home, he'd send someone to search for her tomorrow. In the meantime, he had to get Caitlin away from here.

"Come on." He stretched down a hand to her. "Let's get you back to the ranch."

She took a deep breath, ignored his outstretched hand, and pushed herself up off the stump. "I don't need any help," she told him quietly, with a glimmer of her old stubbornness.

"I can see that."

She shot him a wary glance. "Are you making fun of me?" Her chin angled up in the way he was beginning to know—and more dangerously still—in the way he was beginning to like.

"Are you?" she asked with some of her old feistiness.

"Not right now. Maybe later."

They walked in silence to the roan and suddenly, after one look at the horse, she spun toward him. "Star—"

"Don't worry—we'll find her. Or she'll come home."

"She can do that? Find her own way home, even if she's lost?"

"You were lost, she wasn't." Slowly, he grinned. The color was returning to her face. "Besides, everyone can find their way home eventually," he said in a steady tone. "It might take a while, but they can. Even if they're lost."

She had a strange feeling that he was talking about something other than Star. Caitlin searched his face. There was no anger or mockery in it now, there was only a kind of tension, which she didn't really understand. But there was also something else.

Gentleness.

The usual hard expression on his face had disappeared. His eyes held a warmth that she'd never seen before, and suddenly her own feelings were in confusion.

She felt hot, then cold. Her heart skipped a beat. She wanted to pull away from him—and, good Lord, she suddenly wanted to lean against him and feel those powerful arms go around her . . .

Stop being an idiot, she warned herself, but she quivered as he lifted her effortlessly into the saddle. Such easy, flowing strength. When he mounted behind her and wrapped his arms around her, Caitlin felt a rush of heat that spread through her entire body.

It's the whiskey, she told herself frantically. *It's having a potent effect on you. That's all.*

It had better be all. She wasn't ever going to have feelings—romantic feelings—for any man ever again. Not that her feelings for Alec Ballantree had been anything like these feelings she was having toward Wade Barclay.

There was no comparison between the lovely longing and affection she'd held for Alec and the raw blaze of sensation—much like the hot fire of the whiskey—she felt when Wade was near.

And right now, he was *very* near. He couldn't have been much nearer. Every part of his body touched hers—she felt his rock-hard chest behind her head, his muscular torso pressed against her back, his thighs squeezed against hers.

She couldn't believe how her body tingled. She felt weak all over, but the strange thing was, she also felt oddly invigorated.

Alive in a way she hadn't felt in a long time.

She had meant to pay attention to the trail on the way back, to try to learn her way, but she was too tired, her mind too full of the horrid images of the dead men, of the still-chilling race to escape.

To her dismay, she found herself leaning back against Wade Barclay, resting against his strength. It wasn't at all unpleasant; in fact, it calmed the turmoil inside her, making her feel safer than she'd felt in a long while.

Before she knew it, before she even was aware of passing the gates, they were riding up to Cloud Ranch, and Dawg was bounding out to greet them.

None of the wranglers were in sight.

Weren't they supposed to be here, starting the branding?

Half turning in the saddle, she started to ask Wade, but he cut her off. "They're out searching for you. When you didn't return from Cougar Canyon, I sent them out on a search. Soon as you're settled, I'll go after them and tell them you're safe."

She was silent as he helped her down. To her surprise, his hands lingered at her waist as he set her on the ground—holding tight to her as if he were reluctant to let her go. Funny, she thought. Suddenly she didn't *want* him to let her go. Caitlin lifted her head to meet his keen gaze.

"I've caused a great deal of trouble for you today."

"I reckon so. Just as you meant to."

She bit her lip. She thought back to her picnic with Jake, how she'd tried so hard to antagonize Wade. All part of her plan. But she hadn't planned on getting lost or finding danger—or on Wade and the wranglers having to cease all their work to search for her.

Of course, it was good for her overall plan. She hadn't really been hurt, and she'd disrupted the workings of the ranch far more than she ever could have hoped. So why didn't she feel any satisfaction?

She swallowed. "I suppose I should thank you for finding me when you did."

"That was luck." He shrugged. "No thanks necessary."

"But if you hadn't shown up exactly when you did . . ."
A shudder ran through her.

"Don't think about it." Wade felt the delicate trembling, and before he knew what he was doing, his arm slid around her waist. That was his first mistake. She felt fragile and sweet in his arms. And her eyes widened. Hell, she had the most beautiful eyes he'd ever seen. In the dusty yard, with Dawg frolicking around them, she looked angelic and scared and brave and beautiful all at the same time.

Get away from her. Now.

But those glorious green eyes held him mesmerized. He couldn't drop his arm, couldn't resist the pull.

Caitlin knew she should move away from him. But she couldn't quite bring herself to break the spell that seemed to have come over both of them. She was intensely aware of the hot still day, of how his pitch-black hair brushed his shirt collar, of the rough stubble along that handsome jaw. She sensed the coiled male tension in him and her own blood raced through her veins.

Her lips parted.

"Damn it, princess," he muttered, then both arms swept around her, pulling her close, and as if drawn by an invisible overwhelming force, Wade Barclay leaned down and kissed her.

Oh, how she wanted the kiss.

That was the first thought that flashed through her mind—and the last. After that there was no room for thought. Once his mouth touched hers, she couldn't remember how to think at all.

It was a warm, wonderful, frightening kiss. Frightening

because it felt so delicious. Far too delicious. His mouth on hers was both rough and sweet, demanding from her and at the same time giving to her. He seemed to be tasting her as if she were the most desirable morsel in the world, stunning her with the heat and strength of his kiss and a dizzying tenderness that somehow was hotter than the blazing sun . . .

He broke it all too soon, pulling back from her. He was scowling, Caitlin saw in dismay. Through the thudding of her heart she didn't know whether to scowl back or try to kiss him again.

She gave her head a puzzled shake.

"That," he said in a firm tone that was oddly low and hoarse, "was a big mistake."

And without another word, he turned and left her. He mounted the roan, rode away, and didn't once look back.

Chapter 11

 "Senorita, the hour is late."

Francesca's voice reached through the door, filling Caitlin with a sense of inescapable destiny.

"Senor Wade wishes me to ask you if you are attending Senorita Porter's supper party—or not."

"Of course I am." Caitlin threw open the door. No one had to know that she'd been sitting on her bed, all dressed and ready, for more than half an hour trying to muster her confidence before facing Wade. She swept past the house-keeper in a swirl of spring green silk taffeta and floral French perfume.

She prayed that no one, not Francesca, not Wade, not anyone at this dratted party tonight, would be able to see the uncertainty and confusion churning through her.

"It's about time . . ." Wade began, then broke off, his gaze sharpening as she entered the study where he waited. His glance swept over her and she knew by the tensing of his jaw that she looked more than presentable. She saw him swallow and loosen his string tie and she felt a surge of purely feminine triumph.

But it was short-lived, cut off by the next words out of his mouth. "Another five minutes and I'd have left without you."

Francesca snorted behind her, then disappeared toward the kitchen. Caitlin's delicate brows lifted with practiced haughtiness.

"A pity you didn't. There really isn't the slightest purpose in my attending this party—I won't be around long enough to develop a friendship with Luanne Porter or anyone else."

"I wouldn't be too sure about that." He strode toward her, slow and easy, and Caitlin drew in her breath at the devastatingly handsome picture he made in his white shirt and black string tie, his tanned face clean-shaven, and that dark silky hair falling over his brow. No man had a right to be that handsome, she thought. He stopped right before her—almost, but not quite as close as they'd stood yesterday when he'd kissed her. The memory of it flooded back and she was certain he was remembering too because the corner of his mouth jerked up in a mirthless smile.

"You don't seem to have the knack of annoying me nearly as much as you'd like, princess."

She didn't know how to take that. One delicate shoulder rose. "Then I suppose I'll have to try harder, won't I?"

"Suit yourself."

"As you always do?"

It was a reference to the kiss, and she was certain he realized it. In the lamplit study his eyes gleamed coolly as he took her arm. "Let's go—we don't want to keep Luanne waiting."

There was silence between them during most of the ride to the Circle P Ranch. It was a lovely starlit night, warm, clear, and dazzling with a full moon that dangled low. It shimmered like a huge brilliant pearl in a breathtaking black satin sky. Lightning bugs darted here and there through the trees, adding a magical twinkle.

But the evening's loveliness could not soothe the unrest in Caitlin's heart. Seated so close to Wade, she couldn't think of anything but the way he'd kissed her.

Why in the world had he kissed her? He didn't even like her. And she didn't like him—not one little bit. So why had she wanted to kiss him back?

"Miguel took those corpses to town and wired the marshal in Laramie. He got here today. Thinks they're the rustlers all right. At least, part of the gang. Both of 'em are wanted in Montana and North Dakota."

Corpses. She was thinking of moonlight and kisses, and he was thinking about corpses and rustlers. Caitlin felt as though she'd been whacked over the head with a shovel. She gave her head a tiny shake and reminded herself to be sensible, for once. The kiss had meant nothing to Wade—obviously it was as ordinary an occurrence in his eyes as . . . rustlers and corpses.

She ignored the hollow feeling in her heart and smoothed her skirt. "So does that mean there's only those three left—the ones who chased me?"

"Could be, but doesn't look that way. Looks a lot worse than we originally thought."

"What do you mean?"

"The marshal identified both of the men from wanted posters out of North Dakota. The first man you saw shot was Skeeter Biggs, cousin to Hurley Biggs."

"Who's Hurley Biggs?"

"Big-time rustler. They call him King of the Rustlers. He heads up a cattle-rustling outfit that shifts from territory to territory, and several different states. Never been caught. No one's ever even seen his face close up. Except, now, for you." Wade steered the horses onto a side trail, up a small rise. "Chances are Skeeter was part of that ring, but decided to double-cross Hurley and siphon off cattle to start his own herd. The red-haired man you saw do the shooting might even have been Hurley Biggs himself. Want to know who the other dead man was?" Wade's mouth tightened. He quieted the horses as a squirrel whisked across the trail, perilously close to those flashing hooves. It made it to the safety of untrampled grass just in time. "Otter Jones."

"What?" Caitlin shot up straighter on the seat.

"You heard me. Seems like Jones didn't spend all his nights drinking. When he was sober enough, he worked with the Biggs gang rustling the same cattle he wanted us to pay him thirty dollars a day to round up."

Caitlin flushed. "I had no idea," she muttered.

Wade threw her a curt glance. "Neither did I. If we knew everyone involved in the rustling it would be a simple thing to catch them and lock 'em up. The thing is, the whole valley has been thinking they were a small, pesky band who'd get caught sooner or later. But if they're part of Biggs's ring—operating in all these territories—then they're a lot more clever and organized than we thought. We'll have to take a different tack."

"What will that be?"

"I'm calling a town meeting to propose hiring a gunfighter. Someone to track Biggs down and bring him in, dead or alive. If that happens, the rest of the gang will fall apart—the marshal believes it's Biggs's cunning and leadership that's allowed them to be so wide-ranging. And so successful."

"You're going to hire a gunfighter?" Caitlin stared at the flickering path of a lightning bug. How could she ever have even considered bringing Becky to Silver Valley, even for a moment? Sure there were beautiful mountains, a gorgeous blue sky, wide-open space, and pretty lightning bugs—but also gunfighters and rustlers and all manner of dangerous men.

Including the one sitting next to her.

"Actually," Wade continued in his quiet, even way, "there's a pretty famous gunfighter living not too far from us—Quinn Lassiter, over on Sage Creek Ranch." He grinned. "But he's retired now. A happy family man, so I reckon we'll have to go with someone else."

"You sound like you have someone in mind."

He threw her a sideways glance. "You're right. My brother."

"Clint?"

"Nope, Clint's a sheriff in Colorado. Nick, my baby brother, is the gunfighter in the family. I've already wired him—he should get the telegram within the next week, and soon as he's finished whatever he's working on, I reckon he'll show up here."

"Lovely," she muttered. *Two of them. Two Barclay boys. Reese's "sons."*

He might have been reading her thoughts. "We're not so bad once you get to know us," he said, trying to suppress a smile.

"I have gotten to know you and believe me . . ." She broke off.

"Don't tell me you've found something lacking in my character, Miss Summers."

"More like a dozen things," she informed him darkly.

"Aw, that hurts. After I saved your life—"

"Which is entirely beside the point. You had one good day, one decent moment. Other than that—"

"Go ahead." She could see his grin through the darkness. "Tell me just what you think. I can take it."

"I'm too ladylike to tell you what I really think."

"Or too chicken," he drawled.

Caitlin's mouth dropped. *"Chicken?"*

"You heard me."

The words flew out. "You're a bully. And more stubborn than a mule. Not to mention the most close-minded, irritating, and domineering man I've ever met. Did I mention arrogant? You think you know everything and that no one else's opinion matters. You can't add or subtract—"

"Anything else?"

"And you wouldn't know how to treat a lady if your life depended on it."

"That all? I thought maybe you didn't like me." Wade gave a low chuckle, and suddenly, after a moment of startled silence, Caitlin couldn't help but laugh too.

"You're utterly impossible."

"Want to know what I think of you?"

"No," she said quickly, too quickly, then bit her lip as he chuckled again.

"Chicken," he pronounced gravely.

Caitlin took a deep breath. "Go on—if you must."

"Never mind. I'm not sure you can take it."

"For your information, Mr. Barclay, I can take anything you care to dish out."

"You sure about that, Miss Summers?" His voice was low, deep, and full of a purely male challenge. She felt herself flushing.

And thinking of the kiss they'd shared, of how it had affected her, she suddenly felt warm all over.

"Try me." She forced out the words, hoping they sounded bolder than she felt.

He glanced at her, his eyes glinting in the moonlight. "Careful. I just might take you up on that."

The moment he said the words, Wade regretted them. What was wrong with him? Kissing Caitlin Summers had been the stupidest thing he'd ever done. And if he wasn't careful, he just might find himself doing it again.

It was a relief when they suddenly descended into a sweep of dark-shadowed valley studded with willows, a relief when he spotted the Circle P ranch house set amid stately trees. All night he'd been trying to focus on the rustlers so that he wouldn't have to think about the gorgeous woman seated beside him—or about that big mistake he'd made the other day. But it hadn't been working. She looked so pretty in that dress, he'd hardly been able to think about anything else.

Caitlin Summers was his charge, his duty, he reminded himself. Taking care of her was a job he'd been given— same as chopping wood or line riding or mucking out the horse stalls.

It should be just as ordinary and businesslike as all of those things. What the hell had he thought he was doing by *kissing* her?

Sure, it was a lot more interesting than mucking out stalls, Wade admitted as he pulled up before the Circle P corral. But it wasn't part of his job. Rescuing her was, thanks to his promise to Reese, but from this point on, she was strictly off-limits.

Coming around the buggy to help her down, he loosened his tie yet again. When he lifted her and set her carefully on the ground, he could feel her tremble. Wade stepped quickly back. "We're late," he said gruffly.

At least tonight it would be easier to forget about Caitlin. Luanne would be here. He could just look at her, sweet and kind and pretty as she was, and everything would be fine.

The small parlor of the Porter house brimmed with people in their Sunday best. Caitlin found herself warmly greeted by Edna Weaver, introduced to her husband, Seth, and then Winnifred Dale tapped her arm and began admiring her dress. As Wade and Seth Weaver started a discussion of the rustler situation and the price of beef, Luanne Porter hurried over to Caitlin. She was wearing a soft, cream-colored silk taffeta gown, and her eyes sparkled as she introduced Caitlin to her aunt and uncle, a handsome pair who hailed originally from Boston.

"I'm so happy you could join us tonight, Miss Summers," Luanne exclaimed. She smiled warmly at Caitlin, but her glance shifted almost immediately to Wade. She caught his eye as he was asking Seth a question, and he paused to wink at her. Luanne's cheeks pinkened.

A queasy feeling came over Caitlin. "It's Caitlin, please," she managed. "I'm delighted to be here."

How was it she could speak normally when she felt so icy cold inside. Even her lips felt frozen.

Amelia Porter, Luanne's aunt, gave a chirrupy laugh. "Well, yes, this is quite a nice-sized gathering, isn't it? Perhaps it wouldn't be considered so in Boston or Philadelphia, but for these parts, yes, indeed. Funny it began as a small family dinner, with only Wade included, since he's almost like family," she explained. "He and Luanne, you know . . ." She broke off as her niece blushed and threw her an exasperated glance.

Caitlin's heart squeezed tight—and dropped down to the pit of her stomach.

"Really, Aunt Amelia," Luanne protested, but she looked pleased as well as embarrassed.

"It's the truth, isn't it, dear?" Her aunt beamed at Caitlin, then at Winnifred and Edna. "Anyway, the whole evening just grew into a splendid little party, which is an excellent thing because I believe Luanne truly misses the social life she had back east. You must also, Miss Summers."

Caitlin inclined her head, still painfully taking in the implications Luanne's aunt had made about the school-teacher and Wade. "Why . . . yes, of course," she murmured. She wasn't about to say that she missed nothing back east—no one. The events of the last weeks she'd spent in Philadelphia had revealed all too clearly the superficial nature of the people she'd known there. Only one or two of the young men and women she'd known had even bothered to offer her true condolences and sympathy when Lydia and Gillis had died—the others had merely uttered words that meant nothing while they gossiped and sniped and pitied her behind her back. The revelation of Gillis's debts, owed to half the men he did business and socialized with, had turned the entire town upside down, and also turned its most prominent citizens against him.

And it had made Caitlin an object of scandal and scorn.

"Do you play the pianoforte?" Amelia Porter asked eagerly. "Luanne plays beautifully—and sings as well."

"I sing a little—very little," Luanne corrected her with a laugh. "It suits the children at school well enough—they tend to admire any grown-up who pays the least bit of attention to them—but trust me, my skills are most undistinguished among adult company."

"And you, Miss Summers? Do you sing?" Frederick Porter, Luanne's uncle, regarded her with interest.

"A little, like Luanne." Caitlin smiled in spite of herself. Luanne Porter and her aunt and uncle, like Winnifred and Edna, were warm and genuine and it was difficult to resist their kind interest. "But it's my little sister, Becky, who possesses a really lovely voice. It's most unusual—clear, strong, and yet exquisitely sweet. I wish you could hear her sometime . . ."

She broke off. What was she saying? She wished no such thing—Becky would never set foot on a stagecoach traveling all the way to Hope! And even if she did, her timid little sister would never find the courage to sing before so many strangers.

But they all took her up on the prospect immediately. "Perhaps she'll come visit you," Winnifred put in hopefully.

"Well, if she does, Seth and I will give a dinner party and she can sing for all of us." Edna nodded excitedly at the idea.

"She's quite shy, I'm afraid," Caitlin said quickly, but Edna dismissed that with a wave of her hand.

"We'll let her know right quick enough that she's among friends. That's all she'll need. How old is she?"

"Eleven."

"Oh, I'll bet she'd love meeting the Morgensen twins!" Luanne exclaimed. "Two of the sweetest, brightest girls I've ever met—Katie and Bridget Morgensen. They're eleven too. Oh, you really must invite her soon," she added enthusiastically.

Caitlin found herself swept up in the spell of friendliness and warmth. The bright, simple parlor, the kind, boisterous, happy people, the aroma of tantalizing fried chicken and dumplings and corn muffins and apple pie wafting through the house filled her with a strange sense of peace and belonging. As the older women moved into the kitchen to see to dinner, she found herself seated beside Luanne on a plush gold sofa, discussing the Hope Sewing Circle.

"I was invited to join only a month ago. It's a lovely group of women . . . perhaps you would care to come to a meeting sometime—"

Luanne paused as someone knocked loudly at the door.

"Oh, that must be Mr. Raleigh. Excuse me." With a quick smile, she hurried to the door.

"Do come in, Mr. Raleigh. Let me introduce you to everyone."

The man who entered, sweeping off his derby, was tall, broad-shouldered, and polished as brass. Caitlin recognized the way his gaze swept the room—she had seen many such appraising glances in Philadelphia parlors and ballrooms—a self-important man taking swift account of his fellow guests, deciding which of them might be useful or amusing to him. There was something familiar about him as well, something that stirred an ember of unease within her, but she couldn't place where she had seen him or under what circumstances.

"Dear friends—allow me to introduce Mr. Drew Raleigh," Luanne announced just as Winnifred, Edna, and Amelia Porter returned. She beamed at the handsome stranger in the well-cut eastern suit. "Mr. Raleigh is visiting on business from New York City. Edna introduced him to me yesterday afternoon."

"Yes," the newcomer added with a grin. "Luckily for me, Miss Porter took pity on me. I know few people in town and she kindly invited me to meet some of her friends." Raleigh had a smooth soothing kind of voice, deep and slow as fresh-poured honey, at odds with his sharp, attractive features and keen hazel eyes. His sandy hair was neatly combed, his ruddy skin tinged with a touch of bronze as if he'd been out riding the Wyoming plains for the past weeks.

As the men shook hands and the women murmured, "How do you do?" Caitlin rose from the sofa, and her gaze shifted from the newcomer to settle for a moment upon Wade. She had noticed Luanne stealing glances at him too while they talked and felt with certainty there was much more between him and the red-haired schoolteacher than merely friendship. Especially considering Mrs. Porter's remarks.

Her heart twisted. What kind of a man was involved with one woman and kissed another?

The wrong kind.

She remembered Mrs. Casper's warning, and her stomach tightened. She knew that a man like Dominic Trent would do something so low—in fact, he'd tried to do much worse, but she hadn't thought of Wade Barclay as reprehensible. Until now.

When Wade glanced up to find her staring at him, she

averted her eyes and turned away, angry with herself. Fool that she was, she'd been hoping that deep down, for all his irritating arrogance and stubbornness, he was as steady and honorable as he seemed. Now she knew differently.

She resisted the urge to scrub at her lips, wishing it were possible to also wipe away the memory of that kiss.

Her thoughts were interrupted by Luanne's friendly voice as she and Drew Raleigh approached. "And this is Miss Summers," Luanne said.

"Caitlin, please."

"Caitlin, then. She's a newcomer in Hope also," Luanne explained. "She's part owner, along with Wade Barclay, of the Cloud Ranch."

"Ah, Cloud Ranch." Drew Raleigh smiled warmly. "Now that's a magnificent piece of property. I've heard a great deal about Cloud Ranch."

"Forget it." Wade spoke so suddenly over Caitlin's shoulder that she jumped. Raleigh's sandy brows shot up.

"Cloud Ranch isn't for sale. Not now, not ever." He met Raleigh's glance squarely.

"Mr. Barclay," the other man countered with a faintly mocking smile, "what makes you think I'm interested in buying?"

Caitlin watched him take Wade's measure at the same time that Wade took his. Raleigh's lip curled slightly, but Wade's face gave nothing away.

"Well, Raleigh," Seth Weaver interjected, "the truth is, I just told Wade about the reason for your business in Hope." He turned his close-set, brown eyes upon Caitlin. "Drew represents an eastern business syndicate interested in acquiring a sizable cattle ranch in the territory," he explained. "His outfit already owns cattle interests in Arizona and in Montana. But as I told him this afternoon during our meeting at the bank, out of all the ranchers in Silver Valley, the Barclays, the Tylers, and the Lassiters are least likely to sell. Matter of fact," he added with a pointed look at the easterner, "I made it clear that I couldn't see any circumstance under which Wade or his brothers would ever sell."

"It's true, Barclay. He did explain exactly that." Drew Raleigh nodded. "But he didn't mention Miss Barclay here—er, I mean, Miss Summers. You two share ownership of the ranch—so you must be . . . related?" he asked, fixing Caitlin with a charming smile.

"No. We are *not* related—not in any way," Caitlin said vehemently. The others guests stared, surprised at the forcefulness of her tone, but Wade simply glanced at her with his usual nonchalance.

"And personally," she rushed on, more quietly, "I would be delighted to sell my share of Cloud Ranch, Mr. Raleigh—if circumstances allowed. Unfortunately, they do not."

"So in other words, don't waste your time trying to sweet-talk her into it." Wade reached for Caitlin's arm as if to draw her away but she pulled back from him.

Drew Raleigh's hazel eyes were riveted upon Caitlin's face. "If I ever tried to sweet-talk anyone so lovely, it wouldn't be over a piece of property," he replied softly.

Caitlin read the apparent admiration in the man's eyes. She was unmoved by it. She had met Drew Raleigh's type hundreds of times before. It wasn't his too-obvious charm, but Wade's snort beside her that made her murmur, "You're too kind, Mr. Raleigh. Thank you."

Wade grimaced.

"I insist you call me Drew." The easterner's smile widened. "Where do you hail from, Miss Summers?"

"It's Caitlin, remember? And I'd much rather hear about you."

They began to chat easily, but all the while Caitlin was intensely aware of Wade's glance on her. There was ice in his eyes. And all through dinner, and the card games and conversation that followed, he ignored her and spent his time joking with Seth Weaver, talking cattle prices with Frederick Porter, or complimenting Luanne and her aunt on their cooking.

Shortly before the evening drew to a close, Caitlin noticed she was missing her reticule. She remembered going into the small back sewing parlor with Amelia Porter for a moment to look at a dress pattern the woman had heard was all the rage in the East, and wondered if she'd left it there, so she slipped down the hall to look. To her relief, the reticule was lying upon the cushions of the small tufted sofa. But as she started back toward the front of the house, she heard a sound to her right, and turned.

She was facing the kitchen doorway. And there, upon the threshold, she saw Wade and Luanne standing as close as two candles melted side by side. Luanne's arms were tight around his neck and Wade's hands were at the schoolteacher's waist. As Caitlin watched in shock, Luanne lifted her face to his and they kissed.

Chapter 12

Caitlin's reticule slipped from her fingers. It hit the floor with a thump, and Wade pulled back from Luanne with a start.

His eyes narrowed as they focused on Caitlin, pale and frozen only a few feet away. For one agonizing moment she couldn't tear her gaze from his as silence seemed to thunder around them. Then she heard Luanne murmur and pull away, Wade's arms dropped to his sides, and the dark spell was broken. Sick and furious, Caitlin snatched up her reticule and fled down the hall.

"Caitlin, wait!" Wade's voice called after her, but Caitlin only ran faster. She bolted toward the parlor so quickly she collided with Winnifred Dale as the woman stepped out into the hall.

"Oh!!! My dear, excuse . . ." She stared into Caitlin's parchment-white face. "Heavens, child, whatever is wrong? You look like you're going to swoon."

"No, no, of course not, I . . . never swoon. It's only that . . . I have a headache and I . . . I believe Wade might wish to stay and visit longer with the Porters, so I was wondering if perhaps the Weavers would be kind enough to drive me home—immediately."

"Of course, my dear. I'll ask them this very moment." Winnifred studied her anxiously. "I'm so sorry you're feeling poorly. Just give me a moment to find Edna and—"

"If I had a buckboard, I'd be honored to take you home, Caitlin." Drew Raleigh had come up behind Winnifred and his hazel eyes lighted on Caitlin with concern. "Unfortunately, I came on horseback this evening. Won't you let me escort you to a chair until the Weavers are ready to leave? May I bring you a glass of brandy?"

"That won't be necessary." Wade's voice cut in from behind her. Caitlin whirled around.

Grim and unsmiling, he strode toward her and caught her arm. Deliberately, he hooked it through his. "Sorry to have kept you waiting. Let's go."

"I beg your pardon." She pulled her arm free and met his gaze squarely, her green eyes dark with anger. "I haven't yet said my good nights."

"Say 'em then."

"I will say them when I'm ready."

"I suggest you get ready *now*." Tension crackled through the air between them and Winnifred glanced from one to the other in amazement. Drew Raleigh watched the exchange in silence.

Chaos churned through Caitlin and it was all she could do to hold her gaze steady, directed right at Wade Barclay and his icy blue eyes. She would not look away first—*she* had done nothing to be ashamed of. But apparently he didn't feel he had either because his stare was every bit as hard and steady and relentless as hers.

It was Winnifred who broke the deadlock—she tugged Caitlin away to bid farewell to the Porters. And shortly after that, Caitlin found herself stuck. Stuck in the buggy beside a man she detested, beneath the shimmer of moonlight and a darkness rich with the fragrance of wildflowers and pine. Neither of them spoke until they were nearly at Cloud Ranch.

"Reckon there's something I ought to explain."

She nearly shrieked at the calm tone with which he said those words.

"Really?" She put all the haughtiness she could into the word. "I can't imagine what that might be."

"Let me make it clear for you then," he continued. "Under no circumstances are you to have any dealings whatsoever with Drew Raleigh."

Drew Raleigh! A fog of red fury swept across her eyes. "You want to discuss Drew Raleigh?" she bit out, flabbergasted.

"Of course I don't. He's the last thing I want to discuss. I'm just telling you to steer clear of the man."

"You don't have a right to tell me anything, Mr. Barclay. Anything at all. And the only man I intend to steer clear of is *you*!"

"Now why is that? Is it because of that . . . mistake . . . that happened between us last night?"

"Obviously. And apparently you made another 'mistake' tonight," she retorted. "With Luanne Porter."

"That wasn't a mistake. I meant to kiss *her*," Wade said matter-of-factly.

Caitlin turned to stare at him, anger vying with jealousy in her chest. His darkly handsome face wore a neutral expression as he looked straight ahead at the trail, but she saw the tension in his shoulders and in those big hands that so expertly held the reins.

"Then I pity the poor woman!" she exclaimed.

"She seemed to enjoy it well enough. So, for that matter," he glanced coolly over at her, "did you."

She didn't know whether to scream or slap him. Instead she clenched her hands into fists and scooted as far away from him as the buggy would allow. "Really? I can't recall."

"You don't say."

"That's right. I tend to block unpleasant experiences from my mind. It's much easier than dwelling upon them. So whatever happened between you and me . . . whatever *mistake* you made, might never have happened as far as I'm concerned. It really is only a vague, unsavory blur."

To her astonishment, he pulled the horses up, halting them so suddenly she lurched in the seat. The dark night was thick and dense about them, the trees, moon, and stars their only company.

"Wh-what are you doing?"

"Refreshing your memory," he said, hauling her into his arms. Her tiny gasp of surprise only made him gather her closer against him. As her eyes widened, and she began to struggle, he slanted his mouth down on hers, tasting the dewy rose lips that had been haunting him night and day.

He hadn't meant to kiss her. Not that other time, not tonight. But this exquisite, irascible angel had a way of getting under his skin like nothing else. "So you've forgotten what it felt like when I kissed you," he muttered, and she shivered in his arms.

"Y-yes."

"And none of this seems familiar?"

"N-no . . . not the least little b—"

He kissed her again. She tried to escape but stopped with a small helpless moan as his warm lips captured hers and a sweet dazzling pleasure spun through her.

"Don't you even remember this part?" His voice was low, hoarse, as for one instant Wade lifted his head.

"Mmm . . . no . . . maybe . . ."

"I sure as hell do." The next kiss was even deeper, even more intense. And then she melted against him, her lips catching fire along with his, seeking his with soft, aching welcome.

A kiss hotter than fire rocked them both. Wade couldn't have stopped now if his life depended on it. She was in his blood—her taste, her scent—and there might have been only the two of them in all of Wyoming—in all of the earth.

One kiss led to another, and then another, and then his hands began to slide over her, caressing her, stroking the lush shape of her hips even as his mouth sought and conquered hers, eliciting small breathless gasps and deep kisses from her, kisses so ardent and intoxicating that he burned with wanting.

"Caitlin, what are you doing to me?" he groaned, his lips grazing the slender column of her throat. Then his hand swept up to that perfect gold chignon, his fingers resting gently against the plaits and the pins.

"N-no . . . Wade, don't!"

His chest felt on fire as he heard her say his name, and

even his heartbeat had speeded up in a way that had never happened when he faced snakes or bobcats or ruffians spoiling for a fight in the saloon.

"Can't help it," he growled, and then as one arm clamped around her waist, his fingers closed upon one of those damned hairpins. "Been wanting to do this for a long time . . ."

His touch was gentle but deft as he undid the pin—two, three, four of them—and tossed them into the night. Rich gold curls spilled down in a riotous tumble and sunshine met moonlight as Wade buried his fingers in the vibrant curls and kissed Caitlin with a fierce tenderness that came from someplace deep inside of him he'd never known existed before.

She mewed against his lips, then pressed herself against him, their bodies fitting together, the heated perfume of her like a sensual cloud that filled his senses.

He thought he'd die of pleasure when her sweet mouth parted to welcome his tongue and he delved deeper within her. It was almost heaven . . . but not quite. What he really wanted was to shed her of that gorgeous gown, and take her in the moonlight, kiss every inch of her, and devour her once and for all so he could stop dreaming about her.

Then things would go back to normal, he was certain, and he could stop thinking about her night and day. His fingers tangled in her hair, caressing the silken strands, and then slid downward. Tension and desire pounded through him as his fingers closed gently over her breast. She gasped against his lips, quivering for an instant with a shock of pleasure—but then, suddenly, she stiffened and drew back.

"No!" It was a whisper. And then, as if someone had broken a magic spell, she yanked away, flushed and trembling and staring at him with panic shining in her eyes, right alongside the shimmer of passion. "No!"

Wade forgot his own needs and urges and felt a sudden astonishing urge to soothe her.

"It's all right, princess. We'll call things off—for now. If that's what you want—"

"What I want!" Her voice was a breathless squeak. Her flushed face had gone pale in the moonlight. "Since when has it mattered to you—to anyone—what I want! It didn't matter to Alec—or to Dominic Trent," she cried bitterly, "and you—you have kept me on Cloud Ranch against my will from the moment I arrived. You don't care what I want!"

He held up both hands in the air, concerned because he could see she was trembling all over and trying like hell not to cry. "Easy," he said quietly, speaking the way he had to that wild filly Nick had captured a few summers back and brought in for taming. "Who's Alec—and who's Dominic Trent?"

"None of your business—but you're as bad as they are!"

Wade dropped his hands, studying her panicked face. "Sounds like they hurt you, Caitlin. I'd never do that."

"You already have!" she flung at him, touching her swollen lips, but then wished she could bite back the words.

"How?" he asked sharply.

"You kept me from returning to Becky—she needs me. I have to take her away, we have to run away before . . ."

She caught herself and felt the blood drain from her cheeks as she realized what she'd said. "And you k-kissed me!" she rushed on accusingly.

"That hurt?"

"You didn't mean it. You didn't kiss me because you . . . like me . . . or anything. You and Luanne . . . I saw you . . . so why?"

"Why." He suddenly gritted his teeth. The expression in her eyes tore the honesty from him. "Damned if I know. But I've been wanting to do it ever since that night I found you at the stream."

"Why?"

"The same reason, I reckon, that you wanted to kiss me back."

"I didn't! I never—"

Quick as lightning, but gently, he caught her wrists and tugged her closer. "Do you really want me to prove it to you . . . again? Because if we start, I don't know how easy it will be to stop, not for either one of us."

Their eyes met and locked. *The same reason she had wanted to kiss him back.* Caitlin didn't even dare contemplate what that reason might be.

"Damn you!" she cried. She broke free and shoved against him. Tears shone in her eyes but not a single one escaped to slip down her cheek.

Before Wade knew what was happening she had flung herself from the buggy and was stumbling across the tall grass. She took off running, moonlight silvering the spring green gown that billowed behind her, her hair streaming wildly nearly to her waist.

She ran straight toward Cloud Ranch, like some wild,

beautiful creature of the night, and she never slowed or looked back.

Wade watched her go, his chest tight, his arms aching. Aching to hold her again, he realized in alarm.

What the hell did he think he was doing?

He couldn't tell her that he'd only kissed Luanne tonight because he was desperate to stop thinking about *her*. That he'd thought—hoped—that when he and Luanne kissed he would forget all about the kiss he and Caitlin had shared.

But he hadn't forgotten. He couldn't. And he felt lower than a snake about Luanne. But the whole time he'd been kissing her, it was Caitlin who had filled his thoughts.

Damn everything to hell. Wade slammed a hand against the seat of the buggy, startling the horses. Reese had entrusted him with his daughter, and Wade had promised to take care of her—but he hadn't counted on her stirring up so many different emotions in him. He was a calm man, a steady man, that's what everyone said.

And lately, he'd been behaving like a lout and a fool.

He watched her run, lovely as a vision in a dream, but retreating further and further from him. He wanted to hold her close but Caitlin Summers was running away from him.

And from what else?

"We have to run away," she'd said of her and her sister.

From whom? What? Those men whose names she'd blurted out?

He had a feeling that wasn't all. Caitlin Summers, for all her beauty, sophistication, and courage, was running from herself.

Chapter 13

For a whole week Caitlin avoided Wade. She came down to breakfast after he had already left to begin the day's work, she busied herself in her room when he returned for lunch, and at dinnertime, she carried a tray up to her room and spent the evenings reading or writing to Becky.

It was branding time and he was busy—he made no effort to seek her out. For which she was grateful, she told herself as she stood at the window one afternoon staring out at the empty corrals. Branding was done—the men were all out doing various chores, Dawg was chasing a squirrel toward the stream, and barking, in the way of dogs, as if his life depended on it, and she was restless.

She hadn't ridden alone since the day the rustlers had chased her, even though, just as Wade had predicted, Star had returned from her adventure in the foothills all on her own. It's high time I stop cowering here in the ranch house, Caitlin decided suddenly.

Picking up her letter to Becky, she contemplated it.

She'd written to her sister every day, but still hadn't received an answer to any of her correspondence. Biting her lip, she decided to ride into Hope this very afternoon to mail it, and to see if at last Becky had written back.

The gang of rustlers appeared to have left—there hadn't been a sign of them since that awful day when she'd come upon them—so there really was no danger, she told herself. Except perhaps from wolves, snakes, or bears, she reflected as she drew the strings of her Stetson close under her chin and headed downstairs, her plum-colored cotton riding skirt rustling about her ankles.

She went directly to the kitchen, where she'd noticed a shotgun was kept propped near the door. It was midafternoon and Francesca was just whisking an apple pie from the oven as Caitlin strode over and picked up the gun.

"Senorita?"

The woman's questioning glance annoyed her. She knew the housekeeper was only surprised to see her taking the gun, but she wasn't in a mood to answer questions. She was in a mood to ride clear across this gorgeous land, to be alone, to forget all about Wade, and Cloud Ranch and this difficult situation she found herself in. And about the impact Wade's kisses had had upon her.

"I'm riding to town, Francesca. Do you need me to leave the shotgun here for you or may I take it?"

"We have another, under the shelf in the pantry, if it is needed, but, senorita, what do you know about firing such a gun?"

"It can't be all that difficult." Caitlin shrugged and clasped the shotgun at her side as she crossed to the door. "Do you need anything in town?"

"No. But, Senorita Caitlin, if you've never fired a gun, Senor Wade would want you to know how to—"

"Senor Wade has nothing whatever to say about anything I choose to do." Caitlin met her gaze squarely. "I don't need his permission—for anything."

Unexpectedly, Francesca grinned, her pretty olive-skinned face lighting. "*Su padre*—he could be stubborn too. *Obstinado*. Senor Wade—now he is a more patient man. But still—"

"Patient about what?"

At the deep sound of Wade's voice, both Caitlin and the housekeeper turned and found him leaning his shoulders against the door leading from the hall, his Stetson low over his eyes.

"Never mind." Caitlin gripped the rifle tighter. She spun back toward the kitchen door but his voice stopped her.

"What are you doing with that?"

"None of your business."

She flung the words over her shoulder and let the door slam behind her without glancing back.

She heard him coming after her but kept walking—in fact, she walked faster, refusing to look over her shoulder. He caught up to her just outside the barn and stepped in front of her, blocking her path. Caitlin sidestepped, trying to reach the door, but he moved even faster, his powerful body barring the way.

"Stop this at once and leave me alone," she ordered.

"Not a chance. Not until you tell me where you think you're going with that shotgun."

"I'm riding into town, if you must know. I have a letter for my sister—the one waiting patiently for me to return to her in Philadelphia, remember? I'm going to send it to her—if that's all right with you."

"And the shotgun? You sending that to her, too?"

"I happen to own every bit as much of this ranch as you," she reminded him coldly, "so I guess I own this shotgun, too. That means I don't need your permission to borrow it."

"But you damn well need to know what you're doing when you fire it." He wrenched the gun from her. "I'll bet you've never used a shotgun in your life, have you?"

"What difference does—"

"Do you even know if it's loaded?"

Loaded? She bit her lip. "I didn't check . . . yet. That doesn't mean I wasn't going to—"

"Listen up, you little tenderfoot." Wade shook his head. "You could get hurt firing this thing without knowing what to expect. It has a kick. You have to hold it a certain way, aim it a certain way—if you want to hit anything near what you're aiming at."

"Fine, then I won't take the damned shotgun to town with me. Does that satisfy you? Step aside and let me get my horse."

"Forget it. I'll hitch up the wagon and take you to town myself."

"The last thing I want is your company!"

"Why?" He stepped closer. "Afraid?"

"Don't be ridiculous." She tossed her head. "You over-estimate your powers, Mr. Barclay, if you think that being in your company causes me any *inkling* of fear. I simply don't wish to be bored to death during the duration of the journey!"

And with that she tried to march around him into the

barn, but with a muttered oath, he caught her around the waist with his free arm. "You're the most stubborn woman I ever met. I said I'm taking you into town and that's what I'm going to do."

Caitlin tried to pry herself free, just as another voice, a deep, soft, amused voice, emerged from the side of the barn.

"Reckon I can't wait another minute to meet the lady who has my big brother all riled up. Reckon I just have to shake her hand."

And a man every bit as tall and muscularly built as Wade, with the same black hair but eyes that were dark gray instead of blue, strode up, a grin as wide as Silver Valley upon his handsome face.

"Where the hell did you come from?" Wade exclaimed, still holding Caitlin about the waist, as he gazed into the amused eyes of his youngest brother.

Nick Barclay shrugged his big shoulders. "Washed up at the stream. Wanted to look presentable before meeting Reese's little girl. And I guess, ma'am, that would be you," he said with a slight, gallant bow.

Caitlin stared at him, disconcerted not only at Wade's closeness and the tight way he was holding her—a hold that made her heart beat faster and her pulse quicken—but at the sight of another man who could only be a Barclay.

"You must be Nick . . . or Clint," she murmured, and pushed uselessly at Wade's enclosing arm.

"Nick Barclay at your service, Miss Summers. Just remember, don't believe anything my big brother has said about me. Not a word is true. Now, big brother, why are you holding on to that little girl like you'll never let her go?" Nick Barclay's voice was soft and serious, but his long-lashed gray eyes crinkled with amusement at the corners.

Wade released Caitlin. He didn't even try any longer to hold back the grin that spread across his face as he set the shotgun down and walked forward to shake his brother's hand.

The next moment, the Barclay boys were embracing, clapping each other with resounding thumps upon the back.

Caitlin saw the obvious affection between them. Wade's tension and anger had disappeared and when he stepped back, he looked relaxed. "How long can you stay?" he asked.

"Couple of days. Till you fill me in on those rustlers. Then I'll get started tracking 'em down." He rubbed his jaw. "Nothing Reese hated more than rustlers."

Reese. Always Reese. These Barclay boys had all known him, idolized him, loved him. *Well, why not?* she asked herself bitterly. He had raised them, been a father to them in this big, comfortable house—the house where she was an outsider, a stranger.

The familiar pain twisted through her as she turned away.

"I'll let you two catch up," she said quietly and with a cool glance at both of them, she returned to the house. When she told Francesca that Nick had arrived, the woman's delight sent her spinning into rapid action, preparing food for the guest.

Caitlin set the table with a white lace cloth and pretty blue and white flowered plates, while Francesca rushed from cupboard to stove to pantry like a woman on fire. By the time Wade and Nick entered the house, Caitlin was setting out coffee cups and slicing wedges of apple pie, and Francesca tore, beaming, out of the kitchen bearing a platter of ham slices, beans thick with molasses and onions, and thick slabs of sourdough bread.

"Join us," Nick invited Caitlin when she started toward the stairs. He had the same kind of charisma and air of quiet command as Wade and she somehow couldn't refuse. She felt Wade's gaze on her as she slipped into a chair but she didn't glance at him.

Nor did she speak much during the late-afternoon repast—mostly she listened to the brothers talk as they heaped food onto their plates. There was an easy cama- raderie between them, a warmth she recognized as similar to what she and Becky felt for each other. But they were both men, equals, and for all their good-natured sparring, they both knew it—Becky was only a little girl, Caitlin thought with a pang, someone who needed her big sister to look after her.

"So, Caitlin," Nick turned to her, flashing that gor- geous Barclay grin, as she set her coffee cup back onto the saucer. "How do you like Cloud Ranch?"

"It has its good points, I suppose," she admitted reluc- tantly, aware of Wade's keen gaze upon her.

"Good points? What might those be?"

"Well," Caitlin took a deep breath. "The house is certainly a fine one—large and comfortable. And the land . . . it's very pretty."

"Pretty. That's all?"

Her smile turned to a laugh, despite herself. "Well, all right, it's breathtaking . . . particularly the mountains. And when the sun sets, the sky glows with the most beautiful colors, violet and rose and there's this stunning gold light which is so luminous and clear . . ."

She broke off, dismayed by her own enthusiasm, and threw Wade a stricken look. She finished primly, "However, I much prefer the East."

"I see." Nick nodded gravely. His cool glance, so like Wade's, flicked from his brother to the golden-haired girl Wade had scarcely been able to take his eyes off of.

"And my big brother? Has he been taking good care of you?" he asked slowly.

For a moment Caitlin wanted to say that he'd been absolutely abominable to her, but instead she told the truth. "He saved my life," she admitted, and glanced down at her plate.

"Doesn't surprise me. He's the best man I know of to have around if there's trouble."

"Trouble, unfortunately, is her middle name," Wade said as he leaned back in his chair.

Caitlin's head flew up, her green eyes flashing. "If I'm so much trouble," she countered sweetly, "then why don't you make things easy on yourself and buy my share of the ranch so I can go back to Philadelphia?"

"Reese taught me never to take the easy way out." He studied her flushed face and vivid eyes a moment, then pushed back his chair. "Come on. You wanted to go into town."

"Your brother is here. You'll want to spend time with him."

"Who says?" Wade came around the table toward her chair. "Besides, there's that letter you wanted to send to your sister."

He was gazing at her with that quiet calm, mixed with a

kind of gentleness that never failed to touch off a flickering heat inside her. Such a contradictory man. Tough as rawhide, but possessing a tenderness sometimes that couldn't be concealed.

No wonder her own feelings were as contradictory as he was.

She glanced back and forth between him and his brother, who reclined in thoughtful silence in his chair. "It can wait until tomorrow," she heard herself saying softly as she rose to her feet. "You and Nick must have some catching up to do."

She hurried from the dining room before either of them could argue with her.

When her footsteps had retreated up the stairs, Nick eyed his brother piercingly.

"So that," he said slowly, "is Reese's long-lost daughter."

"What of it?" Wade lifted his coffee cup.

"Damned beautiful woman," Nick remarked as Wade took a long gulp of the hot liquid.

"So?"

"Seems kinda skittish, though. Doesn't want to stay put—if you're around." Nick's eyes were fixed on Wade's face.

Wade shrugged. "You noticed."

"I noticed. And I noticed the way you looked at her."

"Yeah? Like how?"

"Like you'd found yourself a mine filled with shimmering gold and you couldn't wait to get your hands on it. But at the same time, you're thinking if you touch it, it'll disappear."

Wade said nothing, just stalked to the window and

stared out at those mountains Caitlin had admitted she loved.

"So why were you and she tussling out there by the barn? You've usually got a much smoother touch with the ladies, big brother."

"Yeah, well, I never met a lady quite like Caitlin Summers." Wade frowned as he turned back to meet his brother's eyes.

"She wants to leave and sell me her share—and I can't let her. For some reason, Reese wanted her here."

Nick nodded. "I know the terms of the will." There was a brief silence. "So what are you going to do?"

"Keep tussling with her until she gives up," Wade growled.

"Maybe you should think again, big brother. Not that I'm claiming to be more of an expert than you when it comes to women, because hell, I never saw any man who could reel in more pretty women just by saying 'howdy, ma'am,' than you—but . . . remember when I said she was skittish?"

"Yeah?"

Nick steepled his hands on the table. "She reminds me of those wild horses you're so good at breaking. Kind of scared and strong all rolled into one, but sweet as maple sugar once they get to trusting you."

Wade returned slowly from the window, pausing beside the dining-room table. "She doesn't like me," he said.

"Hell, I say she does."

"You're wrong."

"Well, then . . ." Nick cocked an eyebrow, and gave his brother a long look. "Neither did any of those wild horses we captured in Hope Canyon that summer a few years back. Not at first. But you managed to tame every single one of 'em."

"She's not a horse, Nick, she's a woman."

"Yeah, I noticed. So have you."

"And she broke Reese's heart." Wade's jaw clenched. "You know she did."

"I know. She never answered his letters all those years, never would set foot on the ranch. Did you ever ask her why?"

"No. She told me why she didn't come out right before he died, and I guess I can understand it, but I never asked her about all those years before."

"Maybe you ought to."

"Maybe you ought to mind your own business."

Nick shrugged. "Reckon you're right. I didn't mean to—"

"She's exactly the opposite of the kind of woman I always wanted to settle down with someday," Wade burst out almost desperately as his brother stared at him. Groaning, he raked both hands through his hair. "She stirs me up inside something awful and she's too damn beautiful and way too feisty and . . . she's dead set on living in some big city somewhere—and there's this new schoolteacher— you met her at Reese's funeral. Luanne Porter."

"Pretty lady." Nick nodded. "And I reckon she's just what you want?"

Wade couldn't answer. He felt his chest constricting as he saw Caitlin's lovely, high-boned face in his mind, remembered the passionate sweetness of her kiss. He contemplated the sparks that flew between him and Caitlin every time they were in the same room together, every

time he came near that gorgeous body and those mesmerizing eyes, or saw that stubborn little uptilted chin of hers.

"Luanne's the one I *want* to want," he said at last, so
quietly and desperately Nick almost didn't hear.

His brother regarded him gravely for a moment, then
cleared his throat. "Don't know much about these things,"
Nick said. "Thank the good Lord. But it seems to me, and
you'd best remember this, big brother, that things don't
usually happen the way we want 'em to. Not much in life
goes according to plan—and sure as hell, nothing involving a woman."

He clapped a hand on Wade's shoulder, shuddered in
pity for his brother, and strode out to fetch his gear.

Wade dropped his tall frame onto a chair and closed his
eyes.

"Damn." The realization that hit him struck him to his
very core. Caitlin's face, voice, and kisses had haunted
him for days now—not to mention for nights. Luanne
Porter was sweet, pretty, smart, and kind—but to Wade's
way of thinking, she was also tame. Somehow, against his
will, against every reasonable, rational intention, the skittish blond beauty with the clearest green eyes he'd ever
seen was close to doing something no other woman had
ever managed to do—something he'd vowed no woman
would ever do—if he wasn't careful, she'd stampede
through his life and damn well corral his heart.

Chapter 14

The stream beckoned like glistening green silk as Caitlin stripped off her clothes in a sheltered clearing along the bank. Dawg had followed her on her morning ride until she'd circled back toward the water, then he'd shot off in pursuit of a jackrabbit who'd peeped out from some brush. That was fine with her. She was perfectly content to be alone. She was far enough away that she couldn't see the ranch house and she certainly couldn't hear any of the commotion going on there.

Which was exactly the way she wanted it.

There was only the pale early morning sun, a glimmer of amber in the sky, the peacefulness of the dewy air, and the water that flowed gently in the shade of the cottonwoods.

She had slept fitfully all night. She had far too much on her mind. Since the first time Wade kissed her, her nights had been haunted. And since the dinner at the Porters' ranch all efforts for tranquil slumber had been in vain. But it wasn't only the memory of his kisses that disturbed her sleep—there was also Becky.

She planned to go to town that afternoon to post her letter to her sister and hoped fervently that there would be a letter awaiting her in turn. Caitlin prayed that the girl was handling her delayed return without too much dismay. And that the teasing, hushed whispers and pitying stares her sister had endured after word of her reduced circumstances leaked out at the school had subsided.

All these thoughts churning through her mind had kept her tossing and turning. The restlessness drove her out of bed as dawn gilded the sky and the early birds began to sing, and she rode out across the wide grassland, over ridges, along red-rimmed ravines, taking care to note her surroundings even as she lost herself in the fresh beauty of the new day. She spotted antelope on a distant hilltop, and a hawk wheeled overhead. An odd exhilaration came over her at all the wild loveliness that surrounded her. But as the sun rose higher, and her skin grew flushed, her clothes began to feel heavy and uncomfortable and she suddenly thought with longing of the stream.

Here in this secluded spot, the water flowed gently, looking cool and inviting. Wildflowers grew in bright profusion and the willow where Star was tethered swayed gracefully in the breeze. It was perfect, Caitlin thought with satisfaction as she left her riding skirt and white linen blouse folded neatly on top of a tree stump—and far enough from the house so that no one would disturb her.

She peeled off her stockings, set them beside her soft kid boots, and tiptoed into the water, clad in only her chemise.

"Oooh!" she gasped in surprise, for despite the warm

day, the stream water was icy cold. But she drew in a deep breath and waded farther, letting the water rise around her hips. She ducked down, immersing her breasts and shoulders, letting her pale hair flow free. The sun above burned hot—she expected it would dry her soon enough when she emerged, but the cold water felt good against her skin.

The shock of it drove all her problems—even Wade Barclay—from her mind.

But not for long. As she splashed and swam, his lean, rugged image returned to her mind. Again she felt the strength of his arms around her, the hot branding of his kiss.

And then she remembered the sight of him kissing Luanne.

You don't need him. Or want him. He cares nothing for you, just as Alec cared nothing for you. He's a two-timing cad, arrogant as they come, and no different from the rest. Remember what Mrs. Casper said? Never fall in love with a cowboy. Well, what do you think Wade Barclay is? she demanded of herself, her teeth chattering as she dunked her head in the water in hopes that the crystal droplets would wash away every vestige of foolishness in her brain.

Of course he *had* saved her life. He had saved her from the rustlers, and defended her against that awful Otter Jones. But she mustn't think about that. None of it mattered. He was bullheaded and infuriating—not to mention untrustworthy. Oh, but she pitied Luanne. That girl had no idea how insincere those long, deep kisses actually were.

Suddenly she couldn't bear the cold any longer. She edged toward the streambank, stubbed her toe on a rock hidden in the currents, and swore a blue streak as she clambered out. Heavens, it was cold. The sun wasn't quite as warm yet as she'd hoped it would be. Gasping, she scurried across the grass to the tree stump, eager for the warmth of her clothes, then stared down in stupefaction.

The tree stump was bare.

Standing there dripping wet in her chemise, which clung icily to every damp curve and hollow of her body, Caitlin's mouth dropped open. She peered frantically around the clearing—but saw only her boots. And Star, and the wildflowers, and a squirrel hidden in the leaves of the cottonwood nearest her.

But there was no sign of her skirt, blouse, or stockings. Every last stitch of her clothing had vanished.

"Dawg! What the hell have you got there?"

Wade eyed the black dog ambling toward the corral, his ears pricked upward, his tail happily wagging. Beside him, Nick gave a guffaw.

"Damned if it isn't a lady's clothes!" Jake Young, who'd just mounted up, stared down at the pile of clothing Dawg dropped right in front of Wade.

"What the hell." Wade grinned as the animal sat on his haunches, looked up hopefully, and thumped his tail on the ground as if expecting high praise. "Where'd you get these, you thievin' coyote?"

But he already knew the answer. He'd seen the dog trotting up from the direction of the stream, and he knew exactly what he'd find there, somewhere down along the bank. Wiping the grin from his face and plastering on a frown instead, he scooped up the blue cotton skirt and the lace-trimmed blouse—and the delicate stockings—and ignored his brother's unabashed grin.

"Reckon she'll freeze to death if you don't bring 'em back to her pronto," Nick remarked gravely.

"I'll do it, boss," Jake Young cut in. "You and Nick were just about to head out, so I don't mind—"

"You were the one about to head out," Wade interrupted him evenly. "Check the south pasture and then meet up with Miguel. If I sent you down to return these to Miss Summers, you'd lollygag the whole damn day away—reciting poetry and chomping on cookies."

Jake turned two shades redder than his neckerchief as Nick burst out laughing. "Aw, hell, Wade, no, I wouldn't—"

"Get moving." Wade tucked the clothes under his arm, ignoring the crestfallen expression on the wrangler's face as he stalked toward the stream.

"Think you'll need any help keeping the lady warm?" Nick called after him, a chuckle in his throat.

"That'll be the day, little brother," Wade shot back over his shoulder before quickening his steps toward the long belt of trees that lined the streambank.

His boots crunched through the tall grass as he rounded a thicket and emerged near the water's edge.

There was no sign of Caitlin there, so he veered to the right and kept going. Dawg suddenly appeared, prancing alongside, the picture of an obedient companion.

"Haven't you caused enough trouble?" Wade tried to sound cross, but he was strangely looking forward to the encounter about to take place.

He spotted Caitlin before she saw him, less than a quarter of a mile downstream. She was just reaching out to untether her mare in a small, flower-bedecked clearing.

She wore nothing but a thin ivory chemise edged in lace, her streaming pale hair falling in riotous wet tangles down her slender back, and she carried a pair of lavender kid boots clutched in one hand. The lovely shape of her— the high, taut breasts and slender waist and those long, sleek legs shimmering with water droplets—made him stop in his tracks. She might have been a sea goddess, all golden hair and ivory skin and chiseled crystal features. Wade's throat went dry and he felt a heavy searing ache in his loins.

She saw him then. Her shriek, he reckoned, could have been heard in Laramie. She dropped her boots and whirled around and splashed back into the stream, dipping down so low in the water that only her head remained above the surface.

"G-give those back!" she demanded, pointing a shaking finger at her clothes. "How d-dare you take them!"

"Now why in hell would I take them?" He strolled forward as nonchalantly as he could, despite the damned aching desire jolting through him, a desire that heated up even further as he studied her flushed face and fiery green eyes as she bobbed just above the water's surface.

"Because you . . . you thought it would be funny. A j-joke!"

"Do I look like I'm laughing?"

"Y-yes, you . . . do!" Those vivid eyes had darkened with fury. "Now put them down and get the hell away from here. I'm f-freezing to death and you don't even care!"

His amusement faded as he suddenly noticed how her teeth were chattering. She was shivering all over. "Come out of that water, Caitlin." His tone was sharp, the same commanding tone that made his wranglers jump to follow his orders. "Right now."

"Not until you l-leave. Just put them back on that t-tree stump and g-go."

"Believe it or not, princess, I've seen half-naked women before."

"Not this half-naked woman!"

Exasperation tore through him. "I'm damned if I'm going to stand here and argue with you." He tossed her clothes down on the grass and strode forward into the stream. Even as she shrieked again and tried to dodge away, he seized her and dragged her toward him, then scooped her into his arms.

"Let . . . m-me g-*go*!"

Before she finished the last word he had reached the bank and dropped her to her feet. "It's spring, you nitwit. Only a tenderfoot would brave the stream this early in the morning at this time of year!"

"Only a t-toad would steal a woman's clothes while she's swimming!" Gasping, Caitlin snatched up her blouse in quivering, frozen fingers. "T-turn around."

"I didn't do it—it was Dawg."

"T-turn around!"

Gritting his teeth, Wade obeyed. She had to be the stubbornnest female on this earth. But he'd glimpsed her in that chemise that clung to her like a filmy second skin and he could barely keep from groaning with thoughts of what he'd like to do to warm her up. He threw a stick for Dawg, who'd been prancing around Caitlin as she struggled into her garments and fought against the almost impossibly powerful temptation to turn around before she'd donned those prim, pretty clothes.

Dawg chased off after the stick, barking, and Wade glanced around to find her trying to fasten up the shirt with hands that shook so much she couldn't close the buttons.

"Here, let me," he said with rough impatience.

Deftly, he closed the top button, then the one beneath it. His muscles were taut as his hand brushed between her breasts. He felt like a schoolboy who'd never touched a girl.

"I . . . can do it . . ." she said breathlessly.

He pushed her shaking fingers aside. "The hell you can."

Caitlin remained motionless, except for the shivering, as he fastened all the buttons for her. She was cold, so cold. She'd never imagined Dawg would steal her clothes and never imagined the stream would be quite that frigid. When Wade stripped off his own big flannel shirt and wrapped it around her shoulders, she gave a gasp of relief for the added warmth.

Then, without warning, he drew her close against him, warming her against his body. She melted into those iron arms, and nestled against the solid warmth of his bare chest. Heat radiated from his brawny body to her slender one, waves of heat that were as powerful and comforting as he was. She trembled as they flowed through her, along with a complete sense of safety—and something else.

A spark of heat, of pure fire, that had nothing to do with flannel shirts, and everything to do with this heart-poundingly handsome man who always showed up when she needed him. This man whose gaze could be hard, but also unspeakably gentle, whose touch seemed to ignite both her temper and her heart.

She found herself clinging to him, her body fitting effortlessly against his, even as she knew she should be pulling away.

Wade's hands stroked up and down her back with sure, soothing motions and every last impulse to flee ebbed away right along with her common sense.

Caitlin's heart was thudding in rhythm with her racing pulse. It felt too good to be this close to him. Dangerously good.

She took a deep, steadying breath. "We should go . . . back to the house."

"Yeah?" His arms tightened, and his hands kept stroking her back. "Who says?"

"You know . . . we should. Right . . . now," she said as forcefully as she could, but her words came out in a soft whisper, not at all in the determined tone she'd intended.

He knew she was right. But it didn't matter. Holding her like this was having a strange effect on him. "If I didn't know better, I'd think you were afraid of me, Caitlin. I'm not going to bite."

For a moment she was filled with a joyous pleasure at the gentle way he'd spoken her name, but then a most unwelcome thought intruded into her mind: *Does he speak Luanne's name the same way?*

"Let's go back." She pulled out of his arms and saw his eyes narrow.

For a moment she thought he was going to argue with her, or even try to hold her or kiss her again. His gaze dropped to her white, trembling lips and lingered there a moment. She sensed the tension in him, and felt an ache deep within herself. For one wild moment she almost reached up on tiptoe and kissed him. *Madness!*

But then he nodded and spoke in a quiet tone. "Whatever you say, Miss Summers." He started toward Star. "Come on."

By the time she was settled in dry clothes before a fire in the parlor, with a cup of steaming sweetened coffee before her and a blanket Francesca had brought wrapped around her, Caitlin was thinking much more clearly. When Wade came into the room, wearing a clean plaid shirt, and dry pants and boots, his Stetson on his head, she was able to smile quite calmly at him and thank him for bringing back her clothes.

"And I suppose I should apologize for accusing you of stealing them," she said formally. "I'm sorr—"

"No need to apologize." His tone was as calm, steady, and even as always, but she sensed something different in the way he was looking at her. He no longer seemed to be regarding her with anger or resentment, as he usually did. He actually smiled at her, Lord help her, a smile that made every nerve in her body tingle.

"Right now I'm late to a meeting at the Tyler ranch. It concerns the patrols our Cattlemen's Association is setting up just in case the rustlers return—I'll fill you in on it later. During your shooting lesson."

"What shooting lesson?"

His diamond-blue eyes gleamed. "The one you're getting this afternoon. You and me. Right after lunch. Then we'll head into town." He tipped his hat at her and turned toward the door. "Meet me at the corral, Caitlin, and be ready to ride."

He strode out before she could argue or refuse.

By the time she was ready to meet him Caitlin was convinced that there was something very suspicious going on. Wade was being entirely too nice to her. He hadn't scolded her all that much about swimming in the cold stream, he hadn't called her *princess* even once, and now he was going to give her shooting lessons?

So when she met him at the corral, with the hot sun blazing overhead in a burning turquoise sky, she wore a pale gray cotton riding skirt, a puffed sleeve yellow peasant blouse, and a layer of crisp, no-nonsense armor.

"Wait just a minute," she said as he rode up. Ignoring her, he dismounted from his horse and came toward her, ready to help her mount Star.

Caitlin pushed his hand away as he reached out to take her arm. "First tell me why you're so set suddenly on teaching me to shoot."

"Because I thought it over, and if you're going to be sticking around, you'll need to know how to defend yourself."

I need to defend myself against you, Caitlin wanted to shout, but instead she shrugged. "I won't be sticking around that long."

"Long enough."

"But . . . I don't understand. If the rustlers have already been driven off and are going to be tracked down and arrested by your brother, where is the danger?"

He spoke patiently, as if to a child. "This is untamed country still—rustlers or no. It's important to always be prepared. That's rough wilderness out there—you could run into snakes, bears—and human varmints as well." Wade was glad Otter Jones was dead and no longer a threat to Caitlin, but he knew that any stranger she encountered alone could be dangerous.

"Course there's no need for shooting lessons if you want to arrange always to be accompanied by me or one of the wranglers when you go to town or out riding—"

"I don't."

He pushed his hat back on his head. The sun illuminated the blue-black sheen of his hair as he met her gaze. "Then I reckon you'll have to learn how to fire that shotgun properly and how to hit what you aim at."

"Very well." Caitlin reached out a hand and stroked Star's mane. "I'll learn. But I don't want you to teach me."

"Why is that?"

"Because we don't get along." Her eyes dared him to contradict her. When he didn't, she continued briskly. "And because Nick is a gunfighter—he must know all about guns. He can teach me."

"Nick's busy right now, renewing an acquaintance with some ladies who work in the saloon."

"Oh. *Oh.*"

He smiled in amusement at the quick blush that entered her cheeks.

"Well, then, tomorrow . . ."

"Tomorrow, he's leaving. At first light."

"Then Miguel or Jake or Dirk—"

He reached out, cupped her chin, held her captive with the sudden gleam in those diamond-blue eyes. "Do you always have to argue with me about *everything*?"

"I don't argue with you about everything."

Wade chuckled. "See what I mean?"

His touch was firm, but gentle. If she hadn't been on her guard, if she hadn't experienced what she had with the men in her past, if she hadn't seen him kissing Luanne Porter, she might have found herself susceptible to the very potent male charm that emanated from him. If . . . if . . . if . . .

"All right, then, you may teach me," she said quickly, her breath catching in her throat. "But starting tomorrow I'll be riding to town alone to post my letters to Becky."

"Let's just see how you do today."

"You think I can't learn to shoot in one afternoon?"

"Oh, I think you can learn how to shoot all right." He released her, and stepped back, grinning. "Only question is, can you hit anything you aim at?"

Caitlin's eyes darkened to the hue of a storm-tossed sea. *Charm?* The man had about as much charm as a skunk.

"You just watch and see," she bit out between clenched teeth. And turning with a swish of her skirt, she led Star to the corral fence, and used it to mount without any help from Wade Barclay.

She suddenly wished she had a large photograph of Cloud Ranch's foreman—to use for target practice.

Chapter 15

Wade chose a spot deep in the foothills for her lesson. It was open, quiet, filled with goldenrod and buttercups. There was an old scarred pine tree close by, its leaves sighing in the breeze.

"That's what you're going to shoot at," Wade told her, and then showed her how to load the shotgun, how to hold it braced against her shoulder, how to work the safety.

He was a patient teacher, Caitlin had to admit. She tried hard to be a disciplined pupil.

But it wasn't precisely easy to concentrate. The day was soft and lovely, the man close beside her with his arm around her waist, his hand steadying her grip, was too handsome, too . . . male.

And far too distracting.

She did learn how to adjust her sights for the kick of the shotgun, how to aim, how to squeeze the trigger just so. Once she even hit the side of the tree. But only once.

It was frustrating, not only because she couldn't aim better, but because his arms around her reminded her too sharply of the night he had kissed her beneath the moon. And of this morning when he had held her and warmed her beneath the sun.

Stop thinking about that. Where's your backbone? she wondered crossly and yanked the trigger too fiercely, only to find that she'd hit an entirely different tree than the one she'd aimed at.

"Looks like you need a break." Wade took the rifle from her and set it down. He brought out a water canteen from his saddlebag and offered it to her.

Her throat was dry. She took a long sip and handed the canteen back to him, then they sank down together upon the grass.

Wade plucked a blade of grass, then another. "You've got a good eye and a steady arm." He squinted at her through the sunshine. "But . . ."

"But what?"

"You're not focusing on the target the way you should. When it comes to shooting, you can't be distracted, can't let other thoughts or emotions get in the way." He studied her, his voice matter-of-fact. "You got something on your mind?"

What isn't on my mind? Him. Becky. Getting back to Philadelphia. And steering clear of Dominic Trent.

"A few things," she murmured, swallowing.

She should have known he wouldn't be deterred by a vague answer.

"Like what?"

The man was as persistent as a mosquito. And just as annoying. "My sister." She blurted out the words. They were only partly true, though she had been worried over not hearing from Becky. "She has yet to reply to the first letter I wrote her after arriving here. That was two weeks ago! I hope she's all right."

"Any reason why she wouldn't be?"

She ran her fingers through the blades of grass, looking down at the slender green stalks. "The death of our parents was a horrible blow to her. To both of us," she said quietly.

There was a silence during which the only sound was the faint rustle of the bright new leaves. "Yeah." Wade studied her profile. "I'm sure it was." He cleared his throat. "We knew Reese was dying, that his heart was giving out, but it didn't make it any easier once he was gone. Fact is, it hurt like hell."

There was a sorrow in his eyes that stabbed straight into her heart. She nodded, her throat filling with a painful lump, but whether the pain was for him or for herself—or for both of them, she couldn't be certain.

"Reese was prepared," Wade went on quietly. "He was ready to die, said all his good-byes. All his papers were in order."

"I noticed." But she was surprised by how little bitterness she felt at this moment. Every day in this beautiful country, on the awesomely vigorous ranch that ran so smoothly thanks to Wade, it was getting harder and harder to hate Cloud Ranch.

"But your folks," he said slowly, "didn't know what was coming." His gaze was fixed intently on her. "On top of losing them so suddenly, I reckon you had a bundle of headaches trying to get their affairs in order."

Caitlin thought of the way her legs had given out when Gillis's lawyer had told her the facts, the way she'd sunk into the chair, nausea churning inside her.

"You could say that," she whispered.

She heard the trace of bitterness in her own words and felt her cheeks flush. She glanced at him, hoping he hadn't noticed, but of course he had. Wade noticed everything.

"Want to talk about it?"

"There's nothing much to say."

"That little tremble in your lip tells me otherwise."

Her eyes flew to his face. His penetrating gaze seemed to reach into her soul, into her mind, touching every painful secret.

"It was . . . difficult," she admitted slowly.

"Because . . ."

"It's none of your—"

"You said once that I didn't know anything about your life. Well, here's your chance to tell me."

Suddenly the urge to talk to him about what had happened in Philadelphia welled up in her, like water swelling over a dam.

"My adoptive father—Gillis—had apparently gambled away his fortune," she said in a low, quick tone. "That took a lot of doing because his fortune was vast. No one knew—at least, I don't think my mother knew. Certainly not me or Becky." She studied an elk that appeared suddenly, high on a distant ridge. "But after their ship went down, all of Philadelphia knew. Gillis owed money to almost everyone, it seemed. It was . . . quite a scandal." She tried to sound light, sophisticated, and unconcerned as she said these last words, and failed miserably. Beside her, she sensed the sudden tension in Wade.

"Sounds bad."

"Oh, yes. It was. Very bad." It was the merest whisper.

"A scandal, huh? Bet that must have hurt you—and your sister."

"We're going to be fine," Caitlin replied swiftly. She took a deep breath. "It was a great shock at first—as was losing them at sea—but now . . . everything is under control."

Wade watched her face, a study in elegance, pride, and quiet courage. He couldn't help feeling a surge of admiration.

"So . . . the Tamarlane fortune. You don't . . . you're not . . ." He scowled. "He didn't leave you anything, is that what you're saying?"

Caitlin's chin rose and she met his gaze unflinchingly. "That pretty well sums it up, yes. But I have this ranch." Suddenly her arm swept out, encompassing the wild, awesome countryside, the plains of endless sagebrush, the foothills, and all of Silver Valley where Cloud Ranch sat proudly. "Once I can sell my portion of it," she said, enunciating each word, "Becky and I will get on just fine."

There was a small silence. "Where would you go if you did sell it?" Wade asked.

"*When* I sell it," Caitlin responded, emphasizing the first word with some asperity, "Becky and I will travel to Boston, or perhaps Chicago. We'll start over, just the two of us. I'll have money to get started on a new life for us, and I'll find some sort of respectable position."

Wade read the determination in her eyes and he didn't doubt for a moment that Caitlin Summers would manage just fine on her own. He also guessed it wouldn't take long before some man in Boston or Chicago fell in love with her, offered her marriage and a home, and changed the scenario entirely. Hell, half the men in those cities would probably fall in love with her, he thought, scowling grimly. Fools that they were. Not only was she beautiful, but she was brave, and better than most at arithmetic—and she had that air of dignity about her. Not to mention that sinfully lush mouth, he thought desperately, and those high, beautiful breasts . . .

Suddenly the thought of some other man kissing those lips, touching those breasts, filled him with a boiling pain. And a rage that made his chest hurt. "I reckon I still don't understand." He spoke tautly. It took effort to keep his voice steady as he imagined her in another man's arms.

"Why do you have to sell in the first place—just to go to some big city?" He threw down the blades of grass he'd been plucking and stared hard into her eyes. "Why not just stay here on Cloud Ranch? Bring Becky here, like I said before. It's a good place to grow up—you won't find a better one. Your little sister doesn't need some fancy eastern school, if that's what you're worried about. Luanne happens to be a damned fine teacher and Hope has a library now—"

He broke off as she suddenly went pale. Was it the mention of Luanne's name that had made her look that way? Or what he'd said about Cloud Ranch being a good place to grow up?

Caitlin was scrambling to her feet, so he sprang to his, and seized her hands when she would have pulled away. "Hold on. Tell me what I said that made you turn all . . ." He groped for the right word. "Skittish," he said at last.

"Maybe this was a good place for you and your brothers to grow up, but my own father didn't want me here."

"He damn well did!" Wade stared at her incredulously. "He left you forty percent of the finest ranch in the territory, and made sure his will spelled out that you had to stay here and give the place a try—if that's not a sign of wanting you here, I don't know what is."

"He never wanted me before—when he was alive— when I was growing up! Maybe you and your brothers were enough family for him, and so he didn't care about me. I wrote to him and he never once answered—not once!"

She hated that her voice was shaking but she couldn't help it. Once the words had started she couldn't seem to hold them back. "I wanted to visit Cloud Ranch so badly—I used to dream of it, pray for it—every night. I even asked him for a photograph but—"

She stopped, staring at Wade. He appeared stunned, as if she'd thrown a pail of stones over his head, and sharp stones at that.

"You *wrote* to him?" he demanded.

"Of course. Several times. First when I was eight and then—what is it?"

He gripped her shoulders. "He never received any letters from you, Caitlin."

"Yes, he did." Her eyes flashed in the sunlight. "My mother gave me the proper address herself—I wrote it out so painstakingly, every letter clear and as perfect as I could make it."

"Caitlin!" He gave her a small shake. The hard planes of his face were rigid with tension. "He never received a single letter from you!"

The words shocked her. She would have rocked back, dizzy, except that he was holding her so tightly she couldn't move.

"I . . . don't understand," she managed faintly.

"There's more." Steel-blue eyes imprisoned hers. His voice was rough. "He wrote to you. I know he did. I took the letters to the post office myself."

"You did? He really . . . ?" The shock was still flooding through her. How was it possible that Reese hadn't received her letters and she hadn't received his? "When did he write to me?"

His mouth was grim. "Before your birthday—every year from the time you left until you were twelve. And at Christmas. He invited you to Cloud Ranch, Caitlin, I know he did, because he told me and Nick and Clint that his little girl might be coming for a visit. And then, when there wasn't a reply," he said in a low tone, "he'd get quiet for a while. Sad. He grieved for you, Caitlin, whether you can believe it or not. I watched it and felt helpless." He didn't tell her that he'd also felt alarmed at how much love could hurt a man.

"It was a damned unpleasant feeling knowing that no matter how much he loved me and Nick and Clint—and he did—we couldn't fill up that empty spot he had in his heart—the place where you belonged."

Had she truly belonged somewhere in her father's heart? Had there been a place for her here after all?

"What could have happened?" She spoke dazedly. "To his letters—and mine?"

"That's what I'd like to know." Suddenly his hand came up and cupped her chin. "But I don't want you to go one more day thinking Reese didn't want you or care about you. That's so far from the truth, it'd be laughable, if it didn't hurt so much."

Caitlin was trying to take in all he was saying. She was thinking back over the years, when she'd felt that her father had turned his back on her. She'd had Gillis, and her mother—when they hadn't been traveling in Europe—or visiting friends at their Newport cottages—and of course, she'd had Becky, but always deep inside, there had been a tiny forlorn part of her that wondered why her real father had shut her completely from his life.

It changed everything—everything she'd ever thought about Reese, everything she'd ever felt about Cloud Ranch.

Suddenly she saw the terms of the will in a whole different light. "I wonder—do you think he knew . . . about Gillis—that Becky and I had been left . . ." She hesitated, then forced herself to say it aloud, "Destitute? Do you think that's why he left me the ranch and insisted I stay here for a year? So I—we—would have a home?"

"Wouldn't surprise me. I know he had that lawyer of his check some things out back east while the papers were all being finalized. I can talk to McCain. And . . ." Wade suddenly realized something else.

"What is it?"

"When he was lying on his deathbed, he asked me to do something for him." He took a deep breath. "He asked me to look after you. Made me promise I would."

His gut clenched at the agonizing emotions that flashed across her exquisite face—pain mixed with joy and dawning hope, a young girl's hope to be loved, and suddenly his arms were around her and he was holding her so close that he could feel her heartbeat deep in his bones.

"So he must have known," Wade said against her hair, "that you were in some sort of trouble, though he never actually told me. But he wanted my word. Almost the last thing he ever said—he asked for my word."

She closed her eyes, trembling as she tried to picture the father she could barely remember speaking of her with his last breath.

"And there's something else you need to know." Wade didn't even glance up as the shadow of an eagle passed overhead, the great bird swooping up, up toward its eyrie in the mountains. "I'll stand by that promise." His voice was purposeful. "No matter what, Caitlin, you can always count on me. On Nick and Clint, too. We'll take care of you, stand by you. See you through every kind of trouble."

But suddenly Caitlin was remembering other promises made by other men. The sight of Alec Ballantree's pitying face as he turned and left her filled her mind. She pulled free of Wade's embrace and stepped back.

"That won't be necessary. I can take care of myself."

Wade stared at her. "You don't have to . . . that's the point . . ."

"I'm glad to know that Reese wanted you to look after me—that he cared about me. More glad than I can say." There was a tiny quaver in her voice. She swallowed and endeavored to bring it under control. "But I learned after my mother and Gillis died that counting on someone else, no matter who, isn't a very good idea."

Wade wondered with a stab of fury who had hurt her. And how. "Too bad," he said softly. "Because you're stuck with me. And my promise."

He smiled as he said it, a quiet, reassuring smile that made her want to run into his arms. Instead she steeled herself and turned away toward the horses.

"We should get to town. My letter . . . Please?"

He followed her in silence.

Caitlin only knew she couldn't concentrate on shooting anymore today. There was too much to think about—the fact that her letters had never reached Reese, and that his hadn't come to her, filled her with astonishment, relief, and a raging tangle of emotions.

And she couldn't sort them out with Wade Barclay right beside her. She felt too vulnerable around him as it was. She had to stay away from him. She had to think clearly. And she had to come to terms with this revelation and see how it affected her plans for the future.

No sooner had Wade helped her into the saddle than she snatched up the reins. "Which way to Hope?" she asked briskly, and he jerked his thumb to the east.

"But first—one more thing." Wade placed his hand over hers so she couldn't move the reins. "Who's Dominic Trent?"

Caitlin felt the color ebb from her cheeks. She cursed herself for ever having uttered his name to Wade. Or Alec's.

"He's someone I don't want to talk about," she muttered, and yanked her hand free.

As he stepped back, she turned Star sharply and spurred her forward. Toward Hope. Glancing over her shoulder, she saw Wade gazing after her. Tall, handsome, steady, the sight of him sliced through her heart. He had a quiet strength that had drawn her from the first moment she set eyes on him.

And then there's his two-timing nature, she reminded herself. *Don't be a fool.*

Any woman in her right mind would ride away from such a man.

She tightened her grip on the reins and rode faster.

Chapter 16

The first person Caitlin spotted in town was Jake Young. He was in front of the feed store, loading bulging brown sacks into the wagon.

"Howdy, there, Miss Summers."

"Jake." She gave him a warm smile. "If I'd known you were going to town today, I'd have come with you." She paused beside him and he blushed, wiping the sweat from his square-jawed face with his neckerchief.

"That would've been my pleasure, ma'am. You didn't ride here all alone, did you?"

"No. Not today. Wade accompanied me." She waved a hand vaguely in the direction of the blacksmith's shop. Wade had caught up to her easily before she'd ridden a quarter of a mile, but they'd barely spoken during the remainder of the ride to town. He'd tethered their horses outside of the blacksmith's and she'd left him there conversing with Jethro Plum while she headed straight toward Hicks Mercantile.

"If you're too tired to ride all the way back, we could

hitch Star to the wagon, and you could come with me," Jake offered eagerly.

"Oh, how kind. But I'm not tired at all, Jake—I love to ride. Thank you for the offer, though."

But as she smiled and walked on, another male voice called out to her.

"Caitlin!"

Drew Raleigh had just emerged from the saloon, look-ing tall, fit, and prosperous. His neat suit was as immacu-late as his center-parted, handsome head of hair. He strode toward her and she paused once more, but the smile she gave him was cooler than the one she'd offered Jake Young.

"Good afternoon, Mr. Raleigh."

"Drew," he reminded her. The charming smile that seemed somehow familiar flashed and stayed in place. "I've been meaning to come calling. Unfortunately, my business has kept me pretty occupied."

"Oh? Have you found a property to invest in then?"

"Not yet, but I'm an optimist, Caitlin. I think the right opportunity is bound to come along and I can afford to wait. Matter of fact I'd like to talk to you about just that. Would you allow me the pleasure of treating you to a glass of lemonade and some cherry pie at the diner?"

His smile deepened, exhibiting smooth confidence she would concur. In that instant, something clicked inside her head. Something about that confident smile—yes, she had definitely seen Drew Raleigh somewhere before. For some reason she thought of the lobby of the Opera House . . .

"Caitlin?"

She blinked and realized she'd never answered his

question. "I'm sorry, but I'm afraid I don't have the time today. I must get to Hicks, you see, and . . ."

Her voice trailed off as her gaze fell on Luanne Porter in front of the library, right across from the Walsh Boardinghouse. Luanne had just emerged with an armload of books and collided directly with Wade, who had inadvertently knocked all the books from her arms. As Caitlin stared, he stooped to retrieve them and so did Luanne, and they were laughing as they gathered them up together. Wade held the pile of books for her—it was obvious he was offering to carry them to Luanne's buckboard. And a vise tightened around Caitlin's heart.

"Ah, the pretty schoolteacher and the rugged foreman. They make a fine-looking pair, don't they?" There was an unmistakable note of mockery in Drew Raleigh's light tone.

Caitlin spoke through the heaviness in her chest. "Why, yes. They seem . . . quite well suited."

"You, on the other hand, Caitlin, don't seem at all suited to anything here in this crude little town."

"Drew, if this is about selling Cloud Ranch . . ."

"It's about you, my dear. Why, you're beautiful and cultured and sophisticated. Any fool, even these countrified dolts, can see that. You don't belong here with these people, nor should you have to endure the dangers of such a rough, primitive land—or be forced to live someplace as isolated as Cloud Ranch. You'd like to return east, wouldn't you?"

Caitlin dragged her gaze from Wade and Luanne and focused on Drew, trying to ignore the dismal ache in her heart. For all his suavity and charm, Drew Raleigh didn't fool her for a moment.

"If you're thinking that I still might sell you my share of Cloud Ranch, and that you might somehow then convince Wade and his brothers to sell the rest, you may as well forget about it." Her tone was crisp. "I can't sell my shares for a year, and Wade will never sell. He'd rather die, I believe, than turn Cloud Ranch over to an outsider. And that's what you are, I'm afraid, Drew, and you always will be." She spoke the words clearly, for all their softness. "An outsider."

"But a persistent one." He caught her arm as she started to move past him. "I haven't reached my present place in the world because I give up easily," he said. His tone was still pleasant, but there was a hard edge beneath it that made her stare. "I have a gift for inventive solutions to problems, Caitlin, and I'm willing to share that gift with you. From speaking with . . . oh, various people in town, I know that you loathe Cloud Ranch and would like nothing better than to sell your shares. I, in turn, would like nothing better than to buy them. Cloud Ranch is precisely what my business associates and I have been looking for. So perhaps if you and I just sit down together we can figure out a way—"

"There is no way. If you'll excuse me—"

"There's always a way, Caitlin, my dear."

A chill swept through her. "Please excuse me, Drew. I must post a letter to my sister. Good day."

He stepped aside, tipping his hat, but not before she saw the cold glint of anger in his hazel eyes.

She was beyond caring. Once she might have gone to any lengths to sell her share of Cloud Ranch, to seize the money and run away with it, no matter how it affected anyone else, but something had changed. Despite the pain she felt seeing Wade and Luanne chatting so easily, strolling side by side, she didn't want to strike out at him. And she didn't want Drew Raleigh even setting foot on the beautiful land that stretched endlessly beyond her bedroom window.

What was happening to her? Was she actually contemplating staying here for a year—bringing Becky here?

Wouldn't it be cozy, should Wade and Luanne marry? she thought miserably. *All of you living under the same roof.*

Her stomach turned over. No, no, that would be intolerable. She had to leave. She had to return to Becky . . .

With swift steps she made her way to the mercantile. Somehow she smiled and chatted pleasantly with Nell Hicks, and then greeted Winnifred Dale, who was full of talk about the upcoming annual May Day dance at the Tyler ranch.

As Caitlin placed her letter on the counter beside sacks of mail, she interrupted Winnifred suddenly. "Is there by any chance a letter from my sister? I've been expecting to hear from her."

"Well, oh, my, yes! Now that you mention it—I do believe there is a letter, dear." Winnifred beamed at her and began sorting through mail on the shelves behind her. "It arrived in yesterday's batch—from the Davenport Academy for Young Ladies—*here* it is." Pushing her glasses farther up on her delicate nose, Winnifred handed Caitlin a richly textured cream-colored envelope.

"Such fine stationery," she murmured admiringly.

For a moment, Caitlin's heart soared, but then she saw that the prim black handwriting on the front of the envelope did not belong to her sister after all. Foreboding swept over her as with trembling fingers she tore open the seal.

"Caitlin? Is something wrong?" Winnifred scurried around the counter at the expression on Caitlin's face as she scanned the missive.

"No—this can't be!" Caitlin's anguished whisper froze the woman in her tracks.

"My dear, what's happened? Your sister—she isn't ill, is she?"

Blindly, Caitlin shook her head. *Wade. She had to find Wade. He'd know what to do—he must know what to do!*

"I'm sorry, Winnifred, I'll explain later," she cried as she ran to the door.

Her feet flew down the boardwalk until she found him chatting with Luanne beside her buckboard. He'd loaded all the books into it and was about to help Luanne up onto the seat when he saw Caitlin flying toward him, pale and distraught.

He dropped Luanne's hand and started toward Caitlin, grabbing her shoulders as she nearly ran right into him. "What's wrong?" he demanded.

"It's Becky! She's disappeared."

"Oh, my God!" Luanne exclaimed.

"Easy, Caitlin. Just tell me." Wade's calm, quick voice somehow steadied her even though her mind was frantic with worry. "She's disappeared from her school? Did she run away?"

"They think so. This letter just came from Miss Culp, the headmistress. She says Becky has been missing for a week. A whole week, Wade, before they even wrote to tell me! Where could she be? She's only eleven!" Her eyes shone with anguish. "How could she manage a week on her own, with no one to look after her—no one to take care of her? She's so timid, so . . ." Her voice broke. "We have to find her!"

Wade's expression was grim, but the purposefulness in his voice penetrated Caitlin's despair. "We'll find her. I promise you, Caitlin—Becky's going to be all right." Forgetting everything and everyone else, he drew her close, and stroked a hand down her hair as she trembled in his arms.

He heard a sob break from her. Caitlin, who never cried. Something ached, broke, deep inside his chest.

"Shhh, sweetheart, don't worry." His arms tightened around her. He didn't see Luanne staring at them, her face pale, stunned—nor did he notice Jake Young, only a few feet away, watching the embrace with an expression of raw disappointment and dismay. Or Drew Raleigh, who studied the scene with interest. He only knew that Caitlin was weeping silently, clutching him, more distraught than he had ever seen her, more distraught than he could bear.

"Whatever it takes, whatever I have to do," he said quietly, pressing a kiss against the softness of her temple, "I promise you, Caitlin, we'll find your sister."

Chapter 17

Night stole quietly over the town of Beaver Junction, Wyoming. In the barn behind Cleever's Blacksmith shop, a small, slight figure wriggled out from beneath a pile of hay high up in the loft. She made no sound doing so—until a sneeze flew out of her and seemed to her cautious ears loud enough to rattle the rafters of the barn.

But there was no one to hear except the horses.

Becky Tamarlane brushed hay from her light brown hair, shook out the skirt of her wrinkled blue dress, and tugged her small, brass-handled satchel from beneath the pile of hay, then made her way to the ladder.

She felt hot, boiling hot. Sweat glistened on her brow and her flushed cheeks, and she had to cling weakly to the rungs of the ladder as she climbed down from the loft. She'd been sleeping all day, exhausted from the job she'd found yesterday after arriving in Beaver Junction on a farm wagon. She'd become rather good, she felt, at stealing rides in wagons without anyone being the wiser.

She'd traveled a good ways across Wyoming Territory in this fashion. Of course, it wasn't as comfortable as traveling by train and stagecoach with the Kelly family, but that couldn't be helped.

She was rather proud of herself.

She, Becky Tamarlane, who found it painful to look strangers in the eye and who rarely even had the courage to ask for a second helping of mashed potatoes at dinner, had managed to get within fifty miles of Cloud Ranch all by herself.

Now if only she didn't starve to death before getting there, she'd be fine. Fine enough to surprise Caitlin. And fine enough to warn her about that horrible man.

Her stomach growled. She felt weak, and she knew she was dirty, but she tried not to think about it. Not having eaten a bite of food since last night, she ought to have been hungry, but her stomach was roiling something awful and she couldn't imagine eating even a crumb. Last night, after arriving in town tired and alone, she'd gazed longingly at the stewed chicken, dumplings, steak, and oyster stew being served in the Beaver Junction Hotel dining room. But she'd had to wait until after her job washing dishes was finished before tasting any of the food that had flowed so plentifully from the tiny kitchen. It'd been worth it though— she'd been paid a whole dollar plus fifty cents *and* a free plate of chicken and dumplings.

If she washed dishes again tonight, she might get another dollar and fifty cents. Maybe that would be enough to buy a stagecoach ticket for the last leg of the journey to Hope.

Of course, she'd have to make up a story when someone on the coach asked her, as they no doubt would, why a little girl like her was traveling all alone. But that wouldn't be a problem—she'd become rather good at making up stories.

She edged toward the barn door, wrinkling her nose at the smell of horses and manure. Then Miss Becky Tamarlane of the Davenport Academy for Young Ladies slipped outside into the cool sheltering darkness of night.

Her legs felt all funny and wobbly. Maybe, Becky thought, she ought to eat some soup for nourishment before trying to work. Her maid at home in Philadelphia—when she and Caitlin had still *had* a home—had often told her that without nourishment the body and the spirit shriveled up like an old pea fallen under the stove and forgotten. But a cup of soup at the diner would cost her a whole precious dime of the money she'd earned last night—and she wondered if she should spare it.

She tried to think clearly through the thrumming in her head. She needed to be strong, to be able to work again tonight, standing at the sink, washing all those plates and bowls. But most of all, she needed to be clearheaded, able to stay alert and careful. There were bad people in the world—and good, she thought, recalling the kind family who had invited her to travel with them when she left Philadelphia. She couldn't afford to run into any trouble—she must reach Cloud Ranch before that terrible man did and tried to hurt Caitlin again.

Because Caitlin didn't even know he was coming after her.

Becky had always relied on Caitlin—she was so smart,

so pretty, and so grown-up. And she had promised Becky, her eyes filled with purpose, that things would work out all right.

But they wouldn't be all right if that bad man reached Caitlin and hurt her—or worse, had her arrested and put in jail all because she'd hit him over the head in order to get away.

The very thought of it made tears sting her eyes. The night should have been cool, but it felt hot, hotter than an August afternoon. She walked faster toward the diner, but her legs felt so heavy. She would skip the soup, Becky thought, and save her dime, and offer to wash dishes again, sweep the floor, whatever was needed. She had to get to Cloud Ranch. She had to warn Caitlin . . .

She had reached the middle of the narrow street lit only by a hazy half-moon when her legs crumpled beneath her. Becky gave a small wavering cry, but there was no one about to hear. Her cheek struck the scratchy dust as she went down, down, down with a thud—and then the lights of the saloon and the diner and the Beaver Junction Hotel flickered and went out.

Forty miles south in the notorious outlaw town of Dead Man's Bluff, a man in a black duster, black Stetson, and gleaming boots pushed open the door of Whip Muldoon's way station and strode inside.

Through the smoke that clung to the fetid air, he surveyed the dark saloon abuzz with flies and mosquitoes. A few men at the bar or poker table glanced over at him, but no one spoke or paid much attention. In Muldoon's place, everyone minded his own business or risked rubbing the wrong man the wrong way.

So Dominic Trent claimed a seat in the corner and eyed the burly, black-bearded giant puffing on a huge cigar at the next table.

He called for whiskey, and it wasn't until the bartender had brought him a bottle and a glass that the black-bearded giant hefted his huge frame out of the chair and came to stand beside Trent's table.

"Smoke Jackson?"

The giant blew a smoke ring into the air and nodded.

"Have a seat."

The big man folded himself into a chair and stuck the cigar between stained teeth as he scrutinized Trent through shiny black eyes that were too small and clever for his large, fleshy face.

"Well, you look fearsome enough," Trent remarked coolly, "but the question remains, bounty hunter or no, are you as fast with a gun as they say?"

Jackson spat into the spittoon beside the table, then reached for the whiskey bottle. He tipped it to his lips and drank.

"I'm better than they say."

"Well. Let's hope so. I'm going to pay you a great deal of money *if* you're successful at the tasks I assign you."

"I'm always successful."

If a bear could talk, he would sound exactly like Smoke Jackson, Trent thought approvingly. He was pleased with the bounty hunter's fierce appearance. It would frighten his prey. He wanted her frightened. The more frightened, the better.

Trent's head ached, a reminder of what he owed Miss Caitlin Summers.

"Do you happen to know any lawmen?" he inquired,

pursing his lips thoughtfully, even as he signaled the bartender to bring another bottle of whiskey.

"Tend to steer clear of 'em," Smoke snorted. "Except for the crooked ones."

"That's the kind I have in mind."

"Why didn't you say so?"

Jackson drew another long drag on the cigar and blew smoke toward the low, fly-infested ceiling. "Sounds like a complicated job. But for the right price, I can find you a lawman who'll do whatever I tell him to."

"Excellent." Trent couldn't contain a smile of satisfaction. The moment he'd been waiting for, dreaming of, was getting closer. So close he could almost taste the fear on Caitlin's lips, could almost feel the terror freezing every beautiful bone in her body.

Poor Caitlin. But she deserved what was coming to her. He had offered her respite when she was in dire circumstances, he had offered her luxury, wealth, and a life of ease where her only obligation was to please him—and she had rewarded him by nearly scratching out his eyes, and by striking him a veritable death blow with that candlestick. He still grew dizzy sometimes, still had to deal with the throbbing pain in his skull. It might never go away, the doctors said.

Never.

Well, once he had her, a captive at his mercy, once she saw that there was no escape, that her only hope and salvation was at his side, in his bed, doing his bidding, she would learn how long never could be.

"I'll pay you five hundred dollars," he said softly, watching the bounty hunter's face. The man's eyes flitted over him, hungrily, eagerly. "And another five hundred to the lawman who joins our cause."

"And what cause might that be, Mr. Trent?"

Trent shifted in his chair and felt the emerald ring slide across his deep duster pocket, secure in its pouch. "You—and your lawman friend—must help me apprehend a most dangerous criminal. A would-be murderess—and a thief."

"What'd she steal?"

"An emerald. A family heirloom. Most valuable."

The bounty hunter grunted.

"I want her caught, dragged to justice, locked in jail." Trent's eyes glittered in the gloom of the way station. "When I say so, and not before, she will be released to my custody, to stand trial back east."

"Well, we can hang her right out here if you want," Smoke Jackson growled. "Why bother taking her all the way back?"

"No questions," Trent murmured pleasantly. His mood was lightening as for the first time he voiced aloud his splendid plan. "I want her frightened, helpless, trapped like a rabbit in a cage. But I don't want her broken. You and your friend will leave that part of it," he finished with a small, cruel smile, "to me."

Chapter 18

"How much farther?"

Caitlin tried to ignore the ache in her thighs and backside as she waited for Wade's reply. They'd been riding for two days now—two endless, nerve-wracking days—passing through as many neighboring towns as possible. And they'd keep riding until they received more information from the Pinkerton detective Wade had hired, or until they found Becky themselves.

"I'd say Beaver Junction is no more than ten miles ahead." Wade pushed up his hat and studied her with concern. "Want to rest a bit?"

Caitlin shook her head. "No, I'm fine. Let's keep going."

The first wave of panic that had swept over her when she learned Becky was missing had gone—leaving behind a cold, hard knot of fear. Her sister—small for her age, shy, and so terribly vulnerable—was out in the world all alone, with no one to protect her, look after her, or care about her.

The very thought of it made her shudder.

But shuddering and fear wouldn't help her find Becky. Wade had known exactly what to do. He'd taken action, calm, quick, decisive action.

First he wired the Pinkerton Detective Agency and initiated a search. He instructed them to begin at the Davenport Academy and to try to trace Becky's path from the time she left.

Using the description Caitlin included in the telegraph message, the detective came up with their first real lead when he checked at the railroad station in Philadelphia. A young girl matching Becky Tamarlane's description was seen buying a ticket on a westbound train on the same day Becky had run away.

The stationmaster noticed her traveling with a family. She stood out because all of the other children with these parents possessed bright red, curly hair—and they were all a high-spirited, noisy bunch—Becky's stick-straight light brown hair and quiet demeanor in the midst of all the rowdiness caught his attention.

"Looks like your sister found herself a nice family to travel with," Wade told Caitlin. "She must have told them a tall tale about why she was going out west all on her own, but the good news is that if we can find that family, we might find Becky too."

After that, Caitlin clung to the hope that Becky was safe and in the company of kindhearted people.

But then her hopes were dashed when the next morning another wire from the detective agency confirmed that the family—and Becky with them—seemed to have traveled on the Union Pacific Railroad as far as Nebraska, then boarded a stagecoach. But on the third day, in Diamond

Springs, Mr. and Mrs. Patrick Kelly raised a commotion when the young girl accompanying them disappeared. The family insisted that the stagecoach driver delay his departure while everyone searched high and low through the town for the young girl in their charge. But there was no sign of her. And no good-bye. And finally, the Kelly family was forced to board the stagecoach and leave without her. The mother and her two daughters were weeping, the detective reported, distraught because they didn't know what became of the young girl they'd grown so fond of.

When she learned this, Caitlin's heart stopped beating. She went white as parchment as she began to imagine all kinds of terrible things which might have befallen her sister, but Wade came up with a different explanation.

"Sounds to me like something spooked her—and she took off on her own again," he mused. "I've got a hunch that little sister of yours has some of the same steel in her spine that you do. And she's obviously headed this way. Reckon by now she could be within a hundred miles of Cloud Ranch."

So they fanned out—Nick riding off to search some of the towns in a hundred-mile radius, she and Wade the others. Though Wade suggested that Caitlin remain at the ranch and wait for word, she staunchly refused.

"I won't slow you down. I can ride as long and as hard as it takes." She faced him with such determination and yet silent pleading in her eyes that he wasn't able to refuse her.

As they covered the last few miles to Beaver Junction, Caitlin fought a growing despair. What if they never heard

another word about Becky? What if she was gone too—
lost in the vast plains of the West, as their parents had
been lost at sea . . .

But as the low frame buildings of the town came into
view she felt hope rise again in her heart. Maybe Becky
would be here, safe—or maybe someone would have seen
her . . .

"You take the general store," Wade instructed as they
dismounted in the center of town and tethered their
horses. "I'll find out if there's a sheriff or a mayor—someone in charge. Then I'll meet you at the hotel and we'll
check with the folks there together."

She nodded, suddenly so grateful to him she couldn't
speak. Wade had pushed just as hard during this search as
she—he'd done everything that could possibly be done to
locate Becky. And during the moments when doubt and
fear nearly conquered her, he took charge with a firm gentleness that she'd never known from anyone before.

"Are you all right?" He paused beside the horses to
scrutinize her, confused by the way she was staring at
him. "Do you need some grub first? Should we start at the
diner?"

"No." She moistened her lips. "It's only . . . I don't
know how to . . . thank you."

He shook his head. "Thank me after we've found her."

Caitlin scanned the boardwalk as she hurried toward
the general store, the hub of every town. When the small
bell tinkled above the door as she entered, she saw two
children eyeing the penny candy set out in glass jars on
the countertop. She smiled at them, turned to the clerk,
and speaking in a voice loud enough for all of the

customers to hear, began asking about a small, thin eleven-year-old girl with freckles on her nose and stick-straight light brown hair.

Wade had just discovered that Beaver Junction had no sheriff, and the mayor lived in a frame house at the end of town. He was headed that way when he saw an office door across the street open and a young girl step out onto a narrow porch. She was blinking in the sunshine, her hand shading her eyes.

The shingle hanging above her head read: HENRY FRANKLIN, MEDICAL DOCTOR. The girl stepping down off the porch looked pale and wobbly.

Wade froze. The girl appeared to be about ten or eleven years old—with freckles marching across a small, upturned nose and stick-straight, light brown hair.

"Becky?"

Her eyes widened when he said her name.

In a heartbeat she whirled around and started to dash back into the office.

"Wait!" He didn't want to frighten her, so he stayed where he was, but his voice reached her, low and soothing. "Becky, I'm here with Caitlin. We've been looking for you. Don't you want to see your sister?"

She spun back. Caught between fear and hope, for a moment she just stared at him. In her small, delicate features he could now see something of the woman who had accompanied him to this town.

"Are you . . . telling me the truth? Because if you're not—"

"You're just like her, Becky." Through the relief rushing through him, Wade gave a dry chuckle. "She doesn't trust anyone either."

The little girl continued to study him, all the while chewing on her lower lip. "What does she look like? My sister?"

A test. He had to hand it to the girl—she was cautious and smart. Just like Caitlin. "She looks like an angel," he said slowly. "A beautiful, golden-haired angel."

And then he heard a gasp behind him, and Caitlin's voice, breathless, shaking with joy. "Oh, my God. Becky! It's you!"

Wade watched, his chest tight, as Caitlin raced past him in a blur and then she was gathering the girl in her arms, and both of them sank down on the porch step, sobbing.

The fair head bent to the brown-haired one and as the passersby in Beaver Junction stared, and the sun drifted overhead through a high brilliant blue sky, the sisters rocked and wept in each other's arms.

"Are you sure you don't want anything to eat besides soup?" Caitlin asked as Becky set her spoon down inside her empty bowl of chicken broth with vegetables.

"I'm sure. It was good though, Caity."

The girl smiled happily first at her sister, then shyly at Wade. "Doc Franklin said I might not feel much like eating for another day or so," she reminded them.

"Yes, so he did." Caitlin sighed. "That was quite a fever you had, young lady. It was very good of the doctor to take you into his own house behind his office and take care of you until you were better."

"But he sure didn't expect you'd be getting out of bed even today," Wade drawled gently. Doc Franklin had explained to them later that when he left his office that morning to see another patient, Becky was sound asleep, with the shutters drawn and the sheets drawn up to her chin. "Reckon I could have knocked him over with a feather when he saw you on those porch steps with Caitlin," he added dryly.

Becky laughed, a rich, high sound that to Caitlin was more beautiful than the chiming of bells. "Yes, well, I was sleeping when he left, but then I woke up and I felt ever so much better. And I remembered for the first time since I fainted from the fever exactly where I was and *who* I was—and where I wanted to go. To Cloud Ranch," she finished as she answered the question forming on Caitlin's lips. Her brows knit. "I needed to find you quickly so I could warn you."

A cloud descended over her thin little face and Caitlin leaned forward across the dining table. "Warn me about what, honey? Is that what made you run away?"

"Yes, that and the fact that they were hideous to me at school. Absolutely hideous." Becky clenched her hands into fists.

"How do you mean?" Wade asked, frowning.

"Oh, they didn't beat me or anything like that," Becky assured him swiftly. Her toffee-brown eyes flashed. "But when Alicia Peabody threw spitballs at me in class, and I threw one right back at her, *I* was the one who landed in trouble, not her. All because her father is president of the Peabody Steel Works Company and has more money than Midas, and mine is . . . was . . ." She broke off.

"I *hate* that school." Her voice shook with a quiet intensity. "Miss Culp ordered me confined to my room until further notice. And there was a tea held in the drawing room for all the girls and their mothers and they wouldn't let me go because I threw the stupid spitball and because I . . . didn't have a . . . m-mother and my s-sister was . . . g-gone . . ."

Sobs broke from her. Instantly Caitlin knelt beside her chair and clutched the girl's hands in her own. "I'm so sorry, dearest," she cried. "I wanted to come back for you, truly I did, but . . ." She took a deep breath, then shook her head. "It's all so complicated. More complicated than I ever expected. But before I explain, you must tell me what exactly made you leave? Surely you didn't run away just because you were punished?"

"No. It wasn't that—it was the man. The man you told me about!"

For a moment, shock swept away Caitlin's every rational thought and she couldn't speak at all. Then she found her composure.

"Do you mean Alec Ballantree?" she asked tersely.

"No." Becky's brown eyes were fixed desperately on hers. "Not him. Not Alec. The other man. The bad man!"

Caitlin tried to draw in her breath. She felt as if someone had punched a fist through her stomach. Beside her, she saw Wade's gaze piercing her as if he would read into her very soul.

"Dominic Trent?" Icy cold all over, she met Becky's eyes. "What did he do? Did he come to see you—did he *threaten* you?" she asked in sudden horror.

Wade's eyes went cold and flat.

"No, he didn't come to see me," the girl hastened to explain, "but he came to the school. I saw him arrive in his carriage—a magnificent carriage, drawn by two beautiful white horses. He's very rich, isn't he? Just like Papa used to be."

"Yes, he's very rich. Becky . . . please, tell me what happened."

"Miss Culp actually curtsied to him when he introduced himself to her and she invited him into her office. I recognized him," Becky added, "from that time he came to our house the day after Thanksgiving, the time you asked him to leave and he followed you into the garden and you had to call for Perkins to help you."

She turned to Wade. "There was this very bad man who bothered my sister and tried to hurt her . . ." She started to explain, but Caitlin interrupted hastily.

"Just tell me what happened at the school, dearest. There's no need to bore Wade with all the details."

"I'm not bored." Wade's gaze seared Caitlin's. She gave her head a tiny shake. *Not now,* her eyes pleaded silently.

He'd been listening intently to every word Becky said—and he'd seen Caitlin's face turn paler by the moment. *Dominic Trent.* It wasn't the first time he'd heard that name. And it wouldn't be the last. Caitlin liked to avoid explanations of her past and certain people in it but all of his instincts told him that Trent was someone who had played a key role in that past—someone who had hurt her, frightened her.

And suddenly he was someone Wade wished very much he could get his hands on. Five minutes alone with the man—that's all he wanted.

No, it wasn't all he wanted. He wanted to be able to erase that tense, drawn look from Caitlin's face. He wanted, he realized with a shock, to hold her and keep her safe from men like Dominic Trent and Alec Ballantree, and whoever else had hurt her in the past. Whatever they'd done, he wanted to undo. Whatever harm they'd caused, he wanted to heal.

"Why did this man come to your school, Becky?" He spoke in his calm, steady way and Becky's gaze centered on him. "Was it to ask questions about your sister?"

"How did you know?" The girl bobbed her head. "That's exactly why he came. You see, I listened outside the door after he went into Miss Culp's office. He told her that Caitlin was bad. And that Miss Culp must know where she was because of me. He said that if she didn't tell him where to find her, he'd send a constable to ask her questions—and how would that look to the parents of the girls attending her school?"

Caitlin's hands shook, but she managed to keep her voice calm. "So she told him I'd been writing letters to you and sending money from Cloud Ranch."

"Yes, she told him the letters came from a town called Hope in Wyoming, and then he left and I just knew he was going to come after you and maybe bring the constable after you, too, so I . . . I ran away. I wanted to get here first and warn you."

At the mention of the constable, Wade's gaze had sharpened on Caitlin's face, but she refused to look at him as Becky rushed on.

"I met a nice family, the Kellys, and I told them that my sister was a famous actress traveling across the West performing plays and giving poetry recitations and that I was finally going to be allowed to join your theatrical troupe—that you were going to be meeting me when I got off the stagecoach in Hope."

"You did *what*?" For a moment Caitlin was so

astonished at the thought of her meek little sister weaving such an elaborate tale that she forgot about Dominic Trent. "How did you ever think up something so . . . so clever?"

Becky's smile brightened her pale little face. "It just popped out," she admitted proudly. "I didn't want to tell the truth in case the school sent someone looking for Becky Tamarlane, so I made up a name and everything else. I said I was Lauralee Jones, and you were Lily Jones, and we came from a family of great actors, and that our mama was a beautiful singer . . ." Her voice trailed off. "But when we got to Diamond Springs, Nebraska, you'll never guess what happened."

"Tell me, dearest." Caitlin threw Wade a quick look. Though he sat silently, leaning back in his chair with his long legs stretched out, she could sense the tension in him. She wished he would leave, that he wouldn't hear any more about Dominic Trent than he already had. Trent was her problem. She had dealt with him before, and she would again if necessary. She wasn't about to start relying on anyone else to help her solve her problems, and she wasn't about to start leaning on Wade, depending on him.

She could take care of herself, she thought silently. And she'd take care of Becky too. She pondered the shotgun and her shooting lesson, resolving to work harder. Next time, if Trent came after her, he might get more than a candlestick beaned across his skull.

"I saw him—Dominic Trent," Becky continued excitedly. "In Diamond Springs. Just as the Kellys and me were heading to the stagecoach, I saw him standing right there in the street. If he'd seen me . . . well, I didn't want him to see me," she said in a low tone. "I was scared and I didn't know what to do, so I told Mrs. Kelly that I'd left my candy behind and I ran back toward the general store, but I didn't go all the way there—I hid in a wagon all the way down the street in front of the feed store. I was too afraid to come out until I felt the wagon start to move, and then I jumped out. Dominic Trent was gone. But so were the Kellys." A single tear slipped down Becky's cheek. Her narrow little shoulders slumped. "From then on, I traveled all by myself. And I did pretty good, I think, Caitlin, didn't I? Until I got sick."

Caitlin wrapped her arms around her sister and hugged her. She had to swallow back her own tears. And the ripple of fear inside her.

"You did just fine, Becky. I'm very proud of you. You were so brave and so smart."

"I'll say." Wade leaned forward and the smile he directed at the little girl filled Caitlin with a rush of warmth. "You've got the makings of a real western cowgirl, Becky. What you did shows grit. We respect that out here."

"You do? You really think I could be a cowgirl?" For some reason Caitlin couldn't fathom, Becky found this notion delightful. She smiled eagerly back at Wade. "Do I get to see Cloud Ranch? Today?"

"No, not today," Caitlin said quickly, rising and holding out her hand to her sister. "It's nighttime and Cloud Ranch is far from here. We'll go there tomorrow."

"Well, I suppose I can wait one more day," Becky conceded. But she chattered with more animation than Caitlin had ever seen as they climbed the stairs of the hotel to the room she and Becky would share.

"I'll be right across the hall." Wade spoke casually, but Caitlin caught his deliberate glance, and knew he was letting her know that if any unwelcome visitors showed up, she had only to call for help.

"Thank you, Wade. We'll be fine."

"Damn right you will be." The words were softly spoken, but there was no mistaking their meaning. Whether she liked it or not, he would be there to protect her and Becky. Or so he wanted her to believe. That might be true for tonight, but she couldn't count on him for tomorrow. Or the day after that.

"Good night, Mr. Barclay," Becky's sweet voice piped up, interrupting Caitlin's thoughts as she stared up at the tall, lean man whose eyes held so much kindness. "Thanks for finding me. And for the soup."

Wade grinned down at her. "Night, sweet pea. Tomorrow I'll take you home to Cloud Ranch. Show you around."

"Oh, boy!"

He bent down and kissed the little girl lightly on the cheek. Then straightened and his glance settled on Caitlin. For a long moment neither of them looked away. Caitlin was all too aware of Becky's small hand holding fast to hers, of the dim, quiet hall, of Wade's warm, intent gaze. His eyes lingered, holding hers, as if loath to let her go. "G-good night," she murmured at last as, beside her, Becky peered back and forth between them.

"Sweet dreams, princess."

She felt dizzy as he pushed open the door for her. Somehow she made it inside, somehow she closed and locked the door, somehow she managed to pay attention to Becky's happy chatter.

She feared she would dream of Dominic Trent that night when she closed her eyes, but it was Wade Barclay who haunted her sleep. His gentle smile, deep, reassuring voice, and those keen hot blue eyes were imprinted on her mind.

Don't ever fall in love with a cowboy.

It's too late, Mrs. Casper, she whispered to herself in the deep indigo hours of the night. *I'm beginning to fear I already have.*

Chapter 19

For the next few days Caitlin managed to avoid Wade. She knew he wanted to question her about Dominic Trent, but she had no intention of discussing that unpleasant subject with him—Trent was her problem, and hers alone. Nor was she ready yet to face her own feelings for Wade, the man who had taken her place in this ranch house and in Reese Summers's life. So she busied herself showing Becky around and helping her get acclimated to the ranch.

She was surprised and pleased by the number of visitors who came to welcome her sister. Edna and Winnifred and several ladies from the Hope Sewing Circle stopped by with baskets filled with cookies and shortbread, Luanne brought the Morgensen twins, Katie and Bridget, to meet Becky, and Alice Tyler from the Crooked T Ranch arrived with a personal invitation for everyone in the household to attend the May Day dance that she and her husband held every year.

And true to her word, Edna Weaver even planned a

small dinner party in Becky's honor and after dessert invited the girl to entertain everyone with a song. To Caitlin's astonishment, her sister was only too happy to skip up to the pianoforte in the Weavers' front parlor, and as Caitlin played, Becky sat beside her on the small bench with its embroidered cushion and in her clear sweet voice warbled "My Old Kentucky Home."

Even Francesca, who had never treated Caitlin with anything but polite reserve, beamed at Cloud Ranch's newest guest and spent her afternoons baking all sorts of cakes and pies to tempt Becky's appetite as she recovered from her fever.

Through it all, Caitlin kept a nervous watch on the horizon. Each day she half expected a towering figure with strange colorless eyes to appear. Trent had made it all the way to Diamond Springs—why hadn't he shown up on her doorstep yet?

Twice she rode out and spent hours at shooting practice—one time with Jake Young, who always seemed like he wanted to say something to her, but kept forgetting what it was, and once with Dirk, who showed her not only how to aim and fire the shotgun, but also a small derringer that Wade gave her when they returned from Beaver Junction.

"Keep it on you every day, and close by every night," was all Wade said when he handed her the derringer.

Dirk, who mentioned that as a gunfighter he had always kept at least two hideaway weapons on him at all times, gave her some useful tips on the use of the derringer as well.

Since Nick had continued on after Becky was found, taking up his pursuit of the rustlers, it was only the three of them at the dining-room table each night. With Becky present, Wade avoided the topic of Dominic Trent. He actually spent most of the dinner hour entertaining Becky with stories of life on a ranch, of his boyhood with Nick and Clint, of the time Dawg had chased a bear up a tree.

Caitlin couldn't help being amazed at how easy and warm he was with her sister. She wanted to warn Becky not to take too much of a liking to Wade, or Dawg, or anything on Cloud Ranch since they wouldn't be staying—but she couldn't. She'd never seen Becky so happy and animated. The little sister who'd always seemed afraid of her own shadow had somehow, through her adventures in running away, burst out of her shell.

It was on the third evening that Caitlin found herself alone in the kitchen several hours after tucking Becky into bed in the oak-floored guest room down the hall from her own. She sat at the table in her peach silk wrapper, staring at the cup of tea she'd brewed, but not once tasting it.

Beyond the kitchen window, the night was soft and dark as a wool cloak. No stars lit the sky and a fuzzy half-moon flung blue shadows along the edges of the pines. From somewhere came the howl of a coyote. Another answered, then more joined in.

Around her, the house was silent. Francesca had retired to her room, which overlooked the vegetable garden. Wade had been down to the bunkhouse playing cards earlier but she'd long since heard him come in, his boots thudding along the hall past her bedroom to his own. He, too, must have gone to bed.

Even Dawg was sleeping in Reese's study, on the rug under his desk. That was his favorite place to sleep, Wade had told her after she'd first arrived at Cloud Ranch.

Reese had always to take a care not to step on him when he rose from the desk, but Dawg had dozed without a care, full of implicit trust that his sleep would be undisturbed.

Trust.

Dawg had trusted his master. Reese had trusted Wade to take care of her—and the ranch. She didn't trust anyone in the world—except Becky.

Or did she? She stared at the cup of tea, remembering how instinctively she had run to find Wade when she learned Becky was missing. How she had watched him ride along that ridge when the rustlers had been shooting at her, knowing in that instant she was safe. How she'd let him kiss her, touch her, hold her as if he'd never let her go—even when her brain had screamed at her to run away.

The tea had been sitting before her for nearly a quarter of an hour and she had yet to take a sip.

It would be cold by now.

When she heard the footfall behind her, she didn't turn around. She knew without looking who was there.

"Can't sleep?"

Wade's deep voice was as quiet and steady as always. The sound of it made her stomach flutter, her breasts ache.

"Something like that." Her voice came out lower, huskier than she intended. She cleared her throat. "And you?"

"Too much on my mind."

At this she turned her head, her hair, loose and golden, drifting across her cheek. Wade strode forward into the room, into the glow of amber lamplight, and she saw that he was bare-chested but for the unbuttoned plaid work shirt he'd tossed on. Aside from that, he wore denim pants, and his feet were bare on the spotless floor. His muscles gleamed like polished bronze in the lamplight, and it was all she could do not to stare at his broad, hard-muscled chest.

She grabbed the teacup and took a gulp to distract herself. It was cold. Bitter. She'd forgotten to add sugar. She gulped it down rather than glance at him again.

Wade came around the table and folded his lanky frame down onto the opposite bench. His sharp, handsome features were totally unreadable.

"Who's Alec Ballantree?"

If she'd still been drinking the tea, she'd have choked. As it was, she gasped. "What makes you ask . . . about Alec Ballantree?" she demanded, and felt her cheeks flushing.

"You mentioned him the other day. And wouldn't tell me who he was. But when Becky told you about the man who came to her school looking for you, his was the first name you guessed."

So it was. She acknowledged the fact with no small degree of irritation. "He's nobody important. At least, not now." Though she prayed he would accept this explanation and move on to another subject, he merely continued to study her, his gaze cool and noncommittal, until at last she could bear it no longer.

"If you must know, he was my fiancé." Why, oh why, did he have the power to wrench words—and feelings— from her she would rather keep to herself? Her chin jutted out. "A man I thought I loved. When I still believed in love," she added with a brittle smile, and stood up. Hurrying to the sink she placed her cup inside and used the pump to rinse it, talking quickly all the while.

"He claimed to love me, promised to love me forever—but forever only lasted until my stepfather's death, and the discovery that Gillis owed more than a half million dollars in all—great portions of that to many of Philadelphia's finest citizens, among them Alec's own father. Suddenly, forever became . . ." She took a deep breath. "Yesterday."

Her lashes swept down, covering, she hoped, the pain in her eyes, but she should have known she couldn't keep it from Wade. He didn't move, and his expression never changed.

"In other words, he's a damned fool."

She looked at him then—his expression held no pity, not even sympathy, just flat-out anger.

"I'm afraid not many people in Philadelphia would agree with you." She tried for an indifferent laugh, a light tone. "It was generally agreed he escaped just in time. Another few months, and it would have been too late—we'd have been wed already and he'd have been stuck with m—"

He moved so quickly she broke off, faltering. He grabbed her by the shoulders before she could even gasp. "The man's not only a damned fool, he's a spineless one. Do you still love him?"

The question took her by surprise. She stared at him blankly. Once, she would have said *yes*. She'd have said it immediately, heartbrokenly. And followed it by saying: *No, I hate him.*

But now . . .

She summoned up Alec's face. Strangely, there wasn't pain at the memory, only . . . fuzziness.

"I—I don't know . . ."

"Do you think about him night and day? See his face in the firelight, hear his voice in your bed in the dark at night? Do you think of him when you're out riding, or saddling your horse, or walking up the damn stairs to an empty bedroom?"

She stared at him, his dark face tight-lipped and pale beneath his tan, his eyes seething with something powerful and dangerous that came from a place deep within. "N-no . . . of course not . . . what are you saying?"

"I'm saying, Caitlin, that those are all the times I think of you. Those—and more. Too many to count in a day. In a night."

Stunned, she could only stare at him. Then she remembered Luanne. She yanked free of him. "Perhaps it would be best if you saved your pretty words for Miss Porter," she said, turning away, heading for the door. "They're wasted on me . . . oh!"

She was shocked when he grabbed her from behind, his arms sliding around her, holding her taut against him. She couldn't escape. His breath rustled her hair as he spoke in her ear. "Miss Porter is quite pretty."

Pain squeezed around her heart. "Yes, yes, she is. Now let me go!"

His arms tightened, his voice grew rougher, sending shivers down her spine. "She's sweet as pie. Kind and easygoing and pleasant to be around."

"Yes, so do go ahead and be around her all you want—"

"And I only kissed her that night to forget about you. To *try* to forget about you." Wade's mouth touched her ear, and a shiver shot through her. "But it didn't work, Caitlin. It only made me think about you more."

He spun her around, still holding her tightly, and one muscle-corded arm coiled around her waist. Good thing too, Caitlin thought dizzily, because otherwise she would surely have fallen. Her knees turned to butter as she searched his eyes.

"You expect me . . . to believe that?"

"I'm going to prove it to you."

"I . . . don't see how," she muttered warily.

"You will," he told her, a strange hoarseness in his tone. His eyes seemed to be devouring her, but those two deliberate words were what struck her with all the force of a hammer smashing through her heart. With her pulse racing, Caitlin tried to struggle against his unbreakable hold.

"I'm going to bed . . . I want you to let go of me right now!"

"Can't, Caitlin." His breath fanned her cheek. "Not yet. There's something I have to prove to you first." He drew her inexorably closer. Panic burst through her as she saw he was about to kiss her again.

Wade saw that fear in her eyes—much like the terror he'd witnessed in wild mares fighting for their lives and their freedom.

Anger jolted through him. That son-of-a-bitch Trent *had* hurt her, hurt her badly—even worse than that gutless fiancé of hers, he thought, and it only made him want to kiss her more, to kiss away the fear and the pain. But searching her eyes, seeing the depths of her dread, he wondered if it was only a man she was afraid of, any man—or if she might really be afraid of herself.

He remembered Nick's words and suddenly swept her even closer, but this time his face softened, and a smile tender as morning touched his lips.

"Tell you what. Let me kiss you once more, Caitlin, just once more. And let's see if a kiss can lie."

She looked stunned, terrified. But she didn't struggle and she didn't say no. Slowly, gently, he leaned down and touched his mouth to hers. Her lips were like satiny pillows and they fitted against his warmly. A powerful need surged through him, a need for this woman, this angel with her sharp tongue and bruised heart, this girl he had sworn to protect.

But how could he protect her from himself?

The kiss deepened. His need grew hotter. One hand tangled in her hair, his fingers dragging through the silken strands until he caressed her nape, while with his other hand he drew her ever closer against his body. With her breasts crushed against his chest and his need for her building to a painful tension that rippled through every part of him, his lips stayed gentle as they played against hers. He felt her quiver, and passion roared through him. She leaned into him, like a leaf nestling against a rock, and everywhere their bodies touched caught fire.

"Caitlin." Hoarsely, he spoke her name and kissed her again, deeper, harder, quicker. "My God. Caitlin."

She trembled in his arms. How could anything that terrified her so much feel so good? She knew she should run from what she was feeling, from what they were doing. For even if he was telling the truth, Wade Barclay was more dangerous to her than Alec or Dominic Trent had ever been—he touched her more deeply, more powerfully, than they ever had, ever could . . . and that meant he could hurt her more.

When Wade kissed her, she couldn't think, couldn't fight, she could only dive headlong into the most delirious pleasure she'd ever known.

And he was kissing her now.

Oh, was he. Fire ignited along her lips as his strong, hot mouth toyed with hers. Coaxing, demanding. Dominating.

Her mouth betrayed her, parting eagerly for his kiss, and the sweet invasion of his tongue. Her own tongue battled his even as her senses swam with pleasure. She clasped her arms around his neck and became one with him in the lamplit kitchen, locked in endless burning kisses that swept them both down a path into the perilous unknown.

Wade didn't even remember scooping her up in his arms, carrying her into the hall and up the staircase, then down the silent corridor to his room.

Inside, there was little light except for the sparkle of the silvery half-moon, faintly illuminating the masculine room with its tall oak bureau and sturdy desk, its rich maroon curtains and the deep blue and scarlet rug on the floor. As soon as Wade set her down upon the four-poster oak bed, he was reaching for the sash of her wrapper.

"I want to see you, Caitlin. All of you." After carrying her all that way, he wasn't even breathing hard, but his chest was filmed with sweat—not from exertion, but from desire. He leaned in closer to her, inhaling the light flowery scent of her, drowning in the wanting of her. "You're too damn beautiful," he groaned as her green eyes glimmered up at him, and that gorgeous hair swirled around her exquisite face. He couldn't even think straight anymore. "You shouldn't be here," he muttered roughly.

"N-no, I shouldn't," she whispered back, but even as she started to rise, the panic bubbling up, Wade pushed her gently back and she went still, staring up at him, her heart pounding, her breath caught in her throat.

"Too late to turn back," he rasped in a low tortured tone, and she knew it was true. It was too late, for both of them.

She didn't want to turn back, she didn't want to leave. And that was as far as her thoughts would take her because in the next instant, he parted the peach wrapper and she saw the flash of pleasure in his eyes, then he was sliding it down her arms and she couldn't think of anything but how glad she was that he thought she was beautiful and how much she wanted him to touch her.

Wade couldn't breathe with pleasure at the sight of her lovely pale breasts, rose-tipped and delicious in the moonglow. She was naked as the morn beneath the wrapper, and as he tugged away the silken robe and sent it sailing in a heap to the floor, he forgot everything but the woman before him, the woman whose smooth skin and lush curves begged for his touch, the woman whose eyes shone like precious jewels, the woman who looked and smelled and felt more delicious than a whole damned field of violets.

As he lowered her across the bed, Wade's body covered hers, his arms bracing beside her narrow shoulders as he captured her mouth in a kiss even more intense than they had known before.

But that was only the beginning. He touched her

slowly, feverishly, everywhere—savoring the softness and shape of her breasts, skimming his hands in slow caresses along her shoulders, her arms, circling between her thighs.

Tortured by the urge to go fast, he forced himself to take it slow, wanting to pleasure her, ready her, savor every inch of her. His brain had shut down—Wade Barclay, who thought through everything he ever did, quite simply stopped thinking and gave himself over to the instincts claiming him, instincts Caitlin Summers had taken by storm. Each little moan she gave as his tongue scraped against her taut nipples, or as his fingers stroked the slick softness between her thighs, sent his urges into full aggressive mode, made him ache and throb for her, but he held back and kissed her until their mouths were bruised and hot, their breathing ragged. Struggling and panting, she tore at his shirt and her fingers trembled at the fastenings on his pants.

Hot need swirled through him, over him, and crazed, he flung his clothes atop hers on the floor. The world was a roaring blur as they tangled and tossed in his bed.

This is madness, Caitlin's brain tried to tell her, but she was past listening. There was only this bed and this man and the delicious things his hands and his tongue were doing to her and she surrendered to the dazzling sweetness, and to the wild, stirring needs of her own body.

Wade Barclay was driving her over the edge of reason and she didn't care. She was driving him, too, she could see it in the hunger deep within his glinting eyes, feel it in the rough and tender handling of her body as he kneaded and tasted and touched. Responsive as a wilted flower to sunshine and spring rain, she awakened as if from a deep slumber, her body revitalized and wildly alive. Gasping, clinging to him, to his sweat-slickened muscles and overpowering strength, she squirmed and moaned and dragged her hands across his chest and through his midnight hair, wanting . . . wanting . . .

She didn't know exactly what she wanted, she only knew she wanted more of it and Wade gave it to her, his mouth relentless on hers, alternately savage and gentle, plundering and soothing.

He studied and explored her entire body and boldly she pushed him over and did the same to him. A deep, tortured groan came from his throat as she touched his huge, thickened manhood and she drew back, alarmed, but he caught her hand and chuckled harshly.

"Don't stop now, sweetheart. The fun is just beginning—for both of us."

A desperate smile broke from her as she gazed into his darkened blue eyes. "I've no intention of stopping, Wade," she informed him, thrilled by the effect her hands were having on him, delighted by her power to arouse him even further, to make this hard-muscled, always-in-control man sweat and burn with the same uncontrollable desire that was jolting like a runaway train through her.

She stroked and teased him then, every engorged inch of him, until he groaned again and suddenly rolled her over, once more trapping her body beneath his own.

"Two can play that game, princess," he told her roughly, his breath warm on her face, and she soon found herself a prisoner of aching need as his mouth suckled cleverly at her breast and his fingers stroked the nest of golden curls between her thighs and slipped inside.

Delicious heat pooled where he touched, sensation

after sensation quivered through her and she began to twist with an urgency that made Wade's lean, dark-stubbled face light with a grin.

"No stopping now, princess," he spoke against her lips, and she sipped at his and pulled him down closer and closer to her.

"I'd have to shoot you if you stop," she gasped desperately, and her heart thrummed as his grin widened, and then he lowered himself over her. His strong body flexed, shifted. Caitlin clung to him, her eyes glazed, her mouth damp as he rained kisses on her lips and her eyelids and began to slide the powerful length of his manhood inside her.

Sweat filmed his brow as he used all of his willpower to hold himself still a moment, watching her flushed, beautiful face.

"Caitlin." His voice was a raw scrape as he gathered her close and twisted his hands in her hair. "Hold on, Caitlin. Hold on."

She clung to him, frightened and eager and wild with that hunger for *more*. Wonder swept through her as he filled her and her thighs parted even more to welcome him. The world was gone, there was only the two of them as he slanted his warm mouth against hers, kissing her tenderly and pushing himself deeper and deeper inside her.

Then . . . *pain* . . . *sharp, splintering pain.* She cried out, but his kisses captured the pain and sweetened it, and then it dissolved into raw sweeping pleasure as Wade began to thrust inside her, slowly at first, then with ever-increasing surges. Caitlin cried out again, this time with a primitive joy that shuddered through her as she clutched at his muscled back, and then sensation built upon sensation and she was twisting and bucking beneath him, lost in the headlong rush of their bodies toward oblivion, in the brilliant, tumultuous explosion that shuddered through her very core and sent her soaring to heights she'd never dreamed existed.

"Wade . . . Wade!" She cried his name, weeping as they rocked and shattered together over a dizzying peak. From a great distance she heard him saying her name, over and over, even as his body claimed hers beautifully and with all-encompassing possession and he branded her forever his own.

Midnight and moonlight and sweet, soaring madness.

These they found in the oaken bed as the moon glittered like a diamond in the perfect sky and the night stood still.

At last, shaking and spent, they collapsed side by side, entangled in each other's arms. After the whirlwind, the storm, quiet descended—and peace.

Chapter 20

Caitlin didn't know how much later she awakened to find Wade holding her tucked against his bronzed naked body, kissing her with slow, gentle kisses. She kissed him back, her body stirring to quick warmth once again. Lovely, gentle kisses. Slow touches. Mmmmm. Smiling, she drew back for a moment to catch her breath and gazed lovingly into his eyes—only they weren't Wade's eyes.

The eyes of the man holding her belonged to Dominic Trent.

Her scream echoed around and around the tousled bed as she fought to wrench away, but Trent held her close and those icy colorless eyes glistened like moonfrost.

"Did you think I wouldn't find you, Caitlin? You and I are part of each other. This is meant to be."

"No!" she shrieked and yanked free. Suddenly she heard the pounding of hooves outside the window and ran toward the blowing draperies. There was Wade—galloping away from her, whipping his roan faster and faster, his broad figure becoming smaller and more indistinct as he rode into the blue-tinged distance.

Wade! She called to him, shouting over and over for help, but he never turned or slowed.

Wade!

Terror bubbled up in her as she whirled back and saw Trent springing from the bed, coming toward her. She dashed toward the bureau to grab the bronze candlestick atop it. It was the same one she had hit him with in Philadelphia: tall, heavy, magnificently carved. But her desperate fingers closed on chill empty air.

The candlestick was gone. *Where?*

"This is meant to be," Trent repeated, advancing with that same small, evil smile she remembered. "No one will help you, Caitlin. You're all alone."

She shook her head wildly. And then she saw it—the shotgun propped against the foot of the bed. She darted past Trent and reached for it, but again, only that cool drift of air met her fingers. The shotgun was nowhere to be seen.

She turned a slow despairing circle around the room. For a moment the faces of her mother and Gillis seemed to shimmer blurrily in the dark bronze mirror on the wall—then the mirror vanished, and so did Lydia's and Gillis's images.

Where the wall had been there was only a swirling gray mist.

They were gone, all of them . . . everything . . . gone . . . gone . . .

No!!!

"Caitlin!"

No!!!

"Shhh. Caitlin, it's all right." Wade's voice, steady, calm. His hands on her, gentle, soothing.

Her eyes flew open.

"You had a dream, sweetheart. Pretty bad one, I'd say," he told her softly.

For a moment she could do nothing but stare into his dark, quiet face, into those diamond-blue eyes so full of concern and warmth.

She was trembling all over, her entire body clammy as he pulled her closer and kissed the silk of her hair.

"Want to tell me about it?"

She shook her head.

Wade stroked her hair. She heard his even breathing beside her and her own ragged breaths slowed. It was still dark beyond the window, and the night was silent. No wind. No mist. The curtains weren't blowing. No one was riding away.

"Then why don't you tell me about Dominic Trent," Wade said.

"Wade—"

"Tell me, Caitlin." He swung up to face her as she lay back upon the pillows, the twisted sheets loose across her body. "You said his name in your dream," he said grimly. "It's not the first time I've heard it. For your sake—and Becky's—it's time for you to fill me in on this son of a bitch who's coming after you."

Shakily, Caitlin dragged a hand through her hair. "He's a . . . former suitor. A would-be suitor," she amended quickly in a low tone.

"And?"

She saw there was no denying the determination in his eyes.

"We met at the opera and he began courting me. Or trying to court me," she said with resignation. Her face was still very pale. "Dominic Trent is a powerful man in Philadelphia—one of the wealthiest men in the country. He was brought up with every imaginable luxury and apparently had never been refused anything he wanted. Until I refused his attentions." She moistened her lips. "I was seeing Alec at the time I met Dominic—but that didn't stop him from pressing his suit." Suddenly chilled as she remembered how he had shown up everywhere she went, and always seemed to be watching her, she pulled the sheets up to her shoulders.

"One day he came to my home—it was the day after Thanksgiving last year, just before Becky was to return to school. Mama and Gillis were away and I was walking in the garden."

She halted and bit her lip.

"Go on," Wade said even more grimly than before.

"He—he accosted me. That's the only word for it. He told me that he and I were meant to be together. That Alec was wrong for me, and he himself was the only man who could ever make me happy. He asked me to marry him and tried to kiss me and to . . ." She shuddered. "I told him no, I wouldn't marry him—I asked him to leave. But he kept trying to kiss me and so I slapped him. And pushed him away. But when I tried to go back inside he wouldn't let me go. He was hurting my arm and my cloak ripped in the struggle, but I couldn't get away . . . so I started screaming and our groom, Perkins, came running and threw Trent into the shrubs and by then more of the servants came running and he—he left."

"But that wasn't the last you saw of him," Wade muttered, watching her drawn, taut face.

"No." Caitlin shook her head, and the thick pale locks of her hair fell across her cheeks. "After Lydia and Gillis died, after Alec broke our engagement, Trent followed me one day as I returned from Gillis's lawyer's office. It was late afternoon—almost dusk. I had stopped at the park near our home and sent the carriage ahead, planning to walk the rest of the way home and have some time to think over what I was going to do, how I was going to manage—but suddenly his carriage pulled up beside me and before I knew what was happening, he had dragged me inside."

Wade's eyes went cold and flat again, Caitlin noticed, the way they had in Beaver Junction, when Becky had told him about Dominic Trent. She drew in her breath at the frightening expression on his face, but he quickly reached out, his hand closing over hers.

"It's all right, Caitlin," he said very quietly. And in contrast to the frightening ice in his eyes, his hands were warm and reassuring.

"What happened?" he asked.

Caitlin swallowed as the ugly memories crept back. "He took me to his town house." Somehow she managed to speak without quavering. "There was no one about on the street, and I screamed, but no one heard and then he pulled me inside the door and—and there were no servants inside—not another living soul. He told me that they all had been given the day off, that he had planned this so that we could be alone."

She suddenly closed her eyes. "He dragged me into the

drawing room and locked the door. He offered me brandy and told me he had a proposition for me." Her eyes flew open and her anguished gaze met Wade's hard blue one.

"He insisted that now I must be able to see that he and I were meant to be together. Everyone had deserted me, my mother and stepfather, Alec—everyone but him. He said I needed him. And that he needed me." She shook her head slowly, horror in her voice. "But there was evil in his face, in the way he spoke. As if . . . nothing would—or could—deter him. I was more frightened than I'd ever been in my life," she went on softly, her fingers clinging to Wade's.

"I ordered him to let me go, and then . . . I begged him to. But he only laughed and said I would learn to love him. He wasn't offering me marriage this time, he wanted me to be his mistress. I would live with him in that house and be his mistress and he would provide for me—and for Becky—pay for her clothes, her tuition and room and board, whatever she needed . . . for as long as I remained with him."

Her voice began to shake. "I had heard . . . stories about him . . . rumors . . . that he had a dark side, especially where women were concerned. And as he circled me there in his drawing room, with the light burning low, I knew that they were all true. He slapped me when I tried to run to the door—he said that I deserved it for having struck him that day in the garden. He tried to tear off my clothes and I fought him. I grabbed a candlestick from the table—it was large and heavy—and I . . . I struck him over the head." Her eyes were huge pools of shining green light in the darkened room. Wade read in them the depths of shock and horror.

"He . . . fell. There was blood. I ran for the door and never looked back. I stopped only long enough to wire Mr. McCain that I was coming to Cloud Ranch and to tell Becky I was leaving. Then I took the last of my money and I came west."

"Caitlin," Wade said in a hoarse tone. Emotion for this woman, and what she'd gone through, surged through him. *It's sympathy,* he told himself, *and concern, nothing more.* Yet as he studied her shaken, pale face, a trace of panic thrummed through him at the intensity of his own feelings.

She clutched at his hands. "I didn't know if he would come after me or not," she muttered. "I only knew I had to get my hands on enough money to take Becky away—for us to start over somewhere else, somewhere far from Dominic Trent."

"What about the authorities? Didn't you think of pressing charges?"

"It would have been useless. My word against his. And who was I? The impoverished daughter of a dead man steeped in scandal." Caitlin gave a bitter laugh. "Dominic Trent had power, connections, friends. And I had left him lying in a pool of blood. I knew I wouldn't stand a chance."

Wade knew she was right. He also knew that if Dominic Trent came within ten miles of Caitlin or Becky all the power, connections, and friends in the world wouldn't save the man's sorry hide.

"You don't have to worry about him anymore." He wanted to gather her in his arms and kiss away every dark memory she possessed. He wanted to tell her he'd keep her safe forever.

But there was no forever. Caitlin Summers would leave Cloud Ranch just as her mother had—as soon as her year was up.

The knowledge sent pain twisting through him like barbed wire. Fear followed. *Whoa, Barclay. You're getting way too involved.*

He released her hands and leaned back, studying her in the waning glow of the moon. "I'll take care of Dominic Trent if he's stupid enough to show up," he said coolly.

"He isn't your problem, Wade." Caitlin resisted the urge to touch his stubble-laden face. "He's mine. And I'll handle it." She took a deep breath, her heart breaking because in his eyes she no longer saw any warmth or softness—instead there was a wariness. He was closing her off, distancing himself from her—after she had poured out her heart. Something shattered deep inside her. Perhaps it was hope.

She wrapped the sheet around her and started to wriggle her way off the bed, intending to return to her own room, but Wade snatched her and pushed her back against the pillows before she had set both feet on the floor.

"Where do you think you're going?"

"To bed."

"You're in bed."

"I meant my own bed." She met his gaze quietly. "Don't think that because we . . . we did . . . *this* together . . . that you owe me anything. That you need to try to protect me from Dominic Tr—"

"Who said anything about *trying*?" he growled. "I damn well will protect you."

"Why?" Her lip trembled. "Because you made a stupid promise to Reese?"

"Hell, Caitlin—I gave him my word."

"And I am releasing you from it," Caitlin whispered. "From any obligation whatsoever." She swung her legs over the side of the bed, still clutching the sheet, but Wade promptly seized them and swung them back. Before she had time to think, he straddled her.

"Damn it, I *am* obligated," he said as her eyes widened and she tried to sit up. Wade pushed her down and held her there with his body. "Not only for Reese—for me. After tonight, well, I guess we're not enemies anymore, right? That makes us . . . friends. And I always stand by my friends."

Friends. They were friends.

She swallowed and spoke with as much composure as she could manage through the pain tearing through her. "I don't want any favors from you. And I don't need them. If there's one thing I've learned from everything that's happened, it's that I need to rely on myself. So when it comes to Dominic Trent—"

"You are the stubbornnest woman alive!" he exploded.

"Thank you, now kindly let me go!"

Wade gritted his teeth. "Sure thing. Go."

He rolled off her and Caitlin bounded up, but in her haste as she struggled to keep the sheet around her and to scamper from the bed, she lost her balance and fell against his chest. Wade caught her and his arms came around her instantly.

The next thing she knew she was flat on her back and he was leaning over her again, but this time his eyes held a glint of more than anger. A hot flutter began inside her as she read the warmth and desire there . . . and a trace of amusement. Suddenly she became aware that the sheet had slipped down, it was now twisted around her waist and her breasts were exposed, but for the strands of hair that drifted across them.

Wade was aware of them, too. Every part of him was aware, Caitlin realized as she wriggled beneath him.

"Wade—"

"You don't really want to leave, Caitlin, do you?" He leaned down closer to her and his lips brushed her eyelids. His smile seared her soul.

"What if . . . I say I do?" But her senses were already swimming. Her heart thudding. She could scarcely breathe as his lips skimmed a hot trail down her throat.

"Then I'd say we'd have to find out for sure."

"And . . ." Caitlin couldn't suppress a moan as he pressed a scorching kiss against the base of her throat. "How do we do that? You . . . mmmm . . . don't seem to believe me when I say . . ."

"Only one way to tell for sure." His eyes glinting into hers made Caitlin tremble with a desire that she was helpless to stem.

"What . . . way is that?" she whispered, fascinated as he brought his mouth up a scant inch from hers.

"A kiss, princess." Wade chuckled, the sound scraping from low and deep in his throat. "Remember—kisses don't lie."

Oh, how her breasts ached for his touch. Her entire body tingled, yearned. His mouth moved closer, closer.

Then, slowly, he slanted his lips to hers and she was a thousand candles bursting into flame. -

Caitlin forgot everything but this man. This moment. This kiss.

The night wrapped around them, and as her arms encircled his neck, the passion and the sweetness all began again . . .

Chapter 21

Drew Raleigh was in a foul temper.

Beside him, the young whore stirred and stretched her voluptuous body, naked beneath the damp sheets. She was stunning, eager, and pleasantly stupid, with her small face, full red lips, and raven-black hair, but he didn't want her again. They'd been at it all night and he still wasn't satisfied.

This was one time a good meal, a good smoke, and a lusty woman in the town brothel weren't going to solve the problem besetting him.

Maybe nothing would.

"Damn it all to hell."

He shoved himself off the bed and dressed briskly in the hazy glow of the moon that slanted in through the window.

The whore didn't do more than turn over, the sheets twisting around her legs as he let himself out of the gold-curtained room.

He needed to walk, to think. It was the middle of the night, the darkest hour, the time he did his best thinking.

Drew Raleigh, immaculate as always in his fine suit that never seemed to wrinkle, his expensive derby, a cigar stuck in the corner of his mouth, strode up Hope's main street.

The town was dead—dark and silent as a coffin six feet under. Up and down the street he strode, back and forth. All the while thinking about Cloud Ranch.

He had to find a way to get the Barclay boys and Caitlin Summers to sell. If he didn't, he might as well start walking straight out into those endless, merciless plains full of sagebrush, wolves, and coyotes and never come back. This impasse was putting his position with one of the most powerful business syndicates in the East in jeopardy—very serious jeopardy—and he stood to lose everything he'd spent a lifetime building—his reputation, his wealth, his prominence—and the respect with which the barons of Wall Street regarded him. His associates at E. M. Piedmont would spread the word of his failure and everything he'd achieved would go up in smoke.

If only he hadn't been so overconfident—if only he hadn't assured his syndicate partners that he'd hand them Cloud Ranch on a silver platter.

Now Edward Piedmont and the others wouldn't be satisfied with any other ranch. At the syndicate board meeting months ago, they'd selected only two cattle ranches big enough and successful enough to fit the bill, qualifying as precisely the type of property they'd been seeking.

Another syndicate had just beaten them to the Wallach Spread in Montana, and that had left Cloud Ranch. When they'd learned that the owner Reese Summers had recently died, they'd been certain that the property was vulnerable for acquisition. Drew had guaranteed them that he'd make the deal.

And if he didn't . . .

Piedmont would cut him loose quicker than a cowpoke cutting out a weak calf from the herd. And his reputation among those in the inner circle of movers and shakers wouldn't be worth a cow dropping.

He paused at the edge of town, hurled the butt of his cigar into the street, and stared up at the sky. "Who'd have thought it would be so damn complicated?" he muttered to the dark heavens.

Caitlin Summers couldn't sell her share. Wade Barclay and his brothers wouldn't sell theirs.

But Raleigh had made it his business to ask questions in town, one here, one there, until he found out the details of the will. He knew that it was Wade Barclay's vote that really mattered—if Wade wanted to sell out to the syndicate, he had the influence and control to make it possible for everyone else to do the same.

The problem was motivating Barclay to sell. The man didn't gamble much—and when he did, he didn't lose. He didn't go on drunken binges, he didn't have any enemies—only friends. The whole damn town respected him, wanted him to be the next president of their Cattlemen's Association. How could someone get to a man like that?

Think, damn it, Raleigh told himself angrily. *You know damn well that under the right circumstances, any man will sell, or give in, or turn tail and run. You just have to find the right circumstances—or create them,* he thought, his eyes glinting in the darkness.

He paced back toward town. Lost in thought, he didn't
see the shadowy figure seated on a wooden bench on the
porch of the Glory Hotel. He didn't know another soul
was awake on this seemingly deserted street until the
silken voice came at him out of the darkness.

"My dear Raleigh, what scheme are you up to now?"

"What the hell . . . !" He nearly jumped out of his skin,
and his hand lurched automatically toward the hideaway
pistol beneath his vest until he suddenly recognized both
the voice and the man.

"Trent! What the hell are you doing here? How long
have you been here?" Raleigh stared at the tall, powerful
figure in the shadows of the porch, his heart still
hammering.

"I'm here for the same reason you are, I expect. There's
something I want."

"Here—in Hope?"

Dominic Trent nodded. In the dimness, Raleigh could
see the gleam in those nearly colorless eyes, and the hair
on the back of his neck prickled. Out of all his acquain-
tances throughout New York, Philadelphia, Chicago—all
the cities where industry was thriving and where he had a
wide circle of associates—Dominic Trent of the Philadelphia Trents was the only man he knew who was more
ruthless than he himself.

Trent would ruin a man in business over a minor dis-
pute or some perceived insult—and when it came to
women, he was rumored to be utterly relentless in his pursuit and domination of those who caught his eye.

There had been stories . . .

But that didn't matter now. He certainly wasn't afraid
of Trent—they'd done business together with perfect

amicability on several occasions. He was merely stunned to find him here in this speck-on-a-map town.

He stepped up onto the porch. "Care for a cigar?"

"Don't mind if I do."

Moments later, they were both smoking, eyeing each other across the darkness. Trent lounged on the bench while Drew Raleigh leaned against the porch post, his mind racing.

"What is it that brings you here—that thing you 'want'? Is it business—or pleasure?" Raleigh asked at last.

"Most assuredly pleasure."

"I see." A woman then.

"I don't need to ask about you." Trent smiled through the darkness. "Having arrived in town only today, I spent an hour in the saloon this evening. In that short time, I learned that you've been sniffing around one of the larger cattle properties in the area."

"Cloud Ranch."

"So," Dominic Trent said softly, "you must have met the lady who recently inherited a portion of it."

"Of course. Caitlin Summers. Of Philadelphia." Raleigh suddenly straightened as things began to fall into place. "You were acquainted with her in Philadelphia, I presume?"

There was such a long silence that he wondered if Trent had heard him. He was about to repeat the question when the other man spoke again, his voice smooth as silk, but tinged with a nearly indiscernible note of menace.

"It seems to me that we perhaps could be of use to each other, Raleigh. There is something each of us wants quite badly—and the lady is at the center of both our desires."

"That may be true, but unfortunately what I want isn't in the lady's power to give." He spat disgustedly into the street. "I'm prepared to offer a veritable fortune for that damned ranch—but it's owned in large part by these Barclays—and the foreman of the place, Wade Barclay, is the only one who could convince everyone else to sell. Trouble is, there's no budging him."

"Come now." A tinge of contempt echoed through Trent's voice. "You know as well as I that everyone can be 'budged' as you say. It's only a matter of finding the proper leverage."

"Well, short of trying to burn him out or rustle him out of business—and they've already been fighting rustlers without any real damage as far as I can see—I'm at a loss. Barclay's a tough bastard—he doesn't give a damn about the money—he's attached to the damn land and nothing else, except maybe . . ."

"Yes?"

"His brothers, from what I hear. They're all close, even though the other two don't live hereabouts . . . but that's not what I was thinking."

Dominic Trent studied the glinting tip of his cigar. "Tell me, dear Raleigh."

"The girl—Caitlin Summers. I saw her with Barclay a few days ago in town—she'd had some bad news about her sister and it looked like . . ."

He took a deep breath. Trent hadn't moved, but suddenly it seemed to him that a feral smile twisted the man's lips. He peered again through the darkness and his neck prickled at the strange sheen of those colorless eyes. Perhaps it was only the odd light coming off the moon, or the late hour, or the smoke of the cigars, but he looked . . . almost eerie, as if he were demented.

"Go on."

"Well." Raleigh cleared his throat. "It struck me that he cared about her . . . more than in a casual way, if you know what I mean. And she about him. A few people in town have noticed and begun speculating about wedding bells," he added somewhat cautiously.

"Indeed." An ominous note had entered the soft voice.

"Of course I could be mistaken. You know how gossip thrives in a small town like this one . . ."

"Do you think Barclay cares enough about Miss Summers to provide some . . . leverage?" There was a banked excitement in the voice now. It was unnerving in a way, and yet, the words penetrated Drew Raleigh's uneasiness.

Leverage. Of course. This whole thing was about leverage. Barclay wouldn't sell for profit, for any reason Raleigh could discover—but if it was something involving the girl—if she *wanted* him to sell, or needed him to sell . . .

"I think our running into each other tonight is going to prove most fortuitous." Dominic Trent rose. At six feet four he was several inches taller than Drew Raleigh, but it was more than his height that made him so imposing. His features were aristocratic and chiseled, his hair pale brown, and he possessed a cold spirit that almost seemed to frost the air around him.

Raleigh felt eagerness surging through him. And for the first time in a while—hope. "So you think you have a way to help me then—and of course, in return, I'd be more than happy to help you."

That was an understatement. Whatever it took, he must

do. And would do. Either that or kiss his future with E. M. Piedmont good-bye.

"I think that you, my dear Raleigh, can provide me with the final and most important piece of the little puzzle I've been playing with for some time. The pièce de résistance."

Trent laughed suddenly, loudly, and the sound screeched through the silence of the night.

Drew Raleigh felt hope beat through him—hope that Trent had truly discerned a way to convince Wade Barclay to sell Cloud Ranch. He sensed that whatever Trent had in mind might be a bit unpleasant, but he'd dealt in unpleasantness before—when the outcome hadn't been nearly as crucial as it was now.

He held out his hand. "I'm certainly interested in whatever proposition you have in mind."

Dominic Trent shook his hand in a grip so strong as to be painful. He squeezed Raleigh's fingers relentlessly, until he saw the flash of pain in his eyes, then he let go.

"Of course you are interested." He gave a low laugh. "I'm going to give you the only chance you have to win at your little game. No guarantees, of course," he murmured. "But a chance. As for me . . ." His eyes glistened in the light of the moon as from somewhere in the distance came the sudden screech of a vulture.

"If things go well, your participation is going to make my own victory utterly complete. Satisfying, final, and perfectly, deliciously sweet."

Chapter 22

"Caitlin? *You're* sorting laundry?"

Becky giggled as she entered Caitlin's room, Dawg trotting at her heels. Caitlin gave a small laugh as she folded the last of the sheets and set them atop the pile of clean linens on her bed.

"It's true I haven't had much experience doing housework, but then *you'd* never washed dishes or slept in a hayloft until recently, either," she pointed out as her sister plopped down in a chair. Caitlin straightened the neat pile of linens atop her quilt, fresh from the clothesline out back. She hadn't wanted Francesca to find the bloodstained sheets so she'd volunteered to do the day's laundry, and had spent hours scrubbing them clean. And thinking about every moment she'd spent with Wade the night before.

"Our lives have certainly changed since Mama and Papa died, haven't they?"

Becky nodded, her brown eyes somber. "I miss them," the girl whispered.

Suddenly Caitlin heard a sniffle. "Oh, honey, I miss them, too," she murmured, hurrying to her sister's side.

"It's all right to cry, Becky." She hugged the girl tightly. "Go ahead."

"But you . . . never cry."

"That doesn't mean you can't."

She held the little girl as her tears flowed, but the sobs that accompanied them were gentle, heartfelt ones, not the wracking and inconsolable sobs that had torn through Becky when the awful news had first been received.

After a few moments, her thin shoulders stopped shaking, and Caitlin gave them a reassuring squeeze.

"Mama and Papa would be very proud of us, you know. We're sticking together, just like sisters should. And we're doing just fine."

"You think so?" Becky gave one last sniff.

"I'm positive." Caitlin smiled as she fetched a handkerchief from her drawer and dried her sister's tears. "What do you say we sneak down to the kitchen and see if we can steal a piece or two of Francesca's blueberry pie?"

"Really? Okay!" A wavery smile replaced the tears. "You know what, Caitlin? I sort of like some of the changes we've gone through. Like leaving school," she said, her eyes darkening. "I don't ever want to go back!"

"You won't have to."

"And I like living here on Cloud Ranch. Who would have ever thought I'd like living on a cattle ranch in Wyoming Territory?" Suddenly she burst into giggles, and in the sunlight, the freckles stood out on her small sweet face. "But I do. I love Dawg, and the wranglers are so funny, and the Morgensen twins are my best friends. And I want Miss Porter to be my teacher," she rushed on, "and

Wade is so nice and he makes me feel calm inside, you know? When I'm with him I feel like . . . like . . ." She pursed her lips, searching for words. "Like the world is safe again," she said slowly. "Like nothing could ever hurt me if he's around. Do you ever feel that way, Caity?"

Caitlin spoke softly. "Sometimes."

She turned away and returned to the pile of sheets on the bed, gathering them up in her arms.

"But you mustn't get too attached to things here," she forced herself to say. "I don't know for certain how long we're staying—"

"Do you mean because of Mr. Trent? We might have to run away again?" A note of panic throbbed through Becky's voice and Caitlin quickly shook her head and sent her sister a firm look.

"No. We're not running away from that man again—either one of us. If he comes here"—*which he probably will,* she thought grimly—"I'll deal with him. I'll make sure he doesn't bother us anymore, Becky. I promise."

"But . . . then . . . why can't we stay here? Your father left Cloud Ranch to you, didn't he? Don't you like it here?"

Caitlin hesitated. "I do," she said softly as slow wonder filled her. "Actually, I like it very much."

"Then why don't you want to stay?"

Because I like it too much. I like Wade too much. I've fallen in love with a man who's never said he loves me, a man who feels obligated to me. She knew Wade was attracted to her, that he wanted her in his bed—their fiery union last night proved that. And she knew that he did care about her. But love?

No. Wade felt responsible for her—hadn't he spent his

entire childhood being responsible for his brothers? It was ingrained in him to take care of those he considered his responsibility, and thanks to Reese, that select group now included her.

Instead of comforting her, the thought filled her with misery. She didn't want Wade to think of her as a responsibility, an obligation.

She wanted him to love her.

But he didn't. And she needed more than heat and desire, more than surface companionship, than friendship and duty.

She needed trust and caring that came from the soul. She needed the giving and sharing of love. Deep, everlasting, solid love, as real as the mountains, the sky, the glowing light of the moon.

She wouldn't ever settle for less and she wouldn't let Wade settle either.

"I have to stay at Cloud Ranch for a while," she said slowly, trying to sound matter-of-fact as Becky peered anxiously up at her. "Because of my father's will. But I'm not sure that it's the right place for us, Becky. I want to make sure we settle down where we'll both be happy—I promised you that, remember?"

"Why can't we be happy here?"

Dawg sprang up then and licked her face and the girl gave a squeal of laughter. "See, even Dawg wants us to stay!"

Caitlin went to the door with the armload of linens. "Let's see about that pie."

Later, as she washed up their plates, and watched through the window as Becky traipsed around the ranch with Dawg, she tried to sort out the myriad feelings enveloping her. It was increasingly difficult to always appear calm and cheerful for Becky when inside, turmoil churned through her. Wade had been gone when she'd awakened in his bed this morning, and she'd felt a shocking sense of loneliness without his arms around her.

She hadn't seen a glimpse of him since. And she had no idea how it would feel to face him this morning, considering everything that had happened between them last night. The very thought of it made her stomach clench.

If Wade had thought their first kiss a mistake, what must he think about last night?

Last night.

It was the biggest mistake I ever made, she thought in dismay, and yet, she wouldn't take back a moment of it if she had the chance. Those hours spent in Wade's arms, making love in his bed, had been the most joyful hours she'd ever known. But perhaps the most foolish as well.

How was it that he had the power to pierce through all of her defenses, all of her facades, and expose her heart's most fragile vulnerabilities? She'd thought she had grown strong, but her love for Wade left her weak.

A sound at the door made her jump and drop the sudsy plate she was holding. It shattered on the floor.

"Senorita, it is only me." Francesca's tone held a note of impatience. Shaking her head, she marched across the kitchen and picked up the broom.

"I'll do it, Francesca."

"No. You've done enough."

Caitlin knelt and began gathering up the larger shards of crockery. "I'm sorry about the plate, but you startled me—"

"This isn't about the plate, senorita. A plate is a plate—it can be replaced."

The housekeeper's color was heightened, her eyes flashed, and there was an edge to her voice. Caitlin slowly rose, setting the shards down upon the counter. "If you have something to say to me, Francesca, please go ahead," she said quietly.

For a moment, clutching the broom, Francesca merely stared at her. Then she shook her head. "Nada, senorita. There is nothing to say."

"I think there is." Taking a deep breath, Caitlin continued in an even tone. "From the moment I arrived, you've disliked me. You said something that first night about how long it took for me to get here."

The housekeeper met her gaze squarely. *"Sí."*

"Perhaps you never really wanted me to come here at all—you certainly don't seem pleased about it. I'm grateful that you've been so gracious to Becky, making her feel at home, but you've never made me feel at home here, Francesca."

The woman's lips clamped together. "This is Senor Wade's home, Senor Nick's, and Senor Clint's. They lived here, grew up here. You have no right—"

"My father wanted me here. That's why he left me a share of the ranch."

"He was a generous man. A good man. Maybe too good."

"He was more generous than I deserve, is that what you mean?" Suddenly Caitlin thought of all the letters that Reese had supposedly written to her—and of the ones she'd written to him, those he'd never received.

She gazed at the housekeeper, who had full run of this house and everything in it. Francesca, who was trusted and counted on, who was treated almost as one of the family by everyone at Cloud Ranch.

"Francesca, did you keep my letters?" The words burst from her suddenly. "The ones my father wrote to me? The ones I never received?"

"What?" The woman's eyes opened wide in surprise, then they grew dark with anger and an angry flush seeped across her olive skin. "I know nothing of any letters."

"Are you sure?" Caitlin stepped forward. "What about the letters I wrote to my father? Did you . . ." She took a deep breath and forced herself to voice the suspicions in her mind. "Did you intercept them? Someone must have. Perhaps you picked them up at the post office, and never gave them to him? Or did you take them from whoever brought them back from Hope and keep them to yourself so my father never knew that his daughter had written to him?"

"Dios, no! Why would I do such a thing?"

"That's what I'd like to know, Francesca—because someone did. Wade told me that my father wrote to me numerous times. I never received a single letter—not until he was dying. And I wrote to him, as well—my mother gave me the address—"

"Su madre." The woman snorted. "Maybe she gave you the wrong address—maybe she didn't want you to know Senor Reese. Didn't she leave and never come back? The poor senor, I never knew him before, I didn't come here until shortly before the *ninos* came. But others have told me, *su madre* . . . she might as well have shot the senor in

the heart. So maybe it wasn't enough for her that she didn't ever come back—she didn't want you to come back either—"

"Francesca, don't you dare speak about my mother that way." Caitlin drew herself up straight. "She never would have lied to me—or stolen my letters. She wanted a different life than the one Reese insisted on having here. But she wasn't evil and she didn't try to keep me from my father. You hated her, didn't you?" she added wonderingly. "Perhaps that's why you also hate me?"

Francesca reached for one of the shards from the plate Caitlin had dropped. Her hand clenched around it.

"After she left and took you with her, your father was like this—broken. When the little boys came to him and needed a home, it was as if he was somehow glued back together, pieces stuck in place, but still . . . never whole. Never just the way he was. *Sí*, he still had his dreams for Cloud Ranch—such dreams—they are what kept him alive, and also the little boys, who needed him—but you . . . you and your mother. So many nights, for year after year, I would go into that place where he did his work and see him holding that photograph, staring at it—as if he could make you real, his *hija*—as if he could make you return, love him . . ."

Her voice broke. She set the shard down and stared hard at Caitlin.

"Never would I do anything to keep you from him, senorita. If you would have written to him, or come to visit him during any of those years, I would have danced for joy. I would have kissed the ground in thankfulness. But you didn't come. Even when the senor lay dying in his bed, even then you did not come. He never saw you again. His heart . . ." Her dark eyes suddenly sparkled with tears. She shook her head.

It wasn't Francesca, Caitlin thought bleakly. *It's plain that she's telling the truth. Then who?*

Before she had time to ponder any alternatives, a firm rapping sounded at the front door.

Both women started. Caitlin hurried from the kitchen and down the hall to find Drew Raleigh smiling at her from the porch.

"Good day, Caitlin."

"Drew! I . . . didn't even hear you ride up." She glanced past him at the handsome gray gelding tethered to the corral post. Her head was still whirling with all that Francesca had said, but she forced herself to smile with as much cordiality as she could muster.

"Forgive me. Won't you come in?"

"Don't mind if I do, but don't worry, I won't stay long." He stepped into the cool spacious hall and followed her into the parlor. But when she offered refreshments, he shook his head.

"No, I only came to ask you a question, and of course, to see how your sister is faring—I heard in town that she was safely found."

"Yes, luckily Becky is fine, thank you." Her words were punctuated by a laughing shriek from outside and the sounds of Dawg barking. "She seems quite taken with life on a cattle ranch."

Caitlin slipped into a flowered chair and gestured for him to be seated on the sofa. But Drew didn't take a seat, instead he walked to the window and stared out, perhaps at Becky and Dawg, racing around the corrals, or perhaps at the wide rolling land surrounding Cloud Ranch itself. "Yes, she seems to have adjusted quite well, I can see that. And so, I think, have you."

He turned and studied her, sunlight gilding his sandy hair, his broad shoulders nearly blocking the entire view beyond the window. "You seem comfortable here. I mean, here in this house, and in town. I've watched you with people. You seem to fit wherever you go, Caitlin, whether you're chatting with that busybody Edna Weaver, or buying beans and flour in Hicks Mercantile. Or making small talk with that little mouse, Miss Dale."

Admiration shone in his eyes. "My grandmother used to say that a true lady can speak as comfortably with a stable boy as with a king." He laughed. "Or something to that effect. At any rate, you, my dear Caitlin, are very much a true lady."

"Such flattery," Caitlin answered lightly. "I'm sure I don't know what to say." She wondered where all this was leading. The next moment, she found out.

"It's not flattery, Caitlin, it's a well-deserved compliment—and the truth. And because I admire you so much, because I think you're every bit as lovely in this rough setting as in a flower-bedecked ballroom, I'd like to humbly ask your permission to escort you to the May Day dance at the Crooked T."

She sat perfectly still, trying to keep her mouth from dropping open. "How . . . kind," she managed to stammer after only an infinitesimal pause. "But . . . I . . ."

"Don't tell me you've already agreed to go with someone else," Drew said quickly.

"Well, no, but . . ."

"Excellent. Then it's settled." He beamed at her. "I'm

vastly relieved to hear that no one else has—uh—beat me to the draw, as they say in these parts."

"Sounds like you're looking for a gunfight, Raleigh."

Wade's voice brought Caitlin surging off the chair. Raleigh spun around. "Didn't know you were here, Barclay." His elegant brows rose. "Don't you have roping or something to do?"

Wade strode into the room, took off his hat, and tossed it on the table before the sofa. Sweat glistened on his face and there was mud on his boots. He looked every bit as dusty, sweaty, and hardworking in his plaid shirt, Levi's, spurs, and neckerchief as Drew Raleigh looked elegant in his dark suit and embroidered silk vest. "Can't say that I remember inviting you to my house. Reckon it must've slipped my mind."

"I came to see Caitlin."

"You don't say?" Wade glanced over at her. "You invite him?"

"No, but really, Wade, visitors are always welcome at Cloud Ranch." *Oh, Wade, why didn't you get here a few minutes sooner and save me from having to go to that stupid dance with him?* she thought silently, but aloud she said with a forced laugh, "He's merely joking, Drew. Please don't misunderstand and think he's being rude."

"Right. When I'm rude, Raleigh, there won't be a single doubt in your mind." Wade tugged the stopper from a whiskey decanter on the mantel and poured himself a drink. He downed it in one gulp, then returned to stand directly before Drew.

"You finished here?" It was more a statement than a question. "I'll walk you out."

"Wade." Caitlin bit her lip. "Perhaps Drew would like a

drink? Or some other refreshment?" she asked, torn between the long-instilled duty to be gracious and her wish to be rid of her unwanted guest. Bad enough that she had somehow gotten stuck agreeing to go to the dance with him—she only hoped he wouldn't tell Wade about it.

She'd already decided she'd better tell him herself. He disliked Drew Raleigh even more than she did and she knew he'd blow up when he heard.

"He doesn't look thirsty to me." Coolly, Wade eyed the other man. "Caitlin's busy."

"I am?"

"Yep." His glance touched her, flickering in one instant from her neatly upswept hair to her white shirtwaist and dark denim skirt. A muscle pulsed in his jaw, then he shifted his gaze to Raleigh, and almost imperceptibly it hardened.

"Caitlin needs to look over our ranch books. I seem to remember I could have made a subtraction error way back in January. Maybe even another one last June. Could be all of twenty cents involved. And you know how women are—they're not happy if they don't get a chance to point out every single one of a man's errors and shortcomings."

"Of which you seem to have many." But she was smiling at him as she said it. Drew Raleigh observed that smile, and saw the way the formidable foreman of Cloud Ranch grinned back at her. Satisfaction coursed through him.

Trent's plan just might work after all. He decided to further test the waters.

"Fine. Then I guess I'll be on my way. I've accomplished everything I set out to do here." He walked around Wade, took Caitlin's hand again, and gently held it. "I'm going to be the luckiest man at the dance."

Caitlin saw Wade's shoulders tense.

Drew Raleigh released her hand and gave Wade a blithe smile. "Miss Summers has agreed to allow me to escort her to the May Day dance."

"Is that so."

Raleigh regarded him with mock friendliness. "You going to the dance, Barclay?"

"Maybe. Maybe not."

"It's fast approaching—if you want to find yourself a lovely lady to accompany, you ought to decide quickly before all the pretty ones get taken."

For one horrible moment, Caitlin thought Wade was going to hit him. She recognized that cold, deadly glint in his eyes. But his voice was low, calm, and even.

"Thanks, Raleigh. I'll remember that."

"I'll walk you out, Drew," Caitlin said quickly.

To her chagrin, Wade followed them through the hall, onto the porch, and across the yard to the corral.

Jake Young was seated on a bench outside the barn, repairing his saddle. As Wade and Drew Raleigh eyed each other with barely concealed dislike, and Caitlin chattered away in the sun-dappled yard, he wiped the sweat from his brow and watched them.

Two of 'em, he thought helplessly. *Damm. She's got both Drew Raleigh and Wade sweet on her. Right along with every other cowpoke in town.* His heart sank. It was bad enough having seen the way she and Wade looked at each other that day in Hope. He'd tried to tell himself that it was only because they were both upset about her sister running away, but he had a terrible suspicion it was more than that. Hell, if he didn't get up the courage to tell Caitlin soon exactly how he felt about her, it might be too late.

Time after time when he saw her, drove with her into town, helped her with her shooting lessons, he'd wanted to tell her. He dreamed of reciting that poem to her—the one she had told him about that day out by Cougar Canyon.

"How do I love thee? Let me count the ways . . ."

He couldn't remember any more of it than that—but he had to. It'd be so much easier than trying to think of his own words. Because when she looked at him, he couldn't think at all. He could barely breathe.

When Raleigh had ridden off, both Caitlin and Wade returned to the house. *Wonder if he's already asked her to the dance,* Jake fretted, staring after them. *Or maybe that son-of-a-bitch easterner Raleigh did. Bet that's why he rode out here today.* His ripped saddle lay forgotten on the bench.

I waited too long.

Despair engulfed him as the sun beat down. But Jake's feelings were too strong. He wasn't about to give up yet.

In the house, Caitlin faced Wade in the parlor.

The last time she'd seen him alone, she'd been lying in his arms. Dawn was glowing outside the window, and her lips were warm from his kiss.

But now he looked anything but loving, anything but tender. His lean, handsome face was set and grim, his thumbs hooked into his gunbelt. Stubble shadowed his hard jaw, and his eyes gleamed clear and cool as slate.

"You really hankering to go to the dance with that son of a bitch?"

"Wade—"

"Tell me. Yes or no."

"It isn't that simple. He invited me. Properly, politely. I could hardly—"

"The hell you couldn't."

She fought to keep her temper. Did he think that just because she'd slept with him—heaven help her—he could dictate what she did, with whom? That he just naturally expected she'd have gone to the dance with him—whether he bothered to ask her or not?

"I hadn't received any other invitations," she said quietly. "Under the circumstances, what was I supposed to—"

"Suit yourself. You want to go with him, that's up to you." Wade strode to the window and then paced back. "The two of you'll have the whole night to cook up some scheme to convince me to let you leave Cloud Ranch and go Lord knows where. And to help Raleigh get his grubby hands on some share of this place he can use as a wedge against Reese's entire will."

"You know I would never do that!" Caitlin admitted there was a time when she would have done anything—*anything* to leave this ranch—but somehow things had changed. She had changed. Didn't Wade see that? She pressed her hands to her throat. Nothing was clear anymore—everything in her life was confused, and far too complicated. Including her feelings for this man who was gazing at her so harshly, his face as grim and closed as the day they'd first met in Hope.

"Reckon I'll wash up before supper," Wade growled. "Come to think of it"—he spun around, snatched his hat off the table, and plunked it upon his head—"think I'll have supper in town. Been a long time since I had a night out."

"A night out?" Her heart sinking, Caitlin watched him stalk toward the door. "What do you mean?"

"Means I'm going to have myself some fun. Don't expect me back before morning."

"You needn't come back until hell freezes over as far as I'm concerned!" Furious, Caitlin glanced around for something to throw but by the time she grabbed up the embroidered pillow from the sofa, Wade was gone. When she heard the thunder of hoofbeats and caught sight of him spurring the roan toward Hope, she forgot about throwing the pillow and hugged it to her chest.

"That went well, didn't it?" she muttered to herself. She supposed she ought to be flattered that Wade seemed jealous about her going to the dance with Drew, but she decided it had more to do with his dislike—and distrust— of the man than it had to do with her.

Well, what did you expect? That he'd get down on bended knee, professing his love? You don't believe in love, remember? And obviously, neither does Wade.

"See if I care, Wade Barclay," she muttered aloud. But misery rolled through her in waves as she sank down on the sofa and tried not to think about exactly what kind of "fun" Wade was looking to have himself in town.

Chapter 23

Jake Young waited on the front porch of the Porter ranch, hat in hand.

"Luanne, dear, there's a gentleman here to see you," Mrs. Porter called in a singsong tone and a moment later Luanne emerged from the small sewing parlor, hope lighting her face as she smoothed her gingham skirt.

"Good evening, Wa . . . oh, *Jake*!" She flushed, and the hope died out of her eyes. A polite smile settled upon her lips and she faltered only briefly before coming smoothly forward.

"How nice to see you. Won't you come in?"

Jake shifted from one booted foot to the other. "Sorry, to intrude, Mrs. Porter—Miss Porter, but I need to speak to you about something. Miss Porter, I mean. It's . . . it's important," he added, and there was such desperation in the look he shot Luanne that she forgot her disappointment that Wade hadn't come to call and invited the wrangler into the parlor.

Curiosity stirred in her as she watched Jake slouch

inside. His broad, clean-shaven face was flushed the color of the poppies Aunt Amelia had arranged in a vase over the fireplace, and he kept clearing his throat. Behind him, Amelia Porter discreetly closed the parlor door.

"Won't you have a seat, Jake." Luanne indicated a spot beside her on the sofa. "What's this all about? Is something wrong?"

"No, ma'am. Well, yes, ma'am. I mean . . ."

With a schoolteacher's patience, Luanne smiled and waited.

"There's this problem I have."

Silence. "Yes?" she prodded after a moment more of throat clearing.

"It has to do with a lady. Er, actually a poem. And a letter." Jake's flush deepened. "I'm not too good at explaining things," he said apologetically.

"Of course I'll try to help you, but I confess I don't see what it is you need from me." It was rather touching to see how earnest and worked up he was. He had the handsome face, height, and muscularity of a grown man—and he must be at least twenty-two years old, the same age as she—but he was almost as awkward right now as the young boys she taught at school. Sympathy flooded her.

Whenever she'd seen Jake before, he'd been doing ranch work or buying supplies in town—and she'd never paid much attention. Now that she thought about it, he'd always seemed quiet, which struck her as unusual in such a good-looking man. He was someone she'd expect always to be surrounded by women vying for his attentions. Luanne had never really conversed with him, except to nod hello.

Jake met her gaze earnestly. "Reckon I should just start

from the beginning. That's what my ma always told me to do."

"It's good advice."

"Yes, ma'am." He swallowed. "You see, it's like this. There's this lady I'd like to get to know better—to court, I reckon you'd say . . ." Jake wiped sweat from his brow. "But there might be this other feller she's interested in." Remembering how Caitlin had clung to Wade that day in town, Jake scowled. "Matter of fact, I *know* there's this other feller she's interested in. But I don't give up easy, especially when I really care about something—or someone—which in this case, I do . . ."

As his voice trailed off, Luanne's smile faded. She suddenly felt she knew exactly to which "lady" Jake was referring. And she vividly recalled that day in town when she and Jake had both been looking on as Wade Barclay held and comforted Caitlin Summers. She herself well recalled the expression in Wade's eyes when he'd tried to reassure Caitlin about her sister.

Luanne hadn't been able to forget it. Because no man, Wade Barclay included, had ever looked at her in just that way.

"You're talking about Caitlin Summers, aren't you, Jake?" she asked softly. "And Wade Barclay."

Surprise flashed across his face, then he grinned. "Well, you're a schoolteacher, so I reckon it doesn't surprise me that you're smart."

Despite her heartache, a laugh broke from her. "What does this have to do with me?"

"Well, I've been wanting to tell Caitlin how I feel about her." He blushed furiously. "Maybe she won't care and she'll tell me to go jump in the stream—but I doubt it, 'cuz she's too nice for that. And if I don't take a chance and let her know, she just might go ahead and get hitched to Wade or someone else. I've been meaning to ask her to the May Day dance for weeks, but I couldn't get up the nerve and then this afternoon, Drew Raleigh rides up and asks her first. So now, she's going with him!"

"I see." Luanne wondered bleakly how Wade felt about that. This entire conversation was painful. She realized in town that day that she had most likely lost Wade. It was clear from the way he held Caitlin and looked at her that his feelings for the co-owner of Cloud Ranch were far deeper than they'd ever been for her. And added to the fact that he hadn't come around much since Caitlin arrived— and not at all since the day in Hope that Becky turned up missing—Luanne had come to the conclusion that her former suitor and she were not destined to walk down the aisle after all.

Now it seemed that Caitlin Summers, however, had not one suitor, but three. All pining for her. *Too bad I like her so much.* It would be much easier if she could despise the blond girl. But she'd found Caitlin to be a warm, kind-hearted person beneath that cool facade she wore. She was loving and devoted to her sister. It wasn't her fault that half the eligible men in Hope were throwing themselves at her feet.

She took a deep breath. "I'm sorry you didn't get to ask Caitlin to the dance, Jake, but I'm afraid I still don't see what this has to do with me."

"The trouble is, I get all jittery around her when I talk to her—I can't think of what I want to say. The words just get all tangled up in my mind. So I thought about writing her a letter," he rushed on, his keen brown eyes alight.

"Telling her how I feel. You know, asking permission to court her. Think that would work, Miss Porter?"

"Why, yes, that's an excellent idea." Luanne found herself nodding. "It *is* often easier to express one's thoughts in writing. And you can perfect exactly what you wish to say so that there are no mistakes or misunderstandings."

"Right. That's what I thought," Jake said, beaming.

"So . . ." Luanne studied him bemusedly. "I applaud your initiative, Jake," she continued, "but what does this have to do with me?"

He leaned toward her. "I need you to write the letter. And to put the poem in it."

"Poem?"

"Oh, I forgot about that part." He grinned again, suddenly so excited by her approval of his plan that he poured out the rest in its entirety. "She recited a poem to me once—real pretty it was too. And I want to put it in the letter and tell her that's how I feel about her—it's exactly how I feel. Confounds me that the lady who wrote it—"

"The poet, you mean."

"Yep, the poet. She knew just how I feel. Imagine something like that."

"What's the name of the poem?"

"All I know is that it begins like this: 'How do I love thee? Let me count the ways.'"

"Elizabeth Barrett Browning!" Luanne jumped up. "Just a moment, I have that very poem in a book in my room."

She slipped out before he could say anything and he could hear her light steps across the hall. Jake wiped perspiration from his face. Good thing Miss Porter was so nice. He was leery of that stiff, pale Miss Ellis who taught school for the children in Hope. He'd never have asked her for help. But there was something friendly and warm about Miss Porter.

She was pretty too. Not as dazzlingly beautiful as Caitlin Summers, but definitely easy on the eyes. Comfortable like. He didn't feel so jittery around her like he did around Miss Summers.

He was daydreaming about Caitlin's reaction when she read his letter, the way her eyes would sparkle and the happy smile that would wreathe her face, when Luanne fairly skipped back into the parlor. She settled on the sofa beside him and quickly thumbed through the book.

"Yes, here it is."

Jake stared where she pointed. His skin had turned red again. He nodded as he gazed at the words running across the page. "Uh-huh."

"Would you like to copy it? There's writing paper over there on the desk—"

"Uh, no, ma'am, I was hoping you'd copy it for me. I could tell you what I want the letter to say and you could write it all down and add that there poem—"

"But, Jake, don't you think it would be better if the letter was written in your own hand? It would be more personal."

"Yeah, well . . ."

He surged to his feet suddenly, stalked across the room to the window, then spun about and stared at her, a muscle working in his jaw. "I don't reckon I want to do that. I'm asking you to do it, ma'am."

"Please call me Luanne. 'Ma'am' makes me feel so old

and stuffy." Tilting her head to one side, she studied him, baffled yet intrigued. He looked so uneasy. Why didn't he want to write the letter himself?

"Never mind. If you don't want to help me, I understand," Jake said stiffly. He strode toward her, frowning. "You're busy and you probably don't have time—"

"Jake." Luanne rose as he came to a halt before her. The top of her head only reached his shoulder, but she met his gaze squarely. "You don't know how to write, do you?" she said softly.

From the night outside came the whistle of the wind, the sigh of the pine trees. Inside the lamplit parlor, Jake Young swallowed hard.

"I'll bet you don't know how to read either, do you, Jake? Can you read this poem?"

He hesitated, then shook his head.

Without thinking, Luanne laid her hand on his arm. "It's nothing to be embarrassed about. There are many people who can't read or—"

"I was the oldest of seven kids on our farm—and my pa said he couldn't afford for me to waste my time in school. My sisters went, and later my little brothers, but I had to help my pa out. And there never seemed to be time for any lessons at home—"

"I understand, Jake," Luanne interrupted. "It's all right."

"It is?" Staring into her soft golden-brown eyes, Jake saw no trace of amusement or pity or scorn—only that nice warmth he'd noticed before, and a sweet, quiet sympathy that made the tension in his neck relax. Hope surged through him. "Then . . . you'll write it for me? Miss Porter, I can't thank you enough!"

"It's Luanne," she corrected him again. And gave her head a tiny shake that sent her gingery-red curls dancing. "But no, I won't write the letter for you, Jake. That wouldn't answer at all. I'll do something even better."

She smiled up at him. "I'll teach you how to read this poem—and how to write that letter yourself."

"Wade, honey." Tessie giggled. "Don't you think you've had enough?"

Seated at a corner table in the Silver Star Saloon, Wade ignored the brassy-haired saloon girl, poured himself another glass of red-eye from the bottle at his elbow, and downed it in one deep swig.

"Aw, now. What's wrong, honey? You can tell me." With practiced ease, Tessie slipped onto his lap as she had a hundred times in the past. She stretched her sleek, perfumed arms around his neck and licked his ear. "Tell Tessie all about it. You never drink like this unless something's real bad-wrong somewhere. Like the night after Reese died—"

"Leave it alone, Tessie."

"Aw, honey, that's not really what you want."

No, Wade thought as she began to nibble on his ear. He wanted a fight. A real down-and-dirty fistfight, with broken windows, smashed mirrors, crashing chairs. But glancing around the saloon tonight, he knew he wasn't going to get his wish. Wesley Beadle was dealing faro to a couple of spindly-legged old miners, and one or two ranch hands he knew were playing poker and minding their own business, and there was no one else in the damned place who looked like they'd put up much of a fight.

He sighed and reached for the bottle again.

Something had to help him forget about Caitlin.

"Like to put my fist through his face," he muttered as whiskey splashed into the glass.

"Who, sugar?"

"Drew Raleigh."

"Him? Now why would you let a fancy eastern green-horn like him get you all riled up? That's not like you, Wade honey."

"You seen Raleigh tonight?" he asked over the lip of the glass.

Tessie shook her head. "But I've got an idea." A smile curved her thin painted lips. "Come on upstairs and I'll make you forget about Drew Raleigh—and whatever else ails you. It's been a long time for you and me, honey. Too long."

Deliberately, he focused his gaze on her. Tessie was pretty all right—with her brassy yellow curls and big blue eyes. And her figure was nothing to sneeze at, he thought, studying the way the low-cut purple and green gown with lace-edged flounces clung to her curves. Always before, her voluptuousness and the pretty red curve of her mouth had ignited hot desire in him—but not this time.

This time he felt only emptiness.

"Come on, honey, what are you waiting for?" She gave a husky laugh.

What was he waiting for?

A vision of a slender angel with flushed cheeks and golden hair bright against his pillow invaded his thoughts.

"Wade, honey? Come on—"

"Nope. Can't do this, Tessie. Sorry."

"What do you mean?" Her smile was seductive. "We're just getting started."

"You're wrong about that." He shook his head, and pushed back his chair, easing her to the floor. "No hard feelings, Tessie, but we're finished. I just remembered someplace I have to be."

"It's that Summers girl, isn't it?" Tessie sighed. "You think she's prettier than me? You like her more than me? Or is it just that she's classier than me?"

"This doesn't have anything to do with you, Tessie. Reckon I never should have come up here in the first place. Reese taught me when I was a boy that you can't run away from your problems."

He glanced at the whiskey bottle, and then at the girl. Both were means of escape. He knew as well as he knew every inch of Silver Valley that neither of them would work.

And in the meantime, he'd left Caitlin alone in that ranch house with only Francesca and Becky.

What if that bastard Dominic Trent chose tonight to show up?

A knot of panic coiled through him. He strode from the saloon without a backward glance, ignoring Tessie's entreaties. The door slammed behind him.

Sprinting toward his horse, Wade cursed himself for a fool.

The cool air hitting him as he rode like hellfire for Cloud Ranch drove the last of the whiskey from his brain. As he approached the ranch beneath a low yellow moon, his fear intensified. What if she was hurt? Or . . . gone? What if Trent had come while he was away and—

He bolted inside and up the darkened stairs. Her door wasn't locked. Shoving it open, he stood in the doorway and stared.

Caitlin lay asleep in her bed. Unconsciously sensuous, peaceful, beautiful. Her golden curls splashed across the pillow, radiant in the moonlight that shone through the open window. The sheet covered her body, but he saw the lace of the lavender nightgown that rose to just beneath the base of her smooth, creamy throat.

She was safe.

And the sight of her in that bed shook him to his very core.

This must have been how Reese felt about Lydia, he thought, and all of his desperation rushed back. *I swore I'd never feel this way. If she leaves here—when she leaves here—*

He wanted with all his heart to go to her, cradle her in his arms, waken her with kisses. To spend the night in that bed and show her how much he wanted her, needed her. To watch the sunrise beside her, to hold her close as night melted away to dawn.

Instead, he closed the door and stalked down the hall. He spent the rest of the night in his own darkened, empty room.

Alone.

Chapter 24

"How many dances have you gone to, Caitlin?"

Seated on her sister's bed, wearing a brand-new pink and white muslin gown, Becky's eyes shone. "At least ten, right?" she asked, drawing her hairbrush through her hair.

"Yes, of course. Probably more." Caitlin slid her rose silk gown over her head and past her shoulders, then let it flounce down past her hips. Frowning, she shook out the skirt and turned halfway to study herself in the mirror.

"If you've gone to so many, why are you so nervous about this one?" Becky demanded. "You've changed your dress three times!"

So it was that obvious, was it? Caitlin threw Becky a dismayed glance. If Becky could see her anxiety, so would everyone else. Including Drew Raleigh. Including Wade.

Stop being so silly, she scolded herself. *Do you really think that if you look your very best tonight, if you smile and dance and charm the whole damn town, Wade Barclay's going to decide he truly loves you?*

For Becky's sake, she tried to smile. "I just want to look nice since this is my first dance in Wyoming."

"It's mine, too. But I'm not a bit nervous," Becky marveled. She tossed her hairbrush onto the coverlet and leapt up off the bed. Coming to stand beside Caitlin at the mirror, she did a small pirouette.

"I do love my dress." Her tone was awed as she watched the long skirt billow gracefully. "It's the most beautiful dress in the world—besides yours," she added generously, slipping her hand into Caitlin's. "Wasn't it wonderful of Wade to buy it for me?"

"Yes, it was." Unbeknown to Caitlin, Wade had taken Becky into town one day and bought her not only a new dress for the dance, but several ready-made Sunday dresses from Hicks Mercantile. He left the girl with Nell Hicks to select fabric and ribbons and patterns to supplement her new wardrobe, since she'd arrived in Wyoming with little more than the clothes on her back, and the few items she'd stuffed into her satchel. When Caitlin later offered to repay him from her next month's stipend, Wade shrugged.

"Think you'll be around long enough to collect that stipend?" he asked, his tone casual.

"It looks that way. After all, now I'm obligated to repay this debt—"

"You don't owe me anything, Caitlin." Wade glowered at her. "Understand? Don't stick around just so you can pay me back. If you stay, do it because you want to. No other reason."

No other reason. He stalked off before she could reply, but his words echoed like death bells in her ears. *No other reason.*

If he told her he loved her, that would be a reason to stay. But he hadn't. He wouldn't. He didn't.

Becky touched the soft silk of Caitlin's skirt. "I want a dress just like this one when I'm a grown-up lady. Can I have one?" she asked wistfully.

"Of course, dearest." She smiled down at the slight, brown-haired girl who was still so innocent and hopeful, despite all that she'd been through. Becky was still very much a young girl, but in a matter of months, perhaps a year or two, she would be teetering on the brink of womanhood. Blossoming and changing. Caitlin wanted so much to protect her from disappointment and pain. She never wanted Becky to go through what she had. Of course she couldn't protect her from all of the pain life might have to offer, but she could at least make sure Becky had a safe, solid home, surrounded by people who cared for her. And that she wouldn't be left alone and vulnerable to lies or betrayal—or to a man who would stop at nothing to possess and control her.

But a man who would fill her with desire, with wild hope when she thought hope was dead, with love, when she thought her heart had turned to stone, a man like that? Only her own inner strength could protect her.

And at that moment, Caitlin felt she had as much inner strength as a spoonful of jelly. She missed Wade with all of her soul these past days when he kept himself distant from her.

Dawg's furious barking and the sound of horses' hooves broke into her thoughts. Becky darted to the window and parted the curtains.

"Mr. Raleigh is here!"

"He's early." Caitlin's stomach clenched. With all her

heart she wished she were going to this dance with Wade, that things between them were different. But they weren't. Yet a part of her hoped that Wade would dance with her tonight—that something magical would happen between them . . .

Magical?

She wasn't a fairy-tale princess and he wasn't her prince.

Magic—love—all that was nothing more than hogwash.

She snatched up her hairbrush and began dragging it through her hair. "Tell Mr. Raleigh I'll be down shortly."

"All right." Becky started to dash toward the door, then halted and slowed her steps, walking sedately. At the door, she turned and spoke almost shyly. "Caity? I wish you were going to the dance with Wade."

Caitlin's hand froze with the brush in midair. "Why, dearest?"

Becky shrugged. "Because I *like* Wade. A lot. And," she said wistfully, "if you were going with him, then we could all drive to the dance together. Don't *you* like Wade?"

"He's very nice."

"Then why didn't you want to go to the dance with him?"

"He didn't ask me."

"I bet he wanted to," Becky declared. "Maybe you should have asked him."

"Becky!" In spite of herself, Caitlin couldn't help but laugh. "Mr. Raleigh is waiting," she reminded her sister. "I have to get started on pinning up my hair."

Caitlin's hands were so clammy she could barely secure

the pins in her hastily arranged coiffure. And by the time she seized her reticule and tossed her black satin shawl around her shoulders, she was in such a state she had to keep reminding herself that this was only a dance, she'd been to dozens of them before, and she didn't care a whit if Wade Barclay asked her to stand up with him or not.

At the sound of her approach, Becky, Wade, and Drew Raleigh all turned and gazed up the wide staircase.

"Oh, Caity, you look beautiful," Becky breathed.

"That she does." Drew Raleigh's smile was wide, and his hazel eyes glinted as she swept gracefully down the steps, one hand resting lightly upon the carved banister.

Wade watched her descent in silence, a muscle clenched in his jaw.

"Please forgive me for keeping you waiting," she apologized to Drew as he took her hand, raised it to his lips, and kissed it.

"She was pinning up her hair," Becky explained, and Drew Raleigh threw back his head and laughed.

Glancing swiftly at Wade, Caitlin saw that he was not laughing. His gaze swept over the low-cut silk gown of pale rose that hugged her curves, then shifted to the delicate amethyst necklace that drew attention to her slim white throat, and then to her face—her *mouth,* she realized, blushing, and then finally to the elaborate chignon of dangling curls she'd arranged. And she knew he was thinking he'd like to take out each of the pins and watch the curls glide down.

"Sh-shall we go?" To her consternation, her voice was unsteady. She didn't want to believe it had anything to do with the way Wade was staring at her, like a hawk watches a mouse. Or with the fact that he looked so devastatingly handsome in his black shirt, black pants, and string tie, his dark hair neatly combed, his lean, bronzed face clean-shaven. She wanted more than anything to tuck her hand in his and tell him how handsome he looked, to flirt with him until he promised to dance with her, but Drew Raleigh was her date and if she knew nothing else, Caitlin Summers knew how to observe the proprieties.

So she pasted a smile on her face as Drew took her arm. She looked back and blew a kiss at Becky, promising to see her at the dance.

"I'll see you there, too," she told Wade lightly as Drew led her to the door.

"Count on it." She felt his gaze burning into her spine as she and Drew left the house and went out into the night.

The Crooked T ranch house was alive with lights and fiddle music. Colored lanterns adorned the large parlor that was so crowded with gaily attired men and women that she and Drew had to squeeze their way through.

"Now, don't you look lovely?" Edna Weaver appeared at Caitlin's side as if by magic. Right beside her was Winnifred Dale and Alice Tyler, hostess of the May Day dance.

"Caitlin, Drew—welcome!" Alice's smile included both of them.

"Quite a crush, Mrs. Tyler." Drew kissed her hand. "I haven't seen this many people together in a room since I left New York."

Alice laughed. "There are so many people here I always worry I won't get a chance to greet everyone! Speaking of which, there are my dear friends, Maura and Quinn Lassiter. Please excuse me a moment."

As Alice plunged into the throng, Winnifred turned to Caitlin. "Isn't your little sister coming tonight?"

"Oh, yes, Becky's on her way. She's coming with Wade."

"Is she now?" Edna pursed her lips thoughtfully, her gaze flicking back and forth between Caitlin and Drew. In the next instant, Alice's husband, Jim, pulled Drew away into a circle of men discussing railroads and the stock market.

Edna's fingers smoothed the lace collar of her bottle-green dress. "Usually Wade's date for this particular dance is a bit *older,* if you know what I mean," she said with a chuckle. "Half the town's been wondering why he didn't ask Luanne Porter. No more'n a month ago folks thought those two were halfway to bein' hitched. But something must have changed, because *she* came tonight with Jake Young."

"Oh?" Glancing in the direction of Edna's keen gaze, Caitlin saw Luanne in a corner of the parlor with Jake. They were deep in earnest conversation.

"They make a fine-looking couple," she murmured. But she wondered to herself why Wade hadn't invited Luanne. Or perhaps he did, she thought, her heart constricting. Perhaps Jake had merely asked first.

"Indeed they do. And so do you and Drew." Edna smiled. "But I'd sure like to see Wade find himself some sweet girl, fall madly in love, and settle down."

"So would I." Winnifred peeped hopefully at Caitlin.

Caitlin lifted her chin. "They say marriage isn't for everyone. And it's my guess it isn't for Wade Barclay. I think Wade Barclay is too ornery and too . . . too arrogant for marriage."

"Wade? Ornery? And arrogant? Heavens, he's the most easygoing, levelheaded, straight-thinking man I know!" Edna glanced again over to where Luanne was still deep in conversation with Jake. "He's going to make some woman a fine husband. And a handsome one," she added, her deep-set eyes twinkling. "For a while I truly thought he was sweet on Luanne, but I guess he wasn't quite sweet enough on her. Or else he's just gun-shy about marriage."

She winked at Winnifred, who took up the thread of the conversation. "Now, we don't mean to meddle, Caitlin dear, but some folks in town have remarked on how nice and kind of *fitting* it would be, if Reese's daughter and the young man he raised as his own son were to find their way to—"

"Winnifred!" Caitlin stared at her as hot color rushed into her cheeks and she felt sure they were every bit as rosy as her gown. "I don't know how you or anyone could concoct such a ludicrous notion. I can tell you right now there is as much chance of that happening as there is of the sun coming out at the stroke of midnight!"

"Really? Hmmm." Edna regarded her appraisingly. "You *sound* certain enough, honey, but—"

"Trust me," Caitlin managed to say with only a slight quaver in her voice. "Wade Barclay is the last man on earth I would ever—"

She broke off because at that moment Wade Barclay appeared in the parlor doorway, filling it with his tall frame. Becky's small hand was clasped in his big one.

Caitlin swallowed. Every other man in the room seemed to fade. Wade, all in black but for his silver belt buckle, stood out from the crowd. He filled her vision, filled her heart. She swallowed as his keen blue glance circled the room, sifting through the throng, and coming to rest at last upon her.

As their gazes locked, she heard Edna's voice, speaking dryly, as if from a great distance.

"Well, now, honey, what was that you were saying?"

But before she could answer, Caitlin felt a hand close around her arm. "Caitlin, my dear, I apologize for abandoning you. Would you care to dance?"

And then Drew Raleigh was leading her toward the dance floor. A waltz had begun, and he took her in his arms.

She saw Winnifred and Edna staring after her and could have sworn they looked mad enough to stamp their feet.

Meddling busybodies. Too bad she was so fond of them or she'd give them a piece of her mind.

Drew Raleigh was speaking to her, smiling at her, and waltzing her across the floor, but her thoughts were centered on the tall man clad all in black whose eyes met hers once more across the room.

Chapter 25

As Caitlin watched, Becky dashed toward the kitchen with the Morgensen twins, and then Wade shot her one last glance and turned away. With Drew expertly guiding her across the dance floor, she could only suffer in silence as Wade approached a tall brunette in yellow gingham.

"Drew." She gave him her most dazzling smile. "Isn't this a glorious night?"

"It is now." He drew her closer. His handsome smile held open admiration.

"This is my first dance in Wyoming," she chattered.

"And with any luck, my dear, it will be your last—and mine."

"What do you mean? Everything is lovely."

"Lovely for a small two-buggy town on the fringe of the prairie. But come now, Caitlin, you can't think it begins to compare with the grand parties you attended in Philadelphia."

"Well, no, not exactly, but . . ." Caitlin glanced around

at the festive room, the colorfully garbed people—a surprising number of whom she knew. And liked. It struck her suddenly that she felt at home here—she'd grown accustomed to the warm bluntness of Edna, to Winnifred's shy, sweet face, to the hearty food, good-humored hospitality, to people saying what they meant and doing their best to be kind and neighborly to others—from the most prosperous bankers and ranchers and businessmen down to the most struggling ranchers and farmers tilling their bit of land. She wasn't quite sure how it had happened, but Hope—and Silver Valley—had found a place in her heart.

And she resented Drew's attitude toward them every bit as much as she resented the possessive way he was holding her, pressing her so close against him she could feel the hardness of his body—his entire body.

"Drew—please, I can't breathe." She pulled back.

"Sorry, Caitlin, but you do have an effect on a man." With a low laugh, he loosened his hold as the music played on.

"This little corner of the world is quaint," he continued, "and the scenery's just fine, but I'll hardly miss it when I return east. Don't tell me you will?"

"I don't know. I haven't thought much lately about returning east."

"I find that quite surprising. It seems to me you most belong in a lovely drawing room—bedecked in jewels and satins, with servants at your beck and call, a silver tea service before you—and lobster patties and champagne to dine upon. Instead of . . . what is it that Mrs. Tyler and her friends are preparing to serve us? Fried chicken, barbecued slabs of steak, and corn on the cob?"

Caitlin's temper flared but she bit back the angry retort

as she saw Wade glance over at her. He and the brunette spun past in a blur. With a heavy heart, she forced her smile back into place.

"Actually, Drew, thank you for reminding me. I really should see if there's anything I can do to help Alice in the kitchen—"

Drew's grip on her tightened again. She nearly winced as he shook his head. "That can wait, can't it? We're in the middle of a dance. I wouldn't think of parting with you—yet."

"This is never going to work. I'm too slow, too stupid, and by the time I'm able to write the damned letter, Caitlin will be married to either Wade or Drew Raleigh with a bun in the oven!"

Jake scowled and slouched against the wall as Caitlin and Drew circled the dance floor amid a rainbow of other dancers.

Beside him, Luanne gave him a poke in the ribs. "Jake Young, you stop that! You're not slow and you're not stupid. Learning takes time. I think you're doing just fine— you improve with each lesson. But if you're going to act like a quitter, then I just can't help you! Look at me. Wade hasn't even come over to say hello to me tonight." For the first time her voice faltered. "But I'm not going to stand here and scowl at the world. I'm going to enjoy myself— with or without you."

Jake straightened and peered at her guiltily. "Sorry about Wade. But if you're not upset that he didn't ask you to the dance or come over to say howdy to you—maybe you weren't as sweet on him as you thought you were."

"Well, for your information, I thought I was—at the time. But the funny thing is, I don't miss seeing him as much as I expected." Luanne smoothed her skirt. "He did pay me a visit the other night, you know. Right after your lesson, not ten minutes after you left."

"He did? What'd he say?"

She was watching the dancers, her gaze following Wade and Sally Hanks, the brunette in gingham. "He told me he was glad we were friends. That if I ever needed anything, I could count on him."

"Well, that sounds like something!" Jake exclaimed. "Maybe he's through with Caitlin—or she's through with him—"

"No." Luanne shook her head. Her curls swayed forward across her lightly freckled cheeks. "It was the way he said it, Jake. He was letting me know that we weren't ever going to be any more than friends. He did it kindly, and very gently. He didn't want me having any . . . any false hopes."

"Well." Jake considered this. "You're sure that's what he meant?"

"I'm positive." Her smile was wan. "A girl knows when a man isn't interested in her . . . in any special way."

She flicked him a quick glance, then looked away. "Maybe you should forget about writing that letter and just ask Caitlin to dance. Then while you're dancing, you could recite the poem. Tell her it expresses how you really feel—"

"I don't know the whole thing yet."

"You almost do. We could practice right now—and then while it's fresh in your mind, you could go over there and give it a try."

His eyes lit. "Maybe you're right. Do you really think I should?"

Luanne nodded. Her cheeks had paled a little, but her voice was strong and sure. "Of course. If you really care for Caitlin—"

"Sure I do! What do you think I've been studying with you all these nights for?"

"Then maybe tonight is the night you should let her know. You look real handsome," she added, and for the first time, there was a quaver in her voice. Jake didn't notice.

He did glance over at her though, and grinned. "You think so?"

Luanne reached up and straightened his black string tie, noting how the red plaid shirt he wore accentuated his fine set of shoulders. "I do."

"Well, thanks. You look real nice, too, Miss Porter." For the first time he seemed to really take in her pale green muslin gown, the pearl drop necklace at her throat, and the dangling pearl earbobs that caught the light. "Real nice," he said again, his eyes moving over the fullness of her breasts beneath the low-cut gown.

"Do you think—just for tonight—you should call me Luanne? I mean, we want people to think we're c-courting and all."

"Right. I keep forgetting." He grinned, and suddenly reached out to brush a wayward curl from her cheek. For a moment his hand lingered alongside her face, then dropped to his side. "That was a great idea you had about my asking you to the dance," he said quickly. "All those times I came calling, your aunt and uncle, the wranglers, anyone who knew, just thought I was sweet on you—not that we were learning my ABCs."

"Yes, it was a good plan, Jake."

Her eyes searched his. She took a deep breath. "I hope you'll continue with your learning, Jake. The ability to read and write—to communicate—is a wonderful thing. You've come so far. A few more lessons would do you a world of good."

"Well, I have to admit I kind of like our lessons." He frowned. "I hadn't thought about stopping 'em."

"Of course, maybe if things work out with Caitlin, you'd want *her* to teach you."

"Maybe." He spoke slowly. "The strange thing is, I've gotten used to having *you* teach me. Reckon I'd miss it if we stopped."

She smiled then, her eyes sparkling. In the glow of the lamplight that illuminated the parlor, Jake wondered at how brilliantly brown eyes could shine.

"Do you want to practice the sonnet now, Jake?"

"Not here." He clasped her arm and tucked it in his. "Too many people around. Let's go outside."

Wade danced with the brunette in yellow gingham. Twice. He danced with every young, pretty, unmarried woman in the room. He danced with Edna, with Winnifred Dale, and with Becky. But not Caitlin. Not once.

It wasn't that she lacked for partners. She was breathless by the time Jake Young led her to the refreshment table and handed her a glass of elderberry wine. But she was as miserable as if she were a wallflower left to wither and die.

"Here you go, Miss Summers."

She accepted the glass of elderberry wine, drank it in one gulp, and requested another.

Jake obliged.

By then Wade was dancing with Hannah Wickes, the well-endowed daughter of one of Hope's leading ranchers.

Caitlin took deep gulps of the wine until the glass was empty.

"Miss Summers, there's something I've been meaning to talk to you about—" Jake began, but at that moment, Caitlin made up her mind.

"Excuse me a moment, won't you, Jake?"

"Sure, but—"

"There's something I have to do," she murmured and started toward the dance floor. Her head felt light, her blood was singing. But her eyes were clearly focused on the tall, dark-haired man doing a do-si-do with Hannah Wickes.

"Pardon me." Caitlin tapped the girl lightly on the shoulder and squeezed out a tight smile. "May I cut in?"

"Why . . . I suppose so . . ."

"Thank you." Caitlin grabbed Wade's arm and tugged him toward her even as the song ended and the fiddle players shifted into another waltz. Wade stared at her in astonishment.

"What's this all about?"

"Do you wish to dance with me or not?"

His hand clamped around her waist. "Well, if you're going to twist my arm."

"Obviously that's the only way," she retorted as they spun across the floor. Wade danced with the same assurance and easy strength with which he did everything else. "You obviously weren't going to ask me."

"The night wasn't over yet. I might have."

"You *might* have?" Her spine stiffened. "How very kind of you."

"I wouldn't have done it to be kind."

Her eyes lifted to his, searching, searching for something she dared not hope to find. "Then why?" she asked softly.

He didn't answer, just held her tighter, and whirled her across the floor.

"Wade. That night we . . ."

"Yeah?"

"Ever since then, we haven't even had a moment to talk."

"So?"

Caitlin's courage failed her. He looked so cold, so distant. Even though she wanted to take that lean, harsh face in her hands, to brush his lips with hers, she knew it was useless. Wade's heart was closed to her—as it always had been, she reminded herself. He had offered her passion, and at times, patience and understanding, but nothing more. Except perhaps pity.

She remembered the expression on his face when he'd heard about Alec—and about Dominic Trent. Wade would never treat a woman that way—and it had angered him, and made him feel sorry for her.

She regretted telling him any of it. The last thing she wanted was for him to feel he had to look after her, as a means of carrying out Reese's wishes.

All along she'd mistaken those kind, decent honorable sentiments for more. She'd even mistaken the desire that had exploded between them for more. She'd hoped with all of her heart for more.

Because she was a silly little fool.

"I'm sorry." She stopped dancing in the middle of the waltz. Edna and Seth Weaver bumped into them, begged pardon, and danced on. Wade's hand stayed at her waist.

"For what?"

"For interrupting your dance with Hannah. You can go to her if you wish and finish your dance."

"Got your permission, do I?"

"As a matter of fact, yes. I must find Drew and—"

She gasped as he pulled her off the dance floor. Caitlin could hardly struggle without making a scene and that was the last thing she wanted to do. She wanted to find Drew Raleigh and ask him to take her home. No matter how many men she danced with, how many compliments she was paid, how many friendly conversations her women friends engaged her in, she felt only emptiness. And pain. A deep shattering pain splintered her heart.

"Please let me go. I just want to—"

"When I'm finished with you, you can go. Not a moment before."

"Wade!"

He ignored her as he dragged her down the hall, into a small back parlor where a kerosene lamp sent an amber glow over the simple furnishings. Wade kicked the door closed behind him. He pushed Caitlin against the wall, seized her shoulders, and pinned her there before she could move.

"What do you think you're—"

His lips closed over hers. It was a long kiss, not a gentle one. A kiss that made her heart stop, her blood burn, a kiss that sent slivers of heart-wrenching pain through her.

When she was breathless and dizzy, he lifted his head. "How's that for talk?"

"It . . . hardly . . . qualifies," she whispered. Her lips felt bruised. And warm. And lonely without his. Still she wouldn't reach for him, wouldn't let him know how much she wanted to kiss him again. Because this was lust. Nothing more. It had nothing to do with love.

"Are you jealous of Drew? Is that what this little demonstration is all about? Afraid I'm going to kiss him good night, that I'll enjoy it more than I enjoy kissing y—"

He cut off her words with another kiss. This one was even hotter, deeper, hungrier than the first. When it was over, her knees were shaking, her heart was pounding, and she swayed in his arms.

Wade held her close, his face only inches from hers. "Yeah, I'm jealous of Raleigh," he said. "Jealous of every time he danced with you, touched you, got you to smile at him. Which was a helluva lot."

"M-men." Trembling, she licked her lips and tried to speak firmly. "You fight over land, over gold, over women. Like dogs fighting over bones. It doesn't mean anything, though. You couldn't care less about me—"

"You're not listening." His hands swept down, pinning her arms at her sides, slamming her against his chest so hard she gasped. "Pay attention."

Again his mouth slanted across hers. This time the kiss was gentle. Gentle as a summer breeze. Tender as the dawn. Wade's mouth explored hers, shaped itself to hers, tasted hers.

"Elderberry wine," he murmured at last. "For the lady who doesn't drink spirits."

"I'm . . . not drunk," she whispered weakly. Not on wine, at least. On love. Heaven help her. She'd rather die than tell him how much she loved him, how her heart yearned for what could not be. She struggled to regain the remnants of her pride, her only defense.

"You must . . . let me go. We can . . . hardly . . . stay in here . . . all night . . ."

"Too damn bad we can't. It seems it's going to take that long before you get it into your head that I care about you. Matter of fact," he added darkly, "more than I should."

"What is that supposed to mean?"

His hand came up, touched her cheek, traced a light path along her delicate jaw and down her throat. Caitlin trembled all the way to the tips of her toes, fighting against the seed of hope trying to spring up within her.

"I've figured out that where men are concerned, you're just prone to trouble," Wade said. He took a deep breath. "And there's only one solution for that. We're going to have to get married so that I can—"

He broke off as he saw all the color drain from her face.

"What is it?" he demanded. "What the hell is wrong?"

"Don't say another word," she gasped. "If you tell me you're going to take care of me, I'll scream."

"What's wrong with that? You need someone to take care of you," he informed her grimly. "Look at all the trouble you've gotten into since you got here—Otter Jones. Hurley Biggs and those rustlers. Not to mention any of those bastards you were mixed up with in the past. And then there's Raleigh."

He grimaced and a set determined expression came over his face.

"I *am* going to take care of you, Caitlin, that's all there is to it. Reese would want me to—"

"Let me go!" she cried. She pushed him away from her. "Don't touch me ever again!"

Wade was only glad that the fiddle music and talk and

laughter coming from the big parlor was so loud it drowned out that scream. He grabbed her as she bolted for the door.

"Caitlin, hold on."

Easily, he yanked her back, his arm snaking around her slender waist, hauling her close against him, so close her prim, pale chignon brushed his chin.

"Running away again? You think that's the answer to everything? Why don't you just stay and fight this out?"

"There's nothing to fight about. I will not marry you."

"The hell you won't. It'll solve all our . . . ouch!"

With no warning at all, her silk-slippered foot shot out and kicked him in the shin.

Wade glared at her, though his fingers only tightened around her wrist. "What'd you do that for?"

"I asked you before not to say another word," she managed to say through the choking lump in her throat. "And you did. You keep talking, and everything you say just makes it worse!"

"Well, how am I supposed to propose if I can't say another word?"

For a moment, Caitlin wished she'd brought her derringer so she could shoot him. Or herself. Through a haze of pain and rage she struggled to appear calm, struggled not to let him see the despair swirling like dark mist around her.

"Tell me again, *why* exactly do you want to marry me?" Her face was as white as milk. "Because you promised my father you'd look after me?"

"That's right."

"And because you always keep your word?"

"That's right."

"And because we have to stay on Cloud Ranch together for a time anyway?"

"Yes, and—"

"Because you don't mind having me in your bed?"

"I think you know the answer to that." His eyes darkened to cobalt and he drew her closer. "It all makes perfect sense." His hand moved up to cup her chin, but she knocked it aside.

"Perfect sense." Her voice throbbed. "*That's* a reason to get married, isn't it?"

"Sure." His jaw tightened. What the hell did she want from him? "If you just stop and think about it logically, like I did, you'll agree—"

"I would rather marry a dead, decaying, putrid, rabid *skunk,* Wade Barclay, than ever marry you." Fury turned her eyes to sparks of brilliant green fire. Wade felt her whole body trembling.

"Mind telling me why?"

"Because I can think of only one reason to get married. Love. Do you hear me? Love! If we loved each other, then I'd marry you. I'd go through hell and back again to marry you. But I won't marry you—or anyone—for anything *but* love. I won't marry you because you feel sorry for me or because you made a promise to my father or because you think I need protecting—I love you too much to ever let you—"

She broke off in horror. For a moment she could only stare at him. Dismay held her mute. Why, oh why, had she lost her temper, let loose her stupid tongue?

If only she could snatch back those words . . .

Wade looked dazed. Stunned. As if she'd cold-cocked him.

"You . . . love me?"

She clenched her fists as tears threatened. "Fool that I am," she muttered, bitterness aching through each word. She had to get out of here. "Now let me pass—"

But at that moment the door flew open and three small bodies tumbled into the room. "Hide—quick!" Becky cried, and then she and the Morgensen twins all stopped and stared.

"Caitlin—Wade!" Her sister was flushed, laughing, her brown hair falling over her eyes. "We're playing hide-and-seek!"

"We have to hide!" Katie Morgensen exclaimed.

"From Jimmy Potter!" Bridget added.

"Becky." Caitlin knelt beside her sister as the twins scrambled behind the winged armchair near the window. "I have a headache, dearest. I'm going to ask Mr. Raleigh to take me home now."

"Oh, no, Caity—before supper?"

"Yes, dear, but . . . but you can stay," Caitlin assured her quietly. "Wade will bring you home later."

"Caity, what's wrong? You look like you're going to cry—"

"Of course not, silly, I'm fine. I just need to rest. I'll see you later, honey."

She gave her sister one quick hug and was out the door, running down the hall, fleeing as hot tears scalded her lashes. In her last glimpse of Wade, he'd still looked stunned, as the three little girls all jumped at him, begging him to hide them.

Alice and Jim Tyler had just called their guests to the supper tables set out back. The house was crammed with people headed that way, laughing and chattering, drawn by the delicious aroma of fried chicken, pies, corn bread. There was no sign of Drew as Caitlin ducked into the spare bedroom behind the kitchen where all the shawls and jackets had been stored. She snatched up her shawl from the foot of the bed, but paused as something fell from its folds and tumbled to the floor.

Kneeling, Caitlin gathered up a ribbon-tied packet. The sight of it penetrated even her pain and she stared in bewilderment. It was a packet of letters. Tied in pink ribbon. And it had been folded inside her shawl.

Her heart began to thud. She moved toward the lamp, holding the letters near the light. With shaking hands, she slipped one from beneath the ribbon and turned it over.

It was addressed to Miss Caitlin Summers at the Davenport Academy for Young Ladies. Written in black, in a man's bold, strong hand.

Quickly she scanned all the envelopes—until she found what she was looking for. One written in her own hand—a more childish hand. Addressed to Reese Summers at Cloud Ranch, Hope, Wyoming.

And another. And another.

Her knees shook. She clutched the letters. "Oh, my God."

Her father's letters to her. And hers to him.

Her mind couldn't begin to fathom how this had happened, who had wrapped the letters in her shawl.

She only knew she had to leave this house, go home, try to take in what had happened.

And read the letters.

Somehow she managed to stuff the packet into her reticule, stumble from the room, and find Drew Raleigh in the hall.

"Caitlin, what's wrong?" Instantly he was at her side as people hurried past them. "You look as if you've seen a ghost."

"Can you take me home, please? I'm not feeling well."

"Of course. Let me help you with your shawl—"

"No, it doesn't matter," she cried as he began to lift it from her arm, where she'd draped it in careless haste. "Please, let's just leave!"

"Whatever you say." His head bent in concern, Drew took her by the elbow. "This way."

Chapter 26

No wind stirred the trees as Drew Raleigh's buggy rolled across the matted grass of the trail, crunching over twigs and rocks, bouncing over the occasional rut. Cool night air settled over Caitlin's shoulders as her shawl lay draped, forgotten, over her arm. She stared down at her reticule through the faint light cast by the stars, and tried not to think about the letters inside it. About who had tucked them in the folds of her shawl. The same person who must have kept them from reaching her—and hers from reaching Reese.

Someone at the May Day dance. Someone she knew. Someone who all along had schemed to keep her and her father apart . . .

The pain of it wrenched at her, but it was better than the pain she would suffer if she dwelled on what had happened with Wade in that back parlor, better than remembering the stunned expression on his face when she'd said she loved him.

Better than remembering that she'd made an utter fool of herself . . .

A choked sound came from her throat, and Drew Raleigh, who'd been mercifully silent, broke the quiet between them.

"Are you all right, Caitlin?"

"I have a slight headache. It's nothing serious."

"Don't think I mind leaving early. It suits me just fine."

In the darkness, he sounded as if he was smiling. For the first time, Caitlin glanced over at him and peered hard through the dimness.

"You didn't even get a chance to enjoy any supper."

"Believe me, I won't enjoy supper until I'm back in New York," he said with a chuckle. "But that day, I hope, will be coming quite soon."

Caitlin struggled to make polite conversation. All she wanted was to be alone. To read her letters. To try *not* to think about Wade.

"Your business here is almost finished, then?" she asked wearily.

"I believe so."

"I'm sorry it wasn't more successful."

"That remains to be seen."

"Oh?" For the first time, Caitlin heard not only a smile, but a note of excitement in his deep voice. "Have you acquired a ranch then for your syndicate?"

"I'm possibly very close to finalizing an acquisition. But you don't want me to bore you with details, Caitlin. Not when you have a headache," he said softly.

Caitlin studied him again through the starlit darkness. There was something odd about his voice. Suddenly she noticed that the terrain over which they were traveling had become quite hilly. Ahead she thought she discerned the shape of larger, darker shadows, not the open sprawling prairie.

"Drew—this isn't the way to Cloud Ranch. We're in the foothills," she exclaimed. "Are you lost?"

"No, Caitlin, I have an unerring sense of direction. It's almost as keen as my business acumen."

"Then why are we here?" she demanded, a sense of unease taking hold, penetrating even her pain.

"You'll find out soon enough."

"I insist that you take me to Cloud Ranch this instant."

Drew was silent, but he whipped the horses to a faster trot, and the buggy jolted over the steep, rugged terrain.

"Drew, if you won't take me to Cloud Ranch, take me back to the party. Turn the buggy around right now!"

"I'm afraid you're not going to like this, Caitlin. And I'm not enjoying it much myself." He sent the horses into a gallop and Caitlin gasped, clutching the seat. "But in the world of business, every adversary has vulnerabilities, and a good businessman doesn't flinch at using them to his advantage."

"What in heaven's name are you talking about?"

"It isn't as if you are without fault. You committed crimes. Surely you didn't expect that you'd never have to pay for them?"

Cold dread washed over her. She fought the urge to jump out of the buggy and run. They were traveling too quickly and the ground was too rough.

"I don't know what you mean," she managed to say in a flat tone that hid the panic coursing through her.

He sighed. "Come now, Caitlin. Denying it will do you no good. It's time to pay the piper. But as you will soon see, I'm giving you a chance, at least, to escape the punishment that would be meted out by the law. When all this is over, you may yet thank me."

"I'll thank you to take me home immediately. I don't have the faintest idea what you're babbling about, Drew, but whatever it is, surely it can wait until tomorrow and we can discuss it in the light of—"

The words froze in her throat at the sight of what loomed before her. Drew had just rounded a curve in the trail and straight ahead was a clearing where a campfire smoked, and two shadowy figures in the gloom of the trees watched the buggy's approach. She saw a shotgun and the gleam of a pistol and with rising panic she struggled to make out the men's faces.

The buggy halted at the outskirts of the camp, just beyond the fire's glow. Suddenly one of the men stepped forward and the dying flames of the campfire cast orange light upon his black duster and black hat, and the handsome, saturnine features that had haunted her nightmares.

All of the blood drained from her face as Dominic Trent stepped forward to the side of the buggy.

"Why, Caitlin, how charming to see you again."

His smile stretched taut across his face but never touched those chilling colorless eyes.

Somehow she managed to sit perfectly still and meet those terrifying eyes. "I'm afraid I can't say the same. I wish I had killed you."

The smile vanished in an instant, replaced by a feral snarl that made even Drew Raleigh beside her suck in his breath. Caitlin sat frozen, numb with fear, using every ounce of willpower she possessed to hide her terror behind a stony facade.

Dominic Trent fed on fear. She refused to nourish him.

"A confession. Thank you, Caitlin, just what I hoped for—it will seal your fate. You've arrived unfashionably early and Sheriff Piltson isn't here yet, but I think Mr. Jackson and I can manage to keep you in custody until a proper lawman places you under arrest."

He turned and addressed the other man, who waited in the shadows. "Bring those manacles of yours over here. She might look delicate, but this is a highly dangerous female. You'll need to keep an eye on her at all times."

The man who came forward, a set of steel manacles draped over his burly arm, looked like he'd just as soon shoot her as bother with her. He had small, mean black eyes and a sauntering arrogance to his walk. He was huge, dirty, and smelled like horse dung.

"This is Smoke Jackson. He's a famous bounty hunter, Caitlin, and he always gets his man—or his woman, as the case may be," Trent explained. Apparently some of the icy dread flooding through her began to show upon her face, because Trent's self-satisfied smile widened. "Usually he brings them in dead, of course, but in this case, if I give certain instructions, you may actually make it back to Philadelphia alive. I do want you able to stand trial, you know."

"Trial? You're the one who should be standing trial!"

She addressed the bounty hunter. "This is the man who should be arrested. Both of these men!" She gestured toward Drew Raleigh, who sat silent beside her. "They've brought me here against my will."

"Have they, now? Well, little lady, I heard a different

story," Smoke Jackson sneered. "You tried to murder Mr. Trent—and stole from him—and this other feller here helped bring you in. In these parts, that's called justice."

"Stole from him?" White-faced, she stared at Dominic Trent. "You despicable, cowardly liar. I struck you over the head with a candlestick to protect myself—that's hardly a case of murder! And as for stealing, there is nothing of yours that I would ever so much as *touch*—"

"What's this, then?" Suddenly Trent pulled a large emerald ring from his pocket. It shone like green flame in the firelight, its band of gold gleaming. "You remember my great-aunt Hilda's ring, don't you, Caitlin?" He spoke very softly. "You stole it from my home that night when I tried to propose to you. You left me for dead and ran off with this precious family heirloom."

He shifted his gaze swiftly to the other two men. "You both saw me discover this inside Miss Summers's reticule just now, did you not?"

Smoke Jackson spat a wad of tobacco juice into the darkness. "Sure did."

Drew Raleigh cleared his throat. "Ahem. Yes," he said more quietly.

She grabbed his arm. "What kind of a man are you? How can you be a part of this?"

He said nothing, just stared at her.

"How much is he paying you to frame me?" she whispered. "Don't you see he's a monster?"

"It's no use, Caitlin." His tone was sorrowful, but he could no longer meet her eyes. "Are you denying you struck him, left him for dead?"

"He was trying to rape me! To force me to become his mistress!"

"I've been told it was an honorable proposal and you . . . overreacted. Just as you are overreacting now."

Drew sighed, and laid a hand on her arm. "Perhaps there is a way, however, that you can escape a jail sentence. That's where I come in. Perhaps the sheriff and this bounty hunter can both be persuaded to let you go."

"I don't have money," she said with contempt. "I can't afford to pay you off."

"It's not your money I'm after, Caitlin." Drew frowned and seemed to brace himself as Smoke Jackson moved suddenly, hauling Caitlin out of the buggy so abruptly she only had time to gasp.

"Need you be quite so rough?" Drew asked, perspiration shining on his face as he watched the bounty hunter snap the manacles around both of Caitlin's wrists.

"Mr. Jackson's tactics aren't really your concern." Trent spoke softly but there was an underlying edge to his voice that made Drew Raleigh swallow down any more protests. "Miss Summers is merely getting her due."

With that, he turned to Caitlin and surveyed her up and down, his glance taking in the pale rose gown clinging to her figure, the proud lift of her chin, and best of all, the slight quiver in her delectable lower lip.

His blood heated. His pulse began to race.

He'd been waiting so long for his revenge. And now it was here—his victory almost complete.

"When Sheriff Piltson gets here, we'll be riding out, my dear. Are you cold? You're shivering and you seem to have lost your shawl."

He fingered the black satin shawl that had fallen upon the wagon seat, beside her reticule. Then he let it slip through his fingers back onto the seat. "Pity. But you'll be riding with me to our appointed meeting place. The place where your fate will be decided. So never fear, I'll be delighted to keep you warm."

Caitlin's shivering was only partly a result of the cold. Hatred for this man who had tormented and hunted her tore through her. "The last time you tried to trap me you ended up the worse for it." Her voice was low, warning. "It will be even worse for you this time. I suggest you let me go before it's too late. I'm not alone anymore—there are people who will look for me, who will help me . . ."

"Ah, Wade Barclay, perhaps?"

The silken way Trent said Wade's name chilled her blood.

"Yes."

"You think your redemption will come from him?" Contempt flicked through each word. "Your ranch foreman?"

Caitlin thought of Wade's kisses, his sense of honor, the relentless way he'd searched for Becky. "Yes," she whispered again. But at the same time, she was afraid. She didn't want Wade to face danger on her account. If he came after her, he'd be outnumbered three to one—and Smoke Jackson looked like a formidable opponent. Drew had once boasted to her of his shooting prowess, and Dominic Trent—well, the man was good at everything that involved evil and destruction.

If only she'd brought her derringer—but who brought a gun to a dance?

"Wade Barclay isn't involved in this yet." She spoke through dry lips. "Neither is anyone else—including either of his brothers. From what I've heard, you don't want to tangle with the Barclay boys. So if you let me go, this can end right now."

"But I don't wish it to end. We're just beginning. The fun hasn't even started yet." Trent pulled Caitlin against him, twined his fingers in her hair, and yanked her head back. "The question is: will Wade Barclay try to save you—or betray you?" he asked silkily.

His lips touched hers, and as she tried to recoil, he pulled her closer and kissed her again, a hard, brutal kiss that somehow made the pain in his head begin once more to throb.

Drew Raleigh, watching, shifted uncomfortably upon the wagon seat. Smoke Jackson looked on with grinning interest as Trent smiled at the woman who twisted futilely in his arms.

"Make no mistake, Caitlin, my dear. Wade Barclay is going to determine your fate, one way or another. Which way will it be—that is the only remaining question. We'll have the answer quite soon."

Chapter 27

"Winnifred, seen Caitlin anywhere? Or Raleigh?"
Wade had searched all through the ranch house, and had stalked back and forth along the rows of tables and chairs scattered in back of the Crooked T. Despite all the people helping themselves to plates of fried chicken, steak, and corn bread, or seated and happily devouring the repast the Tylers had prepared for their enjoyment, he hadn't spotted a single glimpse of Caitlin anywhere.

"Can't say that I have." Winnifred peered about, her mouth pursed in concentration. "Why, Wade? What's wrong? Is something the matter with Caitlin?"

"I need to find her," he muttered and moved off toward Edna, who was bustling toward the kitchen.

"You seen Caitlin?"

"Why, yes, I caught a glimpse of her just as everyone was lining up for supper. She and Drew headed out the front door."

Wade grimaced. "Much obliged."

He turned before she could ask him any questions, and went back outside to find both Becky and Ina Morgensen, mother of the twins.

It didn't take long to arrange for them to bring Becky home after supper. And Becky surprised him by smiling when he explained that he was leaving. "You're going to see if Caitlin's feeling all right, aren't you, Wade?"

"Seems like someone should check on her."

The little girl bobbed her head. "Good idea. Caitlin is always worried about me—and everything else. She needs someone to look after her."

"She wouldn't agree with you."

Becky laughed. "No, I know that. But," she added, nodding wisely, "that's only because she's never really had anyone to look after her before. I mean, Mama and Papa loved her, of course. They loved both of us. But they were always so busy, they didn't really pay attention. Like the time that bad man came and hurt her—Mama and Papa were away. If it wasn't for our groom, I don't know what would have happened." She bit her lip. "You'll make sure she's all right, won't you, Wade?"

"Bet on it, sweetheart."

There was a lead weight around his heart as he headed around the side of the house toward the buggy. Caitlin, so strong, so stubborn. He'd always had Reese, Clint, and Nick behind him. Not that he'd needed them all that often, but he'd known they were there if he ever needed someone to watch his back. Caitlin had never had anyone. Even when her whole world had collapsed.

And tonight—tonight, when she'd told him she loved him, he'd just stood there. Couldn't talk, couldn't think. Frozen like a block of ice.

And he'd let her run away. By the time the shock had worn off, and he'd come after her, she was gone.

Well, it was time for her to stop running. Hell, it was time for both of them to stop running.

From each other, from feelings that just kept squeezing out no matter how hard he tried to push them back.

Feelings like *love*.

Wade felt himself breaking into a sweat just thinking about that word. *Love*.

Did he love Caitlin? Hell, yes. Why hadn't he faced it before now? He'd faced bucking broncs, rustlers, outlaws, and once, a bear who'd caught him unawares. He'd handled all of it with near fearless calm and a steady eye—but love had sent him skittering for cover.

Love.

Caitlin wasn't her mother, he told himself in slow, gut-wrenching realization. And he wasn't Reese.

He started sprinting toward the buggy that he'd left alongside some willows when suddenly he heard a heavy rustling in the brush toward his left. He tensed, a hand gliding swiftly toward the Colt at his hip. Out of the brush came two figures, brushing twigs and grass from their clothes.

"Um, howdy, uh . . . Wade." Jake Young plopped his hat on his head and a tangle of dirt and grass tumbled down onto his broad shoulders. Beside him, Luanne Porter made a small sound resembling a strangled giggle.

Wade's gaze swung to her. Her dress was wrinkled and she was shaking grass from her skirt. Wade couldn't tell if her face or Jake's was flushed a deeper shade of red.

He stared at them. Jake and Luanne?

"We were . . . uh, just looking for . . ." Luanne's voice trailed off. She glanced desperately at Jake.

"For . . . your . . . earbob, Miss Porter. Tiny little thing," Jake explained to Wade. "She . . . lost it."

"Lost it." Wade nodded. "In the brush?"

"Yep, in the brush, when she was . . ." Jake swallowed.

"What was that you were doing in the brush, Miss Porter?"

"I . . . I was playing hide-and-seek with the children!" she burst out triumphantly. Jake grinned with relief. Very gently he extricated a small twig from Miss Porter's tousled curls.

"There you go, Wade. Schoolteacher. Playing hide-and-seek with the children. That was a right nice thing to do. Too bad we couldn't find your earbob, Luanne—I mean, Miss Porter."

"It's on your ear, Luanne," Wade spoke gently. He started past them, punching Jake in the shoulder as he passed. "Both of 'em. One on each ear."

"Oh, my g-goodness, how did that happen?" Her voice quivered with laughter. Wade grinned. Then he remembered Caitlin heading home with Drew Raleigh. He quickened his steps.

"Leaving so early?" Jake called after him.

"Caitlin wasn't feeling well. Going to check on her."

"Yep, saw her leave with Raleigh." Jake added, "When we were searching for the earbob. Didn't think they were headed home though. They headed west. Wondered exactly where they—"

"*West,* you say?"

An icy draft shot down Wade's spine. He spun back. "You sure about that?"

"Didn't think much about it at the time, but . . . yep, I reckon I'm sure. They went west."

West. Toward the foothills. What the hell was Drew Raleigh up to?

"Hey, think there's trouble, Wade? Need any help—"

But Wade didn't hear. He was already running toward the buggy, his mind racing with possibilities, none of them pleasant.

He had a bad feeling—and it got worse when he saw the note. It was stuck to the painted wood side of the buggy, a square paper pegged with a nail.

He snatched the fluttering page, dug in his pocket for a match and tinder, and by the meager flickering flame, he scanned the elegantly scrawled lines with mounting dread.

Barclay.
If you want to see the lovely Miss Summers alive again, come to Wolf Cave—at dawn. Come alone or the lady will die. And bring the deed to Cloud Ranch.

For a moment he couldn't breathe. Couldn't move. A white-hot fury gripped him, paralyzing every muscle in his body—and then it was followed by fear. A dry-mouthed, choking fear.

He couldn't lose her as he'd lost his parents. As he'd lost Reese.

He couldn't lose his Caitlin.

The next moment he was in the buggy, whipping the horse to a gallop, his face a dark, deadly mask. As stars sparkled across the indigo sky and unseen creatures prowled through the brush, Wade Barclay raced hard and fast for the gates of Cloud Ranch.

Chapter 28

The deep evening chill sliced through Caitlin like a sword as the night drew inexorably toward morning. With her hands still manacled before her, she leaned wearily against a rock, all too aware of Dominic Trent sharing the rock beside her—and of Smoke Jackson, lounging across the campfire from her, his mean black eyes watching her across the flickering orange flames.

Drew Raleigh had dozed off several yards away, wrapping himself in a saddle blanket he'd taken from the buggy. When he'd first tried to offer it to her, Dominic Trent had stepped in, frowning.

"That won't be necessary. Miss Summers's care and protection now rests exclusively in my hands."

"But she looks pretty damned cold—"

"Who's in charge here, Raleigh?" Trent's tone held unmistakable menace. "When we first entered into this bargain, we agreed that this entire matter is under my authority. Are you reneging on our agreement?"

"No. Of course not." Drew swallowed uneasily. "But she needn't freeze to death while we're waiting for Piltson to show."

"Don't interfere, Raleigh." The words were a silken threat. "Or I'll be forced to rethink your participation."

"Fine, Trent. Fine. Whatever you say."

Raleigh threw one fleeting regretful glance at her and retreated, blanket in hand. It was at that moment that Caitlin remembered where she'd seen him before.

She'd been right—it had been at the Opera House. The night she'd met Dominic Trent, Trent had been deeply engaged in conversation with another man when he'd looked over and spotted her for the first time. That other man, she now realized, had been Drew Raleigh.

So he and Trent had obviously been acquainted, probably for some time. But from the moment Trent noticed her that evening, he spent the rest of the night staring at her— she felt his strange chilling gaze on her in the lobby, in Gillis's private box, while mingling with friends along the marble stairway and French-papered corridors. It made her uncomfortable the entire evening.

Eventually, he found a common acquaintance to introduce them. And thus her nightmare began.

No wonder she always felt a vague antipathy toward Drew—deep in her mind, she rightly associated him with that fateful night.

But now it was the end of another, even more dangerous night—and as Drew Raleigh slunk off to the opposite side of the fire and wrapped himself in the saddle blanket, Dominic Trent dropped down beside her and dropped one arm around her shoulders.

"Don't touch me. If you do, I'll be sick."

"Tsk, tsk, my dear. Still so stubborn, so childishly proud." He withdrew his arm, but captured her chin and forced her to gaze directly into his eyes. "If only you'd agreed to my proposition that night, all this could have been avoided."

"If only I'd killed you with that candlestick, we'd have had the same result."

The menace in his smile filled her with sick, throat-clogging fear, but she continued to meet his gaze unflinchingly, even when those colorless eyes seemed to shine like demon orbs back at her.

"You'll have a long time to repent for that night. A very long time," he whispered slowly.

Mad. The man was mad. All of Philadelphia knew him as a ruthless tycoon, a brilliant businessman, a sought-after escort to soirees, but he was also known as a man who kept mistresses in four cities, a man whose darker habits, indiscretions, and secrets were whispered about, but never openly discussed. Even Caitlin had heard some of the rumors, but it wasn't that which had always made her flesh crawl when he was in the same room with her. It was what she herself sensed in the man—and that was pure unadulterated evil.

Now her brain whirled with possibilities. She didn't know what he had in mind for Wade, but she wasn't about to sit still and let him lure Wade into a trap. She had to get out of here one way or another, find Wade and warn him—before dawn.

These manacles would slow her down, but they wouldn't stop her. If she could get to a horse, and mount—she could ride.

She glanced around the clearing, noting the positions

of the horses, Raleigh's buggy, the start of the trail just beyond where Drew Raleigh dozed. The shadows were deep, and dark, the stars fainter than they had been before. How long until dawn?

If only Dominic Trent and the bounty hunter would sleep. But Smoke Jackson looked as wide awake and alert as if it were broad daylight. And Trent . . .

He sipped a cup of coffee beside her, his shoulder brushing hers.

"As soon as Sheriff Piltson gets here, we'll head out to Wolf Cave. That's where Barclay's going to show up—if he cares enough about you to show up." The taunting edge to his voice was meant to wound her, she knew, but it had a strangely opposite effect. Instead of weakening her with doubts, it intensified her resolution to escape and try to protect Wade. He would show up, there was no doubt in her mind of that. Wade Barclay would risk his life for her—for anyone who needed help, she thought, with a twist of pain. He was that kind of man. Just as Dominic Trent was the kind of man who would use and abuse others to satisfy the evil that had eaten into his soul.

"What are you planning once Wade gets there?" She spoke quietly, hoping to lull him into boasts that would enlighten her about what lay ahead. But Trent wasn't fooled.

"You would like to know, my dear, wouldn't you? But you'll have to wait and see. Suffice it to say that I intend to prove to you that your only hope lies with me. No one else. Alec Ballantree was a sniveling little self-interested fool who deserted you when you most needed his support. And when it comes right down to it, Wade Barclay will do the same."

You're wrong, Caitlin thought. *Wade might not love me, but he would never desert me.* Eerily, Trent seemed to read her mind.

"I'll prove it to you, Caitlin. At dawn. You'll see exactly where you rank in importance to Wade Barclay. There will be no doubt of his desertion, his betrayal—"

"Why?" Caitlin interrupted, her eyes blazing into his. "Why do you want *me*—a woman who loathes you? Surely you can find someone, some poor, misguided fool who would go to you willingly and—"

He struck her across the face with the back of his hand, a hard thump that sent her reeling back against the rock. Pain sliced through her skull and tiny lights like blinking red stars swam before her eyes.

"Don't ever question my love for you, Caitlin. I won't tolerate it. You'll understand when this business with Barclay is done—I'm going to break you of this notion that you have anyone else to rely on but me. Even if it takes months to teach you that. Or years."

"Why?" she whispered through the throbbing pain in her jaw. "I don't . . . understand—why can't you let me be?"

"Because I always get what I want, Caitlin. I always have, and I always will. And I want you. I love you. I told you that before, and now you can see to what lengths I'm willing to go. I'm going to prove to you beyond any doubt that I'm the only one in this world who will never let you go, never put anyone or anything above my feelings for you—the one who will always want you by my side—and," he added softly, his eyes glittering into hers, "in my bed."

She shook her head, wincing as it throbbed. A breeze

swept down from the mountains, whipping at her bare neck, her arms.

Trent's eyes narrowed. "Unless you'd rather go to prison." He shrugged. "Perhaps after spending time locked away, you'll appreciate all I have to offer."

"It'll never come to that," she whispered. "If Wade doesn't kill you, I will. If not tonight, as soon as your back is turned. As soon as the opportunity presents itself. You'll never win."

She braced herself for another blow, but instead Trent turned his head toward the sound of approaching hoof-beats.

"Sheriff Piltson has arrived. And it's nearly dawn. Time for our little assignation."

He hauled her to her feet as a rider galloped into the camp.

Drew Raleigh stirred and clambered up, while Jackson dumped the remains of a coffeepot over the flames.

The rider drew up and dismounted. "Howdy, Smoke. Mr. Trent." He nodded at Raleigh. He turned his gaze to Caitlin and grinned.

"This here our prisoner, eh? Well, well, they say it's always the ones who look harmless who are the most dangerous—"

He stopped talking abruptly. They stared at each other.

Slowly, his grin faded. But Caitlin had already seen the two gold front teeth—and the red hair. It was all she needed.

"You're that rustler," she gasped. "The m-murderer. You killed those two men—Skeeter Biggs and Otter Jones—and you tried to kill me. You're no more a sheriff than I am!"

"Wrong, little lady. See this?" He tapped a grimy finger on the silver star that glinted from his greasy buckskin vest. "The good folks of Squirrel Gulch elected me sheriff and that's what I am. You must have me mixed up with someone else."

He grinned again, almost flaunting those glinting gold teeth. The same glinting gold Caitlin had seen on the rustler who'd pursued her. Combined with the red hair and the man's build, she knew with every instinct in her body that Sheriff Piltson was Hurley Biggs, the rustler.

Fury surged through her. And fear. Four ruthless, unscrupulous men, all aligned against Wade.

Please let him come out of this alive, she thought. He didn't deserve to be dragged into this mess—she was the one Trent wanted. Suddenly an idea came to her and she whirled toward Dominic Trent.

"I'll go with you willingly—if we leave right now. Anywhere you'd like, we can go. I won't give you any trouble—you can send these men away and we can leave—just the two of us. We can return to Philadelphia— I don't care. But no one else needs to be involved."

"You're wrong, Caitlin. Wade Barclay is very much involved."

"He doesn't need to be."

"Are you forgetting your sister? You're just going to abandon her?"

Agony shot through her, but she managed to retain her composure. "Of course not. But Wade will take care of Becky. We . . . don't need to worry about anyone but ourselves . . . Dom . . . Dominic." She forced herself to speak his given name, forced herself to ignore the shudder of loathing that ran through her.

For a moment she held her breath, hoping, praying he would accept her offer. She met his gaze hopefully, pleadingly, willing to humble herself if necessary—if it would save Wade.

Then Trent suddenly stepped closer, grabbed her shoulders, and shook her until her teeth rattled. "We do this *my* way, not yours, Caitlin. I'm the one who still suffers pain in my head from that little blow you gave me; I'm the one who has dreamed of making you pay. *I* get to decide how, when, and where it all happens. Starting with Mr. Wade Barclay."

He shoved her away from him and she went sprawling to the ground. She banged her elbow, scraped her cheek, and fought back tears of despair.

Above her, Dominic Trent delivered a series of orders to the other three men. Caitlin scarcely heard.

Cold, aching, and filled with dread, she knew only that in the confrontation to come, there would be blood and there would be death.

And nothing she could do would stop it now.

Chapter 29

As gentle lilac dawn bloomed across the sky, a lone rider wound his way up the trail to the high purple rim of Wolf Canyon.

The tenderness of the new day contrasted oddly with the violence that brewed in the air outside Wolf Cave as those above watched the approach of the rider below. At a nod from Dominic Trent, the bounty hunter Smoke Jackson fired into the sky, and the rider halted and glanced in the direction of the shot.

A moment later, he was riding again—at a faster clip, toward the outcrop of rock from where the shot had come.

Caitlin's heart hammered as she heard the hoofbeats of Wade's roan horse. In frustration, she once again tested the manacles chaining her hands before her. Dominic Trent grabbed a handful of her hair, which had by now tumbled loose of all its pins. He yanked hard on the pale curls that were the same color as the sun gleaming out on the new morning.

"No one cares for you as I do," he spoke against her

ear. "No one will risk everything for you. Except for me. You're about to learn that truth."

Caitlin made no reply. She couldn't speak if she'd wanted to because Wade had just thundered onto the ledge and her heart broke in two as she saw him. At the same moment, Trent released his hold on her hair and, like lightning, snaked an arm around her throat, yanking her against him, her back clamped to his chest. With a thudding heart she felt the cold steel barrel of his gun against her temple.

From beneath the brim of his hat, Wade assessed the scene in one swift glance. Four men—and Caitlin.

His blood pounded in his ears. Red-hot fury threatened to overwhelm his good sense and his fingers itched for the trigger of his gun as he saw the cruel hold the man in the black duster had on her, and the gun pressed against her temple.

Easy, Barclay. Not yet.

The wiser, cooler voice inside his head took over as he met her desperate gaze. She looked so white, so fragile, like a summer flower wilting into the dust. And frightened—Wade would have given anything to end the fear shining in her eyes.

Whipcord tension coiled through him and he fairly vibrated with the urge to charge toward her, tear that bastard away from her, and never let anything or anyone hurt her again.

Instead he took a deep breath and shifted his gaze from her to assess the rest of the scene.

Three other men—if you counted Drew Raleigh as a man. Wade recognized the bounty hunter known as Smoke Jackson—he'd seen him pass through Hope once or twice. Wade's gaze narrowed on the red-haired man wearing the lawman's badge. He didn't recognize him, but there was something familiar about his build and that carrot-red hair.

Wade couldn't spot anyone else hidden behind the rocks or the scrub brush, or even inside the cave, but that didn't mean they weren't there. As he dismounted, his sharp gaze swung back to the man holding Caitlin.

"In these parts, Trent, we have ways of dealing with men who hurt women. You won't like 'em."

For a moment surprise flickered over Trent's face. Then he spoke, his voice as suave and smooth as usual. "Very good, Barclay. For a crude Wyoming ranch foreman, your powers of deduction are strong. Don't you agree, Caitlin?"

He jabbed the barrel of the gun against her temple. Caitlin gasped but said nothing. Her eyes were glued on Wade.

"I reckon you'd best let her go," Wade said quietly. "You don't need to hide behind a woman. I'll hear you out without you using her as a shield."

"Throw down your guns, Barclay. Then we'll talk, not before."

"No!" Caitlin cried as Wade moved to comply.

"Slowlike!" Jackson barked, leveling his Colt .45 at Wade.

But as Wade's fingers closed over his guns, Caitlin cried out again with desperate pleading. "Don't do it, Wade! He'll shoot you down in cold blood. He's capable of anything!"

"Easy, sweetheart." His voice was level and as soothing as the morning sky. But beneath it there was a steely quality that spoke silently to her. *Don't panic. Don't fight. Not yet. Wait for the right chance.*

"Let's hear what the city boy has to say."

"Kick those guns over here, won't you?" Trent sounded like he was inviting him to a picnic. "Ah, good. Very good."

"Now let go of her," Wade ordered coolly.

But Trent only laughed and kept his arm snaked around Caitlin's throat. The gun remained pressed against her head. "I call the . . . er, shots, Barclay, not you."

The red-haired man snickered at the witticism.

Wade's hard gaze never left Trent's face.

"You brought the deed? Show it to me."

The deed. What deed? His words rang in Caitlin's head. *The deed to Cloud Ranch?* Stunned, her blood froze. Suddenly the ground seemed to tilt beneath her feet, the sun whirled in a golden blur, the pounding in her head grew to a roar. Finally, finally, things began to come clear.

This *truth* Dominic Trent had promised her—it was all a test—a test to see what Wade would choose—saving her, or keeping Cloud Ranch.

What an evil, diabolical man. The enormity of his malevolence shocked even her. And what of Drew Raleigh?

She realized in a flash then exactly how Raleigh fit into all this. Of course. When—if—Wade turned over the deed, Raleigh would be rewarded for his part in the scheme with exactly what he wanted and needed for his damned syndicate partners.

That had been the lure to insure his participation.

But what if Wade refused . . .

Nausea rose within her. If Wade refused she would

know without a doubt that Cloud Ranch was more important to him than she was.

Dominic Trent was forcing him to choose.

In frozen disbelief, she watched Wade tug a document from his pocket. "Come and get it, Trent."

"I think not." The other man smiled. "Sheriff?"

Piltson sauntered forward, snatched the deed from Wade, and backed up several paces. He peered down at the document.

"Looks like the real thing, all right."

"You're a smart man, Mr. Barclay. Guess you do care about our lovely friend here, after all. The question is, how much? What is she worth to you, this woman here? From what I've been told, you two are—shall we use the quaint western vernacular?—sweet on each other."

"I'm not going to let you kill her, if that's what you mean."

"Come, come, surely you can demonstrate more affection than *that,*" Trent mocked. "That's no way to win a lady's heart," he added with a low laugh.

"And forcing yourself on her is?" Caitlin snapped. But an instant later she gasped as Trent tightened his arm around her throat.

"Let her go, Trent!" Iron-cold fury surged through Wade. "Stop acting like a yellow-livered coward."

"Let her go?" The other man gave a soft taunting chuckle. "I don't think so, Barclay. The lady stays right here by my side. In fact, she's coming with me. I'm taking her back to Philadelphia to stand trial."

"Trial—what the hell are you talking about?"

"Didn't you know? She attacked me. Stole from me. A

most valuable family heirloom. And she nearly killed me
to get it. I have witnesses and proof. And the law"—he
nodded at Piltson—"is on my side. Justice awaits her back
east—the kind that will keep her locked up in a most
unpleasant place for a very long time. If I choose to pursue it."

"What do you need him for?" Wade jerked a thumb
toward the bounty hunter.

"Added protection, of course." Dominic Trent's smile
widened. "I'm going to be traversing a perilous land, with
a dangerous lady in tow. I don't want anything to happen
to me—or to her—until she's safely installed in jail and
awaiting her trial."

Drew Raleigh stepped forward. He looked the worse
for wear after a night sleeping out-of-doors. His clothes
were wrinkled, his string tie askew, his eyes bleak and
bloodshot, but his voice still held a note of confident
authority. "It doesn't have to be that way, Barclay. I'm
here to broker a deal. Mr. Trent has assured me that if you
sign the deed giving your share of Cloud Ranch over to
the E. M. Piedmont Company, and also sign another document I've prepared in which you urge your brothers and
Miss Summers to do the same, he'll let Caitlin go and
forgo pressing charges against her."

Silence fell outside Wolf Cave. A silence in which
Caitlin swore she could hear her own heart beating—and
Wade's.

Cloud Ranch was his life. His love. As it had been her
father's. He'd devoted himself to it. He loved every inch of
it, every tree, rock, butte, every stone at the bottom of the
stream.

It would be like tearing off his arm to sign the deed over to Raleigh's syndicate. Giving up part of himself. He couldn't do it.

He mustn't.

But she knew the man who stood facing his enemies with such still, effortless grace. She knew the sense of responsibility and honor that drove him, the private code by which he lived.

He would sacrifice Cloud Ranch for her—but it would devastate him. Yet he'd do it anyway.

"No, Wade."

His eyes pierced her as she called out to him in a trembling voice. "Don't do it. I don't mind facing trial. He can't prove anything—I never stole from him—"

"Shut up! This is for Barclay to decide." Trent jammed the gun harder against her head, and Caitlin gave a cry of pain.

"She obviously doesn't know what she's talking about," Trent continued softly. "I have witnesses who will back me up about my family heirloom. I've got a lawman who'll testify that he heard her confess—"

"He's lying, Wade! I never . . . confessed to anything. He's a filthy liar—"

"Now, missy, that ain't true. I heerd you myself." The red-haired man grinned at her, his teeth glinting in the rising glow of the sun.

"*He's* not even a sheriff—not a real one!" Caitlin gasped. "Wade, I think he's Hurley Biggs—I recognize him—he's the rustler who shot those men!"

Dominic Trent spun her around then, and whacked her across the jaw. Caitlin went spinning to the ground.

Even as Wade took one uncontrollable step forward, Smoke Jackson and the red-haired man cocked their guns and pointed them at his chest.

"Hold it right there! Not another step!" the bounty hunter boomed.

Wade's gaze was fixed on Caitlin. Fury ripped through him as she struggled to her knees and lifted her manacled hands to her jaw.

He knew then that every man standing between them was going to die.

"The next man who lays a hand on her is going to be the first one in hell," he said. His deadly glance flicked from Trent to Piltson, to Smoke Jackson, and finally, contemptuously, to Drew Raleigh.

"You're not exactly in a position to make threats," Trent mocked. "You threw down your guns. You're not armed. How are you going to kill anyone?"

"The question, Trent, is are you ready to find out?" Wade's low, steely tone of utmost warning was not lost on anyone. Even unarmed, alone against four, he was an intimidating figure. Something in his stance, his eyes, his very voice, filled the others with that small seed of doubt that he knew could be any man's undoing.

"I'll sign the deed. And whatever papers you want. Just let Caitlin come down here—now."

Caitlin heard his words through a fog of dizziness from Trent's blow. She gave her head a shake, trying to focus. "No, Wade, you can't . . . not Cloud Ranch . . ."

"Caitlin, come here. Come down here to me."

"The hell she will!" Enraged that the foreman had given the wrong answer—that he'd agreed to give up his ranch for Caitlin Summers—thereby denying him the pleasure of having her left solely to his mercy—Trent struggled to maintain his composure.

But some of his smug, self-satisfied assurance slipped as the morning sun grew brighter and rose with more brilliance in the clean-washed sky. The sun's clear, burning light was hurting his head. It was throbbing like a drum. All Caitlin's fault. And Barclay's. All of it.

Because now, Barclay had ruined everything. Instead of being crushed, Caitlin would know that the foreman was willing to make an immense sacrifice for her. Rage surged through Trent, swirling with the pain. As if from a great distance he heard Drew Raleigh's voice, quick and relieved.

"Wise decision, Barclay." Raleigh was giving instructions. "Sign the deed and pass it over here and I'll bring Caitlin to you myself—"

"The hell you will." Smoke Jackson blocked the easterner as he started toward the woman kneeling on the ground.

"You didn't really think I would let her go, did you, Raleigh?" Dominic Trent's mouth pulled back in a sneer. "No matter which decision Barclay made, the end result was preordained. If you didn't guess that, you're even more of a fool than I thought. She goes with me—now, always. You were a tool, nothing more, and now," he said coldly, "your usefulness is over."

Raleigh went pale. "We had a deal. If you don't honor it, I . . . I will have no choice but to withdraw my help and cooperation in this venture as of this moment—"

"That suits me fine, Raleigh. You're no longer a part of this venture in any way, shape, or form."

Drew Raleigh grimaced, his ruddy face reddening still further with anger. "If you take Caitlin back for trial, I'm warning you I'll use all my influence to discredit you and everything you've—"

Dominic Trent lifted the gun he'd held to Caitlin's head and pointed it at Drew Raleigh. Without blinking, he fired.

Caitlin screamed as the shot thundered and Drew Raleigh fell down dead. Then everything exploded in a blur of noise and pain and fear as the clearing erupted into violence.

With a lightning movement, Wade yanked a hideout gun from his boot. He and Smoke Jackson fired at each other simultaneously.

A bullet slammed into the bounty hunter's gut and he toppled backward, crashing to earth like an oak tree chopped off at the roots. But as Caitlin watched in frozen horror, Wade too fell in a spurt of blood.

"No!" With a shriek she scrambled to her feet and started toward him, only to see Dominic Trent wheeling to point his gun at Wade as he lay upon the ground.

There was no time to think or hesitate or plan—she hurled herself at Trent and knocked his gun arm aside as he pulled the trigger. The shot went wide—then she and Trent were stumbling together down into the dirt, and he was trying to pin her beneath him.

But Caitlin was driven by desperation, fury, and love. She wriggled aside, clenched her manacled hand into a fist, and struck Trent full in the face. He grunted in rage, fell back a moment, and then slowly pushed himself up with his hands.

"You're going to pay for this, my beauty—for this as

well as everything else!" The mask of smug, cold control fell away and the mad simmering ugliness exploded from him with a fervor. "You and your crude ignorant foreman are both going to pay!"

But suddenly, more gunshots brought them both spinning around. Someone was firing at Piltson from a high rock above Wolf Cave. The rustler dove into the dirt and returned fire.

Caitlin peered up toward that high rock but the sun blinded her from seeing who was shooting. In a quick instant, all she could make out was a tall dark figure—a figure that she could have sworn was Wade, except that Wade lay wounded and bleeding a dozen feet from her. Suddenly she knew—Nick. It was Nick!

Then all hell broke loose again and the clearing roared with gunfire. Piltson and Nick Barclay exchanged shots again and the next thing she knew Trent had trained his gun upon Nick as well.

It all happened so quickly that afterward, Caitlin never quite remembered it all. All she knew was that she spotted Wade's guns lying on the ground and without thinking, she grabbed up one of them, clutching it in both hands. As Trent squinted against the sun and took aim at the high rock, waiting for Nick to show himself, she lifted the heavy gun over her head and brought it down with all of her strength against Dominic Trent's skull.

There was a sickening crack, and Trent slammed to the ground.

At the same moment came more gunfire. The rustler gave out a scream and he too went down, hitting the earth with a thud, his burly body twitching in the sun.

Caitlin lost no time flying to Wade's side. Her own

hurts and pains were forgotten as she gazed into his gray face, at the blood pooling beneath his still body.

"Wade. Oh, no, Wade, *please.*" She couldn't breathe. Terror, fear, and disbelief rushed through her.

He was still, so still. Still as death.

"Don't you dare die!" She fought off faintness as she saw the blood soaking the front of his shirt and swirling crimson beneath him.

Frantically, she looked around for something to stanch the blood and remembered her shawl in the wagon. She ran for it and scrambled back a moment later, pressing it hard against the wound.

"Wade, listen to me. You can't die. I won't let you!"

"Still . . . as b-bossy and uppity as ever . . ." The whispered words were so low she might have imagined them. Then his eyes slowly opened. She gasped and clung to him as hope flickered in her heart.

"Yes, that's me, Wade. Bossy. Uppity. Now I'm telling you—ordering you—don't leave me, stay with me."

"Not going . . . nowhere."

"That's right, darling, you're not."

She had to stop the bleeding and then, God help her, try to get him into the wagon, to town. He needed a doctor—and quickly. Caitlin's thoughts whirled desperately as the blood soaked through her shawl and stained her trembling fingers.

Terror that his very life was flowing from him on this bloodstained clearing brought tears to her eyes.

"You're . . . crying."

"It doesn't matter."

"You . . . never cry. Did . . . he hurt you?"

"No, I'm fine, Wade. I'm going to get Raleigh's buggy. We have to get you to Hope—"

"Don't . . . go. I have to tell you—"

"I'll be right back, I promise." She spoke fiercely through her tears.

"No. Listen to me. I . . . love you."

His words penetrated the choking fear that gripped her, and her tears flowed faster. "I love you, too—but I have to get the—"

"Listen . . . to me."

She went perfectly still. Her heart broke, shattering into a thousand pieces as she stared into his pain-wracked eyes. "I'm . . . listening," she whispered brokenly.

"I'll leave . . . Cloud Ranch. For you. If you don't want to stay—we'll go . . . anywhere. Anywhere you want. I won't be like . . . Reese. I'll follow you, Caitlin . . ."

She began to weep, dying inside with every harsh breath that came from his chest.

"I love you more . . . than anything." Wade fixed his gaze on her as he spoke the words with effort. "Don't . . . leave . . . me—"

"I'll never leave you, Wade. *Never.* And I'll never leave Cloud Ranch. You're going to be fine and we're going to be a family, darling, you, me, and Becky—and we'll have children of our own, as many as you want, but I have to get you to a doctor—"

A voice that made her flesh crawl cut off her words. "An undertaker, you mean."

Caitlin dropped the shawl and spun around. Dominic Trent stood, swaying on his feet, directly before her. Blood poured from his head, turning his clothes crimson and smearing his face, and there was an eerie glitter in his eyes. Struggling to stay upright, he groaned and lifted his revolver just high enough to take aim at Wade as he lay upon the ground.

"No!" Even as she screamed, she heard the shot, and then Dominic Trent staggered sideways and fell face first into the dust.

Dimly she heard Nick's voice, far off, shouting from the rocks behind the cave. As if in a dream she turned back to stare at Wade.

"Now who needs . . . an undertaker?" Wade whispered.

He gave her a weak, horrible shadow of a grin, then lowered the smoking hideout gun.

And closed his eyes.

Chapter 30

Day blended into night, first one, then the next. And the next. Sunrise, midday, dusk. And all the bleak, endless, empty hours in between. They were all dark, all frightening, all the same.

Caitlin lost track quickly. Her entire being was focused on Wade. Sitting by his bed, watching his fitful, fevered sleep, peering into his glazed eyes that stared at her without recognition during the few brief moments he seemed to come awake. Feeding him spoonfuls of broth, cleansing his face with a cool cloth, talking softly while he lay in strengthless sleep.

And praying in the deepest, darkest hours of the night.

Those were the things she could do for him—the only things she could do.

She watched him from the rocker as the midday sun glided across a gleaming turquoise sky, not even glancing up when the door opened behind her.

I love you . . . I'll follow you, Caitlin . . .

Silent sobs ached in her throat as she remembered his

words in the blood-soaked clearing. Wade would have given up Cloud Ranch for her. Followed her. He *loved* her. More than the ranch, more than the home he'd known all his life.

He loved her.

He had proven it, and saved her life—and, in the course of that horrible terrifying night, he had possibly given up his own. She was the one who had doubted, hesitated, and run away—it was because of her own pride and stupidity that Drew Raleigh had so easily been able to turn her over to Dominic Trent.

I love you, Wade. The words echoed through her heart. *Come back to me, and I'll never hide my love from you again.*

She'd held in her feelings for too long. Now it might be too late.

Please don't let it be too late, she prayed wearily as she clutched the arms of the rocker. *Please let us have our chance . . .*

"Senorita, is there any change?"

Francesca paused beside her, and Caitlin shook her head. She felt the housekeeper's firm hand upon her shoulder.

"You haven't left this chair for more than a moment. You slept here all through the night, *si?*"

"It doesn't matter."

"Come downstairs and eat a proper meal. Senor Nick and Senor Clint have finished their coffee. They will come sit here by his side while you—"

"No, Francesca. Not yet. I want to stay a little longer."

Nick had sent a telegram to Clint in Colorado and Clint had arrived late yesterday, weary and covered with trail dust, his face ashen with worry as he'd flung himself from the saddle and vaulted up the steps to hear news of Wade.

He was every bit as handsome in his own way as Nick and Wade, and somehow, the presence of the two younger Barclay brothers gave her reassurance. They were both so vital, so strong and splendid—just like Wade. And they had something else besides physical hardiness: inner strength, a strength that had been nurtured by Reese. A strength that would stand Wade in good stead as he fought the fever and the wound and the loss of blood.

A strength that would never give up, Caitlin told herself as she'd been telling herself for days.

"Are you certain, senorita? Senor Wade, he would not want you to fall ill from hunger—or anything else."

"I'm fine, Francesca. Perhaps I'll come down in a little while."

Francesca let out a heavy sigh. The senorita had been saying that for days now. She'd taken no nourishment but what was brought to her on a tray, and eaten little of that.

"If you change your mind, there are sandwiches of turkey and cold beef and ham—a basket of cookies from Senora Weaver. And Senorita Porter has brought a fresh peach pie."

Caitlin nodded, and smiled wanly, though her eyes had lost their sparkle. "Everyone has been so kind. You, too, Francesca. *Gracias.*"

"Your sister—she is worried about you. We all are."

"Wade is the one to worry about. He needs all our prayers."

"*Sí.* But, senorita, he is very strong. The doctor, he may have his doubts, but I know Senor Wade since he was a little boy. *Muy poco.* He will get well."

"Yes." At that some of the life seemed to come back into Caitlin's pale cheeks. She squeezed the housekeeper's hand. "Thank you, Francesca—for that. I know he will get well."

Her voice grew stronger as she spoke the words. She leaned forward and cradled Wade's big, callused hand in hers. It was so large, and she well remembered its strength, yet there was no power in his grip now, no will or vitality in the long, capable fingers.

"He will get well," she whispered fiercely to herself. Yet a tiny voice of doubt still drummed in her heart: *Then why do you feel this icy sense of dread?*

She fought to silence that voice. Wade was fighting for his life and she would fight to believe in him. Hope is what he needed now, hope and a reason to live. She must give him both.

"Wade. I know you can hear me," she whispered. "I'm right here, and I won't leave you. We're going to live together on Cloud Ranch until we're very old and gray and we can't even remember our own names. Until we can't remember how to saddle a horse or how to match up our boots. But we'll remember our love for each other. We'll always remember that."

Sweat poured down his face and he shifted restlessly in his sleep, then he seemed to sink deeper, a moan rasping in his throat.

He didn't once open his eyes.

Caitlin caressed his hand. Closing her eyes, she prayed.

"She will not leave him." Francesca shook her head. "It is always the same, she sits there, she watches him. Soon, the doctor will need to visit *her*," she fretted.

"Don't you worry about that, Francesca." Clint pushed back his chair from the dining-room table. "We'll carry her into the kitchen if we have to."

She nodded approval at this and scurried off to the kitchen as Clint glanced over at Nick. "It looks like our big brother found himself a woman as stubborn as he is."

"No doubt about it. Now if only he'd use some of that damned stubbornness to lick this thing." Nick rubbed his bleary eyes. He hadn't slept more than an hour or so at a time since the day Wade was shot. "You know if I'd only gotten there a few minutes sooner. I'd been trailing Biggs for days. Had figured out that the son of a bitch had been using the handle of Sheriff Piltson. But I couldn't catch up to him in time—"

"Good thing you got there when you did," Clint cut him off. "No use whipping yourself over it now—what's done is done. But the least we can do is haul that woman of his out of there and make sure she gets some food into her."

Nick paced around the dining-room table and nodded. "You're right. He'd have our hides if we let anything happen to her. Wish you could have seen the way he looked at her, Clint. The few times I saw them together the sparks flew like someone tossed a mess of lightning into a prairie fire."

"Then we'd best take care of her." Clint headed to the door, followed by his brother. "Why don't you bring her downstairs and make sure she eats and I'll keep an eye on Wade. Maybe if I sing to him, he'll wake up. He always hated my singing."

Nick groaned. "That's 'cause it sounds like braying."

"Then maybe it'll penetrate that thick skull of his and

he'll wake up just so he can throw me out of there." Clint spoke lightly, but his face was grim and drawn as he mounted the stairs.

Nick too struggled to maintain a stoic countenance and to rein in his emotions as he returned to his brother's sickroom. Neither of them could contemplate life without Wade—losing Reese had been bad enough. Wade had to pull through this—but if he didn't wake up soon, the doc didn't think he'd wake up at all.

The house was quiet, eerily quiet. From the window in Reese's study, Caitlin watched Becky and Dawg beneath a pine tree. Becky was seated upon the grass, weaving a dandelion bracelet for Wade. Dawg's head rested on her lap. It was a peaceful scene.

But she'd heard Becky crying in her room the previous night, and left Wade's side briefly to go to her.

"I don't want Wade to die!" Becky sobbed.

"He won't die. He's strong. He'll come back to us."

"Promise?"

She hugged her sister close. "I . . . can't promise," she managed to say in a calm tone, marshaling all her resolve. "But I have faith. You must have faith, too, Becky. Try."

"We lost Mama and Papa—and you lost Reese. It isn't fair." Her sister's cracking voice and tear-streaked face cut at her heart.

"No, but life isn't always fair," she replied quietly. "I guess that's something we just have to learn, Becky. And keep on hoping for the best."

"Wade is the best. The best, the kindest, the handsomest."

She gazed earnestly at Caitlin. "If he gets well, are you going to be better friends with him? Nicer to him?"

Caitlin kissed her cheek. "You could say that. I'm going to marry him."

Now, seated in the leather armchair where her father had worked and planned and devoted his energy to making Cloud Ranch a success, where he'd reveled in the glorious view and smoked his cigars and taught Wade all about ranching, she thought of how her life had changed since she'd come to Cloud Ranch, of how she had changed. And Wade was at the center of all that. So was this place, this house, and this magnificent land.

Before her were spread the letters she'd found the night of the May Day dance, the night Wade had been shot. They'd been retrieved from her reticule in Drew Raleigh's buggy, but she hadn't even thought about them—until today. After Clint and Nick and Francesca had all ganged up on her and forced her to go downstairs to the kitchen and eat a sandwich, she'd remembered the letters and brought them in here to read.

It seemed only right.

She hadn't thought her heart could grow any heavier, but it did as she reread the words of her own younger self—hopeful, eager, yearning to know her real father, the man her mother had left behind. But it was when she read Reese's letters to her that a huge knot seemed to form inside her chest and the pain was almost more than she could bear.

My dear daughter Caitlin,

I know you must not remember me, but I have never forgotten you. You were a baby in my arms and I rocked you to sleep night after night. There were songs I used to sing to you—sitting in my study, gazing out at the stars. Whenever I sang, you'd smile at me as you were falling peacefully asleep.

I know that you're a great big girl now—seven years old. I'd like to visit you—and bring you back here to Cloud Ranch for a spell. It's beautiful here and I think you'll like it. We could get to know each other again. And we could have a picnic down by the stream in back of the house, and take a ride up into the mountains, and I'd introduce you to all our horses. I'd pick out the nicest, prettiest one for you to ride.

How does that sound? If you want to come, write me and tell me and I'll arrange with your mama for a visit. I'd ride all the way across the desert and the plains and the mountains to get you. Because I love you, Caitlin honey. You're my little girl and no matter how far away you are, you'll always be my little girl.

> *Love,*
> *Your papa.*

There were others like that—written a year later, two years later. Each one proclaimed Reese's love. Each one was like a knife through her heart, but the pain was somehow sweet, achingly sweet.

It seemed real at last. Her father had loved her, wanted her, and tried to be a part of her life. He'd never forgotten or given up on her—even after all these years of unanswered letters, unanswered hopes.

Even when he'd been dying, he'd thought of her. He'd found out she was in trouble and had made certain she had a home—and someone to look after her.

Wade. The toughest, kindest, most courageous, and trustworthy man he knew.

The man she had grown to love with all her heart. If only Reese could know . . .

She felt he did. She hoped he did. But there was something she needed to know. Who had kept her and Reese apart all these years? Who had hidden both sets of letters? And then, at the May Day dance, given them to her—all of them?

She rubbed her eyes even as she heard a step in the hall.

"Caitlin, dear?" Winnifred Dale peeked her head around the door. "Francesca told me you were in here. May I come in?"

"Of course."

Winnifred's brows were knit with worry. "How is Wade?"

Caitlin sighed. "He's the same. But I . . . I think he may wake up today. I was just about to go back upstairs—"

"I won't keep you then. I just brought over a pot of stew—Francesca took it to the kitchen. I remember from the times I ate supper here that dear Wade was always partial to stew. Now, Clint, he liked fried chicken best, and Nick loved ham with that ginger sauce Francesca prepares, but Wade . . ."

Her voice trailed off. "What is it? What are you looking at, dear?"

A sliver of ice trickled down Caitlin's spine. "You had dinner here often—with my father?"

"Often? Well, I wouldn't say that—but—on occasion. We were very good friends, as I told you." Winnifred tucked a strand of toffee-colored hair behind her ear.

"But . . . only friends . . . all those years?"

"Yes, that's right. Only friends."

"He was a handsome man," Caitlin said slowly, her gaze flicking momentarily to the photograph of Reese, Wade, Clint, and Nick. "He was kind, and big-hearted—and generous. The kind of man any woman might easily fall in love with."

"Well, yes, I suppose so." Two bright spots of color appeared on Winnifred's cheeks. Her hands fluttered up to her throat and then back to her sides again. "I mean, Reese and I enjoyed each other's company. We always got along well—never once had an argument, but . . . well, everyone in Hope and the whole valley knew he never stopped loving your mother. Not for a moment. Everyone knew it, and certainly I did too—so naturally I never—"

"You never let yourself fall in love with him?" Caitlin's knees were shaking as she came around the desk. She paused before Winnifred, staring searchingly into the other woman's eyes. "But a person can't stop herself from falling in love, Winnifred," she said softly. "It just happens. Isn't that what happened to you?"

For a moment the other woman just gaped back at her, her expression frozen. Then, suddenly, Winnifred's face seemed to crumple.

"Yes. Yes, child—I . . . loved him. How could I not?" she whispered. "He was the finest man I ever met."

The room whirled. Caitlin took a step back to clutch the side of the desk and steady herself. "Is that why you kept his letters from me and mine from him?" she whispered. "I don't understand."

"Letters? I never—I don't know what you're talking about, dear." Then her gaze fell upon the letters scattered across the desk, the pink ribbon curled alongside them, and she went pale as stone.

"Tell me the truth, Winnifred. It's time." Caitlin struggled against the surging anger and confusion that filled her. "These are the letters. Someone returned them to me at the May Day dance. It was you, wasn't it?"

For a moment, Winnifred looked as if she was going to flee, to whirl about and actually run through the hall and out the door. Fear and mortification warred with each other in her sweet, kindly face, then she gave a moan and her hands lifted to cover her eyes.

"Yes, Caitlin. You're right. Oh, how I've wanted to tell you from the start—and yet I dreaded your finding out. You must hate me." Her voice throbbed with anguish. "I hate myself."

Caitlin struggled to remain untouched as the woman began to sob. Silent anger filled her—and with it, confusion. "Winnifred, just tell me why. Did you really think a little child was a threat to you—to whatever you hoped Reese would feel for you?"

"You don't understand, Caitlin. You just don't understand." Gasping, agonized sobs tore from Winnifred's throat. She pulled her hands from her eyes and came forward, tears streaming down her face as she reached out desperately toward Caitlin, but Caitlin quickly stepped back, behind the desk, struggling to maintain her own fragile self-control.

"He yearned for Lydia to return." Winnifred's shoulders shook with sobs. "He spoke of it, he told me he dreamed of it. He kept hoping that once she learned Cloud Ranch was a huge success—and becoming more so all the time—she'd come back to him. And so would you. He dreamed that you'd all be a family again, along with the boys . . ."

She drew in a great shuddering breath, ignoring the tears splashing down her cheeks, and continuing in a rush. "I knew he wrote to you. He told me about it, that he intended to invite you to the ranch for a visit. He brought the letter to me in the post office. You have to understand, Caitlin—I had hopes—such lovely hopes—that if Lydia didn't come back, he might someday begin to care for me. Not as much as I cared for him, I didn't dare hope for that—but a little, even a little, would have made me so happy. Do you understand, Caitlin?"

She peered at the girl, who stood stock-still, listening to every word. Caitlin forced herself to speak, her own voice choked.

"No, I don't understand, Winnifred. But go on—the least you can do now is explain."

"I was afraid that if you came to the ranch, perhaps Lydia would come too. That she would indeed see what a success Reese had made of Cloud Ranch, and that she'd decide to return to him. And she didn't deserve him, child, not a whit!" She spoke in a quavery rush. "She deserted him when things were hard, and I didn't want to see her come waltzing back into his life only when he had proved himself—"

"She was married to another man by then," Caitlin interjected coldly. "Happily married. She loved the life that Gillis Tamarlane gave her."

"I didn't know all that. Besides," Winnifred murmured through eyes still wet with tears, "how could she love that other man—truly—when she could have Reese? No one could be as fine and giving and gentle . . ." She broke off with a gasp. "She had only to come back and—" Winnifred yanked a lace-edged handkerchief from her reticule and wiped at her wet eyes. She was trembling all over as she tried to regain control of herself.

"I . . . took that first letter, Caitlin. I'm so sorry. But . . . I was afraid if you received it, and decided to come to Cloud Ranch, that Lydia would follow, that I would lose any hope of Reese turning to me. After all, she was a great beauty and I . . ." She closed her eyes, her voice growing lower, more dejected. "I had my regrets, after I took the letter. It was wrong, I knew that, but I . . . I hid it, kept it, and never told Reese what I'd done. And when you didn't answer him, he was devastated." She drew in a deep, shuddering breath and her eyes opened, fixing themselves in desperation on Caitlin's face.

"Then, some months later, *you* wrote to *him*. The same fears struck me—and in addition, I worried that he might be suspicious if he learned you'd never received his letter. So I kept your letter too. And then all the rest that followed, from each of you. I intercepted them all." She clutched the handkerchief so tightly, her knuckles turned white. "Once I began, I was afraid to stop, and always, I kept hoping . . . hoping . . . You see, if he had only come to love me, just a little, and we had married—I would have sent for you then, child, I swear it!"

Caitlin could only stare at her in stunned, dazed silence. "Do you know what you've done, Winnifred?" she asked at last. "How you made me hate him? How it wounded him when I never came here in the end, before he died—because I thought he had never ever wanted me?"

"Yes," the woman whispered, and began to sob again.

"I know. I've regretted it—oh, I cannot tell you how I've regretted it. And it was all for nothing, because Reese never turned to me, never once even thought of me . . . that way. I was only his friend. Good, reliable, steadfast Winnifred." She shook her head as bitter tears flowed. "He was so blind in his love for Lydia and in missing you that he never once saw how I truly felt."

Caitlin felt bile in her throat. She stared at the woman she'd met on her first day in Hope, the woman she'd thought she knew. Yes, good, reliable, steadfast Winnifred. She'd never seen more than that—but of course, there was more than that. People were complicated. Good and bad mixed together. Only a few were all evil—like Dominic Trent and Hurley Biggs. Some, like Wade, were good down to the depths of their soul. But so many fell in between—flawed, imperfect people who sometimes made terrible mistakes.

"I finally couldn't stand it any longer. The guilt, I mean." Winnifred crumpled the wet handkerchief in her hand and looked pleadingly at Caitlin. "I brought all the letters to the dance, and put them into the folds of your shawl. I wanted you to have them, to understand how much he loved you. I was afraid you might suspect me, might ask questions and pursue the matter, but I took the risk, Caitlin, so that you'd finally know." Her tone was low, desperate, and weary. "Does that . . . count for anything, child?"

"Yes, Winnifred, I suppose it does." Still too stunned to even know what more to say to her, Caitlin shook her head. "But if you're asking my forgiveness—"

"No, no. I'm not. I don't expect that." Winnifred twisted the handkerchief in her hands. "Just understanding.

If—if you can. And peace. I hope that *knowing* will give you some peace about . . . him . . . and that maybe now you finally . . . *finally* can forgive Reese."

Winnifred Dale turned and ran from the room.

Caitlin couldn't move. Her throat ached. She stood there for she knew not how long, then she suddenly went to the front door, stepped out onto the porch, and kept right on walking.

Chapter 31

The sun broiled down as Caitlin stood beside Reese's grave. She'd sworn never to come here again. But that was before she knew the truth.

"I wronged you, Papa," she whispered, her throat tight with grief. "Perhaps it wasn't all my fault—but I should have known somehow, deep inside, that you hadn't abandoned me. It's too late now. I wish . . ." She swayed a little as emotion welled up in her. "I wish I could do it over, that I could see you one more time." Her voice cracked. "That we could have spoken, understood each other. And I wish I'd come to you when you sent for me. But I hardened my heart," she said softly. "And you never did."

She sank down suddenly beside the grave, kneeling alongside the headstone. "Please forgive me," she whispered.

The tears began to fall and she couldn't stop them. But it didn't matter. She was rocking back and forth as the sun beat down, her mind filled with dim memories of a big man holding her in his arms, of a low, loving voice, of laughter and warmth, of the scent of cigar smoke . . .

Suddenly her eyes flew open. Cigar smoke. She smelled it—the same exact scent she'd noticed that first day when she'd entered Reese's office. She smelled it now in this wide-open space that held his grave.

"Papa?" she whispered wonderingly.

And suddenly she knew. Reese was there with her somehow. For one long dreamlike moment she felt his presence, felt a sense of healing forgiveness and love flow through her, felt a tender embrace that seemed to shimmer all around her.

"Papa, I love you," she breathed and a sense of joy burst through her heart. The next instant she was on her feet, shaking.

Go to Wade. Now. He needs you.

She didn't hear the words. She felt them. Felt them inside her bones, speaking to her heart. She whirled and ran, straight back to the ranch house.

She collided on the porch with Nick, who was just charging out through the front door.

"What's happened?" she cried, her eyes wide and frantic.

"He's awake. He's asking for you—I was just coming to look for—"

She tore past him before he could finish. Nick pounded up the stairs after her.

When she reached the doorway, Clint was standing by the bedside, a grin as wide as Wyoming on his handsome face—and Wade was sitting up. He looked rumpled and pale and weary—and somehow older. But never more beautiful, at least not to her. For a moment she couldn't move, could only breathe a silent prayer of thankfulness, as she sought to take in this miracle.

"Well—it took you long enough—Wade Barclay, I nearly went out of my mind!" Flying to the edge of the bed, she clutched his hand.

His eyes were clear and keen as he studied her face. "You weren't worried about me . . . were you . . . princess . . ."

"Of course not." She was laughing, squeezing his hand, trying to contain the boundless love that welled in her heart and glowed from her eyes, even as she leaned forward and pressed a tender kiss to his cheek, not even minding that the stubble on his jaw scraped her face. "Why would I worry my head about an arrogant, stubborn, infuriating man like you?" she whispered, a catch in her throat.

"She only sat here hour after hour and nearly starved herself to death the past week," Clint commented dryly, but he was grinning so broadly his jaw must have hurt.

"Past . . . week?" Wade still hadn't taken his eyes off Caitlin. Her face was flushed with happiness but he still could see the shadow of a bruise on her cheek and it made him long to shoot Dominic Trent all over again. "I been here in this bed . . . for a whole week?"

"That's right, lazybones." Nick strode forward and hooked his thumbs in his pockets. "And none of us are too damned happy about it either. We've had to do all your work—*and* try to take care of your lady when all she wanted to do was stay right by your side. Can't see why she would," he added, "since you've done nothing but groan and sleep and act like a damned invalid, and a coyote could show a woman a better time—but there's no accounting for taste, is there, big brother?"

His twinkling eyes belied his grumbling tone, and Wade gave a snort of laughter.

"Speaking of . . . running the ranch, little brothers, don't you two have some work you need to do? I want to be alone with . . . my lady."

Clint clapped a hand on his shoulder and gave a gentle shake. "Reckon that can be arranged—if the lady's agreeable."

"Quite agreeable." Caitlin's eyes shone as she gazed into Wade's.

Both Clint and Nick saw the looks passing between them and their grins widened. "Course, I could stay a little longer and sing some more," Clint offered, "since that's what woke you up—"

"Braying." Wade reached out and touched one of Caitlin's curls, pale gold in the sunlight. "Your damned braying could wake the dead . . . and I was nowhere near dead. I got me too much living still to do."

"Reckon we ought to let little Becky know that," Nick commented. "She's been peeping in and out of here like a scared little rabbit for days. And Francesca—reckon she'll want to rustle you up some grub mighty quick so you can get your strength back."

"I've got enough strength to take on both of you—if you don't clear out of here pretty damn quick," Wade warned, but a slow grin played around the corners of his mouth and his brothers chuckled as they stepped into the hall and closed the door behind them.

Caitlin felt joy sweeping through every part of her as Wade stroked her hair.

"I'm not dreaming, am I, princess? You look too damned beautiful to be real."

"I look like yesterday's rags and you know it." She leaned forward, mindful of the bandage across his chest, and kissed him tenderly on the lips. His arms came around her, holding her gently close to him.

"Oh, Wade. You scared me to death. I was so afraid I'd lose you—"

"Not a chance." Though his voice sounded rough and scratchy, it was no longer as weak as it had been when he first awakened. His eyes gleamed into hers with a determined intensity. "It's going to take more than a bullet to make me leave you. Or to let you just walk away. I've got no intention of losing *you*, Caitlin."

"Not a chance," she promised with a smile. "I'm sticking around. You see, I've got too much at stake here. If I left, who'd catch all your arithmetic errors? I can't afford to let this place slide into the red due to sloppy . . . Wade!"

He crushed her to him, and caught her chin in his hand.

"G-goodness, you have a lot of strength for a man who just woke up from a week of fever and with a bullet wound in his chest. Doesn't it hurt? I should really let you rest and maybe eat some broth—"

"Nothing hurts when you're here with me, Caitlin. You got that? So promise me you'll never leave."

"Only if you promise to marry me as soon as you're well."

His hold on her tightened. "I'll marry you tomorrow, if you want."

"You will not, Wade Barclay." Eyes dancing, she pushed her lower lip out in a pout. "I want a proper wedding right here in our front parlor—and I demand a healthy groom."

"I'm plenty healthy."

"We'll just see about that," she murmured, smiling dreamily into his eyes. "In a day or so I'll decide when you might be up to the rigors of a wedding . . . and a honeymoon."

His eyes lit up at the word. Then narrowed on her. "Bossy as hell," he muttered and his hand fell from her chin. "Never thought I'd end up falling in love with a bossy woman. Heaven help me."

Heaven, Caitlin thought, and once again sensed that healing love surrounding her. "Wade—" She broke off. He looked tired. He needed rest. Now wasn't the time to tell him about Reese, about what she'd experienced today at her father's grave, about Winnifred, the letters, any of it. There would be plenty of time to tell him everything, to sort it all out together. Plenty of time to tell each other everything in their hearts.

They'd have the rest of their lives.

"This bossy woman is ordering you to rest," she whispered, and pressed another kiss to his cheek. "You've spent quite enough time looking after everyone else, it's my turn to look after you."

"Guess I could get used to that." That slow heartrending grin made her stomach flip as it always did, and she laughed softly in pure joy. "Guess I could get used to most everything about you, Caitlin Summers. So it's a good thing you're going to be hanging around."

"A very good thing," she agreed as Wade's eyes closed

and he gave a sigh of slow, weary contentment. "Because you're stuck with me now, Wade—like it or not."

"I reckon I do like it." His hand covered hers and their fingers clasped tightly. "Because it just so happens I love you. A whole helluva lot."

Suddenly the future looked as bright and wide open and spectacular as the brilliant Wyoming sky.

"Well, what do you know?" Caitlin whispered happily. "It just so happens that I love you back."

Epilogue

The wedding came off without a hitch.

Surrounded by friends and family, Caitlin Summers married Wade Barclay in the parlor of Cloud Ranch on a glorious June day. While puffy white clouds drifted in the vast jewel-blue sky beyond the parlor window where the guests were assembled, and birds warbled in the trees, and the wind played along the tall grass and sagebrush, Caitlin floated down the staircase feeling as if she were living in an exquisite dream. Except she felt too alive, too happy to be dreaming.

In her glossy white satin gown trimmed with tiny pink silk roses, wearing dainty white satin slippers, and holding a bouquet of pink roses in her hands, Caitlin looked to Wade more than ever like an angel. He could swear she actually shimmered in the morning sunlight that poured in the windows of the ranch, and he nearly forgot to concentrate on the preacher's words as he became caught up in the golden-haired, sensuous beauty about to become his wife.

All her thick pale hair was magnificently curled, held in place by a mother-of-pearl comb that looked almost like a crown, and from which a lacy veil floated—and which he found himself looking forward to removing later—as he would slowly and delightedly remove every other exquisite thing she wore.

With her cheeks flushed a delicate pink and her eyes glowing like stars she spoke her vows before Preacher Thompson, their friends and family, and the love shining from her eyes dazzled her groom so that he nearly forgot to speak his.

But at a nudge from his brother Nick, and a meaningful *ahem* from his brother Clint, both of them serving as best men in the ceremony, he recalled himself with a start and solemnly promised to love, honor, and cherish the woman who owned his heart.

Edna Weaver dabbed at her eyes as she watched them together. Her husband Seth squeezed her shoulder. Francesca smiled through the tears that streamed unabashedly down her olive cheeks as she thought how happy Senor Reese would be if he could see them on this day.

All of the wranglers were there, their hats clutched respectfully in their hands, their gazes both envious and fond as they studied the wedding couple. Reese's lawyer, Abner McCain, sighed to himself as he beheld the bride, and the ladies of the Hope Sewing Circle smiled at the thought of the pale blue and white wedding quilt they would soon present to Mr. and Mrs. Wade Barclay.

Winnifred Dale was not in attendance—she had decided two weeks earlier to leave the town of Hope and reside permanently with her sister in Iowa, whom she'd visited when the Campbell gang had been terrorizing the town. Before she left, Caitlin had driven to Hope to see her.

She told Winnifred that she forgave her. The woman wept, and whispered that it was more than she deserved. Unsure about that, Caitlin only knew that she didn't want to live the rest of her life carrying anger or animosity in her heart toward anyone.

She wanted peace, contentment, happiness—and love.

Wade had showed her how to find those things. He'd made her life a joy. And Becky's too. When Caitlin had first told her sister about the wedding plans and invited her to be the flower girl, the prospect of staying on at Cloud Ranch "forever and ever" had made Becky dance with joy. Wyoming suited her, and so did Cloud Ranch. She and Dawg and the Morgensen twins had become inseparable friends—and she confided to Caitlin that Wade was the best big brother she could ever have hoped for. So Caitlin wasn't surprised when she caught a swift glimpse of her sister's face as the preacher announced that the groom could now kiss the bride, and Wade lifted the veil. The sad, timid little girl who had existed so miserably in the halls of the Davenport Academy was watching the bride and groom with dancing eyes, and grinning from ear to ear.

Then Wade had taken Caitlin in his arms and she hadn't seen or heard or remembered anyone else—the moment his lips touched hers the world spun away and there was only the two of them and sweet, simple joy as they held each other, kissed, laughed—joining lips and dreams and hearts.

Luanne Porter watched them with quiet pleasure, her

hand tucked tightly into that of Jake Young. Just before the wedding began, Jake whisked her out back and proposed beneath a willow tree. He looked at her the way no man had ever looked at her before—with all of his hopes in his eyes and enough love to last them two lifetimes—and Luanne threw her arms around him and said yes. That she and Jake found each other through disappointment and unrequited love made their love for one another all the more magical. It made the gift they'd both been given all the more meaningful. They felt no envy toward the very obvious joy that haloed Caitlin and Wade—they knew that joy themselves and shared in it gladly.

And just as the room erupted into chuckles and applause because the marriage kiss seemed to go on forever—and Caitlin and Wade broke apart, laughing—Caitlin felt a warm shiver down her spine. Once again she sensed that healing, loving presence she'd felt at Reese's grave—once again she caught the faint familiar whiff of cigar smoke that drifted on the air for a moment and then vanished.

She knew down to her soul that Reese was happy for them, and satisfied that the little girl he had lost so long ago, whose picture he had kept on his mantel, had at last come home.

She'd come home and married the boy he'd taken in and raised as his own son, the boy who'd grown into such a splendid man. A man to be trusted through thick and thin, a man she could count on for all of her days.

Thank you, Papa—for bringing me here, giving me my home—and for leading me to Wade, she thought silently just before the crowd of guests converged upon her and Wade and enveloped them in a sea of good wishes.

There was wedding cake and champagne, toasts to the happy couple, and dancing—and then the guests went away and the lovely day ended and the beautiful white moon rose in a sable sky.

And Caitlin and Wade retired to his high-ceilinged bedroom at the end of the hall and she found a ribbon-wrapped box upon the bed.

"It's your wedding gift," he told her as she looked at him questioningly, and her white satin skirt rustled as she stepped forward and lifted the lid.

Inside was a hat—not just any hat, but quite the most beautiful creation Caitlin had ever seen. A confection of pink and lavender ribbons and creamy yellow roses, bedecked with shimmering pearls and a wide orchid silk bow. It nestled in its velvet-lined box like a perfect and irresistible jewel.

"Wade! It's gorgeous," she breathed, lifting it out of the box and gazing at it from every fetching angle. "Wherever did you get it?"

"Paris." He grinned smugly at her gasp of astonishment, looking so handsome still in his elegant black coat, white lawn shirt, and string tie that she couldn't tear her eyes from him. "Nell Hicks managed to get her hands on a fancy New York catalog and . . . oh, hell, it doesn't matter."

He took a step toward her. "Reckon I just wanted to make up to you for the first time we met—when that pretty hat of yours landed in the horse trough."

"The day you walked away from me," she reminded him.

"And nearly made the biggest mistake of my life." Wade lifted her up, the hat still clutched in her hand, and swung her around in a circle until she gasped with dizzy laughter, then he paused and cradled her against his chest.

"I'll never walk away from you again, Caitlin."

"Promise?"

"Word of honor."

Word of honor. Those words had meaning for her again—because of Wade. Because of the man he was.

She laid her hand tenderly across his cheek.

"Shall I try it on?" she asked, glancing down at the hat. Wade shook his head. He set her gently upon the bed, took the hat from her, and tossed it onto a chair.

"Nope." He shoved the box onto the floor and then, grinning, pushed Caitlin down across the coverlet. The white satin rustled provocatively beneath him as he covered her body with his own, and then he spread her hair out with his fingers and gazed down into her lovely, smiling face, his own eyes glinting.

"This isn't a time for trying things on—it's a time for taking things off." His voice was husky in the moonlight that streamed in the window. He grinned down at her and Caitlin felt herself tingling with a heady anticipation almost too much to bear.

His mouth came down, paused an inch from hers.

Her own lips parted.

"Pretty as this dress is, what's underneath is prettier. Reckon we'll start with that." His fingers found the dainty pearl buttons at her bodice and made short work of them.

"If you insist," Caitlin murmured, already halfway through the buttons on his shirt, even as her other arm curled around his neck and pulled him down to her kiss.

They kissed and made love slowly, hungrily, by the light of the moon. The beautiful clothes lay scattered, the dark moments of night slid by, and they gave themselves up to the passion and the fury—and the love. There was tenderness and there was fire, blissful pleasure and agonizing need. But most of all, love.

When their bodies were slick with sweat and trembling, they collapsed and slept at last in each other's arms—and awoke to happiness in the pale lilac glow of dawn.

Dawg was barking—Becky was laughing somewhere off near the barn, and horses were whinnying.

Cloud Ranch, Caitlin thought as Wade tenderly kissed her and her heart soared. *I'm home.*

About the Author

USA Today–bestseller Jill Gregory is the award-winning author of sixteen historical romances. Her novels have been translated and published in Japan, Russia, Norway, Taiwan, Sweden, and Italy. Jill grew up in Chicago and received her bachelor of arts degree in English from the University of Illinois. She has a college-age daughter and currently resides in Michigan with her husband.

Jill invites her readers to visit her Web site at http://members.aol.com/jillygreg.